SHADOW OF THE PANTHER

SHADOW OF THE PANTHER

For Marna

Robert Hurst -

with 2 best wishes

[signature: Robert Hurst]

ATHENA PRESS
LONDON

ISBN 10-digit: 1 84748 086 1
ISBN 13-digit: 978 1 84748 086 6

First Published 2007 by
ATHENA PRESS
Queen's House, 2 Holly Road
Twickenham TW1 4EG
United Kingdom

Although the events of this book are based on real historical fact,
the portrayal of all characters and situations is fictitious, and all
names and places are purely the product of the author's
imagination.

Printed for Athena Press

For Ann, Gary and Jamie

Prologue

On a blustery March night in 1974 a man alighted from the last train into Stoke-on-Trent carrying a large duffel bag slung over his shoulder. He was just a nondescript Yorkshireman in a beige raincoat and flat cap and certainly not likely to attract much attention. He was below average height at five foot six, but had a lean frame and taut muscles. His features were finely honed with a square jaw and deep-set eyes beneath a dark tousled mop of hair. He walked up the platform among several other late-night passengers and passed through the barrier before making for the station buffet.

Inside the almost empty buffet he ordered a cup of tea and a bun and sat at a table to while away an hour or so. He was in no hurry to get the village of Tittensor, just four miles away. He had two or three hours to spare and he wondered how he might fill the time. He could walk round the town for an hour looking at the local landmarks, but there wasn't that much to see in this grey Potteries town.

There were three other customers in the buffet, two young men arguing about politics, and a middle-aged West Indian man with his head stuck in a book. The West Indian he discounted as just another burdensome immigrant who shouldn't really be here. There were too many coloureds coming into the country importing poverty right across the Midlands. The Black Country was awash with them. Birmingham man was fast becoming a Rastafarian. They should all be deported and sent packing…

The reasons for his attitude were manifold, wrapped up in his national service days in Kenya on anti-terrorist campaigns. He hated idlers and dole cheats, and immigrants were the worst of the lot. The country was reeling – with strikes and power cuts imposing a three-day working week – without bloody immigrants flooding in putting a strain on the economy.

The two young men sitting across the room waiting for the

Birmingham train were industrial workers, the hardest hit by the three-day week. Birmingham was being flooded with a tide of Asians, and their argument was profoundly racist, resounding with anti-immigration sentiments.

'If we carry on importing that lot into this country it'll ruin the working man,' one of them said. 'My factory is on a three-day week and still the blacks come in with large families claiming their welfare benefits. I don't get welfare doled out to me to pay the bills like they do.'

'No, Les, but then you wouldn't do half the jobs they do,' his mate said. 'Someone has to clean the streets and the public lavs. Best job going for the Pakis, I reckon.'

The West Indian was not immune to such talk. It was becoming common to heap blame on immigrants whenever there was a crisis of government over Britain's struggling economy. Having arrived with the first wave of immigrants a decade ago, he was settled with his family in Birmingham running a corner shop. But as the argument got heated he decided it was better to leave than risk racial abuse and he made an exit from the buffet room. Five minutes later the train to Birmingham was announced over the station tannoy and the two workers jumped up and left.

Now the Yorkshireman was the only customer left and the buffet was just ten minutes from closing time at 1 a.m. Having travelled all the way from Bradford, he decided he too had better make a move. But first he had to look up his direction on the pocketbook map he carried. Tittensor was one of several villages scattered down the A34 to Stafford. He wasn't happy walking main roads at night – you never knew who you'd meet – but he could always follow the Trent Canal across open country. Slinging the duffel bag over his shoulder, he left the buffet and walked out the station heading for the deserted town centre. The clock on the Town Hall struck one o'clock.

He reckoned about an hour to walk to the village and the blustery weather suited him for his particular task. He walked through the town centre without seeing a soul and made his way along Campbell Road past the Stoke City football ground. The whole town was quiet, with no one about at this time, and as he passed a row of terraced shops he saw a sign that directed him to the London Road for Stone, the next town of any significant size, eight miles away.

Soon he was walking down the A34 towards Hanford, passing large suburban houses where lights glimmered in bedrooms. He wondered who the occupants might be, flaunting their obvious wealth living in grand houses behind locked gates in cultivated grounds. He would never own a house like that – not that he particularly craved such a status symbol – but it would be nice to be able to afford one.

He walked on through open country and in a while saw the sign saying, 'Tittensor, 1 mile'. Then he left the road, seeking the safety of the woods where he could walk unseen. He carried a small torch to watch for potholes and other obstacles as he searched for an isolated spot to change his clothes.

He found it under a canal bridge, where he stopped to dump his duffel bag and remove his raincoat and hat. Then opening the bag he pulled out a military-style combat jacket and pulled it on, zipping it up to the neck. Then he strapped on a belt with a sheath knife which he used for a variety of jobs. Then he pulled out a semi-automatic pistol that he jammed in his right side pocket. But his main weapon which he left in the bag for now was a 12-bore double-barrelled sawn-off shotgun that was his stock-in-trade for armed robbery. He dare not carry that openly, but it didn't stop him from putting on a belt of shotgun cartridges over his chest that gave him a distinctive paramilitary appearance, more suited to an IRA terrorist. Then he pulled on a pair of white linen gloves before the most essential element of all. The last item he donned was the one thing that most added to his terror. This was a black Lycra hood with slits for his eyes, and this is what gave him his most sinister appearance.

Now he was ready for the task ahead. It was 2.15 a.m. He stuffed the raincoat in his bag and set off for the sub-post office in the village of Tittensor. Although miles from home, he knew exactly where the post office lay, as he had been there before, a few months earlier. In fact, there was hardly a village he didn't know in the West Midlands or in Staffordshire, Derbyshire and Nottingham. He travelled extensively through the Black Country.

It was just one month from his last raid at Harrogate in West

Yorkshire. It had resulted in shooting dead the postmaster for nil returns. He was hoping to avoid a repeat of that incident, which amounted to a failed robbery. But you could never tell what resistance you would meet. There was always the possibility of an irrational postmaster brave enough to tackle an armed robber. Or there might be a fierce dog guarding the premises with a loud bark to wake the owner. They were just two of the drawbacks. Sometimes there was two men inside, a father and son, like the two at Harrogate – not to mention a screaming woman making things difficult.

When he reached Tittensor, the village was quiet and he made his way to the small sub-post office on the main road and slipped in around the back, which was wide open. In the pub across the road, a boxer dog was disturbed by the sound of someone moving about and he began to bark. Dogs were a major deterrent to the intruder, which was why he carried a tin of ammonia spray. The first job that required immediate attention was to cut the telephone cable with a pair of wire cutters. One snip and they were isolated. Then he opened his bag and pulled out a brace and bit, his usual tool, and began quietly to drill into the casement window of the lounge.

Inside the premises, the postmaster and his wife were oblivious to the barking dog across the road as they slept on. The wind rustled through the trees, covering the sounds of a break-in as two holes were being drilled through the lounge window to weaken the fastenings. Ten minutes later the window was opened and the intruder climbed inside into the lounge, dropping silently to the floor, and beaming his flashlight round the room. Then he went through to the kitchen and unlocked the side kitchen door before going on through to the post office.

He searched for the safe keys with his torch and, unable to find them anywhere, he made his way upstairs. Halfway up the stairs a board creaked and he removed his shoes before going on up to the landing. He then crept into the bedroom to ruffle through the trouser pockets by the bed for keys, and as he did so the postmaster woke up. He reached for the bedside lamp to turn it on and just as he did it was sent flying, knocked off the table by the barrel of the shotgun.

'*No lights!*' the intruder hissed. 'This is a gun! Keys! Where are the safe keys?'

'Who the devil are you!' The postmaster was flabbergasted at the sight of an intruder in his room.

'Keys! Give me the safe keys!' came the urgent reply.

'By heck I will!'

Without a moment's hesitation the postmaster leaped out of bed and lunged at the intruder, forcing the shotgun barrel up. The two men grappled with each other, but as fast as the postmaster took hold of the intruder's clothing, so it slipped through his fingers. The Lycra material of the combat jacket made it impossible to get a grip. It was like fighting a black devil as the postmaster struggled to pull the intruder's hood off, wrestling with every fibre he could muster.

He thought he was up against an IRA man when he saw the belt of cartridges on the man's chest. A sharp blow to the stomach doubled him over and he let go of the barrel of the gun, enabling the robber to regain control. Then he saw the gun raised over him before it came crashing down on his head, clubbing him to the floor. The postmaster's wife had woken with the commotion and she switched on her bedside lamp. She was horrified to see the black hooded man standing over her husband brandishing a shotgun.

His eyes darted furtively around as he shouted, 'Turn off the fucking light!'

Terrified out of her wits, she turned the lamp off and reached out to help her husband onto the bed. Blood trickled from a gash on his forehead and his body ached with bruises.

'No lights, no tricks! Fetch keys!' the hooded man demanded in a strange West Indian accent. Then he ordered the postmaster downstairs and he followed him down into the post office.

'Open safe and fill bags!' the intruder ordered, thrusting two large leather pouches at him. The safe contained £4,000 in cash and postal orders.

The postmaster did as he was ordered, placing bundles of banknotes and postal orders in one bag and an £80 float of bagged coins in the other. It was the best haul yet of all the post office robberies.

'Now, upstairs!' the robber ordered.

The postmaster padded wearily back up to his terrified wife, who had tried unsuccessfully to call the police from her bedside phone. Meanwhile the intruder slipped quietly out the back door and vanished into the darkness. The two bags of cash hung round his neck from a pair of toggles that enabled him to walk briskly back through the woods to the canal bridge.

In the darkness below the bridge he changed his clothing and repacked his duffel bag more neatly. He placed the moneybags in the bottom, then rolled up his combat jacket and hood into a small zipped package pressing everything in before sliding the shotgun down the side and tying the bag closed. Then he slung it on his back and set off on the four-mile walk back to town.

It was 4.50 a.m. when the Yorkshireman reached the station and bought a ticket. He mingled among the early morning workers and might well have been anyone of them in raincoat and cap waiting for the five o'clock train to Manchester. When it pulled in he boarded the second-class non-smoking carriage and sat in a compartment with two workers, listening to their idle chit-chat but rarely joining in.

He had always kept to himself, from the day he left school with no qualifications to begin work as an apprentice joiner. Within a year he quit and went from one job to another, searching for his niche in life. National service taught him his survival instincts. He'd learned the technology of guns and the art of survival while tracking enemy terrorists. Physical training toned his muscles and made him strong, but he was a loner without companionship and found it difficult to mix the older he got. He shunned society and admitted no self-failure while he sought the perfect crime. Past failures were buried with a burning sense of social injustice and a desire to hit back. These were the memories he carried on his journey through life, wherever he went. Tonight, he gazed out of the window into the dark as the train rumbled towards Manchester.

At every station he worried that the police might come aboard, searching for the serial robber dubbed 'the Black Panther' by a frenzied media. Photofits circulated, but none were even a vague likeness of him, and it seemed very likely that unless he committed a major blunder the police would never catch him.

For over four years he had got clean away with armed post office raids in which he lived out his fantasies. He had a fastidious eye for self-discipline, and it ruled his life. The methods he employed were born of the military training that had carried him this far. He used only the winter months for his criminal activities, and this would be his last job until September. He was thinking of an even greater crime – a kidnapping – which would give him the fortune he needed, and he already had the target in mind.

He changed trains at Manchester for Bradford and made his way home across the moors. They were hauntingly beautiful in the first rays of dawn. They were a place of mystery, brooding and silent like himself, resisting the pressures of the outside world to adapt but able to turn up a mystery at any time. All it required was a set of rules and meticulous planning to beat the odds, and that was something he was good at.

Chapter One

The man watching across the road had the cold stare of a panther stalking its prey. They were the eyes of a fanatic, scheming and calculating, for what he was about to do had taken months of planning. He had kept vigil on the shop in Wellington Road on various days of the week, watching the routine movements of the female proprietor and her assistant. He knew the times they came and went, where they lived, what transport they used, and even the type of customers who called into the antique shop in the prosperous suburb of Reddish Vale, Manchester.

Just two weeks earlier he had called into the shop on the pretence of buying a chess set for his nephew in order to identify the owner from the assistant up close. Despite their obvious age gap they were remarkably similar from a distance, and he could not afford to make a mistake. On that occasion he wore a waxed country jacket, dark tinted glasses and a trilby hat, and used an upper-class refined Yorkshire accent to carry it off.

He was clever at accents and could switch from Yorkshire to Birmingham, from working class to upper class, and even effect an Asian or West Indian one when it suited. Today he would use a West Indian Birmingham accent, and his appearance would be different. He'd be totally working class and walk with a fake limp.

He looked at his watch: 4.55 p.m. It was time to move. Dusk was falling, and it combined with a steady drizzle to slow the traffic just beginning to build up on Wellington Road as the workers made their way home in the Mancunian gloom. Clutching a canvas holdall, the man crossed the street dodging the traffic before striding purposefully towards the shop and entering Woodward's Antiques.

The shop bell tinkled and the female assistant stepped forward to serve. 'My word, sir, you're cutting it fine, we're just about to close!' The man brushed past her with his cap pulled down, avoiding her gaze.

A young dark-haired woman at the back of the shop took over. 'I'll see to him, Mary, you get off home.' She closed the customer account book she had been writing in and smiled. 'How can I help you, sir?'

Julia Woodward, the shop owner, was pretty, at just twenty-five years of age. The shop was her pet project – to collect and sell antique furniture from a bygone age that once adorned the large houses of Manchester's industrial barons. The interest stemmed from her own industrial background as daughter and heiress of the giant Woodward Civil Engineering PLC, bridge-builders and large-scale industrial construction. It was part of her heritage stretching back to the mid-eighteenth century. Single and unattached, Julia Woodward had recently moved out of her parents' country manor at Brighouse, West Yorkshire, and opted for a new house on an exclusive private estate at Hazel Grove on the outskirts of Greater Manchester.

The man placed the holdall on the counter and looked up slowly from beneath his cap, and Julia's smile melted away when she looked into those eyes that were totally without a soul.

'I've got something you might be interested in. Might be valuable, might not,' he said in a clipped voice designed to disguise his Yorkshire accent. 'It's been in the family for generations, but you never can tell, can you?'

'No, you can't. What is it?' Julia felt her voice sticking in her throat as the man slowly unzipped the holdall and reached inside. 'I only buy antiques,' she stammered, looking over at Mary, who was donning her hat, coat and gloves. She suddenly wished she wasn't leaving, but it was too late.

'I'll be off then. See you tomorrow, Julia.' Mary skipped out the door, turning the sign to read 'Closed'. But she hung back, looking through the window for a minute just to satisfy herself that Julia was all right before walking away. Now Julia was alone with the man, suddenly feeling vulnerable, and a shiver ran up her spine.

The man removed a large mahogany box from the bag and laid it on the counter. 'This must surely be antique,' he said, running his coat sleeve over the lid as if to polish the delicate inlaid pattern and the brass plaque etched with the name Howard Staunton. 'It's

Victorian, so should be worth a bit.' He opened the box by its brass catch to reveal a chess set with carved ivory and ebony pieces that stood between two and four inches high, laid neatly in their respective compartments at each end of the chequered board.

Julia recognised its value. 'I don't normally buy games,' she said, keeping a desperate hold of her composure. 'Furniture is my line.'

'Your sign says antiques. This is antique, is it not? How much is it worth?'

'I don't know offhand.'

'Look it up. You must have a book.'

'Have you tried Harringtons in the High Street? They could tell you.'

'I'm not hawking this all over town. I want your price.'

Julia opened a drawer and took out the trade bible, the antiques price guide. 'I might have it here,' she said, turning to the page of games and then finding the name, 'Staunton; 1810–74' with a short description of ebony and ivory chess sets and their respective values.

She glanced up, trying to avoid the man's impassive cold stare, and quickly assessed he wasn't about to be easily fobbed off. 'It might be antique,' she said, returning her eyes to the book. 'Have you any idea of the date? When did it come into your family?'

'I told you, generations ago. Take a closer look at it,' he said, taking the king out the box and holding it up to her face. 'Black ebony. Beautifully carved. How many chess sets do you see like that?'

'Quite a number, actually,' Julia replied in her educated voice before realising it was the worst thing to say to this less articulate man.

'Well, you would, wouldn't you! A person like yourself...' The reply carried a caustic grudge against the rich upper classes. 'You must have people coming in every day with antique games worth more than this one. Just give me a price!'

Julia took the piece in her hand, studied it and then looked back at the box, taking in the quality and average condition of the set. Then she looked at the small rule book by the British Chess Company and concluded by the typeface used that it was made about the turn of the century. For that era, the set was valued at £200 in good condition. It was more than she'd imagined, and it half appealed to her. It had a quasi-antique value, but she would probably pay only half that at auction. 'About a hundred pounds,' she said at last. 'That's top notch.'

'Are you sure? I reckoned on £150 at least. It's early Victorian.'

'No, it's much later, and it all depends on the condition. But I couldn't possibly pay that amount. Harringtons would, though, without a doubt.' Julia was anxious to get rid of the man.

'You couldn't, or you wouldn't? You've got some expensive stuff here. Where do you get it from?'

'Auctions, mostly. Now if you'll excuse me, I really must close.'

'Hold on! Let's talk business. That Georgian bureau over there must have cost all of three grand, I bet. And what about that pair of Victorian chairs next to it. How much are they going for? I see money here – lots of it.' He pointed at a painting of two horses in a field by J H Herring. 'And what about that oil painting up there. How much is that?'

'£1,500. Now look, I really must close.'

'£1,500! Who pays that sort of money for a painting? You must have quite a reputation among the rich upper-class folk. Where do these toffs come from?'

'I don't deal with class. I deal with customers.'

'Make me an offer for the chess set.'

'Sixty-five pounds.'

'Sixty-five quid! It's a Howard Staunton, for Christ's sake. The best there is. Come on, you can do better than that. Make it a hundred.'

'Eighty-five. That's my final offer.'

'Come on, come on! It was worth a hundred a minute ago.'

'But I said I couldn't pay that. Besides, the box is scratched and has ingrained dirt. It would need some restoration before I could sell it.'

'A bit of polish needed, that's all. A hundred quid. You can afford it.'

Julia knew this man wasn't leaving until he got his price. 'All right, I'll give you a hundred.'

'That's more like it. Cash!'

'It will have to be a cheque, I'm afraid.' Julia produced a chequebook and pen from a drawer. 'I don't carry cash. Who do I make it out to?'

'Sutton. George Sutton.'

Julia wrote the name and the amount before signing it and then wrote the date, 14 January 1975. Never had she felt so uneasy in a man's presence. She could feel his eyes watching her. She tore the cheque from the book, and as she handed it up to him she froze, staring into the barrel of a semi-automatic pistol pointing straight at her.

'W-what are you doing?' she stammered.

Sutton snatched the cheque and stuffed it in his pocket. 'Put your coat on, and no tricks,' he said, motioning with the gun towards the back office.

He followed her and stood in the doorway, keeping the gun pointed at her as she donned her three-quarter-length suede coat with belt that pulled into her slim waist and slowly pulled on a pair of leather gloves, glancing at her wrist watch. It was 5.10. Where the hell was her taxi? She had to stall for time.

'What do you want?' she said. 'If it's money you want I'll write you another cheque. I don't keep cash on the premises.'

'Shut up and get a move on! And don't bank on the taxi. It's cancelled.'

'Cancelled! No... it can't be. It will turn up to check. The driver knows me.'

'*No it won't*! Now quit stalling!'

Suddenly the doorbell rang as a man stepped inside. 'Taxi for Miss Woodward!' he called out through the shop.

Sutton grabbed Julia by the arm and put the gun to her head. 'Keep your mouth shut or I'll shoot him,' he hissed, forcing her down into a chair. 'Any warning and he's a dead man.' He poked his head half round the door. 'It was supposed to be cancelled. She don't need it!' he called back. 'Sorry to have bothered you.'

'Where is she? I pick her up regular.' The driver moved hesitantly into the shop where the only light came from the back office. Peering through the gloom he noticed the holdall and chess set lying on the counter beside the open chequebook. 'Are you there, Miss Woodward?'

The man grabbed Julia and hauled her up to stand just out of sight in the doorway. 'Get rid of him!' he hissed in her ear.

'Tom, is that you?' Julia called out, fearing for the man's life. 'I meant to cancel. See you tomorrow.'

'As you wish, Miss Woodward.' The driver turned and left, not entirely satisfied.

Sutton watched him drive away as Julia stepped out. 'I told you he'd check. There will be others looking for me.'

'No, there won't. Sit down!' he pushed her back in the chair while he produced a roll of two-inch sticking plaster. 'Close your mouth!' He pulled off a strip and taped it across her mouth to keep her silent. Then he looked round for the umbrella she carried. 'The umbrella! Where is it?'

She pointed to the door, where it was hanging on a hook, and he removed it looping it over her arm. 'Now, out the front door and do exactly as I tell you. Wait! Do you have an alarm to set?'

Julia nodded and he followed her eyes to the small box on the wall with a numbered panel. 'Set it,' he ordered.

Julia tapped in a four-digit number and set the alarm, which emitted a beeping sound until they were out the door. She locked the front door behind her and slipped the keys in her pocket. If only she had scribbled a note on the chequebook.

He made her open the umbrella before stepping out into the cold drizzle and, with the gun pointing in her side, he gripped her arm, walking her, head down, shielded by the umbrella. They went past the parade of shops before turning into a side street where Sutton's van was parked; it was a battered eight-year-old Ford Transit showing patches of rust. He unlocked the rear doors and twisted her arm to force her in, as she put up a token resistance. Escape was impossible. He was too strong, holding her in a vice-like grip.

'Get in the back!' he ordered, pushing her violently.

He climbed in behind her, shutting the doors. Holding her around the throat, he pinned her against the side of the van as he found a roll of tape and bound her wrists tight.

She began to imagine the worst as he straddled her, and she could smell a trace of brandy fumes on his breath. His face was almost indiscernible in the gloom, but the eyes she would never forget. He was about mid-thirties and appeared to be remarkably fit. The feel and the touch of her legs through the thin material of her trousers sexually aroused him as he bound her ankles and he mumbled an apology. 'Sorry about this, but we can't have you jumping out.'

She was sprawled on a grubby sponge mattress between two padlocked wooden boxes containing tools and outdoor survival equipment. Sutton jumped out to lock the rear doors before climbing into the cab behind the wheel.

'We're going for a short ride. Just relax and you'll be all right,' he said in a bid to reassure her.

The van moved off into the traffic and turned north on to the Wellington Road, heading for the main A62 out of Manchester.

Julia lay back, feeling the darkness closing in on her. She was being kidnapped and had not the foggiest notion why. Why had this man picked on her? What had she done? Was it a random kidnap for sexual gratification? No. It was planned. The timing and the cancelled taxi bore that out. Was he acting alone, or did he have an accomplice?

Thoughts tumbled through her mind like a bad dream. Could she have prevented it if she had refused the chess set? How much would he demand for her release, and how did he know about her wealthy background? That wouldn't be difficult, since her family was rarely out of the news or the gossip columns, revealing the wealth of her father, Sir Charles Woodward. There were even titbits about her father's philandering, which she knew to be true. But the most damning scandal was the fraud inquiry into government contracts awarded to the company, which had exposed a government minister and led to his sacking. The inquiry uncovered a whole string of related events, which included blackmail by persons unknown over her father's plundering of the company assets to buy racehorses and pay for an extravagant lifestyle. Julia's elder brother, Peter, who ran a subsidiary company, was sure the blackmailer was a company insider, but it was never proved and the whole thing fizzled out.

Julia mentally ran through her normal routine for a Wednesday evening. She took a taxi to the station to catch the 5.20 Stockport train to Hazel Grove, fifteen miles from the centre of

Manchester, arriving usually at 5.45 p.m. It was a small country station for commuters on the Midland line. From there it was a ten-minute walk to her new house recently built on a small private estate overlooking the Peak District. She had a small circle of friends whom she met regularly in the village pub for a gossip. There was no new man in her life since she had split up with her partner just three months back. It was a sour relationship mired with business problems. Simon Kingsley used it to dominate her life and she was glad to be rid of him. This Wednesday she was meeting her friend Anthea in the pub, and she suddenly realised that apart from Anthea there was no one who would miss her.

The van drove on leaving the urban sprawl of Greater Manchester behind, heading east for the moors. They had been driving just over half an hour and Julia could see nothing through the back window, which was blanked out with plywood. She tried to imagine where he would take her and how long he would hold her – and indeed, if he would ever release her unharmed.

Darkness had fallen as the van climbed across Saddleworth Moor for several miles and then turned off the main road by a large signboard that read: 'Carsbrook Reservoir – West Yorkshire Water'.

They continued down a dirt road for a mile before stopping at a pair of wire-mesh gates to a derelict pumping station that had long been out of use. A sign on the gate warned off trespassers, saying 'Keep Out' with threat of prosecution.

Sutton got out with a bunch of keys to unlock the padlock, letting the chain hang loose as he pushed open the gate before driving inside the enclosure, drawing up by a brick-built Victorian pump house. Julia's heart thumped as she peered through the windscreen at the grim building in the glow of the headlights before he switched them off and got out to unlock the wooden door marked 'No. 5 Pump House'.

Julia's fear was compounded further as the rear doors were opened by the kidnapper wearing a dark hood with slits for the eyes as he ordered her out. From now on, this was all she would see of him as his face faded from memory and the Black Panther emerged from the shadows.

Unable to speak through her taped-up mouth, she mumbled

her disdain as he bundled her inside the bleak derelict pump house and switched on a torch. The beam fell across the dark shape of a large Victorian steam compression pump that sat over a deep borehole that was now out of use. The six-foot-diameter pipe was sunk to a depth of eighty feet and was planked over at the top and the pump disconnected.

Sutton lit an oil lamp that stood on a workman's bench and an owl fluttered somewhere up in the roof. 'This is where you're staying until I get the ransom. You've been kidnapped,' he said, forcing Julia down onto a pile of old sacking.

He then opened a bag that was under the bench and removed a chain and ankle fetters like the kind used in Victorian prisons. He clamped the metal shackle around Julia's right ankle and ran the chain through an iron ring on the wall and padlocked it.

Then he removed the tape from her mouth before going back out to the van to fetch his holdall and other items. Julia remained silent. She was already feeling the cold, and she had no words for this animal.

He returned with his bag and placed the sponge mattress down beside her. 'You can lay on this. No one ever comes here. You're completely isolated, but you'll be safe.'

'You can't leave me here!' she heard herself pleading, knowing it was useless.

He ignored her, taking a flask of soup from the bag and placing that down by her. Then he took a rolled-up sleeping bag out and Julia saw something glint like the barrel of a shotgun as he raked around for a pair of pliers and a roll of wire. He climbed up on the bench to cover a small window with a piece of cloth and then wired up the catch, even though it was out of her reach. Then he made an extraordinary statement as he jumped down and put the tools back in the bag.

'Nothing comes in life without pain and anguish. We are exploited and deceived with false promises of a better life. You come into this world with nothing and you leave it with nothing. You'll get food as and when I'm able to bring it. In the meantime here's a book to read so as you don't get bored. It's a thriller. Hope you like it.'

'You won't get away with this!' Julia said, summoning reserves of courage. 'They'll catch you, whatever it takes. The same as they caught Brady and Hindley.'

'They were stupid. This is planned down to every detail. You will be released only when the ransom is paid.' He threw her a thickly padded survival blanket and turned the lamp low. 'It gets extremely cold up here. The light will last a couple of hours. Sleep well.'

He remained impassive as he went out of the door and locked it with his own padlock. It would keep out nosy park ramblers and the dog walkers who were known to sometimes visit the area. It was as secure as it could be, and the danger signs on the perimeter fence warning of a disused borehole were additional insurance.

Julia heard the van start up and drive away. Already she could feel the cold as she pulled the blanket round her. The light flickered with a draught and she could hear water dripping down the shaft. She was alone with no means of escape, and for the first time in her life she felt the chilling realisation that she might die at the hands of a maniac.

Chapter Two

Detective Chief Inspector George Kennon swore as he cut himself a second time shaving. He stuck a piece of toilet tissue on his chin and dried his face, taking a closer inspection in the mirror. He had a rugged face with a hint of crow's feet around the eyes, but at the age of fifty-four, with no sign of a grey hair on his scalp, he wondered if he perhaps wasn't getting a bit over-concerned about his age. He was single, with no woman in his life, and he felt there should be before it was too late.

Being single had suited him when he was younger. He never lacked friends or female company – not that he did a great deal of socialising. He was an outdoors man with a keen interest in birdwatching and industrial archaeology – not the kind of pursuits that would interest a woman – but he wasn't getting any younger, and man wasn't intended to be a solitary animal.

But that would have to wait. Today he had more important things on his mind. Chief Superintendent Bradley's call the previous evening informing him of a kidnap in the Reddish Vale area may not have been the most dramatic of cases in Kennon's long career with the Greater Manchester force, but it could prove to be the most baffling.

His visit to the antique shop at 10.30 p.m. along with an area patrol car found no sign of a forced entry and, as far as he could tell, there was nothing disturbed inside. The premises was soundly locked for the night, and he was reluctant to break in and set a burglar alarm clanging for no good reason. Bradley had given no details to go on; the shop assistant couldn't be traced, and the few inquiries made in a nearby newsagent's and an off-licence proved a dead end.

He hurried his breakfast as usual and left his neat Edwardian house in Stretford for the thirty-minute drive into central Manchester. It was Tuesday, 15 January, and a blanket of fog hung over the city. The winter had been harsh and there was no end in sight just yet. Kennon switched on the car radio to hear a fruity voice read out the eight o'clock news.

'West Mercia police have reported the man arrested in Wolverhampton on Monday night in connection with the murders of three sub-postmasters has been released without charge. Assistant Chief Constable John Widmore said the arrest of the man was unrelated with the robberies, but insisted the hunt for the notorious killer dubbed "the Black Panther" goes on.'

The Black Panther. Trust the media to come up with a name like that, Kennon mused as he approached the city. The morning fog hampered the traffic going into Manchester, especially the heavy goods that were increasingly clogging up the roads, to which Kennon cursed every time he got stuck behind a thirty-foot juggernaut.

He arrived at Central CID on Blackfriars Road at 8.35 and parked in his reserved space just as his colleague Detective Sergeant Jack Boyd pulled in alongside in his sporty two-tone Austin Healey with black canvas hood.

'Morning, sir,' Boyd called out as he climbed out the low two-seater. 'Did you catch the news on the way in?'

'I did. Do you get any pleasure driving that damned race car in the bloody traffic?'

'I do. It's nippy and can get through traffic easier than a saloon.'

'Well, I suppose it can always go under an eight-wheeler juggernaut. Bloody traffic gets worse every day.'

'It's not that bad. What do you reckon on the Black Panther cock-up, then? That must be the umpteenth wrong arrest by the West Mercia brigade. I bet there's some red faces down there.'

'Red faces! They've got a tough job to do, Boyd. The man's not leaving any clues and nobody has ever seen his face.'

'But he does. His method of entry is always the same, using a brace and bit. Surely it can't be beyond their wits to check all the odd-job men in the area?'

'I expect they have, but the man's never in the same place twice. His robberies must cover a dozen constabularies, which just proves my point: the regional crime squads are hampered by police boundaries. Better coordination, Boyd. That's what's needed.'

The two men entered the building by the rear entrance and went up the stairs to the first floor operations department buzzing with uniformed police and plain clothes CID personnel. The department held the central criminal records for Greater Manchester, recently being updated onto a central computer bank and indexed and categorised into classified and unclassified material. There was a missing persons bureau, a criminal fraud section and recently added was an unsolved case bureau using new methods of forensic science.

As the two men walked to their joint office at the far end of the corridor they were met by Chief Superintendent Bradley coming towards them. The chief was a stout, broad-shouldered man of above-average height with a round face and receding, swept back hair. He was a typical plain-speaking Yorkshireman who trod on more toes than anyone could remember. 'Ah, George! Quickly, man. My office!' he called out.

'Here we go. I can guess what this is about. Put the coffee on, Boyd.'

Kennon moved swiftly down the corridor and up the next flight of stairs on the heels of his chief and followed him into his office.

'I'm not happy, George, with the way you handled the kidnapping last night,' Bradley said admonishingly, staring out of the window. Even his profile revealed a mood of frustrated anger. 'Why didn't you make an entry into the premises and make a proper investigation?'

'Because it wouldn't have served any purpose. The kidnap details were sketchy, with nothing to go on. I had no forensic with me, and besides the damage to a perfectly sound door, breaking it in would have set the intruder alarm off. What was to be gained by it?'

'We'll never know now! A serious case of kidnapping requires more than a casual look from the outside. There might have been signs of a struggle inside the shop. But we couldn't be bothered to look! I really am surprised at you, George. I never expected that from you.'

'If there's been a struggle inside the shop then we'll find it with a proper forensic team. Half a dozen coppers tramping over the scene of crime last night could have destroyed any forensic evidence and made it a damn sight more difficult today.'

'But didn't you realise there's a deadline to a kidnapping? We may have very little time to investigate! We need every minute available. God forbid we haven't put this young woman's life in more danger.'

'I doubt it. And even a deadline is usually extended, from what I've read on most kidnapping cases in the US and Latin America.'

'Yes, but we're not *in* Latin America! This is Manchester, where things are different. I admit kidnapping is much rarer here than in America, but that's no reason to treat it any less.'

'Of course... but why did Sir Charles Woodward leave it so late to phone you when it was inferred his daughter was snatched at 5 p.m. closing her shop? There was a lapse of five hours.'

'He was debating whether or not to involve the police after the kidnapper issued a strong warning against it. He phoned me personally rather than the desk to get advice, as he knows me. We are old acquaintances from a shared interest in racing. He owns a stud farm at Buxton.'

'Does he indeed? This might have a bearing on the kidnap. But I never knew you were a racing man, sir.'

'Well, now you know. It takes all sorts, even in the force.'

'But why was Julia Woodward chosen? What can you tell me about the family?'

'Sir Charles is the company chairman of Woodward Civil Engineering, founded by his great-great-grandfather, Thomas Woodward. There are two sons, Ian and Peter, years apart. Ian is twenty-one and at Cambridge and Peter is in his mid-thirties. He runs the company's subsidiary, Hydromatics, in Sheffield. Sir Charles's second wife, Veronica, is a society woman of some breeding, ten years younger than him. His first wife, Jane, died just a few years ago – so this is a double tragedy for the family.'

'I've been expecting this to happen,' Kennon said. 'Wealthy families in the north of England are a prime target for criminals getting wise to the potential of demand crime where they can get away with it easier.'

'Get away easier? Whoever has done this will be damned lucky to get away with it at all! I want this given top priority. You're in sole charge of this one, George. No news has been leaked to the media, so keep them away for now. Keep it low profile.'

'It won't take them long to sniff this one out. Has Sir Charles has been advised to cooperate with the kidnapper?'

'Not yet – not until we get more information. But he has indicated he will pay the ransom if it means his daughter is released unharmed. DC Murray is doing a report; she has some detailed knowledge on the daughter, and I've asked forensic to comb the antique shop in Wellington Road for fingerprints as soon as the assistant opens up. I doubt whether she knows anything about this so it will come as a shock to her. The ball's in your court now, George. Don't let me down.'

'Do I have your permission to interview Sir Charles Woodward?'

'You do. He's expecting you. In fact he asked for you by name. First time that's happened in my career. But for God's sake tread carefully. He has a lot of influence with the Chief Constable.'

Something triggered in Kennon's memory as he went to leave. 'Is it possible that the company fraud inquiry a few years back might have a bearing on this? There were a lot of loose ends on that case, if I remember rightly. There was a blackmail never fully explained.'

'That's water under the bridge! I wouldn't drag that up if I were you,' Bradley said sharply. 'The case is closed. Do not open it up again. Is that clear?'

'Perfectly clear. I shan't do anything if it's not relevant.'

Kennon wondered if his version of relevant differed greatly to Bradley's. He was certainly touchy over it. But it was a high-profile case, and politics and police are not easy bedfellows. Nevertheless, if it impinged on the present case he would have to investigate it. This was his first kidnap case, and he was drawing on parallels to the kidnapping of a newspaper executive's wife who was mistaken for someone else. Could this possibly be the case with Julia Woodward – mistaken identity? If not, it might be quite possible that the kidnapper knew his victim.

Kennon entered his office to find Detective Constable Janet Murray waiting for him with her typed report. She was just thirty-three, the only female detective on the Regional Crime Squad, and she was on Kennon's team.

'All ready for you, sir,' Murray said handing him the typed report with a smile.

'Fill me in, Murray. I'll read it later. Where's Boyd?'

'Getting some coffee. There's not much to go on, sir. Julia Woodward ran an antique shop in Reddish Vale, and had quite a thriving business by all accounts. She travelled to auctions all over the place and specialised in Georgian furniture.'

'Yes, yes. Is this relevant to the case, Murray? Let's get to the mechanics. What were the girl's movements. What about boyfriends?'

'She was single.'

'Did she live alone?'

'Coffee, sir!' Boyd said marching in with a tray and three cups.

'Yes, Boyd! Sit down.'

'It is relevant, sir, because Julia Woodward was striving to be financially independent; in fact totally independent. She was the black sheep of the family with her rebellious ways, and Sir Charles Woodward had threatened to disinherit her.'

'How do you know?'

'I do read the local gossip columns. Six months ago Julia Woodward attended an auction and bought a rare Georgian bureau for £1,000 which was later valued at £8,000. The seller was furious and threatened to sue Raymore Auctioneers for misleading him over the price. That man was Nicholas Seagrove, a business partner of Sir Charles, who runs his Buxton stud farm. It caused a huge family rift and led to Sir Charles Woodward disinheriting his daughter for dragging down the family name.'

'I hardly think this is grounds for kidnap, Murray.'

'Could be a valid point, sir,' Boyd replied, handing out the coffee. 'If Seagrove thought that Julia Woodward was in league with the auctioneer to swindle him out of seven grand, who knows what the man planned for revenge.'

'He'd resort to legal action. This kidnap is the work of a lower-class criminal, the dangerous type who resents any capitalist's wealth and wants to make him pay. He probably has a grudge against the whole of society. If he doesn't get what he wants he will kill. What else do we have? Has anyone else reported the girl missing apart from her family?'

'Sergeant Walker has just reported one of his night beat constables spoke to Amber Taxis in the locality. One of their drivers picks up Julia Woodward regularly, but when he called at the address at five o'clock he was sent away by some bloke standing in the back of the shop. The driver thought it was odd and he noticed a chess set and holdall on the counter by an open chequebook,' Murray said.

'Well, that's a start. Where would we be without the beat? So, what do we have. The family is wealthy. Sir Charles Woodward is an industrial magnate, now on his second wife, and Julia Woodward runs her own antiques business in Reddish on the Wellington Road. This kidnapper took a bloody chance snatching her off a busy road.'

'I find that odd, sir,' Boyd said. 'She's wealthy and chooses to set up shop in Reddish not more than a stone's throw from stores in the High Street. Why there, and not some country retreat, where most antique shops are?'

'Maybe she welcomed the competition. How do I know, Boyd?'

'Reddish is quite a wealthy part of town. I have an aunt who lives in that area, and her house is full of antiques,' Murray replied.

'Right, let's get started. We need more information. Is anyone looking at the records?'

'Yes, sir. DC Baxter and Fowley are looking at car crime and burglary. We don't have any kidnappers on file.'

'Is it possible the man might have worked for Woodward Construction, and was sacked from his job, sir,' Boyd suggested, 'and is now out to make the company pay?'

'Highly unlikely, Boyd. Qualified steel workers are in great demand in the industry and if he was sacked you can bet his union would have stepped in. But it's possible, and all these things will be considered. We need a profile of the man from any source we can find. Right, let's get moving. We've got an interview to conduct with Sir Charles Woodward. DC Murray, you come with me. Boyd, you get over to the shop in Reddish and interview the assistant, and the taxi driver, and ask Sergeant Walker for uniform to conduct inquiries into the girl's routine movements from local shops. It's just possible someone might have seen her with the kidnapper.'

It was nearly thirty miles to Brighouse on the A58 leading east out of Manchester. Kennon's unmarked Rover purred at a steady 55 mph on the winding road as the fog slowly lifted to reveal a grey sky. Constable Murray kept a slim briefcase of case notes on her lap. She wore a stylish fawn coat and her chequered silk scarf was probably the only indication she was with the police, in the absence of a uniform. She was one of the new breed of women detectives emerging in the Greater Manchester Constabulary.

'What made you step up from uniform, Constable?' Kennon inquired for some light conversation.

'Solving crime, sir. Isn't that what motivates all detectives?'

'It is. But you can do the same in uniform. I see many motivated WPCs on the beat dealing with criminals.'

'But not to the same degree as the plain clothes branch. I worked hard for my promotion; it wasn't given to me. What made you become a detective, sir?'

'It was a goal I set myself. I was interested in the criminal mind from a psychological viewpoint. It can be devious, often defiant and cunning, sometimes clever and sometimes stupid, and it can be sheer evil. But what motivates it? Money and greed are not the only incentives. Power and influence play a part. But what does the killer want if it's not money? It was none of that for Brady and Hindley.'

'I know. I had just joined the force then. You were on that case, weren't you, sir? You met them. What were they like? Wasn't Brady supposed to be educated?'

'He was. Some even said he was an intellectual. He spoke like one and he acted like one. All confidence and swagger. It was virtually impossible to get him to admit to a crime. It took weeks of interviews in an effort to wear him down. Not even those dreadful tapes played to him could do it. I still cannot fathom the man. Most murderers break when confronted with evidence, but not Brady. He was defiant to the end.'

'Do you see any parallel between him and our kidnapper, sir? Will he have the same mentality?'

'No, I don't think so. There could be an evil in this man, like Brady, but on a more radical plane, whereby the kidnapper thought crime was the answer to his problems. That's a major difference between the two. But we shall find out one way or the other. I should warn you, Constable, you might not like what we find.'

'Yes, sir. I shall just have to cope with it.'

Brighouse was just off the main road between Huddersfield and Bradford, set in the dales of West Yorkshire. It was pleasant countryside, and as they drove through the hamlet with its Anglo-Saxon church, a sign pointed to Bridlington Hall up a narrow lane. Soon it loomed up through the trees and Kennon took the car up a sweeping gravel drive and parked out in front of the eighteenth-century manor house set in forty acres of private land. Once the home of Sir Richard Arkwright, the inventor and cotton manufacturer, the house boasted forty rooms, a billiard room, a library of rare books and an extensive conservatory full of exotic plants.

'So this is what she's done herself out of, struck off the family honours,' Kennon remarked as they climbed out the car and took in the grand frontage of Yorkshire limestone with blue wisteria climbing the walls. 'My, how the rich live! The accumulated wealth of our industrial heritage,' he added as they went up the steps of a pillared porch. 'Here we go.'

The front doorbell rang, and a butler opened the oak-studded door wearing a dark suit and tie, with an equally sombre face, and gave a slight bow.

'DCI Kennon and DC Murray from Manchester CID to see Sir Charles Woodward,' Kennon said, showing his warrant card.

'Follow me, Inspector. Sir Charles is expecting you.'

The butler led them through a marble hall into the main lounge with large patio doors overlooking expansive gardens landscaped with ornaments and fountains.

Sir Charles was standing at the patio doors smoking a cigar looking out over the gardens with his favourite Labrador cross at his side. He was a tallish man of sixty-five, with a sober face and a full head of grey hair, and a plain-speaking Yorkshireman to boot.

'Detective Chief Inspector Kennon and DC Murray from the Manchester Police, sir,' the butler announced.

'Ah, come in, Inspector, Constable… I've been hoping to meet you. Damned affair this is. It's the work of a crank, in my opinion,' Sir Charles said, extending his hand cordially.

'It would seem like it, Sir Charles; but one with a criminal mind. May I ask why you wanted me on the case?'

'You're a detective, and a damned good one by all accounts. I admire grafters in all fields, whether it's building bridges or catching criminals, and that's why I asked for you. My wife will be here shortly. It was she who phoned your Superintendent Tom Bradley and insisted that the media weren't to be informed. She's a very forceful woman, Inspector.'

'A wise decision. This must be quite an ordeal for you both. Kidnapping is rare, fortunately, not that it's any consolation for you, but it's also a risky business for the kidnapper. At what time did the kidnapper make contact with you, Sir Charles?'

'Around 8 p.m. yesterday evening. I took the call personally in the hall. I was just about to leave for my golf club at Thornhill. Another five minutes and I would have missed it. Take a seat, both of you.' Sir Charles motioned to the large sofa, while he chose a stiff-backed upholstered chair by the grand piano.

'What exactly did he say?'

'It was a short message, blunt and to the point, spoken with a strange accent. It sounded almost Pakistani or West Indian. "I've got your daughter," he said. "She's pretty, dark-haired, about five foot three and wears nice clothes. It would be a pity to ruin them in blood. I want £50,000 for her life. You've got two days to get it. No tricks and no police. I'll be in touch." And that was it. He put the phone down before I could say a word.'

'He never mentioned her by name?'

'No, he didn't. Is that significant?'

'It might be. What friends did your daughter have, Sir Charles?'

'A damned rum lot. This is my daughter, Inspector,' Sir Charles said lifting a framed photograph off a bookcase and bringing it over. 'She was the original deb party girl of the social circuit, mixed up with a bunch of young fools! God knows I tried to tame her.'

'You don't appear to have a favourable impression of your daughter, Sir Charles,' Kennon said, looking at the photograph of Julia in university gown holding a diploma.

'I don't have one, Inspector. My daughter is the most stubborn person I've ever met. She would try the patience of a saint! She went from an innocent eighteen-year-old college girl to a university rebel in less than two years and now she's making a hash of the antique business. That photo was taken at the graduation ceremony at Cambridge University. She got a degree in history. I reckon that's where she picked up her rebellious ways with the intellectual set, no doubt smoking pot. Damned rabble the lot of them.'

Kennon stifled a smile. 'Have you got any idea as to why someone should kidnap your daughter?'

'For money, I assume! Isn't that the usual motive?'

'Of course. What I meant to say is do you know of anyone who might have had that motive as a revenge for some past grievance or other?'

'No, I don't. Although I daresay I could soon find someone. Do you have a daughter, Inspector?'

'No, Sir Charles. I'm a single man. I never got round to marriage.'

'Really! I am surprised. Why's that? Never met the right woman, I suppose.'

'Probably. Although the job doesn't leave much time for socialising.'

'Your daughter caused quite a stir a few months back, Sir Charles, over an auction,' Murray inquired. 'Did she have any business enemies?'

'You believe the papers, young lady. She had some rum business partners and dodgy associates that the media like to get their teeth into for the gossip columns. My daughter leads her own life in Hazel Grove, a once quiet rural retreat and now a trendy little "village" taken over by the new breed of fashionable entrepreneurs.'

'Strange why the kidnapper didn't snatch her there rather than in a busy street,' Kennon said, hoping he might get an answer, but none was forthcoming. 'Could this auction business, in your opinion, bear any relation to the kidnap?'

'No. It was a storm in a teacup, Chief Inspector! Typical media nonsense that claimed I disinherited her. Superficially, I did. I had to show she couldn't get away with it. But between you and me,' Sir Charles said, leaning forward with a telltale wink, 'I think she made a bloody good business deal. Sort of thing I would have done. But it really was all blown out of proportion, and can't possibly have anything to do with the kidnapping. Besides, the man's a business partner of mine – Nicholas Seagrove, he runs Buxton Stables. It's a stud farm that rears thoroughbreds.'

'Interesting. What made you branch out into the racing world, Sir Charles?'

'It's in the blood, Chief Inspector. My father owned a stable of thoroughbreds years back. Four years ago I received a letter from Nicholas Seagrove inviting me to join a consortium to save Buxton Stud Farm from its financial straits. I didn't know the man, but he claims he heard of my racing interests through a third party. Anyway, I paid him a visit, looked over the place and liked what I saw. I invested into it and became the majority shareholder. I effectively bought Seagrove out, but I kept him on as manager as he knew the business.'

Mention of a third party cast Kennon's mind back to the fraud inquiry and the blackmail. There was more under the surface. Bradley's words came swimming back. *For God's sake tread carefully*. 'Can you tell me anything about Seagrove's background, Sir Charles?'

'No, I can't. All I know is he came out of the army in 1968 and sunk his entire capital into buying Buxton Stables with a consortium of backers. And within three years he almost managed to fold it through sheer bad management.'

'If he was such a risk, why did you invest in it and keep him on?'

'Someone had to manage the place and he knew the business inside out. His talent is with horses but his business attributes were hopeless. But there was a good staff to keep things going. Things are looking up, and we now have a good stable of geldings, and the racing season will soon be here. Look, Chief Inspector, what's this got to do with my daughter's kidnapping?'

'Nothing directly, Sir Charles. But I have to explore all avenues,' Kennon said, unable to resist digging further. 'It could even relate to the fraud inquiry that's on our files. I believe there was some blackmail involved, albeit on a small scale, that was never fully explained.'

'By God, man! Don't push your luck!' Sir Charles exploded. 'That's settled and done with! What do you mean by "on your files"? I shall have to see my solicitor about it.'

'No need for that, Sir Charles. It's classified material, but it has to be kept on file for a statutory period. You want the kidnapper caught, don't you?'

'Of course! But I don't want muck raked up!'

'Of course not. But blackmail's an ugly business, and even if resolved it is never quite finished, especially if the blackmailer sees another opportunity. It's possible that Seagrove read of the fraud inquiry and used it for his own ends.'

'By that I take it to mean you think he was the blackmailer! Say what you mean, Chief Inspector!'

'I'm being as tactful as possible, Sir Charles,' Kennon replied. 'I cannot rule Seagrove out of my inquiries at this stage.'

'Well, you're barking up the wrong tree! My blackmailer was using it over an affair I was having with my secretary. It had nothing to do with the fraud inquiry – nothing whatsoever! I was hoping to avoid this, but now I've said it!' Sir Charles exclaimed, his brow beginning to sweat. 'Nicholas Seagrove is a former Hussar officer. A man like that doesn't go in for kidnapping!'

'I'm not saying he does, but his bankruptcy gives a powerful motive. He might even have colluded with another person. I have to look at every possibility. It may be necessary to question him over his business dealings, Sir Charles, but I'll let you know.'

'He will be damned angry at any suggestion he might be involved, I can assure you.'

'What kind of man is he?'

'He gambles. I've known him fall heavily into debt, but that's part and parcel of the racing business. I've had to tell him to pull himself together on several occasions.'

'And what's his reaction to that?'

'As you'd expect. An angry retort littered with expletives.

Nick's a plain-speaking Yorkshireman who doesn't mind his Ps and Qs. You have to be in his business.'

'Was he bitter over the money he lost at auction involving your daughter, Sir Charles?' Murray inquired, earning her a cold stare from Kennon.

'Of course he was! What else would you expect!'

The door opened and Veronica Woodward entered with a maid carrying a tray of coffee. She swept into the room, dressed in flowing chiffon scarves, totally ignoring the two detectives, and slapped a diary on the lid of the grand piano.

'Have you seen this diary, Charles? It's Julia's! She blames us for all her problems. Listen to this: "January 1973. There's a bad taste in the air. If only Veronica wasn't bleeding Daddy dry, I might have my own business by now!" Damned cheek! Who put her up to it?'

'Not now, Veronica! The CID are here.' Sir Charles introduced the two detectives.

'How do you do, Inspector. Have you any news about my stepdaughter? This is really a truly dreadful affair!'

'Not yet, madam, but we're working on it. Kidnappers normally leave a trail.'

'Well, I did stipulate no media involvement to your chief superintendent, but perhaps I was wrong. They might even help. Help yourself to coffee, Inspector. You too, DC Murray. I must say I find it strange to see a woman detective in plain clothes. I thought that was all Agatha Christie stuff.'

'Oh, you'd be surprised, Lady Woodward,' Kennon answered. 'Constable Murray is one of a new breed of officers pushing the barriers of police work. We couldn't do without her.'

'Well I can't say I'm surprised, with all this women's lib nowadays. So what are we to assume from this ghastly business, Inspector? Who are we dealing with? Could it possibly be this Black Panther madman? I've never heard of such a ridiculous name.'

'It's always possible, but I don't think so. Can you shed any light on the kidnap? It's a hefty ransom he's demanding, and the man has obviously done some homework on your daughter and her background. Do you know of anyone with any reason to attempt this audacious crime?'

'No, I don't. And you can rule out Julia's business rivals, tempting though it might seem among some of them at making a quick buck. Whoever it is, is doing it simply to extract a large amount of money. He's probably got Julia held in some dingy basement in Oldham.'

'I share that conviction, Lady Woodward, if it helps. But I must look at all other perspectives. Has Julia got a boyfriend, a live-in partner perhaps, or maybe she had a volatile relationship with a man?'

'Simon Kingsley was her last volatile relationship. He was a good deal older at forty, but handsome enough. They rowed and broke up, that's all I know.'

'Any idea what they rowed about?'

'He dealt in antiques and he pressured Julia to merge their businesses in order to expand, but she refused. It reached a point where they fell out and she broke off the engagement. But he would never do a thing like this.'

'I shall need to talk to him. Do you have his address?'

'I have his business address. Acorn Antiques, Walton Street, Cheadle. Not the most respectable of districts, so I've heard.'

'Thank you, ma'am. Did you ever meet him, Sir Charles?'

'No, I didn't. But then I didn't bother with any of these so-called art experts. I doubt whether any of them has ever done a decent hard day's work.'

'They don't all have to go down the mines, dear,' Veronica said sarcastically. 'So what's next, Inspector? What happens now?'

'I shall make further inquiries among the names we've collected. But we need the kidnapper's next contact. I have a suspicion the man is known to Julia, or knows someone who has a connection to her which he has latched onto. Kidnappers usually do.'

Suddenly there was a shrill ringing of the phone in the hall and everyone froze. The butler answered and then entered the room. 'It's for you, Sir Charles. The man would not give his name. Shall I hold?'

'Yes, yes! Hold, Thomas. What do I do, Inspector? This might be him.'

'See what he wants. Resist any pressures to follow his

instructions if they're too demanding. Stall him if you can. Is there another phone?'

'In my study. Veronica, show the Inspector, please.'

Sir Charles went to the phone and relieved the butler, while Kennon was shown to the study, where he carefully lifted the phone and listened to the sinister voice.

'I see you've called in the police. That wasn't a wise move, man! Don't you want your daughter back?' the caller said in a West Indian accent.

'Of course I do! I couldn't keep them out! You won't get away with this, you know.'

'Get rid of them! I won't tell you again! Have you got the money?'

'I have the money. But before I hand over a penny I must hear my daughter's voice.'

'Naturally.' There was a muted click. Then, 'Daddy, it's me, Julia! I'm all right. Help me, Daddy! Please do as he says.'

There was another click and the voice came back. 'Satisfied? Now do as I say or you won't hear it again. Get rid of the police. You will deal with me alone! I'm watchin' every move! The money is to be parcelled up into bundles of tens and twenties and placed in a holdall weighing no more than thirty pounds. It's possible, I know. You will get more instructions tomorrow.'

The phone cut dead and Sir Charles was left stunned as Kennon returned to the hall. 'Did you get that, Chief Inspector?'

'I did. Julia's voice was on a tape; I'm sure I heard a click.'

'So did I. But it was her voice. I'd know it anywhere. How the devil is he watching us?'

'He could have seen us leave our headquarters and followed us here. He could even have an accomplice watching. But I suspect he's bluffing. Was the kidnapper's voice at all familiar to you, Sir Charles?'

'No. But it was the same as before. A West Indian Birmingham accent, as far as I could tell. But it sounded contrived, not natural. But where the devil is he phoning from?'

'That was a public call box by the tone. I'd say he's urban-based, north of the city – but where exactly? We've got to learn his movements and find his base of operations. He will have one.

Now let's cooperate with him. You've got rid of us, Sir Charles – outwardly, of course. All further contact will be made by phone only. I'll arrange a tap on your line, with your permission.'

'Most definitely. But you will probably pick up business calls. I'm not sure that's a good idea. It could distract your police work.'

'No, it won't. I'll have trained officers on the line who will be told what to listen for. There can be no mistakes. We can't afford them. Prepare the money he asked for, and leave the rest to us. Our best hope is to lay a trap when we do the handover.'

Chapter Three

Two policemen stood at the front door of Woodward Antiques in Reddish Vale. Inside the shop the forensic team was at work, and Sergeant Boyd was gathering more information from the assistant, Mary Smith, who was adamant the man she saw walked with a limp.

'Well, not so much a limp, but a peculiar walk as though he had a stiff knee joint,' she said, running a cloth over the Georgian bureau as Boyd pressed her for details.

'Are you sure, Miss Smith? What knee was it – left or right?'

'The right one, I think… or was it the left? It's a job to tell, really. I only noticed as he came in the door. Then again it might have been his hip. But the most prominent thing was his eyes. They glared like a wild cat. I only caught a glimpse but it was enough. If only I'd paid heed to it and stayed behind. I could have waited while Julia dealt with him, but she insisted I went home. What a fool I was to go and leave her!'

'You weren't to know. Any idea how old the man was, and how tall?'

'Average height, about forty-ish. It was difficult to tell. But he was not the type of customer we're used to. He was distinctly working class. Not that I've got anything against the working class, you understand. Some of my best friends are working class. But they are not the usual customers we get in this shop.'

'I'm sure. But the working class are a bit more affluent these days, Miss Smith. We've moved on a bit since the cloth-cap days. But nothing was stolen, you say. That surprises me. I mean he could have easily taken those silver spoons there or that small French clock. But then that wasn't his game.'

'Yes, he could have, but nothing has been taken, except of course for the chess set that your forensic team carried away. I shall want a receipt for it, Sergeant. Julia was most adamant we kept the books in order for tax purposes.'

'That's hardly necessary. Anyway, it's evidence now. But why did he leave it behind? That was careless of him. You're sure it was him who brought it in? Is it possible it was already here and you missed it?'

'I miss nothing, Sergeant. I know every piece in this shop. I do all the stocktaking. I know exactly what we have, right down to those silver Victorian spoons. I know every customer by name. I know their taste and I know what sells and what doesn't, and chess sets are definitely not on the list. Julia must have been pressured into buying it.'

'Well, of course she was. That was the man's excuse to get in here and keep her talking. But how did he know who to make for? You say he bypassed you.'

'Yes, he did, but then Julia is quite well known. She was in the local paper when we opened last March with a bit of a fanfare. Then three months later she was in the press again over this Georgian bureau she bought at auction for a fraction of its real value. It was a lot of fuss over nothing. But that was Julia. She had an eye for a bargain.'

'Yes, I've heard about that. Caused a family rift, I believe. Did Miss Woodward ever meet the seller?'

'Not as far as I know, but she knew who he was through her father's business connections. She comes from a wealthy family, Sergeant.'

'I know. That's what made her an obvious target. So it had to be someone fairly local who read of her family connections; but I reckon he knew a bit more than just what was in the paper. How would Julia have paid for the chess set. Cash or cheque?'

'Neither, I should imagine, Sergeant. If she's being abducted she's hardly likely to pay the man for doing it.'

'This might answer your question, Sergeant. This chequebook was left open on the table.' The forensic expert, Ray Johnson, was holding a polythene bag with the chequebook inside. He went on, 'When we get this back to the lab we can put it under ultraviolet light, which will give us the imprint of the last written cheque. Only the date and the amount was written on the stub. She was obviously in a hurry.'

'Obviously. Have you finished now, Ray?'

'Just about. There wasn't much in the way of fingerprints. The man wore gloves, but I imagine he's left a few on the chess box. He must have handled that without gloves.'

'Only problem with that, Ray, is if it's antique it could have hundreds of fingerprints on it.'

'Fingerprints don't last for ever; besides, they would have been wiped off. The clues are thin on the ground, I'm afraid. Whoever did this was very careful.'

Raymore Auctioneers of Fine Antiques was tucked inside Beasant Street in Ashton-under-Lyne on the outskirts of Manchester, where Kennon and Murray were now heading as they pursued their inquiries into the mysterious Nicholas Seagrove.

Seagrove's taste for the good things in life, which included women and gambling, came at a heavy cost. Not only did it cost him his stud farm but it broke his marriage up with an expensive divorce and further fuelled his financial problems, which was why he was still holding Gerald Raymore to account over the auction of his bureau and phoning him with his latest threat to sue for embezzlement.

'Damn the man, I say! Damn him! Who does he think he is!' Gerald Raymore raged as he slammed the phone down inside the office of his auction rooms. 'That was that damned idiot, Nicholas Seagrove! He's just had the affront to tell me that unless I reimburse him the loss on his bureau he will inform his lawyer to sue for fraud, and we could not afford the scandal it would cause.'

'Ignore him, Gerald,' Raymore's live-in partner, Julian Crouch, replied sorting a box of chinaware for the display cabinets. 'The man's bluffing.'

'But what if he's not? We can't afford the scandal of being labelled frauds. I knew it was a mistake to undervalue that bureau!'

'That's what auctions do. He agreed. What does he expect?'

'I know, but it doesn't look good for us. We are supposed to be the experts in the field, and to give sound advice – and we failed him as a customer.'

'That was six months ago. Why can't the man drop it? And

anyway, Julia Woodward said she would reimburse him, didn't she?'

'Yes, but she didn't. About a month ago he called in here to broach the subject once more… you were out at the time. He was in a foul mood. He said he'd written to Woodward's Antiques with an offer of double what she paid for the bureau but was refused, and in the process had been doing a bit of sleuthing and discovered the dirty tricks of the auction business – like faking antiques and running a ring to dupe honest customers. He said he had proof and denounced us all as crooks and swindlers, and said he was considering legal action to sue us for fraudulent trading.'

'The man's mad. He shouldn't be allowed out.'

'All the same, it's disturbing. Look what happened to Simon Kingsley. He was plagued with accusations of fraud and is now practically bankrupt. The scandal alone could ruin us.'

'Oh, come off it, Gerald. We've had enough scandal thrown at us and survived.'

'Julia Woodward could have sorted this out.'

'Why should she?'

'She was well aware of the trouble it caused and she could have put it right. If she'd accepted Seagrove's offer she could have saved us all a lot of bother.'

'Don't be so ridiculous! What was she supposed to do? Admit she bought it by mistake and give it back? We lost out in commission as well, but we're not complaining. Seagrove's stupid accusations that we defrauded him would not stand up in court, and he knows it. He's just trying to scare us.'

'There is one way we could get him off our backs. We could sell him that fake Georgian bureau we've got out the back. It's as good as the real thing and he'd never know. We could sell it to Seagrove for the grand we paid, then if he wants to re-auction it somewhere else, that's up to him.'

'Are you mad! What's he going to do when he finds out that one's a fake? He'll come back and blow our heads off!'

'Not if we tell him it might or might not be genuine. It's still a beautiful piece of furniture, expertly made in satinwood, and looks in better condition than his one. We might even be able to swap it for the original if we approach the assistant in Woodward's and ask her nicely, when her boss is out. She's got nothing to lose. We could even try a bribe on her.'

'It's worth a try, I suppose – but why should she help us out?'

'It's called loyalty, Julian. It's bound up in the antique guild of trades.'

'And what is she going to say if her boss comes back and wants to know where her cabinet's gone? It's too risky, Gerald. I should just forget it.'

'It's too late for that, Julian. The police have arrived. Seagrove has gone and done it.'

A black Rover pulled up outside the shop and Kennon climbed out with DC Murray, both visible through a pile of furniture in the front window. Even in plain clothes it was easy to spot Kennon for a detective. He wore a belted fawn raincoat with the collar turned up, and he projected the aura of a detective with a serious expression on his face.

'They're coming in, Julian. Leave the taking to me,' Raymore said while his partner carried on sorting a shelf of chinaware.

'Mr Raymore? DCI Kennon of Manchester CID. We're investigating the kidnap of Julia Woodward,' Kennon said, glancing at several military swords displayed in a rack on the wall. 'You had business dealings with her, I understand.'

'*Kidnap*! Did you say kidnap? My God! Seagrove has gone too far this time! When did this happen, Inspector?'

'Last night. We believe she was snatched from her premises in Reddish Vale at closing time. You mentioned Seagrove. Is that Nicholas Seagrove, the thoroughbred horse breeder, by any chance?'

'Yes, Inspector. Nicholas Seagrove, the racehorse owner at Buxton Stables, who should be committed in my opinion. You don't think he's responsible, do you?'

'Not as far as we know, but I have to follow every lead. I understand Miss Woodward bought a bureau in your auction around six months ago, over which allegations of fraud were banded about by the seller, Nicholas Seagrove. What can you tell me about him?'

'Oh no! What has he said? The man's a pain in the backside, Inspector. He called us to give him a valuation of his Georgian writing bureau that he was considering for auction. He said he needed the money for his divorce, would you believe. Anyway, I went to his manor house at Buxton and examined it and expressed doubt that it was Georgian. You come across a lot of fakes in this business, I can tell you.'

'I don't doubt it. But you should know if it is or it isn't, shouldn't you?'

'Not always. Even the experts can be fooled. The forger is a master at his craft, don't forget. He'll use the same materials with methods to age it and even as far as forging the maker's name and trademark. Anyway I expressed doubts about it and told Mr Seagrove I would be happy to auction it, but it was no guarantee to make him rich. We agreed a reserve of £1,000. I told him if it was the genuine article the bidding would soon reflect it. He was happy with that. But the buyers can be just as canny when it comes to auction. Anyway, the bidding was slack and it sold for £1,000 to Julia Woodward. Afterwards, a few weeks later, it turned out to be worth much more. More like £8,000. Now Seagrove is threatening to sue me for fraudulent dealing. He's even had the cheek to accuse me of running a ring.'

'A serious allegation. So who valued it as the genuine article?'

'I've no idea. Julia Woodward must have taken it to Sotheby's or somewhere like that and had it examined more closely. When it was confirmed as genuine George III, 1778, the news hit the Manchester press, and that sent Seagrove into a spin. He phoned here demanding I pay the difference or he would ruin me. The man's off his trolley, Inspector.'

'But that was six months back... and he's still demanding recompense?'

'He is indeed, Inspector. He's plagued us for months with accusations of running a ring. In fact he phoned here not more than ten minutes ago threatening to sue if we didn't make good his loss. The man's mental.'

'Ten minutes ago! What did you tell him?'

'I told him straight that if he didn't stop the threats I'd go to the police. I was going to call you anyway. I've had it with the man. I'm registering an official complaint of harassment. Arrest him, Inspector! Haul him in and get him off my back.'

'I'll question him and warn him, but I can't arrest him over a civil dispute. I'm looking for evidence to a kidnapping. People who have had dealings with Miss Woodward. Do you know Simon Kingsley? He was an ex-boyfriend of Julia Woodward. He runs Acorn Antiques at Cheadle. He was trying to get Julia Woodward to merge her business with his.'

'Simon Kingsley… Now there's a man I wouldn't trust as far as I could throw him. If you're looking for a faker he's number one in the business. Fake paintings was his speciality. We come across a lot of them in this business. Isn't that right, Julian?'

'We do, Inspector, we do. But some are better than the real thing. It's hard to tell.'

'Well, every profession has its rogues. But kidnapping takes a particular kind of rogue, a ruthless individual who bears a grudge against society and hits back in unpredictable ways. Is Seagrove capable of that?'

'Most definitely, Inspector. He's like a raging bull when he gets going. Run a trace on him, or whatever it is you do. Find out his background. I know he's ex-military. His house was stuffed full of ceremonial swords and guns.'

'He collects guns? That's interesting. But I suppose a military man would. Did you by chance happen to see a chess set in his house?'

'Do you know, I believe I did. Is that significant?'

'It could be. The man who walked into Julia Woodward's antique shop just before she went missing was selling a chess set.'

'Well, I never! So there's your man, Chief Inspector. Ex-Major Nicholas bloody Seagrove!'

'It could be. But he doesn't sound the kind of man who would resort to kidnap. But then you wouldn't have suspected Doctor Crippen of murder, either.' Kennon walked to the door. 'Greed is a strong motive for kidnap, Mr Raymore. It drives some men over the edge. If you hear of anything that might be connected to the kidnap, no matter how small, please let us know at Central CID.'

Outside in the car, Kennon sat for a minute thinking on the next route to take.

'What way now, sir?' DC Murray asked. 'Do we pay Seagrove a visit at Buxton?'

'No, Murray, we don't. He's not our man. Eccentric he might be, but his grudge is with Raymore.'

'But we'll have to see him at some time, sir, if only to eliminate him.'

'Later, Murray. I think Simon Kingsley would be more useful to our inquiries. But I'm trying to imagine the most likely place the kidnapper would have taken Julia Woodward. It helps build a mental picture of the man. A basement would seem the most obvious – but where?'

'Large houses have basements in them, sir. How about we check out Seagrove's manor house at Buxton?'

'No, it's too obvious. Apart from the man getting steamed up over the sale of his precious bureau, we don't have much evidence to rope him in for kidnapping.'

'But there's a link through the sale of the bureau, and the man's in serious debt. That's a good motive, wouldn't you say? You said yourself it's often the most unlikely person who commits the most horrendous crimes.'

'If it's a cold calculated killer, it usually is, but not always. Most crimes come about from harbouring a resentment that festers in the mind. But I can't see that in Seagrove.'

'Well, until we question him we won't know. If he lies he will slip up. We're here to solve a kidnapping mystery, sir. How else can we do it?'

'By getting to the right people, for a start. Simon Kingsley of Acorn Antiques is next. We've got more legwork to do yet. And no more daft questions like how did he take losing the money. That's plain obvious, Constable. Concentrate on motives!'

'I am, sir. That's what I'm here for to investigate. By the way, sir – who was Dr Crippen?'

It was nine miles to Cheadle going through the busy suburbs of Stalybridge, Dukinfield, Bredbury and Stockport. The traffic clogged up at lights and junctions and Murray handled the multi-channel short-wave radio. She called up control at CID head-quarters to give their position and asked for any reports that were linked to the case. Sergeant Walker was in charge of the radio room and they heard his familiar voice come over to say that DS

Boyd had returned with forensic and he'd reported the suspect walked with a limp.

'Did you get that, sir? According to DS Boyd, the man had a limp,' Murray said.

'I did. It could be crucial evidence, although I find it hard to believe. I imagined our man to be physically fit.'

Kennon's words were lost to the sudden roar of a motorcycle overtaking them and the black-leathered rider swerved round a van that was pulling out, narrowly missing a bus. 'But anything's possible,' Kennon added. 'It could even be that idiot.'

The rider weaved in and out of the traffic, leaving everything standing, as they heard the wail of a police siren in the background. Kennon smiled a flicker of satisfaction as he imagined the biker being chased by an irate copper of Traffic Division.

Twenty minutes later they were in the sprawling borough of Cheadle driving through the High Street. Kennon had a rough idea where the shop lay, as he knew the area well, and he turned into Walton Street pulling up outside of Acorn Antiques, set in a row of small shops. A second-hand car sales stood on the terrace with several cars parked on the wide pavement.

Kennon switched the engine off and checked his wristwatch. 'Note down the time, Murray. Arrived Acorn Antiques at 1 p.m.' Time was important for logging hours on crime sheets.

'Right, let's see what Mr Kingsley can tell us of Julia Woodward's last movements,' he went on, surveying the antique business. It had a run-down appearance, with the blind pulled halfway down the window.

'It looks empty to me, sir,' Murray said as they climbed out of the car and approached the shop. 'There's not much in the window.'

'It doesn't look promising, that's for sure. It's damn well closed,' Kennon said, trying the front door while peering through the dirty glass. 'And it's not for lunch, either. It looks to me as if Mr Kingsley has done a runner. Look at the bills piled up on the mat. Let's make some inquiries.'

Two doors along was a newsagent, and they went inside.

'DCI Kennon, Manchester CID,' Kennon said, showing his warrant. 'Could we have a word, sir?'

'Good day, Inspector. I am Rafel Singh Patel. Always obliged to help the police.'

'We're looking for the owner of Acorn Antiques, Simon Kingsley.'

'He's been gone over a fortnight now, sir,' the Indian proprietor replied. 'I notice when he stopped coming in for cigarettes and daily paper. Not a word said to me either.'

'Any idea where he might have gone?'

'No, Inspector. He was a very private man. Not say much at all. But lately I notice him become sullen. I think he had business problems.'

'Was it a good business? Had he been here long?'

'As long as I have. Ten years at least. He had a very good business with lots of customers. He would drive off meeting clients regular. Then it stopped suddenly a year ago. Very strange.'

'A year ago. What happened to it?'

'It began with a burglary in the middle of the night. No one heard a thing. They must have cut the alarm. He lost a lot of valuable stuff. When he arrived next morning he was in a very distressed state. He was not insured. Then shortly after he had woman problems, and all seemed to go downhill after that. Very strange.'

'Yes, strange indeed. You don't happen to know who the woman was, I suppose.'

'I know, Inspector,' the proprietor's wife said stepping through a curtain with a smile. 'Oh, yes, I know.'

'Keep quiet, Indira – it's none of our business.'

'It is our business! We all look out for each other on Acorn Terrace. Now I'm telling you, Inspector, it is a very strange affair. Mr Kingsley and Miss Julia Woodward were business partners. Both were very wealthy and he would lavish her with gifts.'

'They were not business partners, Indira.' He turned to Kennon, 'She doesn't know, Inspector.'

'Well, they made pretty damned good impression of one! She was a regular caller at Acorn Antiques, Inspector. I see them go off in the car together meeting clients and come back carrying bottles of wine. Antiques would flow in and out all the time. Paintings and chinaware, all shipped to America, so I was told. Then it stop suddenly and we don't see her as much. Mr Johnson of Johnson Car Sales tell me they had a falling-out over business merger, in which he threatened to sue her.'

'He didn't! It's not true, Inspector. It was another woman. He was having affair. It had nothing to do with business merger. He used to disappear for days on end and then come back again. Several times he put shop up for sale and then change his mind.'

'He was hiding something, Inspector,' Indira interrupted. 'He didn't want estate agents poking their noses into his affairs. He was a fly-by-night catcher.'

'Character, madam. So he wasn't as straight as he led you to believe. Would you say he could be deceptive?'

'Very deceptive. He once said to me all Manchester was a dump, only fit for pigs to live in. But I knew what he was implying, Inspector. He was against immigrants coming in. He said they were pulling down Cheadle with cheap takeaways.'

'So he was a racist as well... Any idea how old he was, or where he came from?'

'About forty or forty-five, I would guess. He said he was local but his accent was Birmingham, Chief Inspector. I could tell. Very strange.'

'Birmingham? Well, thank you, Mr Patel. You've been most helpful. If he comes back, give us a call if you would, please, at Manchester CID.' Kennon handed Patel a card and they left.

'Birmingham accent. This sounds more likely our man, Murray,' Kennon said as they walked to the car.

'How would he know a Birmingham accent?' Murray replied, hearing the radio crackle. 'There's a message coming through, sir.'

They reached the car and heard Sergeant Walker's voice calling them. 'Central CID to DCI Kennon. Come in, please.'

'DCI Kennon. Come in, Ted.'

'George. We've had a breakthrough. I'm directing patrols to Blackley. Suspect lives on the Headly Estate. 22 Barton Avenue. Over.'

'We're on our way, Ted.'

They leaped into the car and Kennon pulled away sharply into the traffic. He sped through the high street before turning into the Manchester Road and headed for Stretford, going in a westerly direction to avoid the city's midday rush hour.

They made Stretford in good time and went straight on through the leafy borough to pick up a short section of the M62 that was still being extended as part of the Manchester ring road.

'Hold tight, Murray,' Kennon said, putting his foot down as he joined the motorway. 'I may well have to break the bloody speed limit.'

As they raced along, the radio crackled with a gabble of voices from several squad cars relaying their positions, then Boyd's voice came through.

'Sir, I'm on the Headley Estate at Blackley. Suspect is known as George Sutton. He lives at 22 Barton Avenue. Over!'

'Message received, Sergeant Boyd. This is DC Murray. We are on the ring road. Stay on the channel. What do I tell him, sir?'

'Tell him we're on our way. No, give me that.' Kennon grabbed the mike. 'Boyd! Do not make an arrest. We're on our way. I'm calling for back-up. Over and out.' Kennon handed the mike back as Sergeant Walker's voice came over.

'Central HQ. Sergeant Walker to DCI Kennon. George, do you want armed back-up?'

Kennon took the mike again. 'No, Ted. Not at this stage. Call Number 7 Regional Crime Squad and alert them for standby on the Headly Estate. Over and out.'

'DS Boyd did a good job, sir,' Murray said, taking the mike.

'Providing he's got the right man. It all seems a bit obvious.'

'Can I ask why you didn't request the armed back-up, sir?'

'Not now, Murray, not now.'

They approached a large overhead motorway sign pointing towards Liverpool.

Murray stayed on the short wave listening to the radio traffic of squad cars in the area coordinating their positions. Things were moving very quickly.

A large roadside sign loomed up indicating the M62 for Liverpool, Kennon pushed his speed up to 75 mph, aware that he was going in the wrong direction. He passed the heavy lorries going flat out for the Liverpool docks and Murray felt a surge of adrenalin coursing through her veins. It was times like these she was glad to be in the CID. No boring office job for her.

Four miles on, they reached the Worsley slip road and left the motorway to double back. Kennon took the roundabout at speed and prayed for a clear road heading north of the city. He was lucky it was a clear dual carriageway.

It took a further fifteen minutes travelling at breakneck speed to reach Blackley and they headed on to the sprawling Headley council estate. It was a new estate built in the sixties to take Manchester's bombed-out war victims. A fresh fall of drizzle sent residents scurrying under shop awnings gazing out at the squad cars flashing by as the police descended on the area.

Boyd was waiting at the junction of Barton Avenue with two uniformed men when his boss came into view. The black Rover pulled up beside a police car and Boyd came hurrying over with a sergeant as Kennon climbed out.

'The house is the blue front door just behind that third hedge over there, sir,' the sergeant said, pointing it out. 'I've got a dozen men round the front and back.'

'Any sign of the suspect?'

'He's in all right. The curtains have moved several times upstairs in the bedroom window. A neighbour says he's a loner and lives with his invalid mother.'

Kennon turned to Boyd. 'How do you know this is the man we're after, Boyd? What put you on to him?'

'From the taxi firm that Julia Woodward used regularly. The boss told me a man that called into the office giving ten minutes' notice to cancel her taxi walked with a limp. His description matched Mary Smith's. I called up forensic to see if they could give me anything on the chess set and had the most incredible piece of luck. On the base of the box they found under a microscope faintly carved into the wood the name George Sutton, 22 Barton Avenue. Blackley.'

'Seems too good to be true. Right, let's go in. Sergeant, have you got a door rammer if he refuses to open up?'

'No sir. We'll have to resort to boots.'

'Give me the loudhailer. You have got one I presume?'

'Yes sir. Reynolds! Bring the hailer over.'

PC Reynolds dashed over with the electronic hailer and passed it over for Kennon to use. He switched it on and held it up.

'Sutton! George Sutton! This is Chief Inspector Kennon. Manchester CID. Come out with your hands up!'

The house remained quiet with no movement and no reply. Kennon repeated the message and a curtain twitched in the window upstairs. Then the window opened and a man's face peered out. 'What do you want?' he shouted down.

'Are you George Sutton?' Kennon called back.

'That's me. What do you want?'

'We need you to come down to headquarters and answer a few questions into our inquiries.'

'What inquiries?'

'Kidnapping inquiries.'

'I've said all I'm saying. It's nothing to do with me! Now buzz off! I've got a sick mother to look after.'

'Are you coming out or do we have to come in? It's up to you!'

Sutton stayed silent glaring down. 'All right. I'm coming out.' He closed the window as the police moved in.

Kennon was glad he hadn't called for armed back-up. The thought of the man getting shot and not being able to say where he'd put his captive would have been a disaster. The police moved in and two constables stood at each side of the front door waiting to grab the man as he came out. The minutes ticked by. Then a constable shouted, 'He's gone out the back!'

There was a scramble of police officers dashing up the front path and round the side of the house in hot pursuit. An old pram had to be dragged out the way. Then they had to struggle through a pile of household rubbish and boxes stacked against the wall that blocked the narrow space. The rear garden was no better, littered with junk ranging from old bicycles, car parts and spare wheels, all spilling round a garage that covered the width of the garden. The police entered the garage, which contained a Ford Escort that was under repairs, and found the rear door ajar. It appeared as though Sutton had gone through the garage that led to a back yard with more garages, and disappeared – despite three constables being there. In actual fact he had leaped over the fence to next door and gone across several gardens, where he hid in a shed.

The police went along checking the locked garages. One was unlocked and filled with rubbish, another was left open, but was empty while the residents were at work. The whole area, plus the surrounding gardens, was searched, yielding no sign of the man. The police had lost him.

'Strewth! There will be hell to pay,' an area patrol sergeant muttered.

The search continued as Kennon called for more patrol cars to comb the estate, and neighbours came out of houses to watch. Boyd and Murray entered Sutton's house through the back door and found his eighty-year-old mother sitting bewildered in a wheelchair in the front room.

'What's going on?' she asked. 'What's my George been up to now? He's a good lad, really. He looks after his mother.'

'I'm sure he does, Mrs Sutton. But what made him run off like that?' DC Murray asked in a quiet, unassuming manner.

'He was afraid you'd take him away.'

'We only wanted to ask him a few questions. Do you know where he was yesterday afternoon between the hours of roughly 4 and 8 p.m.?'

'He was making my tea. He always gets tea ready at six o'clock. He's a good boy.'

'Does your son play chess, Mrs Sutton?'

'Not to my knowledge. He plays darts in his bedroom. He doesn't go out much. He has a knee injury from a motorcycle accident.'

'Can we take a look upstairs, Mrs Sutton?'

'No. It's private. I can't let you rake through my son's bedroom.'

'I'm going to have to take a look, Mrs Sutton. This is a police inquiry into a kidnapping,' Boyd explained.

'You'll need a warrant. It's private, I told you.'

'I've got one,' Boyd replied, before disappearing into the hall and upstairs. What he found when he entered the back bedroom was revealing. A pile of soft porn magazines scattered by the bed; a pile of clothes dropped on the floor in a heap ready for the launderette; a dartboard hung on the door and a radio-cassette player on top of a chest of drawers. Next to the cassette player was a dirty tea-stained mug with an electric kettle and two dirty ashtrays overflowing with cigarette butts. But more revealing was a newspaper cutting of Julia Woodward pinned on the wall.

Suddenly there were loud voices outside and Boyd went to the window. Pulling back the curtain, he saw half a dozen police officers escorting Sutton down the garden path. The man looked to be middle-aged, of slim build and gaunt, and was limping as he was led round the side of the house to a waiting patrol car. The kidnapper was caught... or so it seemed.

Chapter Four

The press were gathered outside of Central CID headquarters on Blackfriars Road. Police inquiries had leaked the news of the kidnapping, and the arrest of George Sutton was the high point for the regional press, who had homed in like vultures. One attractive young woman journalist among them was well known to Kennon.

Suzanne Thornton, the 36-year-old chief crime reporter of the *Manchester Evening Standard* was poised with pen in hand as Kennon approached the front entrance.

'Chief Inspector, can you give us some details on the arrest of the kidnapper just brought in?' she asked. 'His name and where he comes from?'

'Not until he's been questioned I can't.' Kennon paused as he noticed a twinkle in the reporter's eyes. 'You should know that, Miss Thornton. Are you still with that rag the *Evening Standard*?'

'For my sins I am. What's the latest on the kidnapping? Is it Julia Woodward, the wealthy heiress?'

'Yes, it is. There are no further details except to say she is unharmed.' Kennon turned to the reporters crowding in. 'You will get a statement later!'

He entered the building and made his way to the interrogation room, reflecting on the slim chance of a relationship with Suzanne Thornton. As far he knew, she was single, and their careers were well matched, even though their ages weren't. But that was a trifling detail, he thought, as he entered the interrogation room to find Sergeant Boyd waiting.

'I've sent for the police solicitor, sir,' Boyd said. 'He should be here soon.'

Kennon sat opposite Sutton and was struck with doubts the moment he saw him. No one catches a kidnapper this fast… but the man had a criminal record, and he was the only suspect they had, and so had to be questioned.

After an hour of interrogation, in which Sutton denied everything put to him, Kennon was no nearer to knowing the whereabouts of Julia Woodward, and the doubts he'd had from the start were now overwhelming.

The evidence on the cheque that Julia Woodward signed and the news cuttings that Sutton had in his possession was convincing, but still Kennon had his misgivings. The man walked awkwardly, with a fractured knee injury. He also had a police record of sexual assaults, indecency and aggravated burglary. But the man's age of fifty-five didn't fit in with Kennon's image of a kidnapper. He just didn't look capable of it.

Sutton sat impassively with his solicitor, Edward Laing, smoking one cigarette after the other, until Kennon snatched the packet away in exasperation. Sutton was not an educated man, but he was wily and shrewd enough to dodge awkward questions. The solicitor called in by the police was showing impatience as well.

'Either charge my client or let him go, Inspector.'

'I'll ask you one more time,' Kennon said, ignoring the solicitor. 'Where is Julia Woodward?'

'I don't know! I don't even know the woman!' Sutton snapped angrily.

'Then why did you have a newspaper cutting of her? And don't give me that cock and bull of being interested in antiques!'

'I *am*. I collect military medals and badges. Ever since I was a kid I've cut out and saved the news articles that interested me. I've got dozens of items stuck in a book. I save them like some people collect stamps. Is that a crime?'

'I'll put it to you once more. You entered the shop in Reddish to sell a chess set right on closing time. But that was just an excuse to go in the shop and get her alone so you could abduct her and take her away. You knew who she was from newspaper articles, and you saw an opportunity. She comes from a wealthy family and you're unemployed – what better way to get money? She was your meal ticket. Isn't that right?'

'No, it isn't right! I don't own a chess set! I don't even play the poxy game! Someone else took that chess set into her shop, and it wasn't me. Somebody is trying to frame me!'

'Oh yes? And who might that be? Who knows you well enough to impersonate you when you hardly leave the house? Someone down the labour exchange, or some bloke in the pub?'

'It could be someone in the factory I used to work at. Fuller's Foods at Middleton. You go there and question that lot on the packing line. There were some oddballs there. Charlie Shaw and Bob Redman used to wind me up with sexual innuendos. But the worse one was Steve Bradford. He was a bragger and a bully. He was done for rape. You check him out.'

'And how long is it since you last worked?'

'Two years. I was sacked for thieving a jar of pickle. I was searched by security going out. But I wasn't the only one. They were all at it. I was just unlucky.'

'Unlucky! You've got a record for thieving and for sexual assault. Tell me about that.'

'Look, Inspector. Are you going to charge my client or not?' Laing intervened. 'He does not have to answer questions for past offences, which he has paid for. He is innocent, and you are overstepping the mark.'

'I'm conducting a serious case here, Mr Laing. A charge of kidnapping. This man ran from the police and resisted arrest. Does that sound like the actions of an innocent man?'

'He's explained that. He thought you were going after him for something else – the pub break-in, which he had nothing to do with.'

'So why did he run if he had nothing to do with it?'

'Come, Inspector. You know as well as I do that a man with a criminal record is never innocent in the eyes of the police. He's under suspicion of every break-in going. Now, either charge him or release him on bail.'

'I'm holding him in custody for twenty-four hours. I shall get all the evidence I need from forensic. If I can't charge him after that he can walk out of here a free man.'

Kennon put Sutton into custody and went back to the incident room that had been set up for the kidnapping, where a team of six detectives were searching records and tracing Julia Woodward's last known movements. Only two other suspects' names were displayed on an incident board: Nicholas Seagrove and Simon Kingsley.

'I'm holding Sutton in custody for twenty-four hours. That's all I can do,' Kennon said as he came into the incident room. 'Though it pains me to say so, I think he's innocent.'

'Innocent? With all the evidence we've got stacked against him?' Boyd said. 'How do you make that out, guv?'

'What evidence? Forensic can't match his fingerprints on the chess set. His name scratched on the box could have been falsified, and the same goes on the cheque. It's doubtful a man like Sutton would even have a chess set, let alone an antique one. And his knee injury could have been imitated by the real kidnapper.'

'That implies the real kidnapper must have known Sutton and has set him up. Which means he bore him a grudge – but at least it gives us another lead.'

'That's what it looks like. This has been well thought out by someone who knew him, and obviously not a friend. Which means it's highly likely Sutton won't know the person who did it either. That's the dilemma we're facing. Has anything come up on files?'

'One possible, sir,' DS Anderson of the Fraud Squad replied. 'Former bank manager Tom McDonald who swindled his own bank out of half a million and served two years. He came out eight months ago and set up his own insurance brokers in Leeds.'

'What made you pull him out?'

'He fits the profile. North Yorkshire man, age forty-seven and ex-professional soldier invalided out the army with a fractured knee. If a man can swindle his own bank out of half a million he has to be one clever person. He has to be totally in control and know he can beat the odds. Trait of a kidnapper, I'd say.'

'Is he a sexual pervert as well? We're looking for a man who's something of a fantasist, someone who likes to be in control of women and make then suffer. He's a loner. He probably frequents prostitutes for bondage. He will be fit. He could well be an ex-soldier who can survive on the moors in all kinds of weather, and he'll know the area like the back of his hand. Do we have anyone on file who fits that bill and is roaming free?'

'Dozens of them, sir,' Detective Constable Sue Baxter replied. 'But I came across a special one. Stanley Winstone, now thirty-six.' She pinned his photo file to the board. 'We know him as the Railway Rapist. He went down for ten years in 1965 on four counts of rape. He would lie in wait at stations in North and West Yorkshire and follow his chosen victim before pouncing at a lonely spot to drag her into the bushes. I checked the prison service release department and he's out. He came out last year on early release and is believed to be living in the Greater Manchester area in a hostel. I'd say this man fits the bill perfectly, sir.'

'Well done, DC Baxter. Check the hostels in the area. That's the type we're looking for! A man who is fit and young, in his late thirties. A man constantly on the move over the moors, like Brady was. A man searching for solitude and carrying a gun like Brady did, to shoot wildlife.'

'That's a damned big area to search for a kidnap victim, guv,' Boyd chipped in. 'Do you think he's holding her on the moors?'

'He could well be, but we can't call a large search party yet. First we have to catch the man, then we'll find his victim. Wherever she is, she must be terrified, and she's counting on us to rescue her.' Kennon looked at his watch. It was already 4.30. He couldn't believe where the time had gone. 'Keep checking the files looking for the man we've identified. He has to be fit, and may have a record for sexual offences. I need a fingerprint check with the ones found on the chess set and I need forensic to look for other clues on the box. If you'd like to chase that up DC Murray and Boyd, you come with me and we'll make a statement to the press.'

'Do we tell them Sutton is out the picture?'

'Not yet we don't. We want the real kidnapper to think we've caught him – and what better way than to inform the press we have?'

Less than a dozen miles away on Saddleworth Moor the kidnapper read the story of his arrest in the *Manchester Evening Standard* that blazed 'KIDNAPPER ARRESTED'.

The Greater Manchester Police have made a dramatic arrest of the man believed to be the kidnapper of heiress Julia Woodward. The police are refusing to reveal the name but the 55-year-old Yorkshire man from Blackley is being held in custody. Leading

61

the hunt for the kidnapped heiress is Detective Chief Inspector George Kennon, who led the hunt for the moors murderers Brady and Hindley.

'I am impressed. Detective Chief Inspector George Kennon,' the kidnapper said, as he poured a cup of soup from a vacuum flask. He laid the paper down and looked at his victim chained to the wall. 'Did you hear that? The man who caught Brady and Hindley is on the case.' He gave a mocking laugh. 'Well, he won't catch me! He thinks he already has.'

His Yorkshire accent was clearly audible even through the black hood he wore. In the light of two oil lamps, Julia was seeing the Black Panther in all his regalia, though she didn't know it. The camouflage combat jacket he wore with leather belt and sheath knife concealed other items of his trade, from razor blades to wire cutters. But the most telling piece of apparel was the black Lycra hood that showed the pink darting eyes through the slits.

'They will catch you. They won't give up,' she said. 'They will be searching the moors right now. How long do you think you can keep me here?'

'As long as I want. They won't come here. Nobody does. This place is derelict. Do you know where you are? You're in an abandoned borehole of the West Yorkshire Water Company. The whole site has been closed down ten years and moved to the Marsden Reservoir.'

'Why are you doing this? And why do you wear that ridiculous hood?'

Suddenly he turned on her in a burst of anger. 'Don't tell me I'm ridiculous!' he shouted. 'This is my identity. My persona! No one knows who I am. No one!'

She watched him pace back and forth like a panther in a cage, gradually calming himself.

'You wouldn't understand the reason behind this. I don't myself, sometimes. I can't give a rational explanation, any more than Hitler could explain why he hated Jews. It's something that grows on you.' He was tense and apprehensive.

'Will you let me go when the ransom is paid?'

'That depends on how cooperative your father is. I may have to coax him with another tape. If things go wrong, blame him, not me.'

He picked up the portable tape recorder and set it down beside her. 'I want a more pleading tone from you this time.' He ran his hand up her leg and left it resting heavy on her thigh. 'You know what I mean. How about this: "Daddy, he's going to rape me." ' He placed both hands on her thighs. 'I can do what I want with you, poor little rich girl,' he said, squeezing them.

Julia felt revulsion sweeping over her. She turned her head away to avoid having to look into his glaring eyes. This was his second visit of the day; the first was at noon when he delivered a flask of soup. He was wearing his beige raincoat then but he still hid his identity beneath the hood. He stayed just fifteen minutes before leaving her to her silent solitude for another six hours before returning with the tape recorder.

He leaned forward with lust in his eyes and she held him at bay with her hands pressed against his chest. 'I'll say whatever you want. Just get it over with and get out.'

'Oh, there's fight in the lady! I misjudged you. But you're no virgin. You're a whore like the rest of them. I can get sex from wherever I want. The Manchester whores are only too willing to sell themselves for a few quid.'

He got off her and switched on the tape. It played the first message of Julia's voice pleading to her father, and it sounded even more desperate now as she listened inside the derelict pump house with a hollow echo sounding off the walls.

'That wasn't bad. Now let's do the next one; they'll be expecting it. But this time we'll have a bit more desperate pleading for your life. Say I'm going to harm you… a bit of sobbing should do it. I'm sure you can sob. Make no mention of this place. You're in a cellar; I've written the words on this card. This is the ransom drop, so get it right.' He plugged in the small microphone and handed it to her. Then he held up a card and pressed the record button.

'Daddy, this is Julia. I'm in a desperate place.' Julia sniffed as though sobbing. 'I'm in a cellar somewhere. But I'm OK, just a bit wet. Please do as he says. Go to the phone box opposite the Red Line bus station at Nottingham town centre and wait for a call at midnight. Have you got that, Daddy? That's the Red Line bus station at Nottingham town centre.'

He signalled her to cut and switched off before playing it back. The words had the same hollow echo, adding to the tone. 'Good. That's good. If that doesn't move him, nothing will.' He closed the lid and placed the tape recorder in his bag. 'I should play this over the phone tonight. But how can I? I'm in police custody. Maybe I should wait another day and make them sweat.'

Julia was horrified. Another day in this rat-hole was unthinkable. 'They will widen the search if they don't hear from you! The police are not fools. They'll soon discover they've got the wrong man.'

'I know that. They probably know already. Kennon will soon realise he's got the wrong man. George Sutton hasn't the wit or the capability to pull off a kidnapping. He couldn't kidnap a cat. It's a pity I had to leave that chess set behind. We could have had a game.'

'You must know him well.' Julia suddenly found the will to keep him talking. 'What did he do to make you pick on him?'

'The bastard sold me a duff van! It cost me hundreds of pounds to get it fixed but there was no comeback on him. He didn't give a toss! In the end I had to scrap it and get another one. I never forgot that bastard!' He thumped the open palm of his hand. 'Nobody gets the better of me. I set him up good.'

Julia could almost feel the rage in him. 'Was he a proper dealer with a garage?'

'Nah. He bodged up old cars and flogged them from his house. I bet he swindled loads of people. It's wasters like him with no ambition that pull down the working class. I met blokes like him in the army.'

'You were in the army?'

'National service. Long time ago now. I was only a teenager, but it teaches you how to be a man. I wanted to join the SAS, but they wouldn't have me. Said I wasn't fit enough. So I trained for it bloody hard. I did cross-country running, physical exercise, weightlifting. I did the lot. I'm fitter now than I ever was.'

In the dull light Julia could see the fitness in him. 'You must be proud of yourself,' she said, trying a little psychology on him. 'Why didn't you stay on in the army?'

'I wish I had. When my time was up I came out and wasted

five years going from one job to another. I took delivery driving jobs. I started my own taxi driving business, but that didn't pay. I had big ambitions once and it all came to nowt. Life's a gamble, and when you lose out you find yourself dumped at the bottom of the heap!'

'What went wrong for you?'

'Nothing! I don't want to talk about it! You wouldn't understand.'

'Try me! I know people who think the same as you. I have done myself.'

'You! What would you know about life? Oh, I'm forgetting. Daddy's crossed you out of his will, hasn't he? Poor little rich girl.'

'Yes. But I'm not worried. I'll make my own life. You face the challenge. That's what life is about. It's a challenge.'

He turned on her suddenly and seized her by the shoulders. 'I spent fifteen years facing life's challenge, scraping a living trying to acquire a better life. I was handy at repairing things, so I became self-employed as a jobbing carpenter. I worked all the hours God sends but I could never make enough money to pay the bills. There were always the bills that had to be paid, and you spend your life working to pay them. So don't tell me how to face a challenge!'

She looked up into his eyes trying to comprehend what drove this man filled with so much hate. Then it suddenly came to her who he was. He was the Black Panther!

She hadn't realised until now. She could hardly believe it. She wondered if the police had come to the same conclusion, and it gave her a glimmer of hope. She didn't know why it did, but she felt the man was in control and would be less likely to harm her.

'So you turned to crime, is that it?' she asked softly.

He calmed down and took a half-bottle of brandy out his pocket and then, turning away, he took a swig. It did the trick. He took another swig and offered her the bottle. 'Go on, take it.'

She held her hands up and shrugged. 'Oh, I see,' he said. He cut the tape with his sheath knife and offered her the bottle. He watched her take a swig and then continued his discussion.

'I made the effort to go it alone self-employed. I was never one to sit around on the dole waiting for handouts. For a while things got better. I had a good wife who was always there for me. She understood me and indulged in my fantasies. We went on manoeuvres together over the moors and it helped me raise my self-esteem.'

'You went on manoeuvres?'

'That's right. Army manoeuvres, using field equipment with air rifles shooting wildlife – rabbits and hares, mostly. We even had a camouflage jeep. She wore battle fatigues the same as me. Even my daughter comes. She loves it. Bet you didn't think I had a daughter.'

'No, I didn't.'

'Yeah, I thought so. I'm doing this for my family. Not just for me.' He crouched over her and she could smell the brandy fumes on his breath. 'You know, you're not bad-looking. I could fancy you. Have you got a bloke?'

'No. I did have, but not any more.'

'Shame. You need a bit of excitement to liven things up.' He came closer and stroked her thighs. Then his hands were on her and she felt revulsion.

'Get off me!'

'Come on, you like it.' He pinned her down under his weight. 'All women like it. Show me what you've got.'

His hands were everywhere inside her coat and she brought her left knee up sharply into his crotch, throwing him off so that he went sprawling. He curled on his side with aching testicles.

'You fucking bitch!' He got to his feet raising a clenched fist and came back at her.

Julia's stomach churned as she feared his wrath, when suddenly there was a noise outside that checked him. They heard voices and the rattle of the chain on the outside gate.

He moved quickly, extinguishing the light from the oil lamps and staggered to the small window. He looked out through a dirty cracked window pane and saw two men at the gate with a torch, rattling the lock and chain. On the road behind them, a van of the West Yorkshire Water Company was just visible with its lights on. The two men were checking the site after a man walking his dog at midday had reported seeing a van parked inside the pump house enclosure. It was a one in a million chance in this remote area, and since the man knew the site was abandoned he phoned the water company and told them about it. Belatedly, two officials came to check it out at 7 p.m. when it was dark.

'Get the bolt croppers, Fred,' one of them said, shining a powerful torch into the compound. 'I can see a van at the back of the compound.'

'Bloody queer. How'd he get in there? This looks like a new padlock. Here, you don't reckon it's the kidnapper?'

'How can it be? They've caught him.'

'But they haven't found the girl yet. I'll get the bolt cutters.'

The man watched the two men snap through the chain and enter the enclosure. He had to act fast; the door was not locked. He rushed to his bag and pulled out his double-barrelled shotgun and darted back in the shadows behind Julia with his hand tight across her mouth. Julia watched helpless as the torchlight came under the door and it opened inwards with a creak on its rusty hinges.

As the two men stepped inside an owl fluttered somewhere up in the roof. A plank leaning against a wall was nudged and fell over with a crash as a rat scurried away.

'Who's in here?' one shouted as the torch swept the walls before falling on the crouched figures, and in that instant the gun fired over Julia's shoulder. The nearest man was hit in the chest with a blast from the 12-bore that threw him back against the wall.

Then the second barrel was fired into the glare of the torch as the second man turned back. The kidnapper leaped out, putting another cartridge into the breech, but he had lost vital seconds. The water company man was out the door and slammed it shut, holding his foot against it as he searched for the padlock. It was by his foot and as he bent to pick it up the shotgun fired with a deafening bang. The pellets went through the rotting wooden door and struck the official in the stomach with a searing flash, and he collapsed with a two-inch hole in his abdomen.

The sound of the shots echoed around the walls as Julia shouted her anger. 'You bastard! You've killed them!'

'Shut up!' The kidnapper opened the door and dragged the

second man inside and then felt the men's pulses for signs of life. The first man was dead and the other was still breathing. He looked round like a wild animal and raised the gun at Julia. 'You're next,' he said making a mock execution of her.

Then he put the gun down and turned to the thick planks that covered the top of the borehole. He dragged two of the planks off and looked down inside the well into a bottomless black hole. Then, going back to the first man lying prostrate, he dragged him to the edge of the well and heaved his body up over the low wall before pushing it over. It fell like a stone, dropping seventy feet into a well of cold water that surged up under the hills in natural springs.

Julia had seen the other man reach out for the torch and she had enough free movement of chain to help him. She reached out with her left foot and kicked the torch over to him. Then, removing her shoe, she stood in the shadows, still shackled by the ankle, firmly gripping her shoe as a weapon. As the kidnapper turned his attention back to the second man he was suddenly blinded by the glare of the torch directed in his face. In that instant Julia launched herself at her abductor and struck him on the head with her shoe and he let out a pained yell.

It was a brave attempt but it wasn't enough to stop the man, who was acting more like a caged animal let loose. He threw her against the pump housing so she fell back and hit her head, while the shackle snatched and bit into her ankle rubbing it raw.

The kidnapper turned his attention back to the official and was struck a glancing blow from the torch to the side of his head. But he parried the blow by ducking to one side, dissipating its force, and he came back with a headbutt in the pit of his stomach, charging at him like a rhino. The man went down, dropping the torch as the kidnapper seized his semi-automatic from the workbench. Demented and guilt-ridden, he fired another bullet into the man's head to silence him for good. He leaned against the bench, panting, and his warm breath froze in a vaporous cloud in the torchlight.

The silence was palpable, with just the man's heavy breathing and Julia crouched frozen in fear. She watched as he dragged the dead man across the floor and heaved him over the low wall, pushing him down the deep borehole to his fate.

In a matter of minutes the kidnapper had disposed of two men. The side of his face was throbbing and he grabbed Julia, hauling her to her feet.

'Thanks to those two we are forced to move! And don't you ever try that again!' he shouted, slapping her hard across the face.

He picked up the torch and went outside to look for the van of the West Yorkshire Water Company. He found it just a few yards back on the road with its keys in the ignition. It was a maintenance van loaded with all the necessary equipment of tools and boxes of spare valves for pumps that broke down regularly. But the item that caught his eye was the test alarm for the presence of gas in drains and sewers. This was a vital bit of equipment for his second choice of hideout. He had looked for one, but had been unsuccessful in obtaining it, and he put the meter in his pocket. Now he had to dispose of the van, and he hurried back to relock the gate before setting off up the road. It was less than a mile to the Carsbrook Reservoir, and he stopped on the edge of the natural lake before climbing out. He then released the handbrake and pushed the van down the steep grassy slope, wet and slick with rain, and watched as the vehicle careered down through the wild gorse, dropping thirty feet before plunging into the deep lake. It was almost lost in the darkness. He watched it sink beneath the surface. Then he turned and walked back in the rain with cap pulled down and the collar of his waterproof combat jacket turned up.

Twenty minutes later he was bundling Julia, with her mouth taped over with Elastoplast, into the back of the van, having cleared everything out and replaced the boards over the borehole. There was hardly a sign that the water company officials had ever been in the pump house. All evidence was eradicated, he thought, as he drove away along the country lanes, heading south across the moors for his next hideout, which was even more hideous than the first.

Chapter Five

The kidnapper drove in inky blackness across the rain-swept moors with only the occasional car passing in the opposite direction heading for the villages around Holmfirth on the road to Huddersfield. Haunted by failure, he felt more like a fugitive on the run, sweating and uneasy at having to move his victim under circumstances he would rather forget. If the water company had sent more men to search the pump house his game would have been up. He was beginning to doubt the wisdom of his first choice; he hadn't reckoned on maintenance men showing up.

He had three possible locations that had all been carefully observed for their security and remoteness. The abandoned pump house he thought would be the safest but that proved wrong. The second hideout carried the risk of gas below ground, but now the meter he had would solve that problem.

The rain was still lashing down when he reached the small village of Woodhead and joined the A628 that crossed the Peak District National Park. He was now headed south-west for the Manchester suburbs.

He was heading in the direction of Denton, south of Manchester, with the ominous thought of running into a police road check. So far he'd always managed to dodge the police checks, but there was a first time for everything. He glanced round at Julia. She was lying in the back with her mouth taped to gag her and her hands and feet tied, and knew he couldn't risk it. It only required one slip and his plan would be in tatters. He had to avoid the built-up areas as much as possible, and he turned off at the Hollingsworth roundabout. Now he was on a small B road heading for Romiley. He knew the area well from the days of his work as a self-employed jobbing carpenter.

Even now, five years later, he reckoned they were the best years of his life. It gave him the freedom he craved for. He could go where he liked and pick and choose his jobs in places he would never have otherwise visited. But always there was that underlying anxiety that no matter how hard he worked he would never earn enough. He would always be scraping a living, always be just getting by until the next job came along. It infuriated him to think of all the skivers and dole cheats getting more money than him while he worked all hours. Then there were the immigrants from Asia and Africa coming in and getting social security handouts, when they had never paid a penny in taxes, or done a day's work for it.

He looked at the fuel gauge showing just a quarter of a tank and knew he'd have to stop and fill up. Three miles further on he reached the Hazel Grove BP Station and he pulled in on to the well-lit empty forecourt beside a pump. He put five gallons into his tank, watching the figures add up to two pounds, and then switched off.

He clipped the pump back and walked to the small shop to pay, when he was suddenly brought up with a start that brought him out in a cold sweat.

A poster was stuck on the window with the words, 'Have You Seen This Man?' above a police photofit of himself with thick dark hair and glaring eyes. It wasn't a bad image. He'd seen it before in newspapers but this was the first time he'd seen it on a poster. Below the picture, the reward of £25,000 stood out with a central phone number to the Greater Manchester Police. He stood transfixed looking at it and wondered whether to go into the shop when a police car pulled in and stopped within ten feet of him.

The cold sweat now turned to panic as two traffic cops got out and walked towards him. He turned his back to them and watched them enter the shop. There was no way he was going in now. Paying for petrol was out of the question. He rushed back to his van and was mortified to hear a battering on the rear doors.

He jumped into the cab and saw his captive violently kicking the doors with her feet. The steel rods, top and bottom, were working their way out. He started the engine while reaching for a length of rope to lash her across the face just as she gave another almighty kick and the doors burst open. She managed to throw her signet ring out of the back, and it bounced across the forecourt as he drove off with a screech of tyres.

He accelerated down the dark forest road heading for Macclesfield, searching for a lay-by while constantly checking the mirror for a police car following, but the road was clear. He drove five miles on the lonely road with the rear doors flapping until he found a lay-by and was forced to pull in and stop.

'I could kill you for this!' he shouted as he got out and slammed the doors closed. He locked them, even though the lock was defective and the doors could still be wrenched open. He reckoned it wouldn't be long before the police were on his tail and he scampered back behind the wheel. As he accelerated out the lay-by he saw a blue flashing light in the side mirror and he broke out in another cold sweat.

There was no turn-off anywhere after he missed the first lane on the opposite side of the road. He simply had to outrun his pursuer. The rain had stopped, which gave him a clear view as he drove at 60 mph on the dark road, not even slowing for the bends. His eyes were transfixed on the blue flashing light in the mirror and he was approaching a fork in the road at Macclesfield.

This was his best chance of losing the police and he never let off the accelerator for a second. As he approached the small village, he turned off his lights to take the right fork, so that his tail lights would give no clue to his pursuers as to which direction to follow.

Driving blind for half a mile, he was forced to switch his lights back on and narrowly missed running off the road. He had thirteen miles to go, and he was constantly looking in the mirror for the blue light of the police car. He never saw it again, and he reckoned correctly they must have taken the left fork. He was out of danger for the moment.

He was heading for Kidsgrove and a place called Bathpool Park. He would have preferred a much later hour, although he was reasonably certain the place would be deserted. There was nothing there except playing fields.

It was nine o'clock when he arrived at the small town of Kidsgrove in Staffordshire. He was twenty-five miles south of Manchester inside the boundary of the Staffordshire Police

Authority, which he had outfoxed on numerous occasions. He took the road that ran along the London to Manchester railway line heading for Bathpool Park, which lay on the far side of the town, arriving at the open entrance on the south side of the railway that bordered the park segregating it into two distinctive areas.

But it was beneath the surface that Bathpool Park hid its deadly secrets. The park stood over a redundant coal mine that had shut down a decade ago, and the slag heaps were grassed over and planted with saplings.

The result was a landscape of hillocks, with one side of the park higher than the other, and plenty of trees all round to screen him as he drove slowly into the park in pitch darkness along a twisting track. He crossed the railway cutting that ran through a tunnel, still following the track with headlights switched off and not a single light to be seen anywhere. The park was as remote from the town as the old coal mine was.

At one end of the park was the Kidsgrove Reservoir, with an overflow drainage system which was unique in that the water was carried along one of the old coal tunnels into a subterranean canal.

The Panther had recalled this place from memory after reading about it years before during its construction. It was most unusual, for the drainage system was constructed over the old colliery with three vertical shafts, and only two shafts were openly visible. The third was buried on Coal-Pit Hill.

He drove past a concrete pillbox that covered the entrance to the first shaft, known as the spillway, and continued to the next less visible opening of the central shaft on the railway embankment. Even in darkness he knew where it was. He drove another twenty metres along the shallow railway embankment to the next concrete plinth and stopped. Then climbing up to the plinth he stooped over the manhole cover with a T-shaped key and heaved it open.

It was heavy, and only a strong pair of hands could lift the cast iron cover up on its hinges, where it hung back on a slight angle. Then he took the toxicity meter and tied it to a length of rope and lowered it down to test for gas. He listened for the telltale beep that would indicate a toxic atmosphere as the meter went halfway down before stopping on a platform. There was no signal, and he let go of the rope to let it fall.

Now came the job of transferring everything underground down a forty-foot ladder that plunged into darkness. He worked methodically, first taking down all the survival equipment in a large holdall, which included a sleeping bag, the sponge mattress and two survival blankets inside plastic sheeting. Then he took down two oil lamps and a bag of hand tools with some steel wire and roll of tape. He piled it on a platform ten feet from the bottom and then went back for his victim who was shivering with the cold, left tied up in the van. This would have been her only chance of escape. She was left unattended for ten minutes or more… if only someone had passed by. But that chance was very remote.

'Where are we?' Julia asked as he pulled her out the back of the van, blindfolded.

'I'm not at liberty to say, and you should know better than to ask,' he gruffly replied. 'Now, do as I say and you won't get hurt.' He marched her towards the open manhole. 'Get on the ladder. It's quite safe, you can't fall.' He guided her on to the ladder and held her as her feet found the rungs. Then he removed her blindfold. 'Now go down slowly. You won't fall.'

Julia stared down the black hole, terrified, and knew it was no good arguing. If she didn't go down the ladder he'd throw her down. He released his grip as she began her descent into darkness. She was petrified and acutely anxious as she felt the cold air coming up. The torch gave small comfort as she went down, her heart beating like a drum. She descended to the first platform halfway down and gingerly stepped on it.

He shouted after her, 'Carry on down the ladder!' His voice echoed down the shaft.

She reached for the next ladder behind her on the opposite side and continued on down until she reached the next platform at the very bottom where the gear was stacked. She stood shivering in the darkness and looked up to see if he was coming, but all she could see was the torch glaring down hung from the ladder by a piece of wire. He had made sure she was down before moving the van further along the road to avoid suspicion and then returning to enter the shaft.

Now he was on the ladder and descending after closing the lid. He came down with the powerful torch lighting the way and stopped just above her. 'Carry on down,' he told her. 'You won't drown. The water you can hear in the tunnel is only a few inches deep.'

Julia reasoned he must be telling the truth, having brought all the stuff down, and she stepped off the ladder into the freezing water that came halfway up her legs. It was more than a few inches deep, more like a couple of feet on a slimy bed of coal slag.

'Take hold of this,' he said, handing her the lantern and a small kitbag. Then he followed on down with the rest of the equipment until they were both standing in the tunnel feeling the rush of cold water and a cold draught blowing in from somewhere.

'Follow me!' he grunted. He went ahead carrying his load and the torch to light the way.

The concrete-lined tunnel was 150 metres long and six foot in diameter, so they could walk without stooping. They came to a set of concrete steps near the end of the tunnel and he motioned her up. Julia looked down into the blackness where the tunnel dropped away below her like a bend in a pipe. It went down to another short length of tunnel that ran into the subterranean canal. She was being held in a huge drainage system.

At the top of the steps they entered a dry culvert going along towards the main shaft to a platform at the foot of a ladder. He motioned her onto the ladder and they went down just ten feet and stepped onto another platform. They were now sixty feet below ground, and this was to be Julia's hideout until the ransom was paid.

'You won't be here long,' he told her, unpacking the survival gear. He threw her a small towel to dry her feet as she removed her shoes.

'You can't leave me here!' There was a note of desperation in Julia's voice. 'Don't leave me down here, please.'

'Shut up! It's perfectly safe. I had no choice after the pump house.'

'Was it necessary to murder those two men? Couldn't you have just tied them up?'

'It was unfortunate, but I had no choice. I haven't come this far to fail now.' He spread the mattress out and unrolled a sleeping bag. 'Get into this,' he said, and watched her struggle into it as she sat on the grubby mattress.

'It may be necessary to leave you a day or two. You have a flask of soup and a bottle of brandy. I think that's reasonable. I will return around this time tomorrow. I will either have the ransom, in which case you will be free, or you will be spending another night down here.' He thrust two survival blankets at her.

'It's all in the hands of your family, whether they choose to cooperate and follow my instructions, or not.'

'They won't give you anything until they see me released.'

'That's up to them. But they'll do as I tell them.'

'How can you can sleep at night?' she said in a baleful appeal. 'What would your wife think if she knew?'

'That doesn't concern you,' he said unrolling a length of wire. 'I'm sorry to have to do this, but it can't be helped. Bend your head.'

He looped the wire round her neck, twisting it with a pair of pliers until it formed a hangman's noose. Then he let out five feet of wire and wrapped the other end round a stanchion beneath the platform well out of her reach. Then he meticulously wrapped insulation tape round her hangman's noose so that it didn't cut into her neck.

'Do not attempt to take this off,' he told her as he took the meter out of his pocket and tested again for gas. It registered a safe level for lighting the oil lamp.

'You're lucky. You won't die of carbon monoxide poisoning, and you can have a lamp burning.'

'Is this wire necessary? I can't go anywhere…'

'I told you it was. Now I must go. Sweet dreams.'

He went up the ladder of the main shaft, higher and higher, with the torch getting dimmer until it was a faint glow at the top. He opened the manhole cover and climbed out and she heard the lid slam down with a shuddering clang. Then he was gone like a cat in the night.

Julia was entombed. She looked forlornly round at her new prison in the glow of the lantern, trembling with the cold, and pulled the blanket round her. She poured herself some warm soup in the cup and sipped it slowly trying to gather her thoughts. Where was she? Would she ever see the light of day again?

She finished her soup and then put the bottle of brandy to her lips to feel the warming effects giving some comfort in the pit of her stomach. She felt tired and eased herself slowly into the sleeping bag before pulling the blankets over her. She must have laid there for an hour, wondering whether anyone was missing her and what her family were doing, before she finally fell into a deep sleep.

Chief crime reporter Suzanne Thornton, of the *Manchester Evening Standard*, was about to leave for her first assignment when a small package from the internal mail landed on her desk.

It was addressed to her personally and when she opened it she found a cassette tape inside with the name 'Julia Woodward' on the label. She looked at it curiously and then slipped it into her coat pocket before leaving with Bill Royston, the news photographer, for their first assignment at Manchester CID.

'I got this in the post,' she said, showing the tape to Royston as they made their way out the building. 'I'll play it in the car before we go.'

Outside in the car she pushed the tape into the car radio-cassette, and they listened to a male voice speaking with a heavy North Yorkshire accent.

'Hello, Suzanne. I see the Black Panther has branched out into kidnapping. Perhaps now you might take him a bit more serious and give him a bit more attention in your newspaper. That way you can keep one step ahead of the police who are no nearer to finding him than they were when they started four years ago. You take my tip and give it front-page coverage. You can't ignore the facts when they're staring you in the face, can you?'

'Bloody hell, Suzanne! Was that the real Panther or what?' Royston said incredulously.

'I've no idea, but he's clearly telling us the Panther is the kidnapper. I wonder if Chief Inspector Kennon knows that.'

'I shouldn't think so – not if the guy they brought in yesterday is anything to go by.'

'How do you know that?'

'I can't imagine the Panther living on a council estate. He'd have been shopped by his neighbours long ago.'

'But why is this man seeking publicity? I thought we'd given him fair coverage? …Unless this tape is meant to deceive us. It's a spoof, Bill. I'll warrant ten to one it's a spoof. I'll hand it to the police and they can sort it out.'

Kennon drove into work the same morning, deeply puzzled. The kidnapper hadn't made the expected phone call to Sir Charles, and he wondered what new game the man was playing. Was it because Sutton was still in custody and the kidnapper was using it to his advantage, or had something gone wrong with his plan for collecting the ransom? But whatever it was, he sensed the advantage of gaining an extra day for tracking him down.

He pulled into his usual place in the rear car park and walked round to the front of the building straight into a crowd of news reporters in the reception area. They were pestering Boyd for details of the arrest when they suddenly turned at the sight of Kennon coming in.

'Chief Inspector!' They surged round him with a barrage of questions.

'Will you be releasing the name of the man you are holding in custody?'

'Is this man the kidnapper?'

'Is there any news on the heiress, Julia Woodward?'

'Gentlemen!' Kennon yelled above the hubbub. 'The man we are holding will be released today. He is not the kidnapper. It's my belief the real kidnapper set him up to divert us, and we are now seeking a new suspect.'

'Who are you looking for, Chief Inspector?'

'Do you have another suspect in mind?'

'We have no suspect other than a North Yorkshire man, probably in his mid- to late-thirties. I hope to issue an artist impression from a profile later today.'

'Chief Inspector!' Suzanne said pushing to the front. 'I have something here that may help your inquiries.' She handed Kennon the tape. 'It arrived on my desk less than an hour ago.'

Kennon was pleasantly surprised. 'A tape! It's probably a spoof. May I borrow it?'

'Of course. Let me know what you think. I have my own suspicions about it. You know where to reach me.'

'Thanks, I will. That's all for now, ladies and gentlemen.' Kennon appealed to the throng. 'Please clear this area.'

Kennon turned and bounded up the stairs with Boyd as the press were ushered out the door.

'Are you sure we can let Sutton go, guv?' Boyd asked.

'He's no more the kidnapper than I'm Jesus Christ.'

'But there's been no further contact from the kidnapper on the phone taps.'

'I know, Boyd. The staff keep me informed as well.'

'What do you reckon is on the tape?'

'Probably a bogus claim looking for a reward,' Kennon said, stopping at the coffee machine. 'I never noticed before what an engaging smile that woman on the *Standard* has. I think she might be useful to our inquiries. Coffee, Boyd?'

They entered the Kidnap Incident Room, which was busy with the extra bodies that Kennon had requested, and were met by Barry Hodges, the Regional Crime Squad Coordinator for the whole of Greater Manchester.

'Morning, George. I got your request for extra staff,' Hodges said. 'Only three at the moment from Number Four squad: Sergeants McBride, Brown and Roberts.'

'Thanks, Barry. That's a help. I see Doctor Erwin's arrived.'

The police specialist profiler, Dr James Erwin, who was attached to the cold case department of unsolved crimes, was sitting studying a book of male faces used to construct an identity of a suspect for a police photofit.

'Morning everyone,' Kennon said, putting his coffee on the desk and going to the incident board, where suspects' names were displayed.

'Right. What have we got? Not much, by the look of things. Just three witnesses who saw the kidnapper: Mary Smith, the shop assistant; the taxi driver, and Peter Amber, the boss of Amber Taxis. Not forgetting, of course, the star of the show, George Sutton, who knows nothing and will have to be released from custody. But he's not quite out the picture yet. He may know the kidnapper from past employment at a food factory. But he's vague about it and that was two years ago since he worked there.'

'Well, surely that's reason enough for holding him, sir,' DS McBride remarked. 'He could be an accomplice of the kidnapper.'

'Hardly likely, if the kidnapper scratched Sutton's name on the chess set.'

'But not so unlikely if he wanted to get rid of him?' McBride countered.

'If Sutton thought his accomplice was leaving him to take the rap he'd be singing like a canary. I should have thought that was obvious!'

'Not necessarily, guv,' Boyd replied following McBride's lead. 'Not if he knew we couldn't charge him with anything for lack of evidence. If that was all part of the plan he will walk out of here laughing.'

'And so will the real kidnapper, if we waste time on the wrong man. This is a one-man job, in my opinion. I know most kidnappings are carried out by a gang, but I don't think so in this case.' Kennon took a swig of coffee from the vending machine and winced at its bitter taste. He'd forgotten to add sugar.

'But we'll follow up on the names of Sutton's former work colleagues. You can do that, McBride, seeing as you're so keen. It's my belief the man is a lone wolf. He stands more chance of success working on his own. You'll agree with that, wouldn't you, Doctor Erwin? Have you done a profile on the man?'

'I've constructed one as far as is possible, George, on the limited information,' Erwin replied, feeling it was necessary to enlighten the detectives with a few scientific facts.

'In a nutshell, gentlemen, I would say the man you want is white, middle class, in his late thirties and reasonably well educated. But he suffers from delusions. Call it the forty-year itch, if you like. It's usually brought on by the uncertainty of the future. He's most probably failed at something, or everything, and is unemployed, and for that he bears a grudge against society. He's a loner, possibly married, and more than likely to have done national service. He will be a forceful character with a strong sense of discipline and he will be physically fit.

'I would hazard a guess he's a Yorkshireman, and fairly astute. He will not want others involved for fear of leaking his plan, which has taken considerable time to put together. As for the man's traits, he will be the person sitting in a pub on his own, brooding and planning his next move. He will be silent, staring into the middle distance, not seeming to notice anyone around him… but he misses nothing. You could pick him out by his furtive actions. But he will have an underlying confidence.'

Erwin looked at all the perplexed faces staring at him and smiled. 'I know what you're all thinking. I can read it in your faces. How the bloody hell does he know? It's a psychological profile of the man's character based on his actions using different viewpoints.'

'How does he treat his victim, Doctor?' a voice called.

'Good question. The victim will be isolated somewhere. She will be in a fair amount of distress and he will have to treat her with respect to lull her into a false sense of security. After all, he may need her cooperation at getting the ransom. Harming her would be counterproductive, but at the same time her life is threatened by a deadline. He will demand a timescale of a few days for the ransom to be paid. The longer he holds her, the weaker his position is and death more likely for the victim. But the one thing this man will have as an advantage is the ability to escape and disappear when you think you've got him. And now we ask the million-dollar question: who is he? Do we have a man like that on our files?'

'What about the tape, sir?' Boyd said. 'I think we should hear it.'

'Yes, Boyd. I'd forgotten it. I'll put it on.'

Kennon took the tape from his pocket and inserted it into a cassette player.

'This tape has come from the *Evening Standard*,' said Kennon, switching the tape on. 'I haven't heard it myself yet.'

'Hello, Suzanne. I see the Black Panther has branched out into kidnapping. Perhaps now you might take him a bit more serious and give him a bit more attention in your newspaper. That way you can keep one step ahead of the police who are no nearer to finding him than they were when they started four years ago. You take my tip and give it front-page coverage. You can't ignore the facts when they're staring you in the face, can you?'

'Well, it's certainly a Yorkshire accent. But it's a spoof,' Kennon said, switching the tape off, 'sent in by some crank who gets a kick out of this sort of thing.'

'Don't you believe it, George?' Dr Erwin said. 'It's a genuine attempt by the Black Panther to get publicity for the kidnapping.'

'Why would he do that?'

'Because he craves it. It feeds his ego, as simple as that.'

'I'll back you on that, Dr Erwin,' Hodges said, stepping up to the map. 'West Mercia are dealing with the biggest manhunt on record for a phantom serial robber who is incredibly fit. He leaps four-foot walls in one bound. No one knows him, no one has seen his face and yet he wakes his victims in the middle of the night. He is hooded on every raid and he is as agile and swift as a panther. We have photofits in every newspaper. There are detailed descriptions of his height, weight, accent, and even the clothes he wears – and still he evades capture. You all know who I'm talking about. I'd go so far to say, Doctor, that the man you have just described is the Black Panther.'

'No, it's not,' Kennon replied. 'This man might share the same profile as the Black Panther, but not the same motive. Until I get evidence to the contrary we cannot let these two cases get entangled or we'll end up chasing rainbows.'

'But he's a plausible suspect,' Hodges replied.

'For post office robberies he is, but not for kidnap. The man who kidnapped Julia Woodward knew her by sight. She's been in the media and is well known as a wealthy heiress. She was a prime target for kidnapping. I have two suspects in mind. One is Nicholas Seagrove of the Buxton stud farm which Sir Charles Woodward is chairman of, and the other is Simon Kingsley, who wanted to merge his antique business with hers. Both these men had a strong motive and are in a far better position to carry out a kidnap.'

'So where do we search for the victim, sir?' DS Roberts inquired.

'My hunch is she is hidden on the moors around one of the reservoirs. There are a few redundant pumping stations in West

Yorkshire, especially around the Saddleworth and Marsden reservoirs. I can't think of anywhere better to hide a kidnap victim.'

'That implies she is sometimes left unguarded, sir,' Roberts replied. 'Isn't that taking one hell of a chance for the kidnapper?'

'Not if it's a place no one visits, like a closed pump house. The kidnapper can afford to leave her, which means he will be going back and forth from his base. That's how we catch him – while he's on the move. Our first task is to get out and talk to people who knew Julia Woodward. Concentrate on the areas of Reddish and Hazel Grove where she lived. Constable Murray has the names of her known friends and associates.'

'Andrea Peters and Julie Goodchild,' Murray said, waving a sheet of paper across the room. 'One has her own hairdressing salon in the main street and the other is an air stewardess. Both women live on the new private Woodley Estate in an exclusive area.'

'Don't forget Simon Kingsley, Murray,' Kennon prompted.

'Yes, sir. Also in the frame is Simon Kingsley, Julia Woodward's former boyfriend, who used to run Acorn Antiques in Walton Street, Cheadle. He has now mysteriously disappeared. He put pressure on Julia Woodward to merge their business enterprises and when she refused he threatened to sue her, or so we are led to believe. He has been described as shady and untrustworthy.'

'But not a serious kidnapper,' Doctor Erwin said sardonically. 'And certainly not the Black Panther. The man you want, Chief Inspector, will be a psychopath without a doubt; but not so you'd notice. He will be adept at covering it up. He will appear normal and will have a good level of intelligence.'

Dr Erwin was suddenly interrupted by the shrill ring of the phone. Boyd picked it up and listened intently to the duty sergeant downstairs in reception spill out a message that set alarm bells ringing.

'Sir! That was Sergeant Walker. The West Yorkshire Water Company have reported two of their maintenance men gone missing on Saddleworth Moor. They were responding to a call from a member of public claiming he saw a van parked in the Number 5 pump house at the Carsbrook Reservoir.'

'Since when?'

'Since 8 p.m. yesterday.'

'They've taken their time to report it! Follow it up, Boyd, and designate scenes of crime up there to take a good look round for any clues that will help us with the search for Julia Woodward. McBride and Murray, you two investigate the men behind those names Sutton gave us, and then talk to the women at Hazel Grove. OK. Let's go!'

Everyone scrambled out, and Kennon went to a filing cabinet marked 'Classified'. He unlocked it with a combination number. He flicked through the files under 'Investigative Fraud' until he found the one he wanted and pulled it out. It was headed: *Investigation into the Woodward Cash for Ministers Inquiry. February 1970*. Kennon knew of the case but was not involved in it. The investigation, which was triggered by a whistle-blower, revealed that Woodward Engineering had systematically bribed government ministers into awarding them contracts for lucrative building projects.

The investigation also revealed the state of the company finances. They were in dire straits, with a black hole in the company pension fund. Sir Charles had been found guilty of plundering company assets and deliberately inflating the company shares to meet the merger requirements with Caulston Steel. The case dealt Sir Charles and the company a severe blow. But Kennon wasn't interested in that. He was looking for the blackmailer who came to light during the inquiries but was never found.

As Kennon sat reading the report, he suddenly became aware of Chief Superintendent Bradley standing in the doorway with a face like thunder. 'George! My office as soon as you can! We've got a storm brewing!'

'Yes sir!'

Bradley disappeared, and Kennon read through the summary, which condemned the company for unlawful practice. The scandal caused the resignation of the Minister for Transport, and two junior officials were sacked. But it was the allegations against Sir Charles Woodward, that he was systematically falsifying company profits precipitating a merger with a rival company, that dealt the biggest blow. The merger with Caulston Steel would have projected Sir Charles to head of a major industrial conglomeration enabling him to expand his stud-breeding enterprise and build the biggest racing stable in the country. The inquiry also uncovered an affair between Sir Charles and his secretary, which was open to a blackmailer who was never revealed.

Kennon felt a tenuous indication from Sir Charles and his siphoning off profits to buy out Seagrove that pointed to the kidnapping. Could the blackmailer also be the kidnapper?

Kennon was pulling strands from all directions and treading on dangerous ground. He was seeking a pattern of events that somehow led to the kidnapping of Julia Woodward, and he felt Sir Charles could hold the key – maybe unwittingly and maybe not. He would have to tread very carefully. He returned the file to the safe and left for Bradley's office.

Kennon found the Chief Superintendent in an agitated state when he arrived in his office. 'Sit down, George. This man Sutton you've arrested, I hear you're letting him go.'

'I am, sir. He's innocent. There is nothing to connect him with the kidnapping.'

'But you cannot be one hundred per cent sure! The chess set links him to the crime. The man has a police record. What more do you want?'

'A lot more. The chess set was a ruse to finger Sutton. He's just a petty thief. He's not even capable of doing a kidnap. We've done a profile with Dr Erwin. The man we want is more like the Black Panther.'

'Yes, and that's the storm that's brewing. I've got half a dozen chief constables on my back right across the Midlands asking me why I didn't inform them we had the Black Panther on our patch. They point out that they have expended thousands of man-hours in interviewing and gathering information on the biggest manhunt going, and we had the man in custody and were stalling their investigations!'

'But we don't have him. Sutton is nothing like the Black Panther. And furthermore, we don't attribute the kidnapping to the Panther. The two cases are not related.'

'Yet you've just claimed he could be the most likely suspect.

Make your mind up! Is the kidnapper the Black Panther or not?'

'No, he's not. My suspicions rest with two other men who had dealings with the Woodward family: Nicholas Seagrove and Simon Kingsley.'

'How the devil do they fit in the picture?'

'Both were on the verge of business failure. One was the owner of a stud farm, which you already know of, and the other appears to be a rogue of an antique dealer who was after Julia Woodward's business. They would have both been in a position to plan the whole thing.'

'So they might, but kidnappers don't abduct people who know them.' Bradley stood and gazed out the window, seemingly on edge.

'I've got Sir Charles coming in this morning. He's got something he thinks I ought to know loosely connected to the kidnapping. I've no idea what it is. I've arranged for Sergeant Walker to escort him to my office.'

'I should point out, sir, that Sir Charles figures predominantly in my investigations.'

'What the devil do you mean by that?' Bradley exploded.

'This case is a bit more than a simple kidnapping. I believe its roots go back to the investigation by the Fraud Squad into the cash for ministers inquiry, which uncovered a lot more than Sir Charles would have liked, and subsequently leads to him withholding information that is linked to the kidnapping.'

'You will not bring that up in front of Sir Charles! I absolutely forbid it!' Bradley thundered. 'Are you suggesting he had his own daughter kidnapped to silence his critics?'

'Of course not. But what I am suggesting is that the case uncovered serious fraud within the company, and Sir Charles was implicated in it. He was living a lavish lifestyle, pouring money into breeding thoroughbreds, and there was even a hint of blackmail over an affair he was having.'

'Yes, I know, but that was four years ago, and he's emerged with a clean sheet. What are you getting at, George? What's this got to do with the kidnapping?'

'I'm coming to that, sir. Also at the same time there was speculation of a merger with Caulston Steel, but the scandal caused Caulston to pull out. It triggered a share collapse in the company in January 1970 and there were calls for Sir Charles to step down as Chairman. A year later the owner of Buxton Stables, Nicholas Seagrove, went bankrupt and sold out to Sir Charles, who then took control of the whole enterprise – yet kept Seagrove on. It all fits too neatly to be a coincidence.'

'Pure speculation! There's nothing there to suggest Sir Charles knows who his daughter's kidnapper is or the motive.'

'Nevertheless, the connection between Julia Woodward's abduction and Sir Charles's takeover of Buxton Stables could well have something to do with it.'

'Follow that line of inquiry if you must, but I insist you do not drag Sir Charles into it! Is that understood?'

Suddenly the phone rang on Bradley's desk and the Chief Superintendent listened in stunned disbelief as he took the message and put the phone down. 'That was Sergeant Walker. Traffic patrol have just reported a shooting on the A672 at Booth Wood at Holywell Green. Sir Charles's car was stopped by a gunman. He's been shot and rushed to hospital in a critical state.'

'My God!' Kennon was struck with the thought of dire consequences looming. 'What lies in store now for Julia Woodward?'

Chapter Six

A small army of police surrounded Sir Charles's dark blue Bentley parked in the lay-by at Booth Wood. Forensic were removing a .22 bullet from the back seat and searching for other clues. Traffic control had put a cordon round the car as uniformed police examined the ground for clues to the assailant's vehicle, and George Kennon was speaking to the chauffer, Sidney Porter.

'I was certain it was a police motorcyclist that forced us over, sir.' Porter was still visibly shaken by the ordeal. 'I wouldn't have stopped otherwise. It had a white fairing with chequered stripes, a tall radio mast on the pillion, and the rider continually flashed his headlight to pull us over.'

'Then what happened?' Kennon asked.

'I told Sir Charles we were being stopped by the police and he replied that it was a damned nuisance but I had better see what he wanted. So I pulled into the lay-by and he stopped just in front of us. He was wearing a dark weatherproof jacket and a police motorcycle helmet with goggles, but I noticed there was no police label on the back of the coat. He got off and walked back to us, removing his gloves as he came. I lowered the window and asked him what the problem was and he said I was speeding. He asked for my licence and as I searched my pocket he suddenly pulled a pistol and fired three shots into Sir Charles on the back seat. Then he said, "Give me the money!" He rapped it out sharp, like an order. I said there is no money. But he made me get out and open the boot. It was empty. Sir Charles wasn't carrying anything when he left the house.'

'Did you see his face?'

'No. He wore a hood with slits for the eyes. I didn't notice until I got out because he was wearing motorcycle goggles and helmet, and his chin was buried in his coat collar. But it all happened so quick. I didn't have the time to react or anything. I just remember the three shots being fired over my shoulder before he forced me out to open the boot. He could see it was empty. Then he swore, saying, "The bastard's tricked me." '

Kennon mulled over the words. They could only point to one man. 'He must have known Sir Charles's movements. Did you notice where he came from when he followed you?'

'It must have been close to the house. I saw him following just after we joined the main A58 at Hartshead. He followed for about three miles then came up flashing his headlight.'

'Sir – we found this,' said a traffic constable. He came up holding a small plastic bag.

'What is it?'

'A cassette tape. It was in the grass by the litter bin. It looks like it's been deliberately dropped.'

'Deliberately dropped? Is that where the police bike stopped?' Kennon asked Porter.

'Yes, sir, by that bin. But I never saw him drop anything.'

'You wouldn't have done, not after the shooting. I'll take that constable. It looks promising. Anything else?'

'Nothing else, but forensic have found a .22 bullet buried in the back seat which they say missed the target.'

'The target was a human being, Constable, not a dart board. Careful how you note the evidence. Take a written statement from the chauffeur.'

Back at HQ, Kennon played the tape in the cassette and sat listening to the chilling sounds of Julia Woodward's voice in a new message.

'Daddy, I'm all right, just a bit wet. When you get the money together go to the phone box at Denton outside the bus station at midnight and wait for it to ring. Go there, Daddy, please.'

Kennon played the tape three times to confirm whether Julia was under duress from ill-treatment, or if she had left any clue as to her location. He could find nothing to tell him where she was or if she was being treated well. Her voice had a slight tremble, but that could have been from the cold. Kennon wracked his brains trying to think where she could be held.

She was 'a bit wet', she said.

From being outside in the rain.

Two days after she was taken?

No, highly unlikely.

Was she in a damp cellar?

No, again.

Was she on the moors in a cave?

Possible, but… Inside a pumping station! Yes! That was more like it. She was up at one of the Carsbrook Reservoirs, where the two water company officials were missing.

'By God, I've got her!'

Kennon rushed to the map on the incident board and drew a circle round the Carsbrook Reservoir system on Saddleworth Moor. There were several lakes set between two major roads in a remote wilderness. Then he looked at all the other locations around Denton and Oldham, where he assumed the Panther would be based in a house. The man had to be working from a secure base within a few miles from where he held Julia Woodward. But where was the money to be delivered? And why shoot the man who was supposed to bring it?

Kennon heard a noise outside and went to the window. He looked down on a gaggle of reporters crowding round Boyd and his colleagues as they arrived back from the Carsbrook Reservoir.

He went downstairs anxious to learn of new developments and found Sergeant Walker holding back the reporters crowded round the front doors as Boyd slipped through.

'There's been foul play up there, sir,' Boyd stated grimly. 'There's a deep borehole inside a derelict pumping station with strong indication that someone was held there. There's no sign of the two missing men, but I've requested a diver to go in. We found two cartridges from a 12-bore shotgun recently fired. But here's the damning evidence.' Boyd removed a page from the evidence bag torn from a book with writing scribbled on it.

Kennon looked at the torn page and saw the name Julia Woodward scrawled across it. 'She was there! Get the team upstairs, Boyd, while I talk to the reporters.'

Kennon went to the door to address all the anxious newsmen.

'Gentlemen! There's been a shooting, which may or may not be connected with the kidnapping. Sir Charles Woodward has been shot by a man on a motorbike at Holywell Green this morning. He's alive but critical in Manchester General Hospital. He was on his way here with information to the kidnap of his daughter, Julia Woodward.'

There was a collective gasp from the assembled reporters as the questions flew. 'Is this connected to the two missing water board officials, chief inspector?' … 'Do you have a suspect?' … 'Is the Black Panther in the frame?'

'I can't say at this moment. But I think not.'

'Is there any news of Julia Woodward? What are the demands being made?'

'There is evidence to suggest Julia Woodward was being held hostage at a reservoir on the moors. That's all I can give you. There will be a press conference as soon as we have more information. That is all!'

There was no sign of the *Standard*'s crime reporter as Kennon left the newsmen to kick their heels. He hadn't thought that Manchester General Hospital would be her venue, and when the rest of the press brigade realised they would do the same.

As Kennon went upstairs, Sergeant Walker called out, 'They won't let this Black Panther story die, George. They're certain it's him.'

'He's not even remotely connected, Ted, but I could be wrong.'

Kennon wasn't happy with two more murders added to his caseload, if that's what they were, and it certainly looked like it. But how to meet the ransom demand at Denton bus station was the next problem.

Back in the Incident Room the tape recorder was switched on and the team sat round listening to the hollow voice of Julia Woodward relaying the ransom instructions.

'It's unusual for the victim to do it and not the kidnapper, isn't it, sir?' one of the team said.

'He doesn't want his voice recorded, for obvious reasons,' Kennon replied. 'Forensic can match voice recognition with a radio scanner.'

'But why drop the tape on the ground when he could have thrown it in the car and made damned sure?' a young rookie detective inquired.

'He knew we would find it,' a detective sergeant replied. 'It was lying almost in full view. Dropping it in the car would have been too obvious, especially if he was laying a false trail.'

'Don't be so cocksure,' Kennon said looking at the other objects found up at the reservoir, which included a brown button from Julia's coat, a strip of Elastoplast and two empty cartridges from a 12-bore. 'This man might be playing a mind game, but one slip and he's out. He's taking every precaution at getting us to back off. He knew Sir Charles was on his way to us with information and he wasn't prepared to let it happen.'

'But why shoot the man who's bringing him the ransom money?' a detective asked.

'Because then he wouldn't have to go through the process of arranging a delivery, which is more risky,' DS Buckley replied.

'How did he know, sir?' Boyd asked. 'How could he possibly know?'

'He could have guessed by simply watching Sir Charles's movements. He would have assumed Sir Charles would come to us, either with the money or simply to assist us with our inquiries. It's possible he could have even planted a bug in Sir Charles house as a previous visitor. It wouldn't be that difficult. A small listening device such as a radio bug can be bought through a mail order magazine. The difficult bit is planting it in the right place.'

Kennon paused at the possible scenario of a business confidant. 'Unless the man who shot Sir Charles already knew him and had spoken to him about the kidnapping.'

'Who the blazes could that be?'

'A business partner springs to mind,' Kennon replied. 'But I'm surmising, and that won't do. We need hard evidence. Forensic will have to match the shotgun cartridges, for a start.'

'Doesn't the Black Panther use a shotgun?' DC Pembrook inquired.

'Yes, Pembrook, he does!' Kennon replied, his patience fraying. 'But so do most armed criminals. We need evidence and a motive. This inquiry is already splitting into two sections. I don't believe it's the same man.'

'In that case, sir,' Boyd interjected, 'we have two different motives and two different crimes: one of kidnapping and one of manslaughter. The kidnapping was for money, but the shooting of Sir Charles was for some other reason. But what reason?'

'What's the most obvious, Boyd? Someone wanted Sir Charles out the way so as he could take over his outside interest. Now who does that sound like?'

'Seagrove?'

'Yes, Boyd. Nicholas Seagrove. The man has made a desperate attempt to get his stud farm back by taking over control of the business.'

'But he's not the kidnapper?'

'He could be. Let's assume he carried out the kidnapping in order to engineer the ransom delivery by Sir Charles and then shift the police inquiry on to the Panther. It's a diabolical plot, and certainly feasible.'

'It could still be the same man,' DS Buckley replied. 'We can't rule that out, sir. If the kidnapper thought Sir Charles was carrying the ransom, it would be easier to snatch it in transit than to go through a delivery process.'

'That's assuming the kidnapper knew in advance! Good Lord, that's what I'm driving at, Buckley!'

'But he didn't get it, boss,' Boyd replied. 'Will he try again?'

'It's quite possible. It was arranged that Sir Charles would bring the money here as soon as he got the instructions, and since he had not received them then I assume the money is still at Bridlington Hall. So now we have to bring in the son, Peter Woodward, and I'm told he's not very obliging. Why, I don't know. I believe DC Murray has the details.'

'I do, sir,' Murray replied. 'Peter Woodward is the Financial Director of Woodward's subsidiary firm, Taylor-Hydromatics, based in Sheffield. He lives in Harrogate and I'm told is a very private man, married with two children. He keeps his stepmother at arm's length and is said to be frugal in money matters. In fact I don't even know if he knows of Julia's kidnap.'

'He will know if he reads the paper or listens to the radio. We now have to get in touch with him and bring him in. He could even be at the General Hospital at his father's bedside right now. I know Sir Charles's wife, Veronica, is there. Just hold on while I ring them.'

'I've already done it, sir,' Murray said. 'I got a direct line through to the ward. Sir Charles is stable and in a satisfactory condition. They removed two bullets from his chest and spleen and have him on a cardiac monitor. Veronica Woodward seems to be taking it well, but she has not been able to get in touch with Peter, who is in Birmingham. She's left a message with his wife. The other son, Ian, is on his way from Oxford, and she says after he has seen his father he will come straight here. The money is ready in the family safe at Bridlington.'

'Well done, Murray,' Kennon said. 'That definitely needed a woman's touch. I have authorised a police escort to take her back. In the meantime we have roughly twelve hours to work out a plan before the next call from the kidnapper. We must search the moors for Julia Woodward. The West Yorkshire reservoirs are the starting point. Yes, I know it's a daunting task, but we'll have the Water Board to assist. I'm positive she is being held in a disused pumping station somewhere.'

'Do you reckon he's moving her around, sir?' DS Buckley asked.

'He could be. If you look at the Ordnance Survey map you'll see just how many reservoirs there are scattered across West and North Yorkshire. Every one of them has pumping stations serving a dozen towns. I'm told there are small number out of use. So we need search only the disused ones on the Carsbrook and Marsden reservoirs serving Manchester and Huddersfield.'

The search was on. Police operations centred from Rochdale as 300 police were drafted in from the regions. Search teams were assembled with dogs, and each team was given an area to cover aided by the West Yorkshire Water Company officials, who held the keys to pumping stations. Some of the teams had dogs as they set off in grey weather to begin the painstaking search for Julia Woodward – held captive, as they thought, in a disused pumping station.

At Carsbrook Reservoir, Kennon and Chief Superintendent Bradley watched as the bodies of the two maintenance men were hauled up the deep borehole by police divers and laid out for forensic to examine. The two corpses held the evidence of the

Panther's weapons: the sawn-off double-barrelled shotgun and the semi-automatic pistol he carried on his raids. The shells would be matched with those used against the sub-postmasters when all the evidence was collated.

'How the devil did he intend to get the ransom delivered to this remote place?' Bradley said, looking around the desolate pump house.

'I don't believe this was the place he would have used, sir,' Kennon said, staring bleakly at the two corpses. 'He would have arranged for the money to be handed over somewhere else. Only then would he reveal where his victim was by leaving a trail of messages. He made it clear there would be no handover until the money was cleared.'

'But that's not the way kidnappers work, George. They know they won't get a penny unless the victim is exchanged pro rata!'

'I know, sir. But we're dealing with a ruthless man who's taking no chances. He won't give in to convention. We play by his rules.'

'We'll have to damned well change the rules, then! We'll follow his damned rules only until the phone contact is made, and then we issue an ultimatum. The exchange takes place only when we know the victim is about to be released.'

'It won't work, sir. He's holding all the aces. All we can do is follow his instructions.'

'It will damned well have to work! I'm not letting him call the tune,' Bradley retorted sharply. 'We have to have assurances. If it was your daughter, would you hand over a fortune not knowing if she was safe or not? Of course you wouldn't!'

'I would if there was no other way. But I'm just as concerned in finding out who the kidnapper is. He has stipulated no police are to be involved. If we start laying down rules he's just as likely to abort the operation and then we've lost him.'

'What do you suggest, then?'

'Stall him while we search him out. We lose his instructions, make a foul-up of them so he has to set new ones, and all the time we delay him we carry out our investigations. We've got 300 men out there searching for Julia Woodward. If she's there, it's a fair chance the kidnapper is making plans right now to move her.

He'll be forced into taking a chance and it gives us a better opportunity of catching him on the road.'

'How do you know he won't kill her first?'

'He won't kill her unless she can identify him.'

'You're assuming then that this is the work of the Panther, who wears a mask. I thought you said it wasn't the Panther.'

'I'm not sure. All I know is the kidnapper won't throw it away yet, not all the time there's a chance of pulling it off.'

Bradley looked at his watch. 'We've got three hours of daylight left. If this search fails to find her I'm prepared to go along with your idea to stall him. But I'm seriously thinking we might have to call in Scotland Yard. I don't want to, not yet, but we may have to.'

'I've got a team hard at work combing the criminal records for a suspect. I've also sent two detectives to central army records at Catterick to ferret out Yorkshiremen who did national service around 1958. That's based on the Panther's assumed age at about mid- to late-thirties.'

'That won't help without a name.'

'But it narrows the field. This is the work of a fit man who's had military training. It's a long shot, but it's damned quicker than making hundreds of door-to-door inquiries for odd-job men.'

'Odd-job men?'

'Sergeant Boyd reckons the Panther is an odd-job man, from his method of drilling through window frames for entry. I have to admit he has a strong point. The two other suspects in mind are Julia Woodward's ex-boyfriend, who has disappeared, and Nicholas Seagrove.'

'You're still hanging onto that fraud case! You won't find nothing there, I can assure you. What do you base your theories on?'

'Nicholas Seagrove was a man in a lot of debt. I felt Sir Charles was holding something back at the interview, and it was his mission here to give us information on Seagrove that got him shot. Until I interrogate the man I can't rule him out.'

'And what about the other man – Kingsley?'

'He was intimately involved with Julia Woodward. He knew

her movements and knew who she was. His motive is greed. He liked the good life and whisked her round the auction rooms. He took her to meet clients to impress her, and all the time he was after her business.'

'Yes, I have to admit I thought you were off beam with him. But a kidnapper who knows his victim... How can he let her go? She would have recognised him if they were that close.'

'Yes, she would have recognised him, and that means he has no intention of letting her walk free. That makes him doubly dangerous.'

'Let's see what happens when the son gets here and we have the kidnapper's next instructions. I propose we put a man in the son's place to carry the money and handle the phone calls while we have a net closing in on him.'

'I'll leave that in your hands then, sir. In the meantime, with your permission I'll go to Buxton and interview ex-Major Nicholas Seagrove over his business affairs with Sir Charles.'

'No, you won't. That's an entirely different inquiry. If you've got evidence he's the kidnapper, then show me. So far, all you've got is circumstantial.'

'So it might be, sir, but what else do we have? Can we afford to let a suspect slip through the net just because we don't have enough evidence?'

'All right, you win. But you can't make an arrest in Buxton without the Derbyshire Constabulary's permission. You'll need their own Regional Crime Squad with you.'

'I want Seagrove in a one-to-one interview. If I roll up with a squad car he's just as likely to make a bolt for it and go into hiding.'

'And if he's as dangerous as you think, you could get shot! You'll have to carry a one-way radio transmitter with a concealed microphone. It will transmit on the police surveillance frequency, but you won't be able to receive instructions. Let's get back to HQ and get you kitted out. I'll sort out the back-up with Derbyshire CID and arrange to have men within range of the stables to move in quickly. But remember, George, this had better prove right.'

Chapter Seven

The blast of a shotgun sounded over Burbage Woods, followed by a man's throaty voice barking orders as a partridge fell in mid-flight.

'Fetch it, Caesar!'

The man let the large Dobermann off the leash and the dog bounded into the woods after the fallen bird. It was the third one of the shoot in just half an hour. Nicholas Seagrove was a solid man, five foot ten and broad-shouldered, with a heavily pockmarked face.

An ex-army major with an arrogance to match, Seagrove was fitter than most men half his age. He kept to a rigid regime of exercise, with polo and other country pursuits, not all of them harmless sports, either. It was women who boosted his ego and kept him in shape, but he was careless with it, and made no attempt to disguise it from Doreen, his new mistress and business partner.

He reloaded his double-barrelled shotgun and snapped it closed before lifting his tally of two pheasants over his shoulder. Then he walked off along the track towards Burbage. As he walked, he thought deeply on the morning's work, which could reinstate him as head of Buxton Stables. There was no one else to take over. It would be all his.

The shooting of Sir Charles was an impulsive action but one he had to make if he was ever going to recoup his losses. The debts were piling up, and he was still fuming over the Georgian bureau that could have kept them under control.

The trouble was, he missed the prestige and salary of being an officer in the 19th Hussars and all the perks it brought. His career was on safe ground and pay was assured. Out of it, he was like a fish out of water. He never realised Civvy Street could be so tough on the finances. Here, life was a lot different, and nothing was guaranteed in the competitive rat race.

He reached the bridge where his Land-Rover was parked and looked down into the foaming waters of the river, thinking heavily on the uncertain future in front of him. He felt life slipping out of his grasp, and if he didn't grab hold of it firmly he could kiss goodbye to Buxton Stables and the Manor. But there was still the subsidiary plan to go for, as long as Doreen went along with it.

As he gazed down into the foaming waters he thought of the girl. She really was a disappointment. Why couldn't she accept his offer of thirty per cent commission of her trade? It was her fault and she had to go. By God, first her and then Doreen. The demands were becoming too much…

He looked up to see the Dobermann bounding towards him with a partridge clamped firmly in its jaws and he went to meet it.

'Good boy, Caesar. Good boy!' he said, retrieving the bird. 'My, if only women were as faithful as you. I think we've got time for a few more. Then we'll have a drink in the Cat and Fiddle.'

Kennon's Rover roared out of Manchester heading for Buxton with the detective racing against time. In all his career he had never been under such pressure to solve a case as this one. He had a distance of around thirty miles to travel and he would be crossing the county border into Derbyshire, which meant if he needed to make an arrest he would have to call on the Derby police to do it. But if Seagrove was the Panther, then it would require more than one man to arrest him.

When Kennon cleared Stockport he was heading for Hazel Grove, and became aware of the Woodley Estate, where Julia Woodward's house was under police guard. He was still puzzled why the kidnapper had not seized her in this quiet corner under darkness when she would have been more vulnerable. But it was irrelevant because she was abducted from the city and the kidnapper had got clean away. As he passed through the village approaching the petrol station he saw a Panda car on the forecourt and decided to pull in on an instinct just to check if they'd seen anything relative to the kidnapping.

The two constables were just coming out the shop as he pulled up and climbed out to meet them. 'DCI Kennon, Manchester CID,' Kennon said, flashing his warrant card. 'I'm on my way to Buxton investigating the kidnapping of Julia Woodward, and wondered if your patrols had turned anything up.'

'We could have a breakthrough for you, sir,' the taller constable said. 'Last night a van pulled in here for petrol. The man filled up with five gallons just before an area traffic car pulled in on routine inquiries. According to the report the man was about to pay and then panicked. He jumped back in his vehicle and drove off without paying. The patrol gave immediate chase but lost him at Macclesfield, where the road forks. He was going like a bat out of hell.'

'That sounds ominous. Did they get a description of the man?'

'We have now, sir. He was caught on CCTV. It was a white Ford Transit, registration AKL 454E. We've just checked the tape and are taking it away for closer inspection. It's a bit fuzzy.'

'Brilliant! This could be a breakthrough. Take it to Manchester Central CID at once. Forensic should be able to enhance it. Have you checked the registration yet?'

'Not yet, sir, but we will do. I'm pretty sure it's a Bradford licence.'

'When you get all the information there is available leave it with the investigating officers in the Kidnap Incident Room.'

'One more thing, sir. The assistant says when the van pulled out, the back doors swung open. Nothing came out, but I thought I'd mention it.'

'It gets better. Make a search of the road. You're looking for anything that could lead us to the kidnapping. A cassette tape, a roll of insulation tape, or even tools that might have fallen out – anything of significance.'

'It's a long road, but we'll do our best, sir. You want the left fork here for Buxton. Good luck, sir.'

Kennon drove on for Buxton and already he felt the journey was worthwhile. A CCTV picture of the kidnapper. He couldn't have wished for better. The road ahead was clear with stretches of dual carriageway going through the Peak District, an area of outstanding beauty, but looking bleak in the grip of winter.

Halfway along the route he began to think of Julia Woodward and the circumstances she was now in. She must be in a fearful state from her ordeal in the abandoned pump house, and could be in an even worse place now. Kennon couldn't think of anywhere worse than the moors to be held prisoner in an abandoned pump house or down a deep well. It would take a large army to search for someone hidden in every vale and reservoir across the moors, and the thought of Julia Woodward lying dead in such a place filled him with dread.

Dark rain clouds were forming as he went through Chapel-en-le-Frith on the last stretch of the journey, crossing small streams heading into the National Park. Then the town loomed up and the signpost said 'Welcome to Buxton'. It was an old market town famed for its annual music festival in the midst of some of the finest scenery in Derbyshire.

Kennon followed the sign for Buxton Stables up a twisting road to Wormhill that led to a country pub, the Harvester Inn, situated three miles from the stables. Kennon pulled into the car park, where a dark blue van was parked among several vehicles. He sat in his car and waited for his contact to show, and within a few minutes a man left one of the cars and came over to meet him carrying a raincoat. Kennon wound down his window and gave a thumbs-up sign as he recognised his contact, DCI Jack Taylor.

'Morning, Jack! Lovely weather you have in Derbyshire,' Kennon said, offering a handshake.

'Not as good as Manchester's, I bet. You're ten minutes early, George. Have you got your equipment on you?'

'All wired up and raring to go. How far is the stud farm from here?'

'About three miles. You're going to need more than a radio, George. Try this mac on for size.'

'What the devil for? I'm wearing a perfectly good one.'

'Does it have a padded sleeve like this one?' Taylor showed the sleeve, firmly padded. 'Seagrove keeps two faithful Dobermanns. You will need this if you're making an arrest.'

'I thought you were doing that…'

'Officially we are, but you're just as capable. See that blue van over there? That's the radio listening post. Turn on your mike and say something so they can tune in.'

'This is DCI George Kennon. Can you hear me? DCI George Kennon. Can you hear me?'

They waited a few seconds and the headlights flashed. 'They've got you, George. You'll have back-up the minute you need it. We'll be picking up every word. Let's hope we get a result. The Black Panther is driving us all round the bend.'

'I'm after a kidnapper, Jack. Whether Seagrove is the Panther or not, I don't know. I don't care. But at least we'll have someone in the bag.'

Kennon changed raincoats and drove out, knowing he was in radio contact with his Derbyshire counterparts. Three miles up the road, and another signpost directed him up a lane to the stables. Then he was pulling into the rambling stud farm, with its manor house surrounded by trees, courtyards and stables. Here, some of the finest racehorses in the country were reared.

The place appeared orderly but had nothing exceptional about it. There was a smell of damp straw in the air; a young girl in jodhpurs and riding boots was saddling a horse, a stable lad was mucking out with fresh straw, and two more hands were brushing down a Chestnut mare with a glistening coat. One of the hands approached as Kennon climbed out the car.

'Afternoon, sir. Are you Doctor Morley?'

'No, I'm Chief Inspector Kennon of Manchester CID. Is Mr Seagrove at home?'

'I don't think so. He's hardly ever here. You'd best see Ted Ainsley. He's the accounts bookkeeper. You'll find him in the office.'

'Thank you. Who's the doctor required for?'

'It's a vet, sir. One of the horses is lame.'

Kennon walked on past the stable blocks and paddocks and approached the office in one of the outbuildings. He stepped inside, where a thin grey-haired man sat writing accounts at a table.

'Ted Ainsley? I'm Chief Inspector Kennon of Manchester CID. I'm looking for Nicholas Seagrove.'

Ainsley was startled, displaying a nervous twitch of his face. 'He's not here. Can I be of any help? Take a seat, Inspector.' Ainsley put down his pen and relit his pipe.

'What's he been and done now – robbed a bank? God knows how he gets into the state of affairs he does! He's paid enough but is never satisfied.'

'What's his position here?'

'Jack of all trades: manager, buyer, trainer and breeder all in one. That's aside from his shooting and military field games. He's an ex-army major.'

'I know. Have you any idea where I can find him?'

'Newmarket, Doncaster, Aintree… he could be anywhere. He travels a lot. He shows up every so often, and then he's off in his Land-Rover playing the country squire.'

'He must have a good knowledge of the county, then. How long have you known him, Mr Ainsley?'

'I've been here over forty years from a stable lad. Harry Bishop was the owner back then before the war. He reared a few winners in the Doncaster flat races, including a Derby winner twice over. Then his son, John Bishop, took over in '52, but his heart wasn't in it. He let it run down and sold out in 1960 to Jack Laker, the boxing promoter. Laker did a good job rearing fillies and won two Cheltenham Gold Cups. Then he retired and sold out to a dodgy consortium run by Nick Seagrove in '68. Seagrove was just out the army. But he came blundering in like a sergeant major, laying down rules that were more suited to a barrack than a stud farm. What he was going to do and not do was nobody's business. Needless to say, he hadn't a clue how to run the place. He spent more money buying horses than we earned and soon ran up a pile of debts. We came close to collapse but were saved when a new consortium took over. That was Sir Charles Woodward, the big industrial magnate. We couldn't have had a better stroke of luck…' Ainsley suddenly stopped in mid-sentence. 'You're here over the shooting of Sir Charles, I've just realised.'

'Not just the shooting. I'm investigating the kidnapping of his daughter, Julia Woodward. But go on tell me more, I'm fascinated.'

'You're not the only one, Chief Inspector. Seagrove lost his controlling share to Sir Charles and was effectively made bankrupt. But they kept him on for his expertise as a trainer, and so far we've managed to stay afloat with money poured in. In fact it's got better over the last year, with a Derby winner. But Seagrove's a bitter man. I don't think I've ever seen a man so screwed up as him. He shouts at the stable hands and the young jockeys. He shouts at me over the most trifling things. We've had two good jockeys leave. He's reckless as well. More than once we've had the police here investigating vehicle theft or checking the gun licence for his 12-bore. But he must give the right answers because they go away satisfied.'

'So, he owns a 12-bore. Does he have other guns?'

'I've seen him with a rifle on occasions. Don't know about any others. Is he in trouble, Chief Inspector?'

'That's what I'm here to find out. Has there been anything more serious than vehicle theft? Money laundering or burglary, like the post-office raids, for instance?'

'I know what you're getting at, Chief Inspector. You don't have to spell it out. I can see it written on your face. Is he the Black Panther?'

'Well, is he?'

'I've wondered that. And to be quite honest I don't know. From what I read in the papers on his description, I'd have to say no, but you might have a strong case for it.'

'Well, I suppose I shall just have to wait until he turns up. I presume he lives in the manor house up the lane?'

'Oh, yes. He clung onto that all right. It goes with the job. But you'll have to see Doreen Chambers in the office. She's his girlfriend, and runs the house strictly on her terms.'

'I'll take a walk up there and introduce myself.'

'I'll have to come with you, Chief Inspector. She won't talk to you otherwise.'

They left the stable yard and walked up the short lane towards the nineteenth-century manor house in its own cobbled court-yards. It was an impressive house of Derbyshire stone, with tall chimneys and gabled roofs going in all directions. The frontage was covered in ivy and as the two men walked up to the front steps a woman came out and challenged them. She was well dressed and about forty years of age with a hard face. She was Seagrove's live-in mistress, Doreen Chambers.

'Who's this, Edward? I thought I said no visitors today,' she said with a haughty manner.

'This is DCI Kennon from Manchester CID, Miss Chambers. He's investigating the shooting of Sir Charles Woodward.'

'What the devil's he doing here then?'

'I'd like a word with you, madam,' Kennon put in, 'if you can spare a few minutes.'

'No, I can't! You will have to wait for the boss. He does all the interviews. I'm much too busy!'

'I can get an enforcement,' Kennon replied bluntly.

But his words were lost by the sound of a car, and they turned to see a Land-Rover gunning up the lane throwing up a shower of mud before pulling into the driveway. A hefty man wearing a flat cap and an all-weather coat got out and walked towards them, holding tight to a fierce-looking Dobermann straining on a leash.

'Who's this, Ted?' he said in a booming voice. 'Is that your car down the bottom?'

'DCI George Kennon, Manchester CID,' Kennon replied, flashing his warrant. 'Are you Nicholas Seagrove?'

'Manchester CID! Bit out of your territory, aren't you? I'm Nicholas Seagrove. What can I do for you, Chief Inspector?'

'I've come about the shooting incident this morning of Sir Charles Woodward. He's managing director of this stud farm, I believe?'

'He is. But we rarely see him. Go inside, Doreen, and make some tea or something,' Seagrove ordered brusquely.

'My inquiries lead me to believe there's a connection with it to the kidnapping of his daughter, Julia Woodward. You know her, I believe?'

'I know *of* her. I'm her father's business manager. We have joint interest in these stables.'

'Sir Charles was on his way to Manchester CID with vital information on the kidnapper when a man on a motorbike stopped his car and pumped three bullets into him.'

'Yes, I know. I heard it on the radio on my way back from Chesterfield this morning. So what the hell's it got to do with me?'

'That's what I'm here to find out. Where were you this morning at nine o'clock, Mr Seagrove?'

'I've just said! I went to Chesterfield.'

'I see. And who did you meet in Chesterfield?'

'What the devil has this got to do with it? I was meeting Jack

Dunstan. He's a captain from my old regiment. We're planning a regimental reunion.'

'I shall need an address.'

'You can't have it. It's a private affair, nothing to do with you!'

'That's because you weren't in Chesterfield at all, were you? You were on the road from Brighouse in West Yorkshire on a motorbike following Sir Charles to rob him of the ransom money he was carrying.'

'Don't be bloody ridiculous!' Seagrove fumed, holding back the Dobermann which was straining on the leash. 'I don't have a damned motorbike and why the hell would I shoot my own business partner?'

'He's not a business partner. He's your employer, after bailing you out of near bankruptcy. I suggest you knew Sir Charles's movements in advance. It presented a perfect opportunity for you to get back this stud farm and take control.'

'Nonsense! Bloody ridiculous! Where's your evidence? Now, if you've finished, I have to get on!'

'I have enough evidence to be going on with. Do you have a licence for firearms, Mr Seagrove? I mean all of them: the shotgun, the rifle and the semi-automatic pistol?'

'I do. They're sporting guns.'

'I'm going to have to ask you to hand them over, if you don't mind.'

'I do bloody mind! I said I have a licence. That covers it!'

'Does it? We'll see what ballistics have to say about that.'

'If that's all you've got to say, then I suggest you leave right now! I'm a busy man.'

'I haven't finished yet. Four years ago the Woodward Engineering Company was hit by a fraud inquiry, and Sir Charles was exposed to blackmail over an affair he was having with his secretary. Following that you invite him to bail you out of near bankruptcy. It doesn't require much imagination to put the two together.'

'Then you've got a wild imagination, Chief Inspector! You haven't got a shred of evidence.'

'The man who shot Sir Charles wore a black hood emulating the Black Panther. I'm going to have to ask you to accompany me to Derby police headquarters, Mr Seagrove.'

'Oh, no! You're not getting me on some trumped up charge! Unless you're arresting me I must ask you to leave. Get off my land this instant!'

The dog emitted a low growl and Kennon could feel the threat it posed.

'I wouldn't make it difficult if I were you. You can either help in police inquiries or I can have you formally arrested.'

'The devil you will!'

Seagrove released the snarling Dobermann and it literally flew off the leash.

'Dog attack!' Kennon barked into his mike turning to offer his right arm to the fierce animal as it sprang at him. In just two bounds it was on him, with teeth ripping through his coat sleeve and pushing him to the ground, snarling and tearing at the material.

Within moments a police motorcyclist and an area squad car came screeching up the lane and drew up within yards. Four police officers jumped out and seized Seagrove, while his dog was held back, and brought under control, barking ferociously.

Two more cars arrived and Jack Taylor leaped out, helping Kennon to his feet, relieved to find just his sleeve hanging in shreds and not his arm. Seagrove struggled with the police as he was handcuffed and Taylor made the formal arrest.

'Nicholas Seagrove, I'm arresting you for the attempted murder of Sir Charles Woodward. You do not have to say anything, but anything you do say may be used in evidence against you.'

'This is ridiculous! You're making a grave mistake.' The sweat poured down Seagrove's face. 'I'll sue the lot of you! Doreen – call my solicitor!'

Seagrove was put in a car, still protesting his innocence, as a collection of stable hands gathered to watch the drama. But the Derbyshire police elation that the hunt for the Black Panther had ended was premature. Even DCI Jack Taylor, leading the hunt for the Panther, was carried away with the arrest.

'Well done, George – that was close,' Taylor said. 'Glad you changed coats now? We heard every word over the radio. So, Seagrove is the Black Panther after all…'

'I don't know about that, Jack. But I'll warrant he's the one who shot Sir Charles this morning. We need this place thoroughly searched. We're looking for weapons, and in particular a .22 semi-automatic pistol. Mr Ainsley here will lend a hand. He's the accounts manager.'

'I can't take you over the house, Chief Inspector,' Ainsley said, looking flustered, 'but I'll assist in any way I can.'

'Thank you, Mr Ainsley. I've got all the authority I need to search the house. I'm looking for cassettes, chequered police tape, balaclava-style hoods, motorcycle gear and a motorbike. Have you seen a motorbike here?'

'Two of the stable lads have one each. Big machines they are, too.'

'I shall want them questioned. The man who shot Sir Charles Woodward this morning was riding a motorbike and he was wearing a black hood like the Black Panther.'

'Seagrove might have a few run-ins with the law, but he's not the Black Panther, Chief Inspector. He can't be. He doesn't even have the same description as the Panther.'

'If he's not, he's certainly emulating him. We can only charge him with the shooting this morning, but it might just lead us to the post office raids carried out over the last four years. They have never been solved to this day.'

Seagrove was driven away to police headquarters in Derby, watched by his hardened mistress weeping crocodile tears. She was the one person who knew Seagrove's devious nature and what he was up to, plotting to seize back his precious stud farm.

Kennon returned to Manchester, pleased with a job well done. Whether Seagrove was the Black Panther or not made no difference; he had caught the man who shot Sir Charles Woodward, and now he could concentrate his energies on finding Julia Woodward. Until then there was no victory to celebrate.

Chapter Eight

That same evening around eight o'clock, under the cover of darkness, the Panther returned to Bathpool Park along the high ridge covered in thick undergrowth and shielded by trees. He moved stealthily through the brambles lighting his way with a torch and carrying his heavy duffel bag over his shoulder. He was pleased with himself about finding this third shaft, virtually hidden from view in a tangle of undergrowth. But he wasn't completely sure it wasn't known to anyone else.

However, he only ever used it at night when the hill was shrouded in darkness. He reached the square manhole cover on a raised concrete platform hidden with branches and he cleared them away to insert his key. He heaved the hatch open and stepped onto the ladder to descend the shaft, closing the lid as he went.

He was going down to check on his victim and deliver her food. He wondered what condition she would be in after twenty-four hours in the hole, for though he remained detached, he couldn't help feeling some sympathy for her.

She lay on the platform listening to him approach as small pieces of loose cement came down pinging on the metal platform with the movement of the ladder. She was lying in her sleeping bag on the sponge mattress, cold and hungry and thoroughly miserable.

When he reached the platform above her she could hear him cursing and she feared what his anger might unleash. Then his boots sounded heavily before he dropped down onto her platform with a thud and she heard the clink of tools in his bag. Then he was standing right over her with his hood on.

'Some stupid bastard has decided to emulate me,' he complained, lighting the oil lamp on the ledge above. 'If he thinks he can load the blame on me he's got another think coming!'

'Get me out of here, please,' Julia pleaded, raising herself up. 'I'm freezing to death!'

'I can't! And don't ask me again... Are you OK?' His voice

softened as he turned to her. 'I've brought you some food.'

'You don't have to keep that hood on. I wouldn't recognise you if I saw your face.'

'I can't risk it! You might do later, and I can't afford that to happen.' He opened the rucksack and produced two flasks of warm soup and a half-bottle of brandy. 'Here, tomato soup. Hope you like it.'

Julia unscrewed the cup and poured some out. It tasted good. 'It's OK. It will keep me going. Have you agreed the exchange with my father? I can't stand another night down here.'

'I'm sorry to tell you I haven't. Your father has met with an unfortunate accident this morning.'

'No! What happened?' Julia felt her world falling apart. 'Was it a road accident?'

'No, it wasn't an accident – far from it. Someone posing as a police officer on a motorbike stopped his car on the Pennine Road, obviously to pinch the ransom, and then shot him. But he wore a black hood to do it!'

'Oh no!' Julia's face crumpled into despair. 'Is he dead… Who did it?'

'He's not dead. He's in the Manchester General. Whoever it was must have thought he was carrying the ransom money but he wasn't. It's a good job too. But it was a stupid move he made. He was on his way to the Manchester police against my express orders. I warned him not to involve the police.'

'How do you know he was on his way to the police? He could have been going anywhere – to my shop or the bank.'

'It was in the bloody paper! He was on his way to the police to help with enquiries. It was a stupid move! Why else would he be on the road to Manchester? Who will bring the ransom now?'

'One of my brothers… Ian or Peter. I expect it will be Peter; he's the eldest.'

'Will they be in the house tonight to take a message?'

'I don't know. Ian's at Cambridge and I don't know where Peter is. We hardly see him.'

'Peter or Ian… I'll have to remember those names. Will they obey my instructions?'

Julia nodded.

'Because they had better if you want to get out of here. You'll have to make a new tape. I've got the cassette with me. If no one takes the message tonight then you're stuck here a bit longer than I planned, but that's not my fault.'

'Can't you move me somewhere else? Have you any idea what it's like being stuck down here all night and all day?'

'I told you, I can't!' he barked at her. 'Anyway, you're safe down here, nothing can happen to you. You've got food and blankets, what more do you want?' He looked at his watch and took the cassette recorder out of the rucksack. 'Let's get this tape made. I've got work to do.'

'What do I say?'

'I've written the words down for you,' he said, handing her a postcard. 'Just change the word "Daddy" to "Ian". That lets them know we're up to date and not using an old tape.'

He switched the recorder on and held the mike for her while she read the instructions on the card in a calm measured voice. She thought the message was badly written and too complicated to follow. It wasn't coherent. When she finished he switched off and played it back to make sure her voice was clear.

'That sounds good. I'm glad you said you're all right. I wouldn't want them to think I'm treating you bad.' He put the recorder back in the duffel bag.

'If you get the ransom tonight or tomorrow, how will you exchange me? Don't leave me here, please.'

'Don't worry, you'll get out the day after I collect. It's four years I've been at this game, robbing to boost my income. The police can't catch me. They don't even know who I am. I lay my plans too good for them. I check out the area before any of my jobs and make sure my escape route is never blocked. I travel on foot across country so their roadblocks are useless. They don't expect a criminal to use public transport.' He pulled the hood off his mouth to take a swig of brandy.

Julia stared at him and realised he enjoyed boasting about his exploits. He had never told anyone else, for how could he? She was gaining a rare insight into his thoughts and what made him tick. 'Why did you do it?' she asked. 'What made you become a lawbreaker?'

'A lawbreaker!' He laughed. 'I like that. It sounds better than a common criminal. That's the upper class coming out in you. Why did I do it? I was fed up working hard and never earning enough. I worked all the hours going to save up and buy a house, and even then I could hardly scrape up the deposit. It's never enough. You struggle to afford things for your wife and kid and you spend your life weighed down with a mortgage. I thought the only way out was to turn to crime. But I don't rob my own class. My target was the state. They take enough in taxes, they can afford to give it back. I don't go begging for welfare like the Pakis!' He took another swig of brandy.

'So I planned, and I planned well. I work in isolation in the early hours and rouse the occupants when they're asleep. When they wake they see a man in a hooded mask holding a gun and a torch on them. It terrifies them. That's why I'm dubbed the Black Panther. I'm armed and I have no accomplice. I work only in the winter months. In between I go back to my trade as a jobbing carpenter. I'm honest six months of the year. Not even my own wife knows what I do in the winter months.'

'Are you ashamed to tell her? Would she leave you?'

'Of course she wouldn't. She's faithful. Husbands don't tell their wives everything. Besides, I've got a daughter to take care of. Eighteen, she is. She's the apple of my eye. She's intelligent and a keen athlete. I train her.' He stopped, realising he was giving too much away.

'You're my last job, then I quit.' He looked at his watch. 'Here, take this brandy. I've got work to do.'

He picked up his tool bag and went up the ladder and back along the tunnel to the centre shaft. He climbed halfway to the first platform with a coil of rope and began work with a crowbar and hammer to loosen the ladder from the wall.

Julia could hear the hammer blows resounding through the tunnel and she wondered what he was doing. She drank her soup and then poured a drop of brandy into her cup. It warmed her as she sat there dreaming of liberty and her father. The wire loop round her neck was a painful reminder of her captivity. It chafed at her smooth skin and she stared blankly into the light of the lantern as night descended, and with it the cold. The world looked a bleaker place with every passing hour.

That night Bridlington Hall was empty when the phone rang at ten o'clock. The butler, Thomas, answered the phone and informed the caller there was no one available, but that the son, Ian, was on his way from the hospital. The butler asked the caller to phone back in an hour. Half an hour later, Ian Woodward came through the front door with his stepmother and Thomas delivered the message they had all been waiting for.

'The caller gave no name, sir,' he said. 'But I'm sure it was the same voice as before. How is your father, sir?'

'He's making progress, Thomas. But he's still weak. So the caller was the kidnapper, you reckon? And he's calling back at eleven.'

'So he said. But you must beware of hoax calls, sir. Inspector Kennon has warned there will be hoaxers.'

'I don't doubt it, but it's a risk we have to face.'

At precisely eleven o'clock the phone rang again and Ian answered it cautiously. 'This is Ian Woodward.'

A man's voice with a Yorkshire accent replied. 'Have you got the money?'

'Yes, but I must have proof of who you are.'

The phone clicked and Julia's voice came over the line with an echo behind it.

'Daddy! It's Julia. Daddy, you must take the ransom to the phone box opposite the bus station at Denton at midnight and wait for a call. Do it Daddy, please.'

'Julia! Wait!'

The line went dead and Ian replaced the receiver with a fazed expression, unsure of just who he was listening to.

'Who was it, Ian?' Veronica asked. 'Was it Julia's voice on the phone?'

'I'm not sure. She said "Daddy".' Ian was perplexed by the tape. 'It might have been her, but it might not. Damn! I can't tell my own sister's voice!'

'Then it was a hoax. Someone is playing on our fears and anxiety for what they can get. The callous swine!'

'But we can't be sure, Mother. We can't ignore the call. I'm going to have to go to Denton bus station and wait for the next call at midnight.'

'Wait, Ian. Let me phone the police.'

'No! If we defy the kidnapper, Julia's life is in danger. I'm going alone! I shall be all right.'

Veronica could see her stepson was determined to go. 'All right, Ian. I'll fetch the ransom from the safe.'

Ian went to the drinks cabinet and poured himself a fair measure of whisky. He took a swig and felt the fortifying effects giving him courage. It may have been Dutch courage, but it worked. He felt ready to face the kidnapper, whoever he was – Black Panther or not.

He left the house at 11.15 and drove out in his dark racing-green Mini Cooper heading for the Pennine road to Manchester. When Veronica returned to the lounge after seeing him off, the butler was holding the phone for her. 'It's Manchester CID, madam. Detective Sergeant Boyd.'

She lifted the phone and answered in a soft voice. 'Yes. Veronica Woodward.'

'Sergeant Boyd here, madam. We picked up the phone call just made to you. We are monitoring the line. Has Ian responded to it?'

'Yes, Sergeant, he has. I had quite forgotten about that.' Veronica's voice picked up a bit. 'I warned him it might be a hoax call but he was determined to go.'

'We shall be tailing him all the way in an effort to catch whoever it was made the call. Can you confirm that was Julia's voice?'

'No, I can't. Ian wasn't sure, either, but he insisted on going. He has gone to Denton bus station, taking the ransom with him. I shall wait up for his return. Goodnight, Sergeant.'

The rain swept in as Ian travelled down the dual carriageway in a determined bid to see through what he had come home from Cambridge for. His one thought was to see the return of his sister, the sister he loved. His mind went back to when they were just small kids getting up to mischief. She was four years older and was supposed to be looking after him. He bowed to her infinite wisdom and took all the blame when she put a cricket ball through the greenhouse glass. They were happy times.

He reached Denton on the outskirts of Manchester in good time and found the Green Line bus station with ten minutes to spare. The rain had eased to a drizzle and the street lights reflected along the Manchester road. It led directly into the city and was fairly quiet, with a small amount of traffic – mostly taxis taking a few late night revellers home.

Ian paced up and down by the phone box, thankful the rain had stopped, and heard the phone ring at one minute past midnight. He stepped inside and answered giving his name to a male caller, who had the same gruff Yorkshire accent as before.

'Take the Reddish road to Stockport. Then take the A6 to Whaley Bridge and wait for phone call by the Red Lion pub.'

'What assurances do I get? I must have some assurance about my sister.'

'Just follow the instructions.'

The phone cut off, leaving Ian to decide whether or not to comply to the instructions without having any assurance. But he had no choice in the matter. He stepped outside just as it began raining again, and he scrambled back into his Mini Cooper and drove off for Stockport. It was a short journey of less than five miles, and was just eight miles south of Manchester. Once there, he picked up the A6 and followed the signpost for Hazel Grove. He was aware of passing through Julia's village, though he'd never made a visit. He drove on down the A6 into open country and arrived at the village of Whaley Bridge just eight miles from Buxton. He was now in Derbyshire at 12.40 a.m.

The Red Lion was easy to spot by its illuminated sign on the main road, and the phone box was nearby. He stopped close to it and, stepping inside, he waited a few minutes for the phone to ring. Again it was the same rough Yorkshire voice he answered to.

'Take the ransom bag across the road to the garage and leave it behind the wall. Then go home. Do not wait, but go home immediately. You will receive a phone call tomorrow telling you where to find your sister.'

Ian had no choice but to comply. He lifted the holdall out the boot and carried it across the road to the garage. It was heavy, weighing almost forty pounds, with the money wrapped in neat bundles inside. There was a three-foot wall by the forecourt petrol pumps, and he lifted the bag over and dumped it down inside. Then he walked back to his car, climbed in and waited a couple of minutes looking up and down the deserted main road.

Nothing moved but the branches of trees in the wind, and then he saw a car headlights pulling off the road a hundred yards away. Was that the pick-up car? he wondered. It made no difference. He started his Mini Cooper and drove away, going back the way he came.

No sooner had he left when a car pulled up by the garage, driven by a woman. A man wearing a black hood jumped out and wasted no time in grabbing the ransom. He lifted the bag back over the wall and dumped it on the back seat of the Ford Consul before climbing back in. Then the car pulled away. It was over in an instant.

Within a matter of a few minutes, the Ford was being followed by two police cars at a discreet distance. They followed the red tail lights for six miles across open country all the way to Buxton. Sergeant Boyd was in the first car and he was astonished to see the car turn off for Buxton stud farm. He radioed the car behind as the driver waited for it to catch up, and then both cars drove up the lane, stopping 500 yards from the house. Eight police officers, including two marksmen armed with rifles and night sights, approached the house on foot where lights glowed in two windows. Two vehicles stood on the drive, the Ford Consul and the Land-Rover, and the police used them as cover as they moved in.

Inside the house, two Dobermanns paced up and down the hall, wary of the sounds outside and sensing that intruders were approaching. The marksmen loaded their rifles with sedating darts and took up positions in the bushes on both sides of the house at twenty yards.

Inside the house, the couple were busy transferring the bundles of money into cash boxes and briefcases before hiding it in secret locations. £20,000 filled a combination safe in an office room. £5,000 went into a locked filing cabinet; another £5,000 was hidden under floorboards, £10,000 was stashed in a bedroom closet and the last £10,000 went up an inglenook chimney in the front lounge.

Suddenly the dogs barked loudly, alerting them to intruders, and the woman scrambled to the window.

'Turn the light out!' she snapped, peering through a gap in the curtains. 'It's the police! Hide it all up the chimney and get out while I let the dogs out.'

She went to the front door, where the Dobermanns were growling to get out, and she released the catch. Then she let them out and stood watching as they bounded down the front steps onto the drive towards the police hidden behind the cars. The marksmen instantly caught the animals in their sights and they fired from both sides. One dart apiece thudded into the flanks of the dogs, releasing a Bacillus toxin, and the effect was an instant drowsiness. They fell at the feet of the police with a whimper.

The police officers rushed the house, forcing their way in as the woman tried to close the door. She was held by two uniformed police while three more barged into the lounge with Sergeant Boyd, catching the man red-handed surrounded by cash boxes.

'Well, well! If it isn't Charley Johnson, known to all and sundry as "Charley the Fixer",' Boyd said triumphantly. 'I thought you were in Spain, Charley. Come back for a holiday, did you?'

'I've been doing business, Mr Boyd. And I can prove it.'

'I bet you can. Monkey business, more like. The banknotes are all recorded. You wouldn't have got away with it. Arrest them both!'

Both were arrested and charged with conspiracy to defraud. The man was known to the police as a flamboyant con man and racketeer, and the woman was Doreen Chambers, former secretary to Sir Charles Woodward. It transpired the man was her secret lover, whom she brought in after Seagrove's arrest.

She had the ransom in her sights as soon as he was out the way. But how she knew about the Denton phone box had to be established. It was assumed that Seagrove must had told her he had deliberately planted the tape on the motorway before his arrest, and that she decided to capitalise on it.

What better opportunity could she have had? With Seagrove out the way, she had the house with her new partner. But she wouldn't admit to it. She acted as though she was an innocent party, roped in because she was gullible. DS Boyd reckoned she was one of the most devious women he had ever met. The call was a clever hoax to steal the ransom. Had her plan worked, the money would have disappeared and possibly never recovered if the Woodward phone had not been tapped.

Chapter Nine

On the next day, Kennon was on the road again to Derby to interview Seagrove at the request of Derbyshire CID. The Denton tape had been Seagrove's faux pas – a blunder whose results not even he could have foreseen.

Kennon saw it as an attempt by Seagrove to throw the blame of the shooting onto the real Panther, but he couldn't shake off the niggling doubt that Seagrove might still be the ruthless serial robber. Such was the aura created by the phantom figure, it created a whirlpool where almost anyone brandishing a gun could be labelled the Black Panther. Anyone acting suspiciously and fitting his description was a prime suspect.

Kennon was disturbed that there had been no phone call from the kidnapper, which created a doubt about him being the Panther. On the other hand, it was conceivable the Panther had changed his plans when he realised he had lost the tape… or did his call go unanswered? The delays were worrying.

Kennon arrived early at nine o'clock to interview Seagrove with his lawyer present. But first he was shown the Incident Room, where Derbyshire CID had amassed the information and exhibits on Britain's number one public enemy. On the main board, five photofits showed the face of the man based on the descriptions of witnesses who actually saw the Panther, or imagined they did. But they were not alike, and bore only a vague similarity to the real man.

But the most telling description was that established by a reconstruction of the Panther as he was seen in the middle of the night by startled postmasters demanding the keys to the safe. The enlarged photo showed a hooded figure in a combat jacket as he pointed a sawn-off double-barrelled shotgun with a torch taped to the end. Across his chest hung a belt of cartridges, a sheath knife hung from his belt, and he wore white gloves that were sensitive to the two triggers on the shotgun. Kennon studied it and realised what a formidable adversary they faced.

'This reconstruction is the image we all have of the Black Panther,' Jack Taylor said as he showed Kennon round. 'It's been compiled from dozens of witness statements. But whether he's the man we're about to interview? Seagrove is bigger than our description of him. The man on the board is five foot six, whereas Seagrove is five foot ten. Seagrove also looks about fifty, whereas our information is the Panther is only about his mid-thirties.'

'Looks can be deceiving, Jack. We won't know for certain until we question the suspect and get a confession out of him. Evidence is the only thing that will nail him.'

'I'm not happy about that raid on Buxton Manor last night, George,' Taylor replied. 'Your men should have informed us about the operation. We had spent considerable effort in taking out evidence and there was still more to come.'

'I know, Jack, but it couldn't be helped. It would have probably been destroyed anyway by that pair of swindlers. But it appears you have it all.'

'I reckon there's more. Have a look at this lot brought in from the house.' Taylor led Kennon over to a table laid out with exhibits.

On the table was a 12-bore double-barrelled shotgun with a belt of cartridges. A .22 semi-automatic pistol; two hunting knives in leather sheaths, two rucksacks; a pair of binoculars; an army chronometer and a pair of motorcycle goggles and helmet that was found in the back of Seagrove's Land-Rover after he had dumped the bike. And in the middle of it all was a black nylon hood with just slits for the eyes.

'This is just some of it. We also found company accounts and correspondences detailing huge bank loans going back five years in a locked drawer. Take a look at this.'

Taylor picked up a folder off the desk and handed Kennon a company balance sheet for 1970. 'I'm no accountant, but there are several large sums between three and five thousand pounds under investments. Could that be the proceeds from the post office robberies?'

'It might be, Jack. But I reckon it's more likely the proceeds of blackmail,' Kennon replied. 'I've been looking at a fraud case involving Sir Charles Woodward, and I'm convinced he was being blackmailed at that time. In fact I know damned well he was now – and here's the proof.'

Kennon was right. Sir Charles was being blackmailed by Seagrove, and Doreen Chambers was supplying the information for it.

'Well, I'm damned! The man was a blackmailer as well. It looks like we've caught one dangerous character,' Taylor said returning to the table. 'This little lot was in a locked room upstairs inside the house.'

Kennon looked at the collection of equipment and then took hold of the hood. 'So this is what the Black Panther looked like to his victims! This is probably the most damning piece of evidence. No sign of the motor bike, I suppose?'

'Not yet, but we're still searching. But it's the weapons that are most crucial. If ballistics can match this pistol here with the bullets recovered in the Langley post office raid and the Freightliner shooting in Dudley, then we've got our man. The Black Panther's reign is over.'

'It also means the description you've got is totally wrong, which doesn't say much for the witnesses. Has Seagrove's lawyer arrived yet?'

'He's with him now. Shall we proceed with the interview?'

'Lead the way, Jack.'

The two men went along to room four where Seagrove and his lawyer, Douglas Pembroke waited. They sat grim-faced at a table with a two-reel tape recorder by it. Taylor switched it on and formally opened the interview naming all the parties in the room.

Seagrove sat poker-faced, inwardly seething at spending a night in the cells, but more concerned what his girlfriend was up to. So far he had managed to get away with his post office raids in the middle of the night, emulating the Black Panther; but now his misdeeds had come home to roost on a careless blunder. He should never have dropped that tape in the lay-by and he should never had trusted Doreen Chambers with his plans.

'Tell me about your business relationship with Sir Charles Woodward,' Kennon asked.

'He's the Chairman of Buxton Stables. I manage the business and meet the clients. They're the racing tycoons with large stables who want the best thoroughbreds. It's a prestige company with thirty staff on the payroll.'

'But it wasn't always like that, was it, Mr Seagrove? There was a time when you were Chairman. You came out the army as a commissioned officer and began looking for investments to maintain your high living. When you saw Buxton stud farm up for sale this was the ideal enterprise. But you needed investors to back your project: money men. Right?'

'That's usual in any big business.'

'You managed to attract a few investors, but it wasn't enough. You were compelled to take out large bank loans. You made mistakes, as any layman would without a sound knowledge of breeding racehorses. You invested in the wrong stock and the business went into decline. In the first two years the balance sheet showed huge losses from 1968 to '70. The backers walked out and you desperately needed new cash injections. Right?'

'Not entirely, but go on.'

'Faced with bankruptcy you turned to crime. It was the beginning of the reign of the Black Panther.'

'Rubbish! You're accusing me of robbing post offices! Where's your evidence?'

'I must remind you, Chief Inspector,' the startled lawyer said, 'this is a new charge you are laying against my client, and one which I had not heard of. I insist you withdraw it.'

'I was merely stating that the two crime scenes coincide, Mr Pembroke. I have not laid a charge of the post office raids on your client.'

'But you clearly assumed it.'

'Assumption is not the same thing, but for the sake of legal process, I withdraw my assumption. It was your good fortune, Mr Seagrove, to attract Sir Charles Woodward, a keen racing man himself, whose company, Woodward Engineering, was hit with a fraud scandal at that time. It was widely publicised during the fraud investigation that it was Sir Charles Woodward's penchant for owning his own racing stable that led him to plunder the company assets. The case also touched on a mystery blackmailer concerning Sir Charles's alleged affair with his secretary, Doreen Chambers. Amazing that she is now in custody after following your plans...'

Seagrove's face turned a sickly pallor. 'She's a liar! She's a conniving bitch! Whatever she says is lies! What has she said?'

'She was the link between you and Sir Charles for dodgy investments. But Sir Charles is no fool when it comes to investments. He got experts to look at the breeding stock and then he bought you out for a song. But he wasn't all mean-hearted. He kept you on at a good salary as manager, but that still wasn't enough for you. You went for the ransom you thought Sir Charles was carrying – emulating the Panther! You figured he had to pay. But you were wrong. He didn't have it with him, so you shot him and threw the blame on the Black Panther. Right?'

'Absolute nonsense! What evidence do you have?'

'How does a black hood sound found in the manor?'

'That was for a fancy dress party. We used to hold regular fancy dress parties at the manor. You can check with my staff.'

'How about a double-barrelled shotgun, a .22 semi-automatic pistol and two sheath knives. Are they fancy dress as well?'

'They are used for sport and hunting, and both guns are licensed! I shoot game and I fish! Is that a crime, Detective Chief Inspector!' Seagrove retorted angrily.

'Is chess another of your pastimes, Mr Seagrove? Do you own a chess set?'

'No. I don't play the bloody game.'

'That's not what I heard from your accountant, Ted Ainsley. He says you used to boast how good you were. He even played you regularly until your set went missing. Where did it go?'

'I don't know! It just vanished from the house. There's a lot of people go in and out at all times. It could have been pinched by a light-fingered stable boy.'

'It was a Howard Staunton. They're the finest chess makers in the country. Was it this one, Mr Seagrove?' Kennon produced an enhanced photograph of the chess set. 'You'll notice the initials on the lid: NS. They're your initials, aren't they?'

'Where the hell did you get that from?'

'You asked for evidence. This is it.'

'Chief Inspector, you must answer my client's question,' Pembroke said, showing his impatience. 'And a photograph is hardly evidence in a court of law.'

'Not on its own, I agree. But I'll have supporting evidence.'

'It had better be good. And it had better be admissible.'

Kennon ignored the lawyer's pedantic remark.

'A man walked into Julia Woodward's antique shop with this set, intending to sell it as an antique on the night she vanished. It was right on closing time just as the assistant was getting ready to leave. It was well timed. The man had Julia Woodward to himself. He kept her talking while he haggled a price for it. She felt pressured into buying it for a hundred pounds. Then while she was writing a cheque he pulled a gun on her. That man was you, wasn't it, Seagrove? It was all part of an elaborate plan to make Sir Charles Woodward pay £50,000 for her return. You've been caught, Seagrove – well and truly caught!'

Seagrove's astonishment turned into anger. 'Never! That man wasn't me! I was nowhere near the shop that night! You can't pin this on me. You're making a grave mistake, Chief Inspector. A very grave mistake.'

'Come on. Admit it! You kidnapped Julia Woodward!'

'I did not!'

The two men glared at each other across the table and the lawyer stepped in again. 'Inspector Kennon. You're with the Manchester police, I'm told. You are dealing with a Manchester case that my client does not have to answer for. I insist he is interviewed by a member of the Derbyshire Constabulary.'

'It makes no difference who interviews your client, Mr Pembroke. I could be from Scotland Yard.'

'In that case I insist some time with my client to discuss the charges, thus so far laid, and I would like to see a copy of the Buxton Stables annual accounts for the years 1968 to '71.'

'You shall have them as soon as we have them, Mr Pembroke. In the meantime this interview is suspended.'

Kennon switched off the tape and left the room with Taylor.

'That was a fiery interview, George. Real dog eat dog,' Taylor said as they stepped into the corridor and walked to a vending machine. 'The chess set convinced me. I didn't know about that. Tea or coffee?'

'Coffee, please. Don't rely on the chess set, Jack. I put that in to test Seagrove's reaction. He could well claim it was stolen, although it seems too much of a coincidence. I'm more concerned if ballistics can match Seagrove's pistol with the bullets fired at Sir Charles Woodward. If they do, then we've got our man.'

'And if they match the bullets used in the post office raids or the Freightliner shooting, then the job is done. The Black Panther's reign is over.'

'Is it, Jack? I'm not so sure. We may have the man who shot Sir Charles Woodward, and it's possible that Seagrove did carry out some post office raids wearing a hood. But whether he's the same man who kidnapped Julia Woodward is another matter.'

'But the Denton tape confirms it, surely— Julia Woodward spoke on the tape to her brother, and it led us to Buxton Stables and Seagrove. Good enough evidence, I'd say.'

'It should be, but what if the voice on it is not Julia Woodward's voice, but someone else? Someone deliberately imitating her voice? Doreen Chambers, for instance. It was a hooded man who shot Sir Charles, but was Seagrove copying the Panther to shift the blame?'

'Well, you certainly like to complicate things, George,' Taylor said. 'You've got me baffled now.'

'I knew it wouldn't be easy the day we got the kidnap message.'

Taylor downed his tea. 'The Black Panther has systematically tied us up for four long years. We have untold amounts of evidence through witness statements and interviews. We have found two stolen cars he used. We know the Panther has used a motorbike at some time. Seagrove is the closest we've got to him.'

'Put out a full-scale search at Buxton, Jack. He could quite as easily have dumped the bike there before returning to the farm.'

'This hunt for the Black Panther is driving us all insane,' Taylor replied with a weary tone. 'Masses of information have been compiled. Every police force keeps its own files zealously locked away, and that hampers the investigation. They miss vital clues, like vehicles stolen in the area, which are hugely important. I've only just learned from Northants Constabulary about a garage rented in Northampton used as a possible supply base. How many more are there? What's the answer, George?'

'A Central Incident Room, Jack. I've been arguing for it all along. I believe Julia Woodward has been moved, but I don't know where, and without a Central Incident Room to filter the evidence the chance of finding her gets slimmer.'

'Well, if she's being held in Derbyshire, we've got plenty of potholing caves and redundant coal mines to hide someone in; but other than that I can't think of anywhere.'

'Precisely. We are currently searching the West Yorkshire reservoirs. I believe a pump house or a drainage system of some kind is the most likely place. Concentrate your searches on that, Jack. I sincerely hope Seagrove is the Panther, but unless he confesses to the kidnapping we have to keep searching. Now I must return to Manchester and see what my lot has come up with. I'll keep you up to date.'

There was a commotion in the corridor and a constable came rushing through. 'Sir! The TV cameras are outside with the press. They want an interview over the Buxton Farm arrests.'

'I expected that. Tell them to wait! Well, George, it looks like we are going to have to oblige the media. I'll take up those issues you've mentioned with the Chief Constable. Now let's see if we can get you through outside.'

Kennon could hardly escape the clamour outside, and after a brief interview he was on his way back to Manchester. On his mind was the next ransom demand from the real Panther. He was coming round to the fact the Panther and the kidnapper were the same man.

Although he had not yet met Ian Woodward, he toyed with the idea of putting an armed police officer in his place to carry the ransom. After all, it made no difference who delivered the money. But the niggling problem was, how would the victim be returned? In fact, Kennon had no way of knowing he was driving away from the kidnapper's lair and that the Panther was making new plans for delivery of the ransom.

When he pulled into Central CID at one o'clock he found Suzanne waiting in her car, and he suddenly remembered he'd forgotten to return her cassette tape.

'Well, you're a fine one!' she said, climbing out to meet him. 'What happened to my tape I lent you?'

'I know, I'm sorry. I'll drop it in the post for you. I keep a cluttered desk, that's my problem.'

'It's OK, I don't want it. So what's the latest? I hear you've made a new arrest in Buxton. Nicholas Seagrove, the racehorse trainer.'

'Who told you? I've only just left there.'

'I had a phone call last night from a guy on the local radio station. It doesn't take long for hot news to get about in the media. We all help each other.'

'Not much chance of keeping anything secret from you, then! Yes, you're right: Nicholas Seagrove of Buxton stud farm. He was the main shareholder until Sir Charles Woodward took control. I've arrested him over the shooting of Sir Charles.'

'Did he have anything to do with the kidnapping?'

'I don't know. And if I did, I couldn't tell you.'

'Oh, you are a stickler. Come on, you know me well enough – I don't disclose my sources. It will come out soon enough.'

'All right, Suzanne, you win. Seagrove has been charged with shooting Sir Charles. He assumed he was carrying the ransom money and tried to hijack it on the Pennine Road. But he was out of luck. Sir Charles wasn't carrying it. As for the kidnapping, he looks the most likely suspect yet.'

'Well, that is a coup,' Suzanne said. 'My editor will love this. And do you think Seagrove is the Black Panther?'

'No, I don't. But he did a good impression of him, and possibly carried out a few post office robberies in his name. Don't you print any of this. You'll get me shot!'

'Why are you telling me then?'

'Because I'm a sucker for a pretty face.'

'Well, that is a compliment. But I must have more information. I can't print until I get all the facts. What I've got so far wouldn't go more than one column. I need a story.'

'I tell you what. Meet me in the Stock Exchange at six o'clock and I'll give you some more on Sir Charles. But it's confidential. You can print Seagrove's arrest for the shooting, but that's all.'

'Well, you are kind. OK, I'll see you in the pub at six o'clock. Don't be late.'

'I'm never late for a good woman.'

They smiled as they parted and Kennon watched her drive

out, giving him a small wave as she went. He hadn't felt so happy in years. He entered the building and bounded up the stairs with a new spring in his step.

He entered the Incident Room, where Ian Woodward was sitting at a table with Bradley and three detectives discussing the previous night's ransom run. On the table was a large holdall containing the ransom money that had been found after an extensive search of Buxton Manor. Everyone else, it seemed, was waiting for Kennon's statement.

'You all want the news, I take it,' Kennon said, looking at faces that showed fatigue from the extra hours being worked. 'So far, Nicholas Seagrove hasn't confessed to anything. Whether he's the Panther or not remains to be seen. I have my doubts. But I'm certain he's the man who shot Sir Charles Woodward in an attempt to steal the ransom.'

A rumble of disappointment stirred through the team, who were all fervently hoping Seagrove was the Black Panther and that the credit would go to Manchester.

'I know, I'm as disappointed as you are. Derbyshire CID are still finding evidence that links him to yesterday's shooting of Sir Charles. But we need the motorcycle, which is probably dumped somewhere.'

'Well done, George!' Bradley exclaimed. 'Now, this is Mr Ian Woodward. He's agreed to carry the ransom money, providing he gets another demand from the kidnapper.'

Kennon shook hands with the 21-year-old student from Cambridge. He was wearing a brown corduroy jacket with a CND badge on the lapel. He was fair-haired with a thin student's beard giving him a Scandinavian appearance, and he bore hardly any resemblance to his father.

'Pleased to meet you, Ian. This must be an ordeal for you.'

'It is indeed. But it must be even worse for Julia. Have you any news of my sister, Chief Inspector?'

'I'm afraid not. But we'll find her and bring her back. Is that the ransom money in the bag? It looks heavier than thirty pounds.'

'It is. It's nearer forty. But it was asked for in tens and twenties.' Ian unzipped the bag and showed it to be stuffed full with bundles of notes. 'It's hard to believe I nearly lost all this last night... if it hadn't been for Sergeant Boyd's timely intervention.'

'Just doing my job,' Boyd said with a red face.

'Is it traceable? The notes can be marked with a special dye.'

'No – and I insist that it is not. I want my sister returned alive, Chief Inspector. If the kidnapper suspects the money has been tampered with, I think he will not hesitate to kill her. I want no bug in the bag, either. From what I hear of this Black Panther, he is ruthless and does not hesitate to kill.'

'We can't let you do this alone. You will have an escort discreetly following at a distance in case the kidnapper is watching.'

'I'm not afraid to do it alone. I'd prefer it that way.'

'I've already explained that to Ian, George,' said Bradley. 'He's ready to appear on national television, and I think it will be a good public relations exercise. Let the public know how determined we are at ending the Panther's reign of terror.'

'I'm not sure it's a good idea, sir. Public relations is all very well, but it could hinder the investigation if we reveal too much. The kidnapper has sternly warned against police involvement, and it doesn't bode well with other forces working on the Panther case if it exposes their weakness.'

'I thought you'd say that! You're a pessimist, George, you really are! We don't get much publicity, and now we're on the biggest case in a decade, and you want to hide our light under a bushel. For God's sake, man, let's show what we can do if we all pull together.'

'I don't believe publicity for publicity's sake is right. Our job is to catch the kidnapper. Showing this case on television will not make it any easier if the kidnapper learns our methods. Let's wait until we've caught the bugger. Then we can talk about success.'

'I disagree, Chief Inspector. The police need good public relations because they are in the public domain,' Ian Woodward interjected. 'It also fosters help from the public, and we need it badly for the sake of my sister if we are to get her back. I want to make a personal appeal on her behalf to show we are doing all we can. And if you believe the kidnapper is the Black Panther, then it can be confirmed by the media and may well assist in his capture by someone who knows him.'

'I admire your courage, Ian. I want her back as much as you. OK, if you feel it's right, we'll go ahead. Maybe it will do some good.'

'That's the spirit, George! I'll leave the script up to you,' Bradley said, as if addressing an actor. 'The moors search never turned anything up. Thirty pumping stations were searched, as well as drainage ditches and reservoirs. Not even the missing Water Board van was found. But my sympathies go to the families of the murdered men.'

'Mine too. Has the CCTV tape been brought in from the filling station?'

'It has, sir,' Sergeant Boyd said eagerly. 'Would you like to see it? I'll put it on.'

Boyd turned on the portable TV and pushed the tape into the video. It was a four-minute fuzzy black and white recording, showing a van pulling into the Hazel Grove filling station. The driver got out wearing a raincoat and flat cap. He was below average height and of slight build, but his face was unclear. He appeared to be in his early thirties and very agile. When the tank was filled he walked to the shop and was stopped by the photofit picture on the window showing the Black Panther. As he paused to look at it, a police car pulled in and a uniformed traffic constable climbed out. The man turned his back before hurrying off to his van and climbing in. He lurched away from the pumps and as he drove off the rear doors flew open and a small shiny object fell out and bounced across the forecourt, then disappeared from view.

'What was that fell out of the back? It looked like a ring,' Kennon said.

'We've made a search and can't find anything,' Bradley replied. 'But was that the kidnapper, or just some bloke running off without paying for his petrol?'

'I would say that's the kidnapper, but it's impossible to tell a description by those pictures. Is that the best forensic could do with it?'

'Chief Inspector,' said Ian Woodward, 'my sister wore a green emerald signet ring on her left hand. I would recognise it anywhere.'

'In that case, Ian, I'll insist on another search. If that was the Black Panther on that tape we may have to move our incident room and share it with the West Mercia force.'

Bradley's face turned pale. 'You're not serious, George! Share our resources with West Mercia?'

'Sir! Take a look at this!' Boyd announced as he tuned the TV after removing the videotape. 'It's Buxton Farm!'

Everyone in the room turned to watch a news bulletin from the BBC. The outside broadcast cameras had descended on Buxton Farm, where the search for Julia Woodward had widened across Derbyshire countryside. The cameras followed the lines of police, with dogs and well-meaning members of the public, all searching acres of woodlands around Buxton in the pale after-noon sun. The scene changed to show potholers descending into caves in several locations scattered all round the area before switching back to the stud farm.

The programme anchor man, Roger Simpson, took the viewers over the manor house and into the Panther's lair. 'This is the locked room where the Panther stored his equipment and planned his meticulous post office raids,' Simpson said, sweeping his hand across a table displaying a camouflage jacket and various other items found on the farm. These included a 12-bore shotgun with a belt of cartridges, a Browning .22 semi-automatic pistol, torches, Ordnance Survey maps, glucose tablets, a roll of tape and a chronometer. Then Simpson held up the infamous black Lycra hood to the camera.

'This is the hood the Black Panther wore to terrify his victims with,' Simpson said with the flourish of a showman. 'Derbyshire police have named the man as Nicholas Seagrove, who managed the stud farm for Sir Charles Woodward, who was brutally gunned down this morning on his way to assist police inquires into the kidnapping of his daughter. This house was also the scene of a dramatic police raid last night to foil a ransom snatch by Seagrove's partner and her lover, Charley Johnson. The search continues for the hiding place of Julia Woodward, believed to be in a disused mine or one of the many caves, as we go live to our reporter, Mark Eaton, at Miller's Dale.'

The scene changed to a craggy hillside, where Mark Eaton was interviewing a potholer at Miller's Dale. 'Thank you, Roger. I have here David Ashley who leads the team at Miller's Dale. David, what can you tell us about this search? Is it possible to keep someone hidden in a pothole such as this?'

'It's not only possible but highly dangerous. These natural limestone "clefts" we call potholes are a veritable maze of tunnels and deep flooded caves. It would require someone with experience to carry out such a task, and there is no guarantee the victim could be safe from drowning. But we will keep searching until we find the missing girl.'

The camera switched back to Buxton Farm, where several workers were interviewed, showing mixed reactions. Some said their boss was full of bluster, while others praised him and said he was a genuine horse breeder. Ted Ainsley described his boss as a dubious character steeped in military tradition, but was doubtful Seagrove could be the Panther, because he came from North Yorkshire and the Panther was widely believed to be from the West Midlands. Then, out of the blue, a character appeared who startled everyone. The suave figure of Simon Kingsley arrived in a luxury car to gatecrash the programme and air his views. He was tall and good-looking for a man of over forty. He made the startling claim that he had been to the house on several occasions buying antiques when the previous owner's son, Jack Laker, sold most of the house contents.

This revelation took the Manchester CID watching the programme by surprise, including Kennon, who had discounted the man from his inquiries. The detectives watched the programme, hoping to learn about Seagrove's background, were further surprised when Kingsley went on to explain that he was one of the original backers to buy the farm in 1968 and had subsequently been swindled by the man.

'Nicholas Seagrove took us all for a ride!' Kingsley said with a bitter tone. 'Myself and several others in the consortium lost a lot of money over Seagrove's mishandling of the business! He convinced us he knew all about horses from his military career in the Hussars and all the time he knew damn all! There's a vast difference between Derby winners and a horse trained by the military.'

Kingsley was playing it for all it was worth, and Kennon could see the real con man behind the words.

'It wouldn't surprise me one jot if it turns out Seagrove is the Black Panther! He got into debt and saw the only way out was armed robbery. He would never explain the investments or talk about the running of the farm. I turned up here early one day and found him counting a pile of cash! He said he'd sold a filly for three grand and there was another in the offing. But there was no receipt, no invoice. I was sceptical then. He had an answer for everything! But that didn't stop our investments from going down the pan. I received only a small return when the business went into administration. I lost five grand to Nicholas Seagrove.'

Last to be interviewed was the Derbyshire Assistant Chief Constable, Daniel Whitmore, basking triumphantly in the limelight.

'With all the evidence so far gathered from this house and from many other crime scenes,' Whitmore said, 'I am certain beyond any shadow of doubt that we have captured the Black Panther. We have ended four years of a seemingly endless manhunt for a ruthless killer.'

When the programme finished, the Manchester team were buoyant.

'It seems very likely we've caught the Panther, sir,' Sergeant Boyd said. 'You can't get much harder evidence than that. I thought Kingsley was the most convincing.'

'Was he? Kingsley was more interested in the money he lost than the fate of Julia Woodward, and he was supposed to be her ex-lover. He never mentioned her once. The man was milking it for all he could get.'

'So you don't believe Seagrove is the Panther after all?'

'No, I don't. He's most definitely the man who shot Sir Charles Woodward, and it's even conceivable that he might have done a few botched post office jobs. But he's not the Panther.'

'So where do we go from here. Back to square one?'

'We go ahead with tonight's TV interview.' Kennon replied. 'I shall be with him on behalf of the CID putting our case forward, and then we wait for the Panther's next set of instructions.'

Kennon was unconsciously admitting the kidnapper was the Black Panther.

Chapter Ten

At five o'clock in the evening a maroon-coloured Jaguar stood on the drive at Bridlington Hall. Inside the house, Peter Woodward, the elder son, had arrived with his wife, Janet, and two children to offer their support to his stepmother; but friction was in the air in the dining room.

'Ian's down at the Granada studios!' Peter said incredulously. 'Whose bright idea was that? It'll ruin our standing!'

'Really, Peter! You could show a bit more tolerance to your brother's efforts. He's doing his best,' Veronica said. She was sitting at the head of the dining table, where the three of them and the two children dined on an early evening buffet of cold ham, potatoes and salad.

'If the police did their job properly the man could be in custody by now. They ferret around in Manchester and Derbyshire looking at Dad's investments as if he were the criminal. They haven't bothered to search Bradford or Leeds, when it's obvious the man comes from that area.'

'How do you know that?'

'Father's shooting was on the A58 that dissects West Yorkshire. What more obvious clue do they want? They should be looking at the immigrant population in Bradford. That's where they'll find the Black Panther – a West Indian from what I've heard about him.'

'He's from the Black Country area, according to what I've heard. That's a long way from Bradford.'

'The man has wheels, doesn't he? You shouldn't have let Ian go ahead with the ransom, Veronica. Father's lying critically ill in hospital and Ian's taking money to pay Julia's kidnapper with no guarantee she will be released! Father would never have permitted it. His golden rule was never give in to blackmail,' Peter emphasised, unaware his father had been blackmailed.

'Well, that's silly, because he never had to – and besides, this isn't blackmail, it's a kidnap. Would you have your own sister murdered just because of some silly principle?'

'She won't be murdered. The kidnapper will have to listen to reason. He won't throw away his chance of a fortune. He will have to produce Julia, alive and unharmed. He can choose the place. I don't care if it's the top of Ben Nevis, but he must produce Julia, or the ransom is totally out of the question.'

'You're as stubborn as your father, Peter. Chief Inspector Kennon says we have to do as the kidnapper says if we want Julia back safe and sound, or we risk losing her to a madman who won't hesitate to kill her.'

'Well, he's wrong! They did that with the wife of the news-paper executive, and look what happened! Her body has still not been found. I tell you the same thing will happen with Julia. And as for going on TV, Ian will make a complete fool of himself. I'm going down to that studio to put a stop to it!'

'You will not! I've authorised it. If you interfere you'll make it worse. I forbid you to do it. Talk some sense into him, Janet, please.'

'Veronica is right, Peter. You'll make it worse if you blunder in like a bull at a gate. The police must believe it will do some good or they wouldn't have proposed it.'

'Oh, take her side, my dear – that's all I need. I shall go down to the studio and speak with them. If they convince me it's right then I shall probably take Ian's place. Yes, that's it – I'll go on instead of Ian! I'm older than him, so it should be me! They can't refuse. You stay here, Janet, and watch me on TV.'

'Don't worry, Peter. I've no intention of coming and seeing you make a fool of yourself.'

With less than one hour to spare, Peter Woodward's luxury Jaguar roared down the A58 heading for Manchester. He drove like a demon and in less than ten minutes he had a patrol car on his tail with its blue light flashing.

'Fucking police!' Peter swore as the car came alongside and ordered him on to the hard shoulder. The cars came to a stop with Woodward hemmed in, and he lowered the electronic widow as the two patrolmen walked back to his car.

'Do you know what speed you were doing, sir? We clocked you doing almost ninety. Now, that is clearly breaking the law.'

'Yes, I know, Officer. My name is Peter Woodward. I'm the brother of Julia Woodward, the kidnapped heiress. I must get to Granada TV studios by six o'clock before they go on air. Give me a ticket, by all means, but hurry. It's absolutely imperative I reach the studio before they go on air.'

'My God!' the officer said, as though he'd just backed a Derby winner. 'In that case, sir, follow us. You've just got yourself a police escort!'

The police set off, with Peter following, and the blue flashing light was enough to clear the way. The traffic was heavy with commuters and they travelled in the fast lane touching speeds of 80 mph, with a wailing siren forcing everything over. They cut through the Manchester traffic like a knife in butter and reached the TV studios with twelve minutes to spare. They rushed through the doors up to the reception, with people clearing a path.

'I want the studio for the kidnap interview!' Peter gasped.

'Who are you, sir? You must have clearance,' the receptionist replied.

'Peter Woodward. Just show me the way. Phone ahead if you must. But give me directions.'

'This way, sir,' a security man said, after getting the nod.

The police hung back as Peter followed the security man into the vast building and led him to the news studio where they were preparing to go on air. When he reached the studio with minutes to spare he was kept in check by security at the entrance to the large news studio 5 as the programme editor came to meet him.

'What's the problem, sir? I'm Chris Hall, news editor.'

'I'm Peter Woodward! Where's my brother? I must see him before he goes on air. It's vital he doesn't go on. I'll take his place.'

'It's too late. The countdown has started.'

'You can stop it. Make an announcement, or whatever.'

'It's too late! It's a special news feature already scheduled. But you can watch from the soundproof observation window and see it all. Follow me, sir. This way.' The editor led the way to a soundproof booth adjacent to the control room as the ITV

National News played its dramatic overture and a close-up photograph of Julia Woodward's smiling face appeared on the bank of overhead monitors.

Peter Woodward watched as the voice of television presenter, Reginald Bosanquet, spoke over the image introducing the special news feature, and then Bosanquet appeared on the screen. His voice had a distinctive quality.

'Good evening. We bring you this special news feature on the kidnapping of heiress Julia Woodward, who is still missing. Never has a crime so gripped the nation and started the biggest manhunt for the man responsible, widely believed to be the Black Panther.'

Then the camera switched to another shot, showing Ian Woodward sitting next to DCI George Kennon on a studio couch against a plain backdrop. Bosanquet sat opposite, and in front of them on a table the canvas holdall containing the ransom money was open for a camera shot. Then the interview began.

'Ian Woodward, you are the younger brother to Julia. What has prompted you to do this special feature?'

'I'm doing it in the hope it will save my sister. I want to make clear the agony that my family is going through. The man who has perpetrated this vile crime has no idea of the distress he has caused. I urge him to let her go and the ransom on this table before us will be his. I will personally take it to anywhere he designates for the drop.'

'In view of the arrest that took place in Buxton yesterday of Nicholas Seagrove by the Derbyshire police, do you have any doubt they have the man who kidnapped your sister?'

'I do. Although we have had no further contact from the kidnapper, I believe those events at Buxton happened for entirely different reasons. I'm told he denies kidnapping Julia, and the police have found nothing at the stud farm to link him to the kidnapping of my sister.'

'Do you believe the kidnapper will make further contact, in view of the shooting of Sir Charles, which has baffled the police?'

'I do. I'm optimistic that the kidnapper, whoever he is, will be in touch very soon. Whether he's the Black Panther or not, if he's watching this programme, I urge him to get in touch.'

Bosanquet then turned to Kennon. 'Chief Inspector, you are

the man leading the hunt for the kidnapper. Do you believe the man arrested at Buxton stud farm is the Black Panther, and in your view is almost certain to be the kidnapper?'

'No, I don't. The arrested man was emulating the Black Panther when he tried to seize the ransom and shot Sir Charles Woodward.'

'Why then has the Derbyshire Chief Constable claimed the Panther is caught?'

'Because of the evidence before him, which points to him being the Black Panther.'

'But you claim that evidence is wrong, do you?'

'I do. I believe Seagrove was impersonating the Panther to throw off suspicion. The real Panther is still at large and much harder to pin down. We have no real leads as to who he is. And I also doubt he's the kidnapper.'

Kennon's reply took Bosanquet by surprise. Up in the control room the editor was having kittens. 'What's he doing? I thought he was going to expose the real Panther! That's what he said, wasn't it?'

'Are you telling us, Chief Inspector, that after four days you have no idea who the kidnapper is, or where he comes from?'

'I am. He's left no clues other than a taped message of Julia's voice instructing that the ransom is paid before he releases her. We don't yet know who he is or where he's holding Julia Woodward. We do know she was held in a redundant reservoir pumping station on Saddleworth Moor and we have carried out a full search on the moors, but she has since been moved.'

'Why do you dismiss the claim by many that this is the work of the Black Panther?'

'There's nothing to suggest it's him, although I don't rule him out entirely. I believe the kidnapper's a Yorkshireman, whereas the Panther is reported to be from the Black Country, with a Birmingham accent.'

'It's been said that the Panther had prior dealings with Julia Woodward through her antique business. Could that be a possible scenario?'

'Highly unlikely. I don't know who puts these stories around.'

'How close are you to catching this man, Chief Inspector?'

'A long way off. He may never be caught.'

'Surely that can't be!' Bosanquet said with surprise. 'This man is in daily contact for the ransom. How difficult is it to track his phone calls?'

'I can't go into that. We have to respect the wishes of the family for the ransom to be paid in order that Julia Woodward is safely returned.'

'I believe it was you, Chief Inspector, who actually tracked down Nicholas Seagrove over the shooting of Sir Charles Woodward. Is Seagrove in any way linked to the kidnapping?'

'No, definitely not. The shooting of Sir Charles was a revenge attack over Sir Charles Woodward's outside interests which I can't go into. But I would take this opportunity to say if I had not shared my information with Derbyshire Constabulary the man would still be free.'

'Are you saying, Chief Inspector, that the Panther is free because of police rivalry?'

'I am indeed saying that. The police forces of this country have got to get away from being the narrow parochial organisations that they have become. We have to determine what is a national crime as distinct from a regional crime. The kidnapping is a national crime, and should be dealt with on that basis.'

Peter Woodward's rage took over. He flew out of the sound booth and charged onto the set stumbling over cables and crashing into Bosanquet.

'Chief Inspector, you are a liar!' Woodward shouted, picking himself up and helping a shaken Bosanquet to his feet.

'The kidnapper is nothing but a pathetic criminal, and he's sitting right under your nose! Have you bothered to question the ethnic communities in Manchester or Bradford? Has it not occurred to you that my sister is probably already dead, and we will never get her back?' He grabbed the canvas holdall. 'The ransom will not be paid without guarantees! This programme should never have gone ahead!'

The studio was thrown in uproar as security men bundled the intruder off the set and wrested the bag from him. The police escort came running to take over and Peter Woodward was dragged away and taken into custody. As calm returned to the studio, a shaken Bosanquet came back on screen, outwardly unruffled, and made a statement.

'That was Peter Woodward, obviously distressed over the shooting of his father, Sir Charles. I'm informed that he is now in police hands, and on that note we now end this special feature and continue with the news.'

The time ticked on towards eleven o'clock and Ian Woodward was getting restless waiting at Bridlington Hall, while his elder brother, Peter, was still in police custody charged with causing an affray.

'For Christ's sake, why doesn't he phone?'

No sooner had the words left his mouth when the phone rang and he jumped up to answer it. As he did so he heard a click and the detectives in the Manchester telephone exchange listened in to the voice of the kidnapper.

The voice spoke in a clipped West Indian accent. 'You are to take the MI to Nottingham, leaving it at exit 26. Take the A6514 to the town centre. Go to phone box outside the main post office and wait for a call at 1 a.m. – there must be no police and no tricks or death will come. I will repeat once more.' The caller repeated the message as Ian scribbled down the instructions on a pad. Then he replaced the receiver and waited a minute for the phone to ring again.

'Ian. This is DCI Kennon. We got the message. There is an area squad car waiting at the end of the lane. They will fit you out with a radio and mike and tell you how to use it. Then it will follow you all the way. Leave now.'

'No! I'm doing this alone. I want no police involvement. Is that understood?'

'Don't be daft, Ian, you can't manage it alone. You're dealing with a vicious killer. We have got to follow you. We would be failing in our duty not to attend. A radio van has been dispatched and is already on its way.'

'OK. You win. But keep well out of sight.' Woodward put the phone down and put on his raincoat while Veronica and Janet offered support.

'Be careful, Ian,' Veronica said, handing him a brolly. 'You will need this. It's teeming down outside.'

'Don't worry. I shan't make the same mistakes as Peter. I just hope the police don't go blundering in and ruin it.'

Ian picked up the bag of ransom money and left the house feeling reasonably optimistic. He climbed into his green Mini Cooper and drove swiftly away. When he reached the end of the lane he saw the dark shape of an unmarked police car waiting in a lay-by. It was Regional Crime Squad 4, and he changed cars to be fitted out with the radio and throat microphone by DS Boyd.

'Can you give me some idea what's going on?' he asked Boyd.

'We're following the kidnapper's instructions. Wherever he tells you to go we follow. This is a precaution. Through this radio you will relay all the instructions for us to follow, but you can't receive us. We will follow in a radio van packed with powerful listening equipment.'

'Is it the Black Panther we're dealing with, Sergeant? Your Chief Inspector Kennon seemed rather vague about it.'

'That was done to deceive the kidnapper as much as it was for hoax callers. We get a lot of sickos trying that on.' Boyd switched on the small hand-held radio and slipped into Ian Woodward's inside jacket pocket. 'There is a radio van parked a few miles up the road. We need to test that they're receiving. Speak softly into the mike so you are barely audible. Say, "This is Ian Woodward. I'm at the main post office." '

Woodward spoke softly into the microphone that was hidden in the lapel of his jacket. A few seconds later the reply crackled through the car's short-wave receiver. 'Hearing you loud and clear, Ian. You're at the main post office.'

'It works. But don't forget we cannot reply through your radio. There's only a one-way contact from your radio to ours.'

Back at Manchester CID a team of detectives were gathered in the Incident Room, receiving final instructions and going over maps and addresses for all the information that had been gathered. DCI Kennon issued a timely reminder before they left.

'We are going into the West Mercia area, therefore we call on them if we need to and share all information. Don't hold anything back out of pettiness. They need to know.'

'How is the Panther gauging the time, sir?' a detective inquired.

'He's starting from midnight. My guess is he's using public transport. We can be in Nottingham in less than an hour in a fast car. After that the times will be tight, and we could be at a disadvantage depending how far away we are. Right! Let's go!'

They travelled across Manchester's deserted rain-swept streets, heading for the A6 to take them across the Pennines to the M1. After a swift journey over the Pennines, they joined the M1 just above Dolsover and were soon hurtling south towards Nottingham in lashings of rain. The total distance to Nottingham was sixty miles.

It was forty minutes past midnight when the police vehicles pulled into the Castle Gate car park opposite the main post office. They were late, but just ten minutes behind Ian Woodward. The green Mini Cooper was parked on the street outside the phone box as Ian waited for his call. It came at 1 a.m. A voice instructed him to pull the Dymo tape out of its hiding place behind the advertising plate. He fumbled all round the board and then he saw it sticking out at the top. He eagerly removed it and read the instructions on it.

Go to Mapperley Park Zoo Gate 3. Take Dymo tape off gatepost.

'Mapperley Park Zoo, next,' Ian repeated into his mike as he stepped out in the rain to look at the Tourist Information Board nearby to get his bearings. He saw it was about three miles away on the edge of town, and jumping into his Mini, he drove off at speed following road signs… and then he got lost.

He had taken the wrong turning off a roundabout, and was now heading for the motorway out of town. He was forced to do a U-turn on a main road and double back.

Twenty minutes later he was pulling into Mapperley Park. It was a large common with a permanent zoo as its main feature, and after parking close by he walked to the entrance and found gate no. 3 clearly marked. Shining his torch all round, he saw the Dymo tape stuck under blue insulation tape right down at ground level, where it was almost impossible to see. He pulled it off and read the instructions.

Go through park subway and look ahead for light. Instructions on post.

He studied the message, shivering with the cold, when a sudden thunderclap shattered the stillness and then the heavens opened. He rushed back to his car and dived in to escape the torrents. This was beginning to look like hunt the parcel, and he relayed the message over his mike, but he could see no sign of any other vehicles in the park.

He sat waiting a quarter of an hour for the rain to ease off and then, when he judged it was easing, he climbed out the car and walked on, looking for the subway. He spent twenty fruitless minutes looking for the subway, squelching through puddles, and gave up. There wasn't a subway anywhere as far as he could tell.

Had he read the tape wrong? He read the tape again under his torch and noticed the badly stamped letters, which on closer examination read: *Go through park archway and look ahead for light. Instructions on post.*

Instantly he realised it referred to the park archway, part of the old city walls. He stumbled back to his car and climbed in, feeling like a wet rag. He started up and drove right around the park perimeter on a ring road until he came to the historic archway that led through to the medieval lanes. Then he saw the instructions taped on the bottom of a lamp post. He peeled it off and read the Dymo tape.

Leave bag by the gate. Return to vehicle and drive away.

The 'gate' he assumed was the arch, and he looked all round for another gate. He was reluctant to follow this instruction to just dump the ransom and walk away. He called out, 'I'm here! Where are you? Where's my sister? Show yourself!'

All he heard was his own echo down the lanes. Everywhere was in darkness – darker than anywhere else, it seemed, as his torch stabbed the night. Nothing moved and the patter of the rain, now easing off, was the only sound as it hit dustbin lids.

Ian dumped the bag and walked away, speaking into his mike as he went, and hoping against hope the contact heard him. But here again he felt stymied. He didn't want the police involvement, and now here he was, relying on them to give him confirmation he was doing the right thing. Should he leave the money? Was the kidnapper watching him walk away? And if not, how could he be sure it was carried out?

He climbed into his car, took a last look at the bag dumped by the gate, and then slowly drove away. But he didn't go far. He drove back into the park, with every intention of returning in an hour to see if the bag was still there. He went as far as the zoo and waited in the car park, fighting against drowsiness; but it was a hopeless task, and gradually he succumbed to the sleep taking over his body.

But even this luxury was to be denied him. Less than one hour later the police vehicles turned up, and DCI Kennon was shaking him out of his reverie. 'Ian! Come on, lad. Sorry to disturb you, but we've got a problem.'

'What…? What's that?' he mumbled. 'A problem… Has the kidnapper showed up?'

'No, Ian, he hasn't. We've been watching the gate from here through binoculars and the bag never moved. So we've retrieved it.'

'Stone me! It was a complete farce!' Ian grumbled. 'I was supposed to see a light and I saw nothing. All I did was wander around in circles getting lost! Could you hear me complaining?'

'We lost radio contact several times. The thunder didn't help. We'll just have to do it all over again.'

'We've blown it! He must have seen you! I said I should have come alone. Will we ever get a second chance? I doubt it.'

'We'll get one more. I think the kidnapper was using this as a rehearsal, to see if we followed you. He held back from taking the ransom because he couldn't be sure. He dared not risk it. But he will be back with another plan tonight. You can bet on it.'

'What's happening, sir?' a detective called. 'Is it all off?'

'For tonight, yes. It's back to Manchester. We try again tomorrow.'

'No, Chief Inspector! I'm not going back! My sister is in trouble and I'm not deserting her. This is the closest we have got to the Panther. I'm positive he must have seen me. I'm staying here all night. He may show himself. If he doesn't, then I want to see what this place looks like in daylight. I'm staying put.'

'Don't be ridiculous! You won't stay awake. There's nothing that can't wait until tomorrow. Believe me, the Panther will not show himself now.'

'This is my show, Chief Inspector, not yours. I'm staying put.'

'By God, I admire your spirit, lad. But you can't stay here, not with all that cash. Besides you need to be home to take the Panther's next call.'

'You reckon he will call again?'

'Of course he will. We still have the ransom. He won't give that up.'

'I genuinely thought tonight I would see Julia again.' Ian's face filled with anguish. His eyes glazed over and a tear rolled down his cheek. 'Where is she, Mr Kennon? Where is she?'

'We'll make a thorough search tomorrow. We'll find her. Move over, lad. You're in no fit state to drive. I'll take the wheel.'

They got into their cars and drove away. It was 3.30 a.m., and as the police vehicles headed back to Manchester the Panther was making his way across the city, cursing his bad luck and blaming the police.

Chapter Eleven

The Panther moved like a shadow in the night heading for the railway station, and by four o'clock he was sitting on the deserted platform drinking coffee from the vending machine. At 4.30 a.m. the shutter went up on the ticket office, and he paid two pounds for a ticket and waited for the five o'clock train to Huddersfield.

He was going back to his base to set the original plan, the one he should have stuck to from the beginning. He would have to iron out a few snags and, though it wasn't perfect, he could not afford a repeat of last night.

Soon he was joined by a few early morning workers. They took no notice of him; he was just another early shift worker. At two minutes to five, the London mail train pulled in, and as he climbed aboard the national papers were being unloaded from the mail van onto a truck. The headlines were bold.

RUMPUS IN TV STUDIO – WOODWARD BROTHER IN FEUD WITH THE POLICE.

The article went on to explain the extraordinary events in the television broadcast that had been sparked off by the police not being totally honest in their dealings with the Woodward family. This was a stigma that weighed heavily on the police, and highlighted the problem on non-cooperation between the regional police authorities.

That suited the Panther down to the ground. By his reckoning, the police forces were parochial organisations that looked inwards rather than outwards, and thus handicapped themselves. He took pleasure in beating them by working across their boundaries to avoid detection.

When he got out at Huddersfield it was still dark at 6.15 a.m., and he walked through the streets, passing early shift workers. The traffic was moderate at this time of the morning and he stepped into a newsagent's shop in Bridge Street. He grabbed a paper and a couple of Mars bars while averting his face from the Pakistani proprietor and thrusting a pound note at him. Then, collecting his change, he left in a hurry and made his way to his rented digs in Manchester Road.

He let himself in with his own key and went quickly upstairs to his room, where he dumped his rucksack. Then he put the kettle on the small portable Primus stove.

As he waited for the kettle to boil he read the leading story about the TV rumpus and managed a quiet chuckle. He was amused at the police saying they had no leads to the kidnapper and knew it to be a blatant lie. Then he was struck with his next idea for giving them a false lead. He would carry out something he'd always avoided, an armed raid on a shop or petrol station with mask and shotgun, while planting a misleading Dymo tape message. The raid would have all the hallmarks of the Panther, but it would lead the police away while he laid the next trail that evening nearer to home. He drank his tea as he finished reading the news on the Woodward family background, which showed up their glaring faults as grasping and vain individuals. He then saw the unions were threatening to cut power supplies again in a battle over pay, and that gave him a fillip: he'd have darker nights to work in. Then he undressed and fell into bed for some much-needed sleep.

As it happened, the Panther needn't have bothered with his latest ruse. That same day, police investigations had shifted back to Staffordshire, to the village of Whitwell, where a girl's battered naked body had been pulled from the River Trent.

This murder – for there was no doubt it was a murder – presented the police with another dilemma. The Trent was a fast-flowing river, which meant the body could have entered the water anywhere along its entire length. But her skin had a multitude of blisters caused by ammonia or some other corrosive chemical. Also, the girl's face had received such a battering that she was virtually unrecognisable.

A mobile incident unit was set up in the village, while police carried out their investigations, surmising that the body was that of Julia Woodward. The forensic lab in Newcastle-under-Lyme, where the body was taken, asserted the girl was aged about twenty-five and had been in the water for at least two days; but she had not drowned. She had been strangled.

Chief Superintendent Rawley of Stafford CID considered it too sensitive an issue to call on the Woodward family for identification. The girl would have to be identified through her dental records. As the police searched for more evidence, a telephone call from a lorry driver to Stafford Central Police headquarters gave the investigation an added impetus. A car had been found abandoned in a lorry park in Holmcroft, on the outskirts of Stafford, by the keen-eyed driver, who noticed the tax disc was out of date. It didn't match the registration, either.

Detectives descended on the lorry park to question long-distance lorry drivers who had stayed overnight in their cabs, while the car was towed away to be examined. It didn't take long to discover this was no ordinary car theft. Detectives found a series of baffling envelopes with road numbers written on them under the back seat. In the glove compartment they also found several strips of Dymo tape that had been typed incorrectly and abandoned. Further inquiries also established the vehicle's owner as a West Indian car worker from Wolverhampton, who had reported the car stolen over two months previous.

The locked boot was forced open, revealing a Primus stove and saucepan, along with tins of soup and a sleeping bag. Could this be the kidnap car? With all this evidence, it was concluded that this car was indeed the Panther's, and he had used the lorry park as his base while he worked on a ransom trail. The numbers on the envelopes were the routes between Leeds and Nottingham, although the Staffordshire force knew nothing of the previous night's journey by the Manchester CID.

A fresh hunt for the Panther was launched across north Staffordshire, from Wolverhampton out as far as Nottingham. Four Regional Crime Squads, working with legions of uniformed police, focused their inquiries on lorry parks, transport cafés and camping shops, and for a while the Staffordshire force conveniently forgotten about Seagrove's arrest, or dismissed it as another wrong identification. They also appealed to freight companies to make inquiries among their drivers who used the lorry park.

The search was broadened by local radio and regional television for anyone to give information on a missing girl who had been found drowned, possibly murdered by persons unknown, pulled from the River Trent at Whitwell. But it was the stolen car that was made the focus of media attention, with all the implications that this was the actual kidnap car. As yet, any inference by the media that the girl fished from the river was Julia Woodward was emphatically refuted.

However, it was prudent to inform other constabularies, and by the early afternoon, the forces of West Mercia, the West Midlands and Greater Manchester were combining to undertake the biggest manhunt ever mounted for the Black Panther.

The discovery of the stolen car was the biggest boost to finding the Panther so far. Police inquiries yielded results of sightings over the past several weeks of suspicious persons, but the most outstanding came from a café proprietor in Kidsgrove.

Rawley sent DCI Bob Morrison, heading the manhunt for the Panther, with two detectives, DS Connley and DC Richardson, to Kidsgrove to investigate their story. They turned up at 2.30 in the afternoon when the lunch-time rush was over.

Morrison's team sat at a table with Dave and Barbara Hodges, the café owners, and Barbara related the incident of the previous day. 'He was a strange man,' she said, recalling the details. 'He was wearing a fawn raincoat and a flat cap. He came in about lunch time and ordered a dinner and a cup of tea. He said as little as possible, in a grudging manner, and avoided looking at me.'

'Did you notice his shoes? What type they were?' Morrison asked.

'I noticed they were a heavy type of boot and fairly well polished, but that's all.'

'And the man's accent, what did it sound like?'

'A nasal accent. Liverpool, although it could have been Yorkshire. A job to tell, really. But he definitely wasn't local.'

'Did you form any impression about what he was doing here?'

'Passing through, I'd say,' Dave Hodges replied. 'There's not much work around here, Chief Inspector, except the chemical works at Chesterson. Not like the old days, when we had the miners coming in.'

'You had a coal mine here?'

'That we did. The Nelson Coal Mine. It's been closed ten years now.'

Morrison was suddenly alerted to a possible hideout. 'Where exactly was it, Mr Hodges?'

'Just outside the town, a couple of miles up the road. Bathpool Park, they call it. It don't look nothing like a park to me. There's a reservoir up there as well.'

'I never knew there was a coal mine in this area. Are any of the buildings still there?'

'Not that I know of. You wouldn't recognise it as ever having been there, although the old entrance up at Coal-Pit Hill is still there.'

'I think we need to take a look at this place. Thank you both very much.'

The detectives left the café and took their car up the road that led out of town. The scenery was pretty dour as they drove into a wooded area skirting the low hills all round the reservoir and it wasn't hard to imagine a coal mine in this area. And then, spotting a sign for the park, they drove into Boathorse Lane for a hundred yards to the park entrance. They were closer than they had ever been before in their search for the Panther.

They followed a dirt track that led them across the railway tunnel and they continued south towards the reservoir. As they got closer to the reservoir they saw the adjacent pump house on the dam that spanned the south end, holding back the Trent and Mersey Canal, and here they stopped.

'Buggered if I can make anything out of this place, sir?' Connley said as they left the car and walked up to the pump house.

Morrison tried the door. 'Locked… I thought it would be.'

'Where's the ruddy park?' Richardson inquired, looking across the cold sheet of grey water.

'I think we just came through it,' Connley replied. 'But it's not a park, more a recreation ground, I'd say.'

'We shall have to reconnoitre on foot,' Morrison replied.

The men came down off the reservoir and approached a small tangled copse on the far side. 'You two take a meander through there and I'll search the park,' Morrison said with a pessimistic note in his voice, not expecting to find much.

'What exactly are we looking for, sir?'

'An abandoned vehicle… a shelter of some kind… I don't know! Just look.'

Morrison walked down the path for a hundred yards, approaching the concrete square-shaped pillbox surrounded by an iron railing. He stood looking at it from a bank and noticed the wide opening on one side. Stepping down off the bank into a hollow, he approached the five-foot railing and gave it a tug. The top of the railing sat in a ridge of concrete which had to be lifted. It was heavy, but he managed to lift it and a three-foot-wide section came away. He pulled the railing along and leaned it against the next one. Now, able to take a closer look, he stepped up to the opening.

He could hardly believe his eyes as he stood looking down a twenty-foot deep dark hole, which appeared to be a drain of some kind. He could just about make out some pieces of junk that had been thrown down it, and then he heard the water flowing though at the bottom.

It's a flood drain of some kind. No one in their right mind would go down there, he told himself. You'd probably need a diving suit, anyway. He gave a shout, only to hear his own echo coming back. But this wasn't deep enough for a mine shaft, and he figured there must be another deeper shaft. He pulled the railing back into place and came away.

He took another meander up as far as the railway cutting and gazed up the hill on the other side of the track. He was looking for a concrete pillbox to identify another shaft, but only the first one, the spillway, had this construction. The second shaft was across the track on slightly higher ground, unseen from where he stood, and the third main shaft was way up on the hill, buried in the undergrowth. He stood looking for ten minutes and then he turned back.

Twenty minutes later the three detectives were on their way back to Whitwell, never knowing how close they had come to finding the real Julia Woodward. Having decided there was nothing in Kidsgrove for them, they centred on the chemical works at Chesterson a few miles farther on. Here was another old Victorian building converted from a cotton mill, and they pulled into the transport yard and made their way to the office.

'DCI Morrison, Stafford CID,' Morrison said, showing his warrant card to the transport manager.

'I know what you want. That poor woman dragged out of the river this morning,' the manager said with a harrowing look.

'That's right, Mr...?'

'Pugh, Donald Pugh. I'm the transport manager.'

'So what do you know about this unfortunate woman, Mr Pugh?'

'I know she was badly scarred, and it don't look good for us. We produce industrial cleaners and we've had a few accidents with river pollution, so that said and done leaves me to conclude she was a prostitute from Manchester. She could have been thrown in the Mersey Canal anywhere and been swept downriver.'

'So why is she a prostitute?'

'Surely you must know that, Chief Inspector. We had one a few years back in exactly the same condition. She was covered in a red rash all up her body from a chemical of some kind, and the police came here to investigate. The firm got done for dumping chemical waste in the river, but it was never that bad. It might have killed a few fish now and again, but that was all.'

'Oh, is that all? Killed a few fish? You're lucky the Health and Safety didn't close you down. But now you mention it, I seem to recall the case. I was in the West Mercia force back then. She was Harriet Saunders, working in the Manchester red-light district. There was foul play involved, but they never did catch her murderer.'

'No, they didn't. But I reckon it was the Black Panther. It might have been a bit before his time, but who knows when he really started. It might even be him responsible for this one. She was dead before she went in the water, the same as the last one was.'

'Have you ever had anyone looking remotely like him working

here? We're trying to trace his background,' Morrison inquired, showing the manager a photofit.

'No, we haven't. And if we did have we'd have turned him in pretty sharp for the reward. I should think anyone would.'

'I should hope so. Well, thank you for your help, Mr Pugh. We'll be in touch.'

The detectives left the office and went back to the car for a review of the case.

'It looks like we could have a repeat crime here, sir,' DS Connley said. 'I remember that case he was talking about. It was August '65.'

'How can you be so precise about the date, Connley?'

'Because it was the same month and year I got married.'

'It's a good job someone's got a good memory! But it was way before the Panther started, and if I remember right it was passed on to the Manchester force. But we can't do the same with this one.'

'Because it might be the Panther this time?'

'Precisely. Even if this girl is not Julia Woodward, she's still a murder victim, and we have to investigate along those lines. I think we'll have to pay the lab a visit and see what else they've come up with.'

The detectives drove out the factory and took the road south to Newcastle-under-Lyme, but Morrison couldn't get Bathpool out of his mind. There was something sinister about the place, and he felt it really needed a proper search. What really bugged him was he couldn't remember a coal mine being there. Although he wasn't a Staffordshire man, he was now living in Cannock, some distance away, and he thought he knew the county as well as anyone. The hunt for the Panther was turning up a whole lot of places he never knew of before, and Buxton stud farm was just another.

As the search for the Panther took a new direction, Kennon was raising a valid point with Bradley in the Kidnap Incident Room at CID headquarters.

'I'm concerned we're missing vital information,' Kennon said. 'This whole inquiry would benefit from one Central Incident

Room where all information could be processed under one roof. It makes sense to pool our resources. It's time we put some pressure on the Panther. It's just as imperative to find the man's base as it is to find Julia Woodward.'

'I don't agree, George,' Bradley argued. 'You can have too much information and get bogged down with it. Our concern is finding the victim, not the Panther. It's her life that is on the line.'

'I agree, but the two are inseparable, and we need her brother to help us. Without him we're blind. At the same time, if he's seen to be helping us, the Panther can halt the whole show, like he did in Nottingham. That's why I played it down on the television interview, so as to make it appear he was not helping.'

'Then we have to outwit him! The Staffordshire force should never have informed the media about the stolen vehicle. They should have left it there and kept it under observation. The Panther has probably gone to ground.'

'Then we need to step up the action. Let's flush the bugger out with the help of the media and the general public – and if necessary raise the reward.'

'And receive a flood of bogus claims,' Bradley countered. 'I don't intend to be submerged by every petty criminal who claims to have seen the Panther loitering nearby in some lorry park!'

'That's why I'm urging a Central Incident Room that can filter out the bogus claims and concentrate on the essential information. At the moment we have a situation where a press conference in Staffordshire gives different information to one in Cheshire. This is not a regional crime any more, it's a national one!'

'We'll have Scotland Yard on us before long; I can see it coming,' Bradley said, gazing out his window as dusk was falling. 'And I have to say that I thought Peter Woodward made a valid point about our failure to concentrate our search on Bradford or Leeds. The shooting of Sir Charles does indeed point in that direction.'

'We haven't done a search of those areas because we had no reason to. We concentrated on the moors as the most likely place and we were right. We know she was there, and we found the two maintenance men.'

'Then we must search Bradford with the public's help,' Bradley declared, showing his authority. 'Let's set up a mobile incident unit in Bradford town centre for the general public's information. We'll have the Panther's face distributed on leaflets and posters and it might jog a few memories. Someone must know him.'

'And who's the most likely?' Kennon replied, realising the potential. 'Shopkeepers! He must buy his supplies somewhere! And it's most probably a local shop close to his base.'

'I'll get straight onto Bradford CID,' Bradley said. 'I haven't spoken with Bob Hastings lately. This will shake him.'

'If just one shopkeeper recognises the Panther, that's all we need to pin him down to an area for house-to-house inquiries,' Kennon replied. 'Just one shopkeeper.'

At just past 5 p.m., DCI Bob Morrison and his team arrived in Cheadle Hulme, Greater Manchester. The Venus Massage Parlour was discreetly advertised and stood on Crescent Avenue, not far from a Jewish synagogue. The dental record of the dead woman belonged to Christine Humphrey, a 27-year-old high-class call girl from that area.

Inside the plush decorated house with its muscle tone massage parlour, Morrison spoke to the redoubtable Madam Celia. 'I run a respectable massage parlour for gentlemen, Chief Inspector. I have a licensed practice for the relief of stiff joints and muscular back pain.'

'I imagine it's fairly expensive. What kind of customers do you have?'

'Men with stiff joints, Chief Inspector! Who else would come in for a massage?'

'They're all geriatrics, then, are they? It's a wonder they make it here. Do you have a girl working here by the name of Christine Humphrey?'

'I do. She is one of my best girls. Highly praised too.'

'Do you know where she is at this moment?'

'No, I don't. I haven't seen her in two days. Is she in trouble? I take great care over my staff, Chief Inspector.' Celia's face suddenly dropped. 'Don't tell me she's the girl they pulled out the river…'

'I'm afraid she is. She's in Stafford CID forensic lab. She's been badly beaten and had to be identified through her dental records. Can you tell me her last movements and who she was with?'

'That would be Saturday night. She went out with a regular client, whose name I have to keep confidential for obvious reasons.'

'This is a murder inquiry, madam. I can close you down if necessary. Your testimony will be treated confidentially.'

'She was with Nicholas Seagrove. He's a well-known figure in racing circles.'

The news hit like a bombshell. 'We know who he is, madam. He's in custody. Is he the last person to have seen her?'

'As far as I know. But she never phoned the next day and I was concerned for her. I was getting a lot of complaints about Mr Seagrove, and was seriously thinking of banning him.'

'What sort of complaints?'

'He thought he owned some of the girls. He took a percentage of their earnings from me for introducing new customers. Then he got greedy and demanded more and more. When I refused he began to cut me out and approached the girls directly. He was so intimidating that they gave in to his demands, all except Christine. She wasn't going to buckle under and she told me she was going to put him straight. That was the last night we saw her. Dear oh dear, why did I let her do it?'

Madam Celia's face crumpled with anguish and tears welled in her eyes. 'Is Nicholas Seagrove charged with her murder?'

'If we can prove it he will be. Can you tell me who the wealthy clients were he introduced? Strictly confidential, off the record.'

A true professional, Madam Celia stalled until she was persuaded it would help the inquiry. 'There were several councillors, an MP, a top barrister… but the most important in my view was Sir Charles Woodward.'

In Manchester General Hospital, Sir Charles Woodward's life was ebbing away in an isolation room. His wife was at his side. Although still on a cardiac monitor he was in control of his faculties and his Yorkshire humour never dimmed. 'You know,

Veronica,' he said with a smile, squeezing her hand, 'I always said I'd go out with a bang. Looks like I was right.'

'You're not going anywhere, Charles, except home! You're making a good recovery. Doctor Henderson tells me you've got a good chance of going home soon.'

'Doctors will tell you anything to lighten the load. But I know what my own body tells me. But I shan't complain. I've had a good life. I've steered the company through stormy weather and built on success. My grandfather, Thomas Woodward, built the first swing bridge over the Tyne, and if Peter has his way, he will build the first bridge over the Humber. The name Woodward will be forever associated with bridges, up there with the giants of civil engineering. What's he up to now?'

'Making a fool of himself on TV. The latest news, Charles, is the police can't find Julia or the Black Panther. Ian's doing his best to help the police. He came home this morning in the early hours, dead beat, after a fruitless effort to hand the ransom over in Nottingham.'

'Nottingham! Is that where Julia is being held?'

'Obviously not. The kidnapper didn't show up at the rendez-vous. Ian blames the police and is now in tune with Peter. The two of them say they will get her back without police interference. I don't know what to think.'

'You must stop them! Don't let them go it alone! They will compromise all the police efforts. It's my opinion that Chief Inspector George Kennon will bring Julia home. He has the experience. He won't let us down.'

'I do hope so.' There was a pause.

'There's something else I must tell you, Veronica.'

'Not now dear. You rest.'

'No. I have to clear my conscience with God. You remember the fraud inquiry that uncovered the cash for ministers scandal, and nearly saw the company into oblivion through my reckless self-indulgence? I was being blackmailed at the time over it by a mystery person.'

'Blackmailed for what?'

'We were fighting a takeover by Caulston Steel that would have wiped out the name Woodward. I couldn't let that happen.

Profits were taking a dive and I was forced to raid the pension fund and falsify figures. My reckless spending trying to manage a thoroughbred racing stable didn't help, and my philandering was being exposed by the media. I was having an affair with my secretary, and I have to confess it went on after we met. I made myself a prime target for blackmail.'

'Nonsense! You wouldn't be the first person to have an affair with his secretary, or fake a company balance sheet to keep afloat. And anyway you were cleared, weren't you?'

'Not entirely. It was glossed over, but it wiped the value off a whole lot of shares. The damage was done, and we are still only just recovering after five years. And Caulston are back again. I want you to tell Peter he must fight it. We cannot let the good name of Woodward Civil Engineering be extinguished.'

'I will. But I'm sure he knows that already. But what about this blackmail. Did it stop after the inquiry?'

'After I paid £20,000 he did. I couldn't work out who it was. But I know now. A year after I bought Buxton Stables my secretary left the company. I believe it was her leaking classified company information to the media, and to the blackmailer. How else could an outsider get hold of classified documents?'

'What makes you suddenly suspect it was her?'

'I was listening to the radio this morning when I heard about the police raid on Buxton Stables. Three people have been arrested. Nicholas Seagrove, who runs the stables, as you know, has been arrested over my shooting. But the other gem to turn up was a 36-year-old woman by the name of Doreen Chambers. The police have not given the details of her arrest, although I can guess. Doreen Chambers was Seagrove's mistress. She was also my secretary.'

Chapter Twelve

'I never knew about this place,' Kennon said to Suzanne as the waiter took their order inside the newly renovated Palace Theatre café.

'That's because you don't get about enough. I always thought a policeman's life was dull. What do you do when you're not chasing criminals?' Suzanne replied in a jocular mood.

'Oh, there's plenty of paperwork, I can tell you. We spend half our time filling out forms: daily reports, crime sheets, witness statements, court correspondences. We get swamped in it. There's no time to investigate criminals. Oh, and there's TV appearances as well.'

'Yes, I saw that. I thought you did rather well. I was impressed with your handling of Reginald Bosanquet. But what on earth was wrong with Peter Woodward? He was outrageous, coming on like a madman.'

'I have to take some of the blame. I had to make it look that Ian Woodward was not cooperating with the police, since he was warned not to by the kidnapper. I played down our part by implying our inquiries were going nowhere, and we had no idea who was responsible for the kidnapping.'

'Well, that's true, isn't it?'

'Not any more, it's not. This is definitely the work of the Black Panther.'

'What's brought that change about?'

'It's a gut feeling from the clues we're picking up. An abandoned car in a lorry park outside Stafford was used by the Panther, and he's leaving a paper trail to the ransom drops.'

'And what about this girl who was fished out the river? Has she got anything to do with the Panther?'

'I've no idea. But at least it wasn't Julia Woodward, as was suggested. But I don't know where she is either. This case is baffling.'

The waiter returned with two coffees and an array of crab

159

sandwiches that were appetisingly fanned out on a dish with small pieces of cut lettuce among them.

'Very tasty. I haven't tasted crab for ages,' Kennon said, taking a bite of one. 'I salute you for your choice, Suzanne. Come to think of it, I haven't been to the theatre for ages either. What do they put on here?'

'Musicals, mostly. Semi-professional, but as good as any London West End show. I'll let you know when the next one comes along. I enjoy the theatre.'

'I'll appreciate that. Suzanne, you're a tonic to me,' Kennon said placing his hand on hers across the table. 'I never thought I'd say that to a newspaper reporter.'

'We're not all just snoopers. If we worked in tandem more often we could be a major asset to the police. I firmly believe that.'

'Sometimes, but not all the time,' Kennon replied. 'So what's your goal? What do you want to achieve?'

'What's my goal? Investigative journalism is my goal. Helping to find missing children. There's hundreds go missing right across the country. You very seldom hear of any turning up. Where do they go?'

'You're treading in murky waters there. Where do they go? London's the attraction, where they end up on the streets with pimps and prostitutes. It's a cruel world, Suzanne. The streets of London are no better than Manchester's.'

'I agree. But until we highlight the dangers directly to teenagers that London is not a haven from poverty it will only get worse. And that's where the media plays its part. We need national campaigns to get the message across that the North is just as good as the South, and could be even better.'

'And start a civil war! That will shake things up a bit.'

'Wouldn't it just. Now tell me your goal.'

'Right now, my goal is to nail the Panther and to save Julia Woodward. Then I can take that trip to Venice I've promised myself. Do you fancy coming?'

'George – don't tempt me!'

'You're an ace, Suzanne, you really are.' Kennon had found his woman at last.

Ian and Peter Woodward sat watching the Six O'clock News on

television in the lounge at Bridlington Hall. Janet Woodward was preparing a meal and Veronica Woodward was still at the hospital, staying out her time as long as possible, giving comfort as her husband's life ebbed away.

The news coming from Staffordshire CID was that the girl in the river was not Julia Woodward, as was first thought, but, although identified through dental records as someone else, she remained anonymous. But the discovery of the stolen car, the news went on, had precipitated the biggest manhunt ever for the Black Panther.

'So much for Seagrove being the Panther,' Peter Woodward remarked. 'I don't think the police have got a bloody clue who the Panther is, and all their talk of catching him is nothing but a load of hot air.'

Ian nodded his head and replied languidly, 'I just hope that girl's body isn't Julia's. They never called on us to identify it.'

'But they've just said it wasn't.'

'That's because they're sparing us the details. The police are desperate to catch the Panther. If the body in the water was Julia the whole case for kidnap would collapse and the police would be back to square one.'

The television report continued with an interview with Staffordshire Chief Constable, Ian Richardson, stating the find of the car had yielded clues to the Panther's movements. 'It's the biggest breakthrough yet,' Richardson said. 'He left clues that make it possible to track him down. We found the road numbers of routes that tie in with the post office raids.'

'Will you be sharing that information with the West Mercia force, Chief Constable?'

'We shall do, after we complete our inquiries, but it takes a little time for that to happen. And you have to remember that the Panther has only just been linked to the kidnap. We had no idea who it was, and even now we are not one hundred per cent sure.'

'Well, that says it all!' Peter Woodward said in disgust, turning the television off. 'They're still not one hundred per cent sure. Who the hell do they think it is – Charlie Chaplin? You see what I mean, Ian? The police are incompetent. They'd soon find out who it is if they were paid on results!'

'They're doing their best, Peter. I can't fault them.'

'Oh, no! What about that fiasco you went through last night? The police buggered that up completely. The kidnapper saw you coming! He couldn't miss a bloody great radio van! And he warned us not to bring the police in.'

'Well, of course. But he must know we had no choice. We'd look pretty stupid if we didn't tell them.'

'If he phones tonight, we keep the police right out of it! We don't follow his instructions and we make sure Julia is still alive. We have to hear her voice and we have to make sure she will be released. There will be no half measures. We want cast iron guarantees.'

'How do we do it? He's holding all the aces.'

'I've already thought of something. He can't expect us to hand over the ransom without our side of the bargain fulfilled.'

'*Bargain*! This is not a bloody tender for some contract! It's our sister's life on the line! We don't bargain, Peter!'

'But we do. We up the ransom by £10,000 if he gives us Julia and we state the rendezvous.'

'Where?'

'I think he's holding her somewhere in the High Peak District. There are hundreds of caves all over the area, and it's impossible to search them all. I suggest he brings Julia to the Castleton caves on the A625 between Stockport and Sheffield. He will have plenty of time to hide her there until the rendezvous hour. Once the exchange takes place there are dozens of forest roads he can escape on, and he can keep a watch on us from the high ground.'

'Sounds reasonable. But he will want to check the money before he hands Julia over.'

'That's no problem. You carry the bag to a spot, put it down and walk away for him to check it. Then he has to produce Julia, or I fire at him with this.' Peter opened a drawer and produced a semi-automatic pistol. 'I bought this in a Sheffield gun store. It's a sporting pistol, but it fires real bullets and will do adequately for our purpose. What do you think?'

'Jesus! It'll never work if he suspects you're holding a gun on him.'

'He won't know. I shall leave the car en route and be hidden in the shadows before he appears. There's no other way, Ian. If we go in with the police he won't bother to show, and that's another opportunity gone.'

'But you're talking about shooting the man! Are you that good a shot?'

'No, I'm not. But it's the best deal we've got. If I miss he'll know I can shoot again.'

'We can try. Are you one hundred per cent sure it will work? Have you looked at it from all angles?'

'Absolutely. It's the best and only chance we've got.'

'There's one thing you've forgotten. If the kidnapper calls here, his call is immediately monitored by the police. They have a tap on the line.'

'I've covered that. Listen to this.' Peter took a cassette from the drawer and inserted it into a portable radio-cassette player. The voice was his on the recording. 'This is Peter Woodward. If you want the ransom, please contact me on 438552 at around midnight. I want proof of who you are.'

'Brilliant! What are you going to do with it? Post it to him?'

Peter looked at his watch. 'It's 6.30. I'm taking this to the local radio station. I know the news editor, Peter Wright. He will play this over the air every hour; he's already confirmed it. The phone box is at the end of the lane. All we do is wait for the Panther's call. Simple.'

'It won't work. You'll have every nut in Manchester phoning that number.'

'I don't think so. We've got huge public sympathy and besides, I will be asking for Julia's voice on the line. Only the real kidnapper can do that.'

Mr Chowdhury was serving in his shop when the Panther walked in and heard the radio broadcast coming from the tinny transistor behind the counter. 'We interrupt the programme for a special bulletin on the kidnap of Julia Woodward…' A second voice came on the air.

'This is Peter Woodward. If the man who has kidnapped my sister is listening and you want the ransom, please contact me on 438552 at around midnight. I want firm proof of who you are.'

The Panther stopped dead in his tracks to listen but he missed the confounded phone number. But he needn't have worried, as the announcer's voice came back.

'That was an appeal on behalf of Julia Woodward, the kidnapped heiress the whole country is praying for. If the Panther is out there listening, this message will be repeated at nine o'clock and on every hour.'

This was a new development, and one he had to consider. He had come here to lay a false trail and carry out a shooting, but it now didn't seem so urgent. Besides, it was a risk he wasn't prepared to take now. He hastily purchased two Mars bars, trying to avert Chowdhury's curious look, and left in a hurry clutching the holdall containing the shotgun. But as he left he dropped the two Dymo tapes with false instructions.

'Thank you, sir. Do come again,' Chowdhury called after him. Then the bemused shopkeeper turned to his wife. 'Do you know, my dear, I see that man every so often and always he avoids looking at me. Funny, don't you think?'

'He's probably a shoplifter. You can always tell them. They keep their heads down.'

'But he always pays. I think he's hiding something. Hold the store, I'm going out.'

'Out? Where to at this time of night?'

'The police are searching for the Black Panther in Bradford. I think I might just have found him in Huddersfield. He lodges with Mrs Downer at Number 46. I'm going down to the police station to tell them.'

Chowdhury put his coat on and left the shop, stepping into Manchester Road at 8.05 p.m. He hurried along the street heading for the police station at Kirkgate and walked right past Number 46, where a curtain moved in the front bedroom.

The Panther, ever vigilant, had rightly suspected the man would run to the police. Now he had to move base permanently from the upstairs rooms and he began packing his holdall ready for the move. Clothes, guns, torches, flasks and all the other gear he carried went into the bag, along with the small transistor radio and cassette player with a tape already recorded. His semi-automatic pistol with silencer went into the deep pocket of his combat jacket. He wouldn't bother telling his seventy-year-old landlady, Mrs Downer, he was leaving. Better she didn't know he'd even gone.

He put his raincoat on over his combat jacket, picked up the heavy bag and went quietly downstairs. He could hear the old lady's television on in the back room at the end of the passage as he opened the front door and left. He walked down the road to the communal car park on a piece of open ground near the greyhound track where he'd parked his van. The tax disc had been altered to match the false registration plates, and so far it had not aroused any suspicion. He climbed in, started the engine and drove out, heading for Leeds just twelve miles away.

A posse of uniformed police with an armed back-up and four detectives from Manchester CID were closing round the house on Manchester Road. The time was just 9.10 p.m.

DCI Kennon stood studying the house while a police cordon was thrown up and he felt a sudden surge of action. Days of waiting and tedious investigation were at last bringing results. The very thought of coming face to face with the Panther gave him a boost of adrenalin.

'It looks too quiet,' he said as two searchlights swept the house. Then he signalled the marksmen. 'Right, let's go.'

Four armed uniformed police with bullet-proof jackets moved towards Number 46. Three were armed with Heckler and Koch machine pistols and one carried a battering ram as Kennon's voice was broadcast through a loudspeaker.

'This is the police. All persons inside the house come out!' He repeated the message, and when there was no response the team battered their way in. The front door was forced and the police surged into the house, upstairs and down, with glaring torches. As lights were switched on in every room, the police burst in on Mrs Downer sitting peacefully watching television. It was the clumsiest operation – enough to frighten the wits out of an old lady, who was actually more bemused than scared.

'What do you want?' was all she could say. 'Couldn't you have rung the bell like any normal person? I don't know what my lodger will think upstairs.'

'There's no one up there,' a police sergeant said coming down the stairs. 'It's empty.'

'I'm Chief Inspector Kennon, madam, Manchester CID. I apologise for our hasty intrusion, madam, but we thought you were in danger. Don't be alarmed. Did you have a male lodger staying here?'

'Me in danger! Preposterous!' the old woman exclaimed. 'I've never heard such rubbish. You say he's gone?' the old lady was at a loss to explain. 'I don't understand. He never said anything. He was a quiet man.'

'Who was he. What was his name, madam?'

'George Sutton. He's been here several weeks now. He was no trouble. Always paid his rent on time. He came and went at the most odd hours. Sometimes he was gone for days. I hardly ever saw him. He was a jobbing carpenter.'

'Did he look like this man?' Kennon showed the old lady the photofit.

'Yes. That's quite a good likeness. My goodness, I know that face! It can't be... is it?'

'Yes madam. Your lodger was the Black Panther. Now you know why we had to barge in. When did you last see him?'

'Yesterday. He came home about 6 a.m. I heard him go up the stairs. I sleep in the front room. But I didn't see him. I rarely saw him, but he always let me know when he was in.'

'Chief Inspector!' Mr Chowdhury came up the passage. He doffed his hat to the old lady. 'Hello, Mrs Downer. I am sorry we had to barge in on you... Chief inspector, I have just found these in my shop lying on the floor. I am sure he dropped them going out the door. He was in such a hurry.'

'Dymo tapes! That confirms it.' Kennon turned to his men, who were crowding in behind. 'We've just missed him!'

Kirkgate police station was crammed with men as the Dymo tapes were examined by baffled detectives. The radio control rooms in Huddersfield and Manchester crackled with a flood of messages to beat officers and a network of Q cars were coordinating their channels from as far away as Staffordshire and Cheshire.

The tapes were baffling: *Proceed to Stafford. From Stafford to Wolverhampton and then to Bridgnorth Swan Shopping Centre. Wait at public phone boxes for call at midnight. Continue on the 458 to Stourbridge. Then the 461 to Netherton...*

The second tape appeared to correspond: *When you come to Freightliner Depot at end of the road turn into Zoo entrance. Go to gate 8 and look for torch light. Instructions on torch.*

'What do you make of that, sir?' Boyd asked, sipping a coffee from the machine. 'This man's got a fetish for zoos. Still, I suppose it's a good place to dispose of a body.'

'Yes, all right, Boyd, we can do without wisecracks. I think these tapes are meant to misguide us. But we can't ignore them! We're going to have to follow them up. Why the hell did Peter Woodward put out that radio message!'

Kennon's normal calm exterior was unravelling with a spiralling impatience as he paced the floor, looked at the tapes again, and then thumped the vending machine. 'He had to go and put his bloody foot in it!'

'Wait a minute, sir,' Boyd put in. 'Wasn't there a shooting at a transport depot in Dudley recently?'

'It's Dudley!' A detective tracing road numbers on the map suddenly saw through the tangle. 'It's Dudley Zoo, sir. The A458 from Bridgnorth to Stourbridge goes on to the A461 to the Freightliner Depot at Dudley. It has to be Dudley Zoo.'

'Well done, Hawkin,' Kennon replied. 'You're right, Boyd. There was a shooting down there. How did we bloody miss that? Do you know that area, Hawkin?'

'Vaguely. But it's off our patch. The West Mercia force linked that shooting to the Panther. The night foreman interrupted a man going through the yard and got shot for his trouble. He's still in hospital, I think.'

Hawkin's words were drowned by a crackle of radios from the control room next door and a female constable burst in. 'There's been a shooting in Leeds! A PC responding to a break-in at the greyhound stadium has been hit. The gunman escaped in a white van!'

'Is anyone dealing with it?' Kennon asked.

'Yes sir. There's an area car on the way. Thought I'd let you know.'

'That's DI Bill Knightly's area, sir,' a sergeant said. 'But he's away on a course. I'm his back-up. Do you want me to deal with it?'

'Yes, Sergeant. But log your area number with the radio room and keep them informed of developments. If it's the Panther I want to know. Hawkin, I'd like you to follow up the Dudley tape and inform Staffordshire CID you're on your way.'

'Yes sir. I'm with Regional Crime Squad 5. West Yorkshire.'

'Log in the number before you go. The rest of you resume normal duties. Boyd and Stacey, we're going back to Central, then it will be a night watch on Bridlington Hall.'

Kirkgate police station gradually cleared of CID, and Kennon left with his two detectives in a squad car for Manchester to check the Central Incident Unit that was belatedly shaping up under his direction. But first he would call on the Manchester telephone exchange to see if the engineers had managed to tap into Peter Woodward's secret number. His intention was to follow Peter Woodward's trail, keeping radio contact with the divisional headquarters of either Stafford or Derby for a joint operation.

As his car sped back to Manchester he reflected on the night's work with his two colleagues. 'You see the problems we're facing. We're not getting all the information quick enough. If that shooting at Dudley had been logged into a Central Incident Unit we wouldn't be chasing around in the dark.'

'I know, sir,' Boyd answered, 'but I don't think even the Staffordshire force knew the full implications of it. And don't forget, the kidnapper and the Panther were two different crime scenes when we started.'

'That's the point I'm making. A Central Incident Unit would have disseminated the information for everyone. By the way, I had a call from Bob Morrison on the Staffordshire force. They traced the woman's body in the river to a massage parlour in Cheadle Hulme.'

'Blimey! Who was she?'

'She was a high-class call girl, last seen with our friend Nicholas Seagrove. Whether it's linked with the shooting of Sir Charles Woodward we shall have to see. But this will serve as another example of information being processed through a Central Incident Unit and made more accessible to the Regional Crime Squads.'

'Isn't there a danger the CIU will get bogged down with too

much information sir?' Sergeant Stacey responded. 'I mean, what's this got to do with the kidnapping case?'

'It's got everything to do with it, Sergeant Stacey! Kennon replied tetchily. 'DCI Jack Taylor probably has more information on the Panther than anyone, and he sends it out with regular bulletins. Now in this case, not only does it help our investigations into the shooting of Sir Charles Woodward but it also discounts the dead girl as Julia Woodward!'

'We're here, sir,' Boyd said as he drove into the telephone exchange. 'It's ten o'clock. We've got less than two hours to intercept Peter Woodward's phone call.'

In an upstairs room of an Edwardian house on Radcliff Avenue in Bradford, the Panther was preparing for a night's work in the small attic room. This was the Panther's lair where the weapons, the kit, and all the paraphernalia of his alter ego were stored and hidden from view. Among the bulk of weapons were two sawn-off shotguns with boxes of 12-bore cartridges, three semi-automatic pistols with numerous live rounds of .22 bullets, as well as three sheath knives, a wire garrotte and a bottle of ammonia spray for dogs. There was a variety of clothing and shoes thrown on the bed in a jumble: jumpers, trousers, gloves and hats, together with two camouflage combat jackets and two black Lycra hoods. Then there were the other essentials for a fugitive on the move: false registration plates, torches, tape, screwdrivers, pliers and a bag full of survival kit with packs of high protein rations. This was his room kept locked at all times. Not even Iris, his wife, came here.

The Panther was now on home ground in his own house where he had lived the last fifteen years with his wife and eighteen-year-old daughter. But even here he was almost a stranger in the winter months. As far as his wife knew he was working all over the country, taking jobs wherever the money was, and his daughter was desperate to leave home. They never went into this room up in the attic. It was his work room, where he kept his tools and did his paperwork.

His duffel bag was emptied of the contents brought from his digs in Huddersfield and repacked for a lighter load. He now had Peter

Woodward's radio message written down but had no intention of letting him dictate terms. Nevertheless, he was concerned that he might pose problems in handing over the ransom, and he might have to change his plans. Then he thought about it and realised he couldn't change his plans. They were set in stone and no amount of hassling could alter them. He would stand firm.

Outside, a police siren wailed in the distance and he switched the transistor on for the local news. The police had issued statements that the Black Panther was being sought in the Huddersfield area and warned people not to approach him. It then went on to say that a shooting of a police constable at the greyhound stadium was not related, and a man was helping with police inquiries.

That pleased him. It meant the heat was off him for the moment and he could probably get across the city without fear of being stopped. These were his worst moments – having to use a vehicle when the danger of being stopped was real. He was happy with public transport but he couldn't use it tonight, not with the transfer of a large amount of money involving two people.

He checked his watch at eleven o'clock and decided it was time to go. He slipped on his raincoat, picked up his bag and left the room to go downstairs. He went through to the kitchen, where Iris was sipping a cup of tea in her dressing gown. Her face had a careworn expression that spoke volumes of uncertainty, but she was a faithful wife. 'When will you be back?' she asked, handing him his two flasks filled with hot soup.

'I don't know. Depends how long the job takes. The bloke wants his conservatory extended. It's going to cost him.'

'You look tired. You're not doing too many hours, I hope.'

'I have to do it when the work's there. Can't turn it down.' He gave her a peck on the cheek. 'Don't worry about me. You look after yourself.'

He stepped out the back door and disappeared into the darkness down the side of the house. He went through the front gate and walked down the avenue thirty yards to a side street, where his van was parked, and climbed in. Then he drove away heading towards the river, heading south out the city, bound for the M1 motorway.

Chapter Thirteen

'I've got it, Chief Inspector!' the phone engineer said as he tapped the line through his headphones. 'It's a phone box in Holywell Green just outside Brighouse.'

Kennon looked at his watch: 11.45 p.m. 'It's early. Probably a hoax call. How long did it last?'

'Less than a minute. It came from a Dewsbury call box. But you can listen in now and get all the calls on that number.'

'Can all three of us listen?'

'Of course. Just put the headphones on and wait for it to ring.'

The three CID men put their headphones on and waited for the call inside the Manchester telephone exchange. They didn't have to wait long. At seven minutes to midnight they heard the box in Holywell Green ringing, followed by a click, then the voice of Peter Woodward came over.

'Peter Woodward.'

'Good evening, Peter. Listen carefully to the tape. You will need a pen and paper.'

'Hold on! I want to hear my sister in person! Not on some bloody tape!'

'You can't. You should know that's not possible.'

'How do I know if she's still alive?'

'Because I tell you she is. You either believe me or condemn her yourself. It's up to you.'

'I don't have much choice. All right, I'm listening.'

'That's more like it.'

Julia's recorded voice came on the line. 'Ian. Go to Bridgnorth Swan Shopping Centre. Wait at public phone boxes for call at 1.30 a.m. If no call by 2 a.m. continue on the 458 to Stourbridge. Then take the 461 to Netherton estate, Dudley. When you come to Freightliner Depot at end of the road, turn into Zoo entrance. Go to gate 8 and look for torch light. Instructions on torch.'

There was a click and the line went dead. The men looked at

each other incredulously. 'That's the same instructions as on the tapes!' Boyd said. 'Half the West Mercia force will be covering that lot!'

'No, they won't,' Kennon replied. 'I stipulated only two area cars will have it under review. What we thought was false is now real. But the Panther is devious. He knows we'll follow and he's laid two different trails to split the force, one at the Swan Shopping Centre in Bridgnorth and the other at Dudley.'

'So which one is the right one?'

'That's the problem; it could be either. One's in Shropshire and the other's in the West Midlands.'

'He's buggered us with the timing as well, sir,' Sergeant Stacey said. 'We'll have to be in two places at once!'

Kennon was temporarily flummoxed. The call waiting at the shopping centre might take a different route and might well be the right one. 'I can't see Dudley Zoo being the right place, somehow.'

'This is ridiculous, sir,' Boyd said. 'If we're baffled, how the hell is Peter Woodward supposed to follow it?'

'He won't, that's the problem. He'll wait at the shopping centre for a call that might or might not arrive. Which means he'll either go on to Dudley or somewhere else – and it certainly won't be Dudley.'

'Why not, sir?'

'Because that's where the Panther shot the freight manager who disturbed him! That trail is now redundant. It has to be a new place.' Kennon looked at the time. 'Right, let's get moving. We'll have to go for the shopping centre and just hope Peter Woodward leads us to the right drop zone. We've got one hour to get there.'

'I told you you wouldn't get him to change!' Ian Woodward said to his elder brother as they got in the car. 'He's the one holding all the cards.'

'The tape threw me. I didn't expect it. I thought I could get him to put Julia on the line; I was wrong.'

'So now what do we do?'

'Follow his instructions. Buckle up. We've got a long drive ahead, all the way to Bridgnorth in Shropshire.'

'I think we should call Chief Inspector Kennon. He told me there's a special incident room that will tell us what to do.'

'I know what to do! There's to be no police involved. I've got all I need in my pocket.'

'I know – that blasted gun! I don't know how you think that's going to work against a man who's already killed and won't think twice of doing it again.'

'If he wants the money he won't. It's time we called the shots.'

Peter Woodward's Jaguar sped silently down the dual carriageway, cutting across the moors heading for Prestwich. The deep hum of tyres on the road was the only sound to breach the silence on the empty road. The car headlights stabbed the darkness, lighting an endless row of catseyes as each brother stared ahead, hypnotically wrapped in his own thoughts.

Mile after mile of darkness was suddenly broken by rows of bright yellow lights as they approached Manchester and went on to Prestwich. They went across the flyovers north of the city, going over the Warsley junction until they reached the M6. The giant overhead road signs directed them south for Stoke-on-Trent, a distance of forty miles, and as the motorway lights ran out they plunged back into darkness for the long journey to Bridgnorth.

Peter turned the radio on low and they listened to the Late Night Show, a programme of jazz and blues, with the unforgettable sounds of Johnny Mathis and Otis Redding drifting out over the speakers.

'How's the PhD going, Ian?' Peter asked at length.

'Pretty good. I never realised molecular study could be so interesting.'

'Neither did I. What's it all about?'

'Thermodynamics, mostly. Did you know that once you dissipate energy it can never be recovered? Take for instance this car. The force driving it is the engine, yet that's not where the energy comes from.'

'How do you work that out?'

'Newton's laws of physics. The energy comes from the motion. Internal combustion is driving the engine, but it's not creating energy. It's losing it by transferring it to the wheels.'

'Brilliant! But how does that help improve life? I mean, what does it make?'

'A whole range of things, from what keeps our bridges and buildings intact to what keeps your beer cold in the refrigerator.'

'Interesting. Could it help us win the Humber Bridge contract?'

'If you can prove your design is better than the competition, it might. But I don't know how you can keep your mind on it. I'm worried sick over Julia... Where's the best place to keep a kidnap victim so they have no means of escape?'

'I don't know. Down a coal mine?'

'Exactly. *Underground*! Not a coal mine, though. A drainage system that people walk over every day and never know it's there.'

'A converted coal mine could have such a system. One that's been closed down by the Coal Board. But I don't know of any in Shropshire or the West Midlands. In fact I don't know of one anywhere.'

'Neither do I. But it's something we should bear in mind. So don't make a balls-up of this ransom handover. I don't want my sister ending up dead in some black hole.'

'Neither do I. We're almost there. See the sign ahead.' Peter flicked a switch on to full beam and the road sign stood out clear: 'Bridgnorth 8 miles'.

'You and your caves! We were way off beam there.'

'Not so far as you think. Most caves have natural underground streams running through them that can be reached by potholers. And there's plenty of disused lead mines in Yorkshire.'

Ten minutes later they were coasting into the small town and heading for the Swan Shopping Centre, deserted at this time, and not even a solitary policeman to be seen. They approached the new shopping mall with its multiplex car park on three levels and stopped at the front on the main street. The sign on the white stonework glittered in a soft neon blue above the main entrance, which opened on to a pedestrian precinct.

Peter switched the engine off. 'We're ten minutes early. The public phones are probably right inside. You take the bag to the phone box and wait for the call. Whatever he tells you, make sure you get absolute guarantee we get Julia back. No ifs, no buts. We see her tonight. Got it?'

'It won't work that way! We have to take his word. Otherwise we could lose her. I'm not risking it.'

'Jesus Christ! We cannot accept blind faith in this man! We have to do what's necessary. Otherwise we might just as well call it off.'

'He'll be the one calling it off, not us. Stay here – I'm going in alone.'

Ian got out of the car clutching the large holdall and walked steadily into the shopping centre.

Peter climbed out and watched him disappear into the shadowy complex before discreetly following him, keeping out of sight. The complex, only recently opened, glowed with soft yellow security lights along the main walkways, but there were dark patches where it was possible to remain hidden. It was possible the kidnapper could be concealed in one of the darkened recesses watching with a loaded gun. There were also several exits leading to external car parks and the high street.

Ian reached the centre of the giant complex, where three public phone boxes stood surrounded by shops under a tall glass domed roof. He looked all around while he stood waiting and the minutes ticked slowly by. He waited for ten minutes, feeling more disillusioned every minute that passed. Then the phone rang in the first box and he dashed inside to lift the receiver, almost dropping it in his haste.

'Ian Woodward!' he panted.

'Do you have the money I asked for?' a voice with a Birmingham accent inquired.

'Yes. Exactly as you asked for in a canvas holdall. I must have assurance that my sister is safe.'

'She is. You will have to take my word.'

'That's not enough. I need more.'

'You will get more after I have cleared the money. Now do as I say! The instructions are behind the panel. Look for it!' The receiver slammed down at the other end and the line went dead.

The Panther had rung off, leaving Ian to search all round the advertising plate. Feeling all round the edges of the panel his fingers touched something protruding at the top and he pulled out a wide strip of Dymo tape. It read: *Go to the lift opposite and take the ransom to the top-level car park. Leave lift and turn left to the outer wall. Drop bag over the edge of wall then leave.*

Ian stepped out of the phone box watched closely by Peter, who was clutching his pistol not more than twenty yards away hidden in a recess. Unbeknown to him, a dozen other pairs of eyes were watching from the shadows hidden all round the Swan Shopping Centre. They were the eyes of the Regional Crime Squads from Manchester and Staffordshire. George Kennon's team of three were in position with uniformed officers, and Sergeant Boyd was on the top-level car park.

As the lift came up, Boyd stood behind a pillar and watched as Ian Woodward stepped out and went to the outer wall. He peered over the top and looked down into the dark precinct, where nothing moved. He lifted the bag up on the ledge, waited a few seconds and then pushed it over the side. It fell with a thump into one of the access alleys used for deliveries. He kept watching and almost immediately a figure darted out of the stairways exit and picked it up. Suddenly there was a chorus of shouts followed by a flash of torch beams flooding the area, and a man went running through the arches beneath the car park. He came out of the underground car park, ran down a cobbled side street chased by half a dozen uniformed police, and turned into an alley at the back of the high street shops, where more police were waiting at one end.

Sensing the alley would be blocked by police, the fugitive stopped briefly to raise his double-barrelled shotgun and fired it down the alley. The police were forced to withdraw and the Panther quickly reloaded two more cartridges from the belt across his chest. Then, running on with his gun held out like a pistol in one hand with his finger on the trigger, he burst out of the end into another side street, and as he did a shot was fired at him. The bullet ricocheted off a wall behind him with a zinging sound. Then he was lit by torches as two constables came at him out of the deep shadows. He swung the bag at them and knocked both men aside before fleeing, as another shot rang out from Peter Woodward's semi-automatic.

The shot whistled close to his head, causing the Panther to stumble and drop the bag. He cursed his luck. As he stooped to pick it up Peter Woodward saw his chance. 'Drop it or I'll fire!' he shouted, stepping out in front of him at twenty yards.

The Panther was already pointing his shotgun in Pete's direction and without a second thought he fired both barrels. The blast caught Woodward in the shoulder and sent him reeling across the road. Scooping up the bag, the Panther ran headlong down the cobbled street, heading for the car park as the police closed in on him. Shouts were coming from all directions as police emerged out of alleys and side streets all round the shopping centre, as the Panther raced for his van parked in a side street. He ran across the car park to reach it and could not avoid running into a post that snagged the bag and tore it from his hands. The bag ripped open and bundles of cash tumbled out, with banknotes blowing from torn wrappers.

Close behind, police torches were flashing his way and he cursed and swore at having to leave behind the ransom money scattered over the car park fluttering in the wind. He reached his van and jumped in behind the wheel with his face still masked. He pushed his shotgun behind the passenger seat to conceal it and then drove away in a fury with a screech of tyres.

Kennon watched him go, silently cursing himself that they might have caught him if he had worked out a better plan. But what else could he do? He had the shopping centre ringed with police, but there just weren't enough of them. Then a squad car appeared, coming down the car park road with a blue light flashing. It squealed to a stop for the Staffordshire men to jump in, and the driver shouted across to Kennon, 'We'll get him, sir!' Then he screeched away. The night's fun was not over yet.

Kennon watched them go while the police were scooping up bundles of money blown all across the car park and putting them back in the bag. Sergeant Stacey came hobbling over on a twisted ankle, and behind him Boyd was helping Peter Woodward along. His jacket sleeve was torn and bloodied from a gunshot wound. 'Call an ambulance!' Boyd shouted.

A police radio crackled as a sergeant called an ambulance and suddenly police messages were traversing the airwaves from Q cars coordinating their positions. Another flashing blue light appeared as a traffic car came roaring up the road before screeching to a stop.

'What's happening?' the driver called out to the police milling about the car park. 'I got a call to go to the Swan Shopping Centre.'

Two detectives threw bundles of banknotes in the bag and piled in behind the two traffic cops. 'We lost him! Head for Wolverhampton!'

The car roared off and Kennon felt better to see the night's work wasn't finished yet.

'What a waste of time and manpower!' Peter Woodward said, leaning on a wall as Boyd tied a handkerchief round his arm.

'You shouldn't be playing with guns, Mr Woodward,' Kennon replied. 'I could have you arrested.'

'Spare me the details, Chief Inspector. How the hell did I know you were going to turn up?'

'You should have guessed we would. I told you to leave this to us. You cannot go after someone as dangerous as this man and expect to get away with it. He's an armed criminal, for God's sake!'

'You can't catch him! What do you expect me to do? We could have had him if it hadn't had been for all your bloody men charging in.'

'You wouldn't have done it. And if it wasn't for us charging in, you'd probably be lying in the gutter dead. We had this place staked out well in advance. We knew he was coming here, and here was where we had a good chance of getting him. But we're not finished yet. He lost the money. He will be back for it tomorrow night.'

'Yes, and in the meantime how many more blunders will be made as my sister's life hangs by a thread? Four years you've had to catch this man. *Four bloody years*!'

'Calm down, Peter!' Ian's voice floated across the precinct. 'Look at the state of you. I told you not to bring a gun.'

'Don't you start! Why did you follow his instructions? He wanted the money! You should have made him come to you for it!'

'Shut up, Peter! I thought you had more sense. We can't gamble with Julia's life. He holds all the cards. Not us!'

'All right, lads. Let's calm down and get a cup of tea.'

'Ambulance is on its way, sir,' a police sergeant said. 'I'll see to him if you want to go down to the station. They'll have tea waiting for you.'

'Thanks, Sergeant. You all right, Stacey?'

'Yes, sir. I must have twisted my ankle on them bloody cobbles. Pity we lost him... but I found this.'

Stacey handed Kennon a folded piece of paper torn from an AA handbook. Kennon studied it and noticed two circled areas. One was around Dudley and the other was around Kidsgrove. 'Interesting. Did he drop this?'

'I reckon he did.'

'He's circled Dudley. That's definitely his mark. But what the devil is there at Kidsgrove?'

Chapter Fourteen

The Panther drove like the wind down dark country roads, frustrated at losing the ransom that had been in his hands for a brief moment. Twice he saw the blue light of a squad car following and twice he shook it off. But it wasn't one squad car pursuing him but several from Shropshire and the West Midlands working in tandem. Radio messages from Bridgnorth went over the airwaves calling for more cars, and the chase was on.

The Panther was familiar with the region and knew exactly where he was heading. He'd see a signpost for Claverley or some other obscure village and he knew where he was from countless previous visits. Twice he was forced to pull off the road up a farm track and hide while the blue light went flashing by.

Gradually he was able to lose his pursuers, but he knew that come daylight it would be infinitely more difficult. The fuel gauge was dipping into the last quarter and he still had a long way to go. His only option was to dump the van and turn to public transport, but the problem was money. He was running short of cash and he was doubtful he had enough for the train to take him to Bradford. In this situation his only choice was a robbery, and he had the tools to do it with.

He kept going north into Staffordshire, heading for a place he knew well. He covered another fifteen miles into the Trent countryside, crossing the A41 near Codsall and carried on to the small village of Horsebrook within five or six miles of Cannock. He cut his speed, searching for a lane or a track to turn into, and when he saw a sign pointing to a farm he turned into a narrow lane and parked under some trees.

He switched on the interior light and opened a toolbox for his next job and pulled out his housebreaking tools. A brace and bit was all he needed. He knew of a sub-post office at Horsebrook that he'd tried once before but failed to get into; this time he wouldn't fail. He opened his duffel bag and took out the 12-bore shotgun loaded with two cartridges, then the semi-automatic pistol with a full clip and a roll of insulation tape. With this he taped the torch to the gun between the twin barrels and then, putting on his hood and a pair of white linen gloves, he was ready to go.

He wasn't happy at leaving the van and wondered whether he should torch it, but then decided against it. There was no point lighting a beacon for the police. He threw his duffel bag over his shoulder and began the two-mile walk to Horsebrook.

He kept off the main road and walked through woods. The time was 3.45 a.m. when he reached the small village just a mile from the M6 motorway. The post office stood opposite a country estate surrounded by a six-foot wall that ran the entire length of the village. Inside the premises, the postmaster and his wife were asleep upstairs with their fifteen-year-old son and the family dog, a faithful Border collie.

The one thing the Panther dreaded was dogs, and he slipped through the side gate and went round the back to peer inside the kitchen. It was dark inside and there was no sign of the dog. It was there the last time he tried. Perhaps they didn't have it any more.

He opened his duffel bag and pulled out the brace and bit already assembled, and commenced drilling through the window frame just above the handle. The brace went silently through the soft wood, drilling a half-inch hole in the frame. Then he pushed a piece of bent wire through the hole and slipped it over the handle, which enabled him to pull it up.

He opened the kitchen window wide, pushed a plate rack aside on the sink top, and then climbed through, dropping silently onto the floor. He unlocked the back kitchen door ready for his escape before proceeding through the darkened house by torchlight and into the post office. He was now behind the counter where the safe stood in the corner. He searched for the safe keys and guessed correctly they would be upstairs in a trouser pocket by the bed.

He went to the foot of the stairs and quietly began to go up. When he reached the landing he faced two bedroom doors. Both were ajar and, keeping the torch beam low, he peered inside. In the front bedroom the postmaster and his wife were sound asleep.

Then he peered in the second bedroom and froze. The couple's fifteen-year-old son was asleep with the family's Border collie curled up at the foot of the bed. The Panther closed the door and turned the key to lock it.

Then he went into the front bedroom and shook the postmaster awake, hissing into his ear. 'Wake up! Don't make a sound. I've got a gun!'

The man stirred himself awake and was immediately blinded by the torch. 'Keys! Where's the keys?' the Panther demanded.

The postmaster knew by instinct who his intruder was. He had been half expecting him for months and he tried stalling. 'Downstairs on the hook.'

'You're lying! I've looked for them.'

'Look again!' he said, shielding his eyes from the glare.

'Quit stalling!' the Panther was losing his patience. 'The keys! Fetch me the keys!'

'They're in my trouser pocket.'

'Get them!'

'Not bloody likely!' The postmaster made a flying dive at the gunman, pushing him back against a wardrobe, and the shotgun went off, sending shots from both barrels through the ceiling. The blast was enough to wake the entire household as the dog leaped off the bed and scratched furiously at the door. As both men wrestled, the postmaster made a desperate grab for the hood as the gun came down across his head and felled him to the floor.

The postmaster's wife, woken by the blast, found herself staring petrified at the dark outline of a man with his face masked holding a shotgun to her husband. 'What's happening!' she yelled. 'What are you doing?'

'Shut up! This is a raid!' the Panther snapped, quickly reloading the gun.

The postmaster hauled himself up onto the bed and searched his pockets for the safe keys. With his head spinning, he tossed them over and they landed at the Panther's feet. He picked them up and threw them back. 'Come down and open it!'

'I'm not going down undressed,' the postmaster replied defiantly.

The Panther motioned with his gun for the man to put his

trousers on and then ordered him out onto the landing. '*Downstairs*!' he said pointing the shotgun at him. They went down the stairs and turned right into the passage to go into the post office. Meanwhile, the son was climbing out of the back window onto the flat kitchen roof, taking the dog with him.

In the post office the postmaster was filling two leather pouches with £2,000 worth of notes and postal orders in one, and £85 of coinage in the other. Then he placed them on the counter.

'Now back upstairs and stay there!' the Panther ordered, pointing with his shotgun.

The postmaster obeyed while the Panther hooked the drawstrings of each bag onto the toggles round his neck and quickly left. He started down the passage and saw a black shape blocking his exit. He had hardly any time to react as the dog leaped at him, knocking him off balance, and he fell with the dog landing on top of him.

Then the son appeared wielding a cricket bat. The Panther regained his feet and swung the gun at him, knocking the bat out of his hand before roughly pushing him out of the way. Then he had to deal with the snapping snarling dog that barred his exit.

He drew the semi-automatic from his pocket and flipped off the safety catch as the collie leaped at him. He fired two bullets into the dog and it fell mortally wounded at his feet. Then the Panther made his escape by the kitchen door.

He went down the side of the house and as he reached the front he was suddenly blinded by the headlights of a car speeding towards him with a flashing blue light.

He cursed, realising he hadn't cut the phone wires. The postmaster's wife had dialled 999 and the Q cars, already out at Bridgnorth and Wolverhampton, were being directed to Horsebrook. He looked to his left and saw another car coming in the opposite direction, and he felt his luck fast running out.

To get caught now would be the greatest of follies. As the car pulled up, the Panther raised his shotgun and fired both barrels, blasting out the windscreen. The driver had already ducked under the dashboard and his colleague, who was half out of the car, dropped down behind the open door. For the very first time he saw the hooded Black Panther with two bags of money hung round his neck.

In less than a minute, the second Q car was rushing towards him and the Panther was caught like a rabbit in a trap illuminated in the beams of the headlights. He turned and fired two pistol shots at the second car, shattering the windscreen, and the driver swerved off the road into a ditch.

He could hear the wail of sirens in the distance as more Q cars were closing in. Never had he come so close to being caught. Throwing down the heavy bag of cash filled with coins, he ran across the road and bounded over the six-foot wall, landing in woods on the other side. He then made off in pitch darkness through the woods and across some open fields that bordered a large manor house. He looked back to see a rapidly moving blue light flashing between the trees as a Q car raced up the road, trying to cut him off.

When he reached the edge of the estate he came out into open country and could see the M6 Motorway at Four Crosses. He carried on across a field bordered by a barbed wire fence tangled with brambles. He threw the duffel bag over before climbing it, and then got tangled up in brambles tearing at his trousers. He cut himself free with his sheath knife and then carried on towards Cannock.

Dawn was less than an hour away, and he felt exhaustion dragging him down as he reached the main road. Not for a minute could he afford to relax as he walked on for Bridgetown. He was now on the edge of the Black Country, leaving the West Midlands behind. By dawn he was walking on to Cannock Central railway station with his shotgun and bag of cash in the duffel bag slung over his shoulder. He had money in his pocket.

He had managed to lose his pursuers, crossing police borders over thirty miles. As he purchased a ticket and waited for the train to Walsall and Leeds, he saw another photofit poster of himself on the station board with the words, 'Have You Seen This Man?' He looked round at the early morning commuters, who were all oblivious to the demon in their midst.

Chapter Fifteen

Any kind of travel for the Panther was potentially hazardous in the daytime, especially a crowded railway carriage. But he had the confidence to brazen it out, sitting back and listening to the conversations of the passengers. The majority were early morning workers going to factories in the Potteries who never gave him a second glance as they chatted about nothing in particular. They were seemingly unaware of the notorious criminal in their midst, in his grubby raincoat and flat cap, looking somewhat dishevelled with a day's growth of stubble.

It was eight o'clock when he reached Lichfield, and had to change trains. He waited on a busy platform with the commuters heading for Leeds and then noticed the news-stands. There again was his face on the front of a newspaper.

He bought a copy and then waited for the train, which arrived promptly at 8.10. It was a corridor train as usual, and he found a near empty second-class compartment where the sole occupant, a young woman, seemed particularly keen on striking up a conversation. It was the newspaper photofit that had prompted it.

'What do you think of this Black Panther bloke?' she asked in a Birmingham accent. 'He's making all the news lately. Nobody knows who he is.'

'He's from the Black Country,' Derek Wilson said, keeping his head buried in the paper. The last thing he wanted was a conversation.

'So they say, but why can't they catch him? That's what puzzles me. My heart goes out to the poor girl he's kidnapped. What must she be going through? She must be terrified.'

'They'll catch him,' Wilson grunted, keeping his head buried.

'Do you think so? They're taking long enough about it. Ee, what about the reward? That would come in 'andy. Twenty-five grand…'

'Aye. It would.'

'If I had that, I could buy meself one of them new houses on the Four Oaks Estate. And I'd still 'ave enough left over for a flash sports car. Where are you heading?'

'Leeds.'

'Are you really? I'm getting out at Derby. I'm a secretary at Rolls-Royce. They have their head office at Derby. What do you do? You don't mind me asking, do you? I like a chat.'

'I'm a locksmith,' Wilson grunted.

'Are you really? What a coincidence. My dad used to be a locksmith. He's retired now, of course. What company do you work for?' She waited for an answer and then leaned forward to tap him on the knee. 'I said, what company do you work for?'

'*For God's sake!*' Wilson slammed the paper down. 'Is it necessary to ask all these questions of a total stranger! I don't know you, and you don't know me!'

'Well, I'm only passing the time!' she replied, taken aback. 'But if you don't want to talk, you only 'ad to say! Here's my station. Enjoy the rest of your journey – I don't think!' She got out and slammed the door.

It was ten o'clock when the train pulled into Bradford Central and the Panther got out carrying all the incriminating evidence in his duffel bag. There were two policemen on the other side of the barrier weighing up passengers as they went through and Derek broke into a cold sweat trying to appear unruffled. He could linger on the platform and wait for them to leave, but how long would that take? He had to get home. He began to falter, feeling uneasy, and he folded his newspaper so as to read it as he walked. He approached the barrier, taking a quick glance up as he produced his ticket, and went on through without a word spoken. He had made it. Then he heard a voice calling him.

'Excuse me, sir!'

He kept walking but the voice was louder. 'Excuse me, sir!'

He felt a hand on his shoulder and turned to see the policeman staring at him. 'You dropped this, sir.' The policeman was handing him a strip of Dymo tape with the words, *Swan Shopping Centre Bridgnorth* stamped out.

'No, it's not mine, Officer.'

'I beg your pardon, sir. I saw it drop out your pocket as you removed your ticket.' The PC looked at it. ' "Swan Shopping Centre", it says. Must be a souvenir. Anyway, it's yours. If you don't want it, chuck it in the bin.'

The Panther took the Dymo strip and walked on, hardly daring to believe his luck. He walked the two miles home to Radcliff Avenue and entered his house by the front door. It was 10.30. He stood for a few minutes taking in the familiar smells of washing and home cooking wafting from the kitchen and then walked up the hallway and called through to his wife. 'I'm home! I'll be upstairs.'

He put his foot on the bottom stair and was about to go up when he saw his wife, Iris, coming down with a large cardboard box in her hand. 'Hello, Derek,' she said with a startled look. 'I didn't expect to see you today. How did it go?'

'Have you been in my room?' he snapped.

'How can I? It's locked.'

'That wouldn't stop you. You could get another key easy enough. What's in that box? Let me see.' He peered inside at old black and white photographs taken on their family weekend military war games on the moors.

'I've been having a clear-out in the cupboards.'

'You're not throwing these out!' He plucked the photos out and rummaged in the box filled with miscellaneous bric-a-brac.

'It's all rubbish.'

'Don't take anything out my room! That room is to be kept locked at all times! I don't want Karen to see it.'

'Don't worry. She doesn't even ask about it. She knows it's your work room.'

'Good. Keep it that way. I'm going up for some sleep.'

'Derek… Have you had anything to do with this kidnapping that's in the papers? They're saying it's you.'

'What if I have. Would it make any difference?'

'It would, Derek. I can't believe you would do such a thing. Tell me it's not you!'

'Of course it's not me! What do you take me for?'

'I'll keep faith with you over the other jobs, but not this one. This is too much. I can't bear to think it's you.'

'You'll stay faithful, Iris, because that's your duty and you don't have anywhere else to go! There's nothing to worry about. This is the last job. There'll be no need for any more. This one will set us up. Now let me get some sleep.'

'Shall I empty your bag?'

'No! I can do it. There's money in it. Another successful job done. The bloke was pleased with his extension.'

'Are you going out again tonight?'

'I am. I was hoping not to, but it hasn't worked out yet.'

'I'll have dinner ready at six o'clock. It's a stew. You like beef stew.'

Derek nodded and carried on up to his attic room. Iris went to the kitchen and sat down with a cup of tea. She unrolled the paper that had been delivered that morning and looked at her husband's picture on the front page in stunned silence. She read the article on the search at Buxton Stables and sat there trying to understand what drove her husband to do the things he did. They'd been married twenty years and though they had the odd row it was a steady relationship; but if she was honest, it was not a blissfully happy marriage. It worked, and that's all she could really say about it.

The name Black Panther, coined by the media, had gripped the nation. The more that was written about him, the more the public wanted to know. A veritable mountain of information was on hand if one chose to look for it, but it was never actively pursued by the crime squads. Half a dozen descriptions all varied, and the man had no criminal record for police to match suspects with.

DCI George Kennon was trying to put the pieces together. It was like a giant jigsaw. He was using every piece of evidence and every scrap of information to reel in the man, who was eluding the police at every turn and stretching police credibility.

'How does he do it?' Kennon asked his baffled team in Manchester CID. 'What gives him the edge over us? He leaves behind clues that an amateur sleuth could follow and still we can't pin him down. Over 3,000 interviews have been carried out, and still nobody can put a name to him. We know he's from West Yorkshire, and yet we've had witnesses say he uses a West Indian accent. What the hell's going on?'

'That's because you're trying too hard, George,' Dr Erwin said, sipping a cup of tea and scattering biscuit crumbs all down his suit. 'It's my opinion that this man is revelling in the fame it's brought him. He craved attention, and to be honest we never paid him much when he was robbing sub-post offices. He wasn't getting away with vast sums and wasn't generating that much publicity. But now he's turned to kidnap he's on the front page of every national newspaper. His ego must be bursting through the sound barrier.'

'What do you mean, trying too hard? This man moves about over half the country to do his work and is tying up every police force in the land. What else can we do other than hunt him down with old-fashioned police work. It usually does the trick.'

'There's nothing wrong with it, but have you thought of a different approach? My advice is to put a blanket ban on all publicity and let him come to you.'

'I don't believe it! You were the one who said rely on the media. They will ferret him out, you said. And now you're saying just the opposite!'

'I was wrong. The media have gone overboard, but they'll still print their own assumptions. They've given him the attention he craved and fuelled his ego. Impose a complete ban on the media, and it's my opinion he will do one of two things. He will either up the ransom for media attention, or resort to terror blackmail by threatening the girl's life by publicly revealing where she is. It's my guess he will choose the latter.'

'And why would he do that?'

'Two reasons. Firstly because he wants to draw attention back to him, and second because he wants the damned money. If he thinks the media have lost interest, or that they are following police orders, he will up the ante. He will reveal the danger that faces the victim, and by that he will almost certainly give a hint as to where she is and give away his own hiding place.'

'With all due respect, Dr Erwin, you don't know that for certain. Your using psychology to unravel the man's alter ego. I have to work on the case notes of evidence and facts that bring us closer to the man.'

'This is a fact. It's been proved that the criminal mind can be analysed through a personality disorder. Take what you know about this man and assess his personality. If he's remotely like the man on that board, he will do what we predict. He will be getting desperate by now, and that's when he will show himself. He can't hold her indefinitely and that's why he will plant a lead by simplifying the details for the ransom drop. I believe I heard someone say the victim was in an underground drain or a hidden shaft, like a coal mine. There are plenty of redundant coal mines that had canals running through them at some time and have since been filled in.'

'You're reading my mind, Doctor. I've been thinking along those lines. We've looked at reservoirs and pumping stations. The Peak District has its caves and potholes. But it's doubtful a kidnapper would choose a cave used by hundreds of potholers. A large drainage system might prove better. But where do we look? There must be hundreds of such systems, without even counting the sewers.'

'That's what the Panther will reveal in his next message. You just be ready to intercept it, and you'll be a lot closer than you realise.'

'Sir, what about Kidsgrove, the place ringed on the map we found?' Boyd said. 'Could there be anything there worth looking at?'

'DCI Bob Morrison of Stafford CID has already done it. I rang him yesterday and he said he took a look around and couldn't see anything out of the ordinary. He did mention an old coal mine that's now buried under a park he didn't know was there.'

'There's your answer, George!' Dr Erwin said. 'The victim is down a redundant pit shaft that's been converted into a drain of some kind.'

'Did DCI Morrison take a proper look, sir?' Boyd cut in. 'Did he have the whole area searched, using teams of men?'

'He told me he found the entrance in a concrete shelter with a manhole cover. He lifted the cover and found lots of scrap metal had been dumped in it. He said it was like the black hole of Calcutta down there, with water rushing through the bottom. He added there was no way you could keep a hostage down there.'

'I wouldn't rely on that, George,' Erwin replied. 'He could very well be mistaken. There could be other entrances much further away that he didn't see that might yield better results. There's more than one shaft to a coal mine.'

'I agree, Doctor. But isn't it the usual practice to fill them in? That's what I've been led to believe. Any hole under the ground will flood in no time if it's not sealed off, according to the miners I've spoken to.'

'Well, then. Maybe our kidnapper's a blundering fool who didn't know that, in which case the victim is already dead.'

Kennon looked at all the information displayed on the wall boards in the Incident Room. 'West Yorkshire CID are carrying out house-to-house inquiries in Leeds. I'm convinced that's where the Panther comes from. We have to cooperate with them. I want everybody over there except DS Boyd and DI Roberts. The rest report to Leeds CID in Westgate. I'll phone there and tell them you're on the way. Chief Inspector Tyler is leading the hunt. Any questions?'

'Yes, sir. Aren't we missing the most obvious place a kidnapper would choose – an attic room or a cellar?'

'No, I don't discount that at all, that's why house-to-house inquiries have been stepped up. Several Manchester districts have been investigated by uniform and all have drawn a blank. Hopefully, Leeds might prove different. Now, let's get to it!'

As the team of detectives rose to shuffle out of the door, Superintendent Bradley intercepted them.

'There's been another sub-post office robbery at Horsebrook in Staffordshire in the early hours. Sources say it was definitely the Panther. He used the same method of entry and he escaped with a haul of over £2,000. Mercifully, no one was seriously hurt. But even more embarrassing – he escaped with five Q cars chasing him! This is just too painful for words.'

Bradley's doleful expression was like that of a man going to the gallows. 'The media are gathering like vultures outside. I'm imposing a complete press ban. No one must issue a statement. Is that clear?'

The team left the room, and Bradley turned to Dr Erwin with a pained expression.

'He's got us beat, Doctor. We're no nearer to catching him than we were when he started four years ago. The Chief Constable is tearing his hair out and I've had Scotland Yard telling me they're coming in to take over. How can one man elude arrest for so long?'

Chapter Sixteen

The Panther's reign had now stretched over five years. He was in police files known as the 'Brace and Bit Robber', from the method he used to gain entry by drilling through casement windows to weaken fastenings or spring open catches. His use of this method had led the police to look up every self-employed jobbing builder over the entire Midlands. But it was a time-consuming effort, and there was still no firm evidence to suggest the Panther and the kidnapper were the same person.

The only person who knew that for certain was the Panther himself, and he was getting desperate at the time it was taking for the ransom to arrive. It was now five days since Julia Woodward had been snatched from her shop, and the longer he held her, the greater the risk of getting caught. Bathpool Park was after all a public place, and although he had hidden the cover of the third shaft, the middle or second shaft was visible and might yet prove to be his Achilles heel.

But nothing could be done about it, and since no one had discovered Bathpool's secrets he would have to rely on it. He rose at 4.30 p.m. after five hours' sleep, and washed and dressed before padding downstairs for a snack of poached egg on toast, while his wife poured his tea.

'I might not be in tonight,' he said whilst glancing at the paper. 'I've got a job in Kidsgrove to do.'

'What about the beef stew, Derek? I've made it specially for you.'

'Save it for me. I must get this job done. Fill two flasks with soup, that will do me.'

Iris didn't argue. She knew better than to antagonise him, and she did as she was asked, filling two flasks with oxtail soup.

'Where's Karen?' he asked whilst glancing down the job adverts in the paper.

'She's staying over at a friend's house tonight. She asked after you when she got in from work.'

'I don't like her staying out. You know that. Her place is here with you. I shall have to have words with her when I see her.'

'She's eighteen, Derek. You can't keep her locked up. I'm all right on my own here.'

'Ee-oop! I see there's jobs going here on my old army base at Catterick. They want carpenters on the new mess hall they're building. I might apply for that. It's not till March, though. Why the bloody hell do they put the ad in so early!' He slammed his fist hard on the table 'The bloody immigrants will grab the jobs before I get there, and it will be cheap labour!'

Iris looked on placidly in the strained atmosphere. What went through his mind, God only knew. At six o'clock she saw him go out of the door into the night as he left for the station with his duffel bag slung from his shoulder. He walked to the station at Forster Square and bought a return ticket to Kidsgrove, changing at Manchester, and waited for a train whilst idly speculating on how to spend the ransom money.

When the train pulled in at 6.45, he boarded a second-class carriage and went along the corridor for an empty compartment. Then he sat back, thinking and planning ahead. He had no contingency if the kidnap failed and he didn't relish a return to post office raids for the remainder of the winter months. But even worse was the thought of failure and having to scrimp through till March when he could apply for the Catterick job, if it was still going.

The possibility of failure gnawed away at him, and when the train pulled in at Manchester Central he alighted and made his way across the platforms for the connection to Kidsgrove. When he arrived at the platform, a group of passengers stood round a large sign announcing train cancellations, with alternative transport laid on. He moved forward to see the sign better and stood staring at the board, mouth gaping like a fish, stunned at the words, which read:

TRAIN DERAILMENT AT KIDSGROVE. ALL TRAINS CANCELLED UNTIL FURTHER NOTICE.

He had immediate visions of a train disaster at Bathpool Park, with the area swarming with emergency services and the discovery of the subterranean drainage system. He couldn't imagine a worse scenario, and he quickly rushed off to find a station attendant to inquire further. He made his way to an inquiry desk crowded with passengers, and stood there listening to the explanations given out by staff.

'The main Manchester line is blocked by a derailment at Harrisheath just this side of Kidsgrove. Rescue services are working to clear the line, which has disrupted all normal service. Buses are being laid on for passengers at the main entrance.'

He came away relieved that the accident was just outside of Kidsgrove and made his way out of the station to where several coaches were loading passengers. Crowds were not his scene, and he was in two minds whether to join them when the next emergency struck.

Passengers were being herded off the station concourse by the police with dire warnings of an IRA bomb planted in the vicinity. People were rushing past him, fleeing in panic, and as he turned to join the bus queue the coaches were pulling away full to capacity.

He turned to follow the crowd heading across the taxi ranks when he suddenly broke into a cold sweat as two armed policemen approached him holding machine pistols across their chests. Surely they wouldn't stop him… He was just another passenger. He tried to avoid their gaze and walk by, but it was too much to hope for.

'Put the bag down, sir, and step away!' one of them barked.

They were wearing flak jackets with bullet-proof vests, and as one policeman held a gun on him the other gingerly approached the bulky duffel bag and pulled it open. He spotted the two flasks crammed in with a large bunch of car keys, a pair of Zeiss binoculars, a roll of Elastoplast and various other items.

'Anything suspicious, Bob?' his colleague asked.

'Could be. What's in the flasks?'

'Soup, Officer, and very tasty it is too,' he answered in a Welsh accent. 'Why, I bet you thought that was a bomb, did you now?'

'Where are you going with two flasks of soup at this time?'

'I'm on my way to Cardiff for a reunion. I always carry soup on a long journey, Officer.'

'And you always carry binoculars as well? I don't like the look of this, Harry. I think you'd better come with us, sir, and do a bit of explaining.'

'Now don't be daft, man. I do a bit of birdwatching in Cardiff Bay. Don't waste your time on me. Look for these IRA buggers.'

'He's right, Bob. We can't waste time on this bloke.'

'That's right, boys. Do the right thing. I've got to press on. Now where can I get a cup of tea?'

He was handed his bag back just as a police car pulled up and two officers jumped out to clear the pub across the road. They had been tipped off to clear the Trafford Arms, and as they began shouting for people to move away the bomb went off.

Twenty pounds of gelignite placed under a seat blasted the pub's interior crowded with drinkers, among whom was a group of soldiers waiting for deployment to Belfast. The IRA picked their targets well and got their timing right. It was a Saturday night, and there were two more bombs ticking away.

The two police officers rushed off to assist the emergency services as sirens wailed in the background. The Panther was left to wander the city centre among the crowds on a night out. He knew Manchester well enough to know where he was going as he headed down Albion Street, which was crowded with restaurants and pubs, looking for a small café. Then he changed his mind and headed for the Stock Exchange pub at the far end of the street.

It was at least a mile from the station, but things were not so calm as he imagined. Police were everywhere, warning of more bombs in the area, and pubs were being cleared rapidly. He found himself being herded along past Mosley, when the next bomb went off in the Stock Exchange pub 200 yards ahead.

The Stock Exchange was popular, offering live music, and twenty pounds of gelignite wrought the same devastation among drinkers who weren't prepared to allow the IRA to disrupt their lives. With police sirens wailing amidst the devastation, people were rushing out of pubs and restaurants in all directions.

Streets were getting clogged with traffic as fire engines and ambulances were fighting their way through to scenes of carnage. The only means of escape was on foot, and it being a Saturday night the pubs were full. Meanwhile, the next bomb, planted in a bar on Princes Street, was counting down in the Station Hotel.

As the Panther veered away from the city centre the third bomb went off ten minutes later, by which time he was well away and drifting through the red-light district. He found himself hovering in the doorway of a strip club that had private rooms above, and like iron to a magnet he was drawn inside.

The man at the desk invited him in with a cheery smile and a sharp wit of repartee for his customer.

'Come in sir! Come in. There are no bombs in here. The management won't allow them.' He chuckled. 'You've chosen well tonight, sir. We've got Doreen on stage in all her sexy underwear. Then there's Rachel with her stunning performance as a dairymaid. But I reckon you want something a bit more than that. I can fix you up with Lulu. This is her.' he said opening a book of photos. 'Or there's Selena, in the black underwear and the riding crop. I reckon Selena will be best for you. She's a cracker. What do you say? Would you like to go up and get to know her? Fifteen quid an hour, that's all.'

'I don't know… I'm a bit short,' the Panther said in a hesitant tone.

'I tell you what then. Ten quid to you, as you're a new member. Give it a try. You won't regret it.'

The Panther fumbled in his pocket for a ten-pound note and handed it over. The man pressed a buzzer, and a woman emerged out of curtained doorway with a ready smile.

'Show the gent up to Selena, Doreen. He's a new member.'

'This way, sir.' She led him up two flights of stairs to a short corridor. 'Number 4. Just knock and Selena will answer.'

He went along to Number 4 and knocked. The door was opened by a tall girl with long glossy brown hair dressed in silk underwear.

'Come in,' she said with a smile. 'I'm Selena. What's your name?'

'Derek.'

'That's a nice name. Take your mac off, Derek, and that silly hat.' She giggled, pulling it off his head. 'You look like that bloke the cops are chasing in this,' she said, putting it on her own head. 'How do I look?' she tipped it back and pouted her lips.

'No – don't it suit me? I didn't think it would. What you got in the bag? Anything good?'

'Nothing to interest you. I don't normally do this, you know. I'm a married man.'

'Ooh, ain't you the lucky one. That's what they all say. *Relax*! Take the jacket off. That's it… now the shirt.' She stood watching him strip to the waist and admired his neat muscular body. 'Nice muscles. I can see you work out.'

She stood six inches taller than him in her high heels and he didn't like it one bit.

'Can we sit down?'

'Sure. On the bed,' she said, sitting on the single divan and patting the place next to her. 'Come on. Don't be shy.'

He sat next to her and slipped his hand round her waist and kissed her hard with a passionate force. He almost stopped her breathing, as they were glued by the lips for a full minute while he fumbled at her breasts. Then they broke away and he stood up.

For a brief moment she felt stifled by him, as if he wanted to harm her. Her anxiety grew as she watched him walk round the room, occasionally glancing out the window behind the heavy curtains on to a walled garden. Sirens were still wailing in the distance and he could see the glow of flashing blue lights making their way to the city centre.

'Terrorists! They don't ever give up,' he said, turning back. Then he approached her and stood directly in front, gazing down at her and placing his hands on her shoulders. He stayed like that for several minutes, quite content just to gaze at her with his staring eyes, transfixed. She looked up into his eyes and thought she recognised something in them.

Suddenly he was jolted by a sharp pain as though an electric shock had gone through his entire body. It was brought on by nerve ends at the base of the spine. It happened only rarely, but made him sweat like a pig, and he was forced to crouch to the floor.

'What's up?' she said. 'Are you all right?'

His eyes watered with the pain and he looked up at her with a doleful expression.

'You're a strange bloke, Derek,' she said. 'I don't get many real charmers, but you're one. I can tell that.'

'How can you tell?'

'There's a lost boy in you somewhere. I reckon you're a bit of a loner. You've never done this before, have you? Don't worry, I'll show you the ropes.' She reached behind her back and unclipped her bra. It fell away revealing her pendulous breasts and she smiled. 'That better for you?'

His face remained subdued, brooding and silent. Then without a word he seized her by the shoulders and squeezed hard digging his fingers into her flesh until she felt the pain.

'Hey, not so rough!' she said, wriggling under the pressure. 'You're hurting me!'

'Don't tell me I'm a lost boy!' he snapped. 'Don't ever say that again! I'm a man! Highly skilled. I could strangle the life out of you if I chose to.'

'All right, Derek. Let go, please, you're hurting me.'

He dug his thumbs deeper into her shoulders until her eyes watered with the pain and then slowly released his grip, leaving red marks on her pale flesh.

'Oh my God!' she gasped, moving away from him. 'You don't know how much that hurt. What's up with you, for God's sake?'

'Nothing! Nothing you'd understand. I'm the only one who can deal with it.'

He was brooding again in silence and then she saw a fresh wave of anger welling up in him and she feared for her very life. She had to get out of the room. In another minute he would turn on her.

She made a sudden move for the door and he pounced on her, grabbing her by the arm, and forced her back on the bed. She could sense the uncontrollable anger in him.

'Do you know what it's like to feel undervalued!' He was spitting with rage. 'Do you? I bet you bloody don't. I've worked bloody hard at making a decent life. But it's never enough! It always falls short of what people expect.'

He glared at her with fiery eyes. 'Everybody wants something for nothing! You do the work for them and then they don't want to fucking pay you!' He kicked the bed in his temper.

'Please, Derek, don't,' she whimpered. 'Tell me about it.'

He let go of her and went to his duffel bag and pulled out the black Lycra hood that was tucked right at the bottom. It was a miracle the police officer missed it.

'What's that you've got?' she asked feeling a fresh wave of trepidation creep over her.

He pulled the hood on over his head and stood glaring at her through the eye slits. 'Do I still look like a little boy lost?' His voice was muffled, but louder and more aggressive. 'I'm the centre of attention with this. I take command over everything!'

She stared at him without saying a word, again fearing for her life. She shook her head and stayed silent, secretly wanting to run from the room screaming.

He stood back with hands on hips and inclined his head. Then he raised his hand and pointed a mock gun at her like a highwayman of old. He was minus the three-cornered hat, but his smooth chest glistened in the pink light of the room like a silk cravat. He stepped forward and seized her by the shoulders once more, squeezing hard, digging into her flesh.

She looked up nervously, fearful at what he might do. Then without any warning he dived on top of her and smothered her with kisses through the hood. They writhed on the bed like two pythons wrapped in combat, each fumbling at the other's clothes until they were stripped naked. Then they made love. The final act came with waves of ecstasy and lasted a full five minutes.

When he climbed off her he felt completely satisfied. He removed the hood and lay back on the bed breathing heavily while she stroked his chest.

'Was that all right?' she asked. 'Do you feel better for it?'

'Aye, I reckon I do, lass,' he said in a soft Yorkshire burr. 'But I've got to get going. I've got work to do.' He began getting dressed as she pulled a sheet round her.

'Three IRA bombs have hit this city tonight. I wonder how many more they will bring. That's what brought me here. I wouldn't be here if it wasn't for them,' he said, repacking his duffel bag. He looked up at her and saw the look of alarm on her face.

'You're IRA?' she said nervously.

He realised now what impression the hood had made and he laughed.

'IRA! Not me, love. No, I use the hood for undercover work.' He slipped into his mac and put the cap back on. 'Recognise me now do you? No? Never mind, it will come. See you, love.' He slipped out of the door and went back down the stairs to the desk.

'All right, squire?' the doorman said. 'Didn't I say she was lovely? Come again.'

He nodded and then he was gone down the street searching for a decent vehicle. The sirens were still wailing in the background as the rescuers were clearing away debris from a night of carnage. The police were all concentrated in the city centre, and he walked further and further away, leaving the city behind and going into the suburbs. In his hand he held his bunch of car keys for a speedy snatch. He stuck mostly to Fords, but he had keys for Vauxhalls, Austins and Morrises.

Vehicles were parked all over the city so he had plenty of choice, but he needed a reliable car and so he steered away from poorer districts. The Stretford suburb seemed reasonably middle class, and he tried several cars before coming to an Austin A40 in a quiet side street. The key turned in the door lock and he climbed in and started the engine and pulled away. It was just past 11.30 p.m.

The journey was quicker than he thought down the A34 under good road conditions, and when he reached Church Lawton just outside of Kidsgrove he saw the rescue crews were still working on the train derailment under arc lights. Four carriages had jumped the track, and as he approached the village he could see the cranes lifting them back on the line. All the passengers had long gone and the rescue services had been scaled down, so that he could drive straight through without stopping. He could have avoided the village altogether but it was important to see the area, since he needed all the details for laying a ransom trail and his subsequent escape.

Kidsgrove was quiet when he entered the small town just after midnight and drove on through to the park. He turned off just before it to go up Coal-Pit Hill. The road wound round to the head of the old coal mine and he came to a pair of rusty gates at what was the pit entrance on a bleak hillside. He parked by the old transformer house that was still there and climbed out to walk down the tall picket fence half hidden by trees. It was a short way along, and by the light of his torch he found the gap where he could slip through by pulling one of the metal slats aside.

Then it was a lengthy walk through the tangle of undergrowth to the head of the main shaft. This was by far the most difficult way to enter, but since he had disabled the ladder to the centre shaft of the drainage system he had no choice. To the untrained eye it could be easily missed, but he knew it by heart, and when he reached the raised concrete plinth that housed the heavy manhole cover he opened it up and peered down into a black hole.

No matter how many times he came, every trip was an experience that gave him a buzz. He climbed onto the ladder, and after closing the hatch he began his descent into the bowels of the earth. Halfway down he stopped at the first platform to open his bag and fish out the black hood. He pulled it on to cover his face as a precaution, but if he was honest it was done more out of habit to boost his credibility. Then he carried on down, shining the torch as he went and feeling the cold that chilled through to the bones.

When he reached the next platform he looked over and saw his victim sleeping below wrapped in her sleeping bag. It disturbed him, for though it was natural for her to be asleep, he could never be sure she had not died of hypothermia, though he doubted it. She was after all a young healthy woman and more able to withstand the hardship.

He clambered down onto her platform and shook her awake. As she stirred in the sleeping bag, he lit the two oil lamps, and the glow seemed to cheer the squalid atmosphere.

'Sorry I'm late. Got held up by a bloody train,' he said in a friendly manner. 'Then the bloody IRA decided to pick this night to blow up three pubs in Manchester!'

She raised herself up in the sleeping bag and leaned back against the curved wall, careful that the wire noose round her neck did not pull too tight. Her face was pale and her eyes ringed with red. 'Was anyone hurt?' she asked in a flat, hollow tone.

'I should imagine so. But I couldn't get close enough to see for bloody police all over the place. I saw the ambulances going in so

I daresay there would have been quite a few casualties. Problem now, though, is that it's delayed my schedule, and I'm afraid you'll have to stay down here a bit longer than I intended for you.'

'Oh no! Can't you move me somewhere else? Please.'

'No, I can't,' he said pouring her a cup of hot soup. 'Here, take this. It'll warm you up.'

'Do you know what it's like down here all alone? It's cruel and barbaric. I can't take much more.'

'You'll have to!' he snapped. 'I can't do anything about it. You've still got some brandy, have you?'

'Yes. It helps keep the cold out. What's happening? Is Peter bringing the ransom, or Ian?'

'Don't know which one, but they're making trouble over it. If I get another fiasco like last night I shall call the whole thing off! If they had followed the rules last night you could have been free today – but no, they had to call in hoards of police at Bridgnorth.'

'What happened?'

'I won't go into details. Suffice to say I never got the money and you're still here until I do get it. I've got to lay a new ransom trail for them to follow. So I'm spending the night down here with you. I shall sleep up on the next platform, but I shall be gone before dawn. I'll leave the lamps burning.' He climbed back on the ladder. 'Goodnight.'

Then he was gone, climbing up to the next platform, and Julia sank back into her sleeping bag, hoping someone would rescue her soon… before she died without anyone knowing where she was.

Chapter Seventeen

After the IRA bombings the Greater Manchester police were stretched to the limit and Kennon felt his resources dwindling. The kidnapping did not seem quite so important now, especially after six days had passed without a positive result.

Seagrove was not the kidnapper, and Kennon was sure he wasn't the Panther either. He pulled into the Hazel Grove filling station at 9 a.m. with Sergeants Boyd and Roberts to begin a thorough search for a woman's signet ring. Using still photographs from the CCTV tape they were able to trace the direction of the ring thrown out the back of the van. Allowing for bounce it would have hardly rolled far.

They searched under the front hedge among a collection of sweet papers, drink cartons and empty cigarette packets that had been blown under by the wind and after twenty minutes they found it. The ring had a single emerald, oval-shaped and beautifully cut, set in 18-carat gold.

'This must be Julia Woodward's ring,' Kennon said. 'Her brother says he can identify it. So, she came this way three nights ago. I think Kidsgrove is looking more likely than ever.'

'A redundant coal mine seems almost farcical to me, sir. How the devil would the kidnapper know about it if it's been closed ten years?'

'I've no idea, Roberts. He could be an ex-miner or an industrial archaeology buff like me. But I didn't know it was there myself. Take the wheel, Boyd.'

'We take the right fork here, sir, for Macclesfield,' Boyd said climbing behind the wheel. 'We should be there in half an hour.'

They set off down the road for Macclesfield. The grey sky had parted to allow some sun to break through and as they crossed the misty dales into Staffordshire their minds were preoccupied. After six days they all feared that Julia Woodward must by now be murdered. But it was the Black Panther that gave them the most worry.

'We are absolutely sure, are we, sir, that the kidnapper is the Black Panther?' Roberts inquired. 'We still have no proof.'

'We don't have a bloody name either, Roberts, but you can take my word the kidnapper is the Black Panther.'

Five miles further on, the short wave radio crackled with Sergeant Walker's voice. 'Manchester CID for DCI Kennon.'

Kennon unclipped the microphone. 'DCI Kennon here. Come in, Ted.'

'George. There's been an accident at Macclesfield. A petrol tanker has turned over.'

'That's all we need. OK Ted, thanks. By the way, we found the girl's signet ring. We are continuing to Kidsgrove. Over.'

'If we had a name,' Roberts continued, 'we might find a bloody parking ticket with an address. It's as though the bloke doesn't exist. No record whatsoever.'

'He could have changed his name or just never got caught,' Boyd replied. 'That's the difference. This man is something special, the likes of which we've never seen before.'

'Changing his name wouldn't make any difference,' Kennon observed. 'It's the identity that's important. You can't change identity. The problem is tracing it. Doctor Erwin was right. We're dealing with a pathological criminal in a permanent state of paranoia. He wears a mask to disguise himself, but he also uses it to become someone else. He becomes a fantasy of his own imagination, which takes him over.'

'If we find this hidden mine shaft or drain, or whatever, with Julia Woodward in it, we shall have to take her out, and the ransom is stopped. Right, sir?' Roberts inquired.

'Yes. Go on.'

'It's then almost certain the Panther will vanish.'

'No one can just vanish, Roberts. But it will make our job easier if we catch him whilst he's still trying to extract the ransom. My biggest fear is how the victim will survive down a deep shaft, maybe a hundred feet underground, without suffering hypothermia. Logically, she shouldn't survive more than two or three days.'

'And this is the fifth day,' Boyd said. 'If we knew the company that did the mine conversion we might have a better chance of rescue.'

'I'm ahead of you, Boyd. I did some digging and found out the contractors who built the site. It wasn't easy going back ten years. It was a Lancashire firm. Bathpool Park, it's now called. I asked if they could send me a list of all the men who worked on it.'

'That was smart thinking, sir. Have you got the list?'

'I have. It came this morning. It has more than 300 names on it with addresses. I haven't checked it yet.' Kennon took the list from his briefcase and handed it to Roberts on the back seat.

'Take a look at that, Roberts. See if you can see a name there that might ring a bell. A known offender, maybe.'

Roberts took the list. 'Shouldn't be too difficult. Blimey, there's a few foreigners on it! There's a Shultz, a Schmitt, a Casserani, and here's one I can't even pronounce... This Lancashire firm wasn't a POW camp, by any chance?'

'It might have been. Just keep looking, Roberts.'

'It's possible a lot of these names could be men working on the lump to avoid tax.'

'What difference does that make?' Boyd asked.

'They give a false name and a false address. I know a bloke who did it everywhere he worked. It's quite common. I'm surprised the company let you have this list, sir.'

'I told them I'm not interested in any illegal workers. I spoke to the manager and he told me the place was converted from the Nelson mine in 1965. He's trying to find me a plan, but he believes there were three shafts left in place for ventilation and maintenance.'

'Who does the maintenance?' Roberts asked.

'I've no idea. I never asked him. But I would imagine it's the local authority's responsibility. Steady on, Boyd – not so fast.'

Boyd negotiated the sharp bends in the road just before Macclesfield. He was driving fast and as he came out the bend he slowed a fraction, but it still wasn't enough. The tanker loomed up large and he hit the brake, screeching to a stop. He ended up sideways alongside the overturned petrol tanker, which had slewed across the road with fuel running out.

The three detectives stared incredulously at the two traffic cops coming towards them, one of them carrying a danger sign. He walked past to place the triangular sign in the middle of the road while his colleague came to the car and Boyd wound down the window.

'A bit bloody late with the warning!' Boyd said.

'Sorry about that, sir. We've only just arrived. The driver's stuck in the cab. It looks like he lost control. There's no other vehicle involved. We're going to have to close this road off to traffic. Where are you headed for?'

Boyd flashed his warrant card. 'Manchester CID. We're on our way to Kidsgrove.'

'CID? I do apologise, gentlemen. Can we be of assistance? I'm Sergeant Davidson. I can get a traffic car here in no time. Is it urgent?'

'Very urgent!' Kennon replied. 'Is there no way we can get round this obstacle?'

'No, sir. Not on this road. You could turn around for Prestbury, but it will make a long-winded journey. Let me get you a traffic car, sir. It will be quicker.'

'No thanks, Sergeant. We need an unmarked car. We'll turn around. Prestbury, you say?'

'Yes sir. If you go back half a mile, take the left fork. You'll see the sign.'

Boyd reversed up the grass verge with a bump and turned the car around as the traffic cops held back oncoming traffic. There was a strong smell of petrol fumes from the overturned tanker carried on the prevailing wind.

'I wouldn't light a match within a mile of this place,' Roberts remarked as they headed back the way they came.

'How the devil did the driver manage to turn that over?' Kennon said as they sped down the road. 'Watch your speed, Boyd. We don't want to end up like that tanker.'

'Yes, sir. Did you bring a map with you, by any chance?'

'No, I didn't. I assumed you knew the way.'

'Not on this route I don't,' Boyd said. He took the left fork for the village of Prestbury down a twisting narrow country road.

Two miles of clipping the hedgerows, and they went straight through Prestbury to a place called Kirkleyditch, where they came to a stop. The road sign pointed straight on for Alderley Edge and left for Nether Alderley. 'What do you reckon?' Boyd asked. 'Left or straight on?'

'Alderley Edge sounds familiar,' Roberts said. 'I've never heard of the other place.'

'Straight on it is, then,' Boyd said, accelerating away. Two miles on, they were confounded by a maze of country lanes with village names coming up they had never heard of.

They tracked the lanes from Alderley Edge to Knutsford for over half an hour moving further away until they arrived at a junction of the A50 at Parkgate. The road sign pointed left for Congleton and right for Macclesfield.

'Turn left, Boyd!' said an exasperated George Kennon. 'We should have entrusted ourselves to the traffic division.'

'You know where we are, sir?'

'Yes! Bloody Parkgate – ten miles off course.'

'Right sir. Left it is.'

'Look out!' Kennon shouted as Boyd pulled out.

The driver of a green Austin A40 sounded his horn as he came straight on and swerved round them, missing them by a whisker. But in the instant that he passed, the eyes of the three detectives fell on the face of a man whose description was imprinted on their memories. Although made less conspicuous by the flat cap he wore, it matched that of the Panther's.

'By God! Did you recognise him?' Kennon blurted.

'I should bloody say so!' Boyd replied as he found the gears and accelerated away.

'Did you get a good look at him, Roberts?'

'I did sir. Was it him? Was that the Panther?'

'I'd bet my bloody pension on it! That was the Black Panther.'

'He must be heading for Kidsgrove! I shall have to put my foot down, sir.'

Boyd accelerated down the A50 flashing his lights on the single carriageway for everyone to move over. The chase was on for the man who had been sighted dozens of times but never identified in person.

The Panther knew they were police. There was no doubt about it. He knew the instant he passed they were CID detectives looking for him. He had no choice but to change direction, and as he reached the Holmes Green roundabout he turned right for the M6 and filtered into the heavy traffic going into Staffordshire.

'He's gone onto the motorway!' Boyd declared narrowly closing the gap.

'Follow him! Keep him in sight, Boyd.' Kennon reached for the radio. 'He can't outrun us in that thing. CID Stafford Division. DCI Kennon of Manchester. Come in, please!' Kennon called on the short wave transmitter.

'Divisional Headquarters, CID Stafford,' the radio crackled. 'Sergeant Bull. Come in, Chief Inspector.'

'Black Panther suspect is heading your way on the M6 approaching exit 16. He's driving a green Austin A40, registration TTV something. We are chasing him! Over.'

'Message received. I repeat, Black Panther in green Austin A40. Is suspect armed?'

'I should bloody think so!' Kennon replied.

'Thank you, Chief Inspector. I'm putting a call out for cars on all exits. Over.'

The Panther was driving flat out at 75 mph. He had seen the car chasing him as he joined the motorway. Now he had no choice but to outrun them. He swept past exit 16 for Kidsgrove, and carried straight on pushing his speed past 80 mph. Keeping his foot pressed hard down on the pedal he passed the heavy freight lorries going into the Potteries, heading for Stoke-on-Trent. He cursed at having to miss this exit as he passed by at 85 mph and went straight on for Stafford.

Now he was beginning to sweat as he looked in his mirror and saw the black Rover following in hot pursuit. The gap was closing as the two cars sped down the motorway in the outside lane. Boyd was constantly flashing his lights and sounding his horn as everything moved over. It was the greyhound chasing the hare as both drivers pushed the speed still further, and soon the two cars were touching 90 mph.

The gap closed and Wilson was pondering whether to come off at Stafford. He knew that if he kept to the motorway he'd soon have more than one police car on his tail. He ignored the indicator and cut recklessly across three lanes, heading for exit 14.

'He's coming off!' Boyd said excitedly as he tried to cross the lanes. The inside traffic kept him penned in until he managed to nudge into the centre lane Then he noticed a car transporter coming up on his inside and he was forced to slow still more to let it go by.

The Panther had just entered the long slip road when he saw an opportunity to dummy, and he crossed back over the white road stripes back onto the motorway right in front of the transporter. There was a long blast of the horn from the driver, and the two vehicles were almost touching.

Boyd was running neck and neck alongside the car transporter with the long sixty-foot trailer blocking his exit. He was forced to slow down still more, and those vital seconds cost him the chase. He fell behind the transporter and crossed to the slip road to come off the motorway.

'Where'd he go? We've lost him!' he said, as they travelled down the slip road.

'He's gone over the flyover!' Roberts shouted, looking out the rear window. 'He's in front of that bloody car transporter!'

Two police cars were waiting at the exit on both lanes with flashing indicators and their radios crackled to a frantic call. 'DCI Kennon, Manchester! Clear the road! Suspect has gone over flyover! Clear the road!'

Boyd flashed his lights and slowed dramatically, keeping his eye on the outside car. It pulled over just as he arrived and came to a stop holding everything up behind him. Kennon leaned out the window to shout a message to the astonished traffic cops.

'Suspect has gone straight on over the flyover!'

Then Boyd sped away for the large roundabout below the flyover and kept going back up the slip road to rejoin the motorway. Now the chase was back on, with the two Stafford cars following up in hot pursuit.

Back on the motorway, the cars were hurtling towards Birmingham twenty miles on and Kennon was back on the radio. 'West Midlands Divisional HQ. Come in please.' The radio crackled in reply. 'West Mercia Police. Walsall Central. Over.'

'This is DCI Kennon of Manchester CID. We are on the M6 chasing Black Panther suspect in green Austin A40 heading your way. Registration TTV something. Over!'

'West Mercia Walsall Division. Message received. Putting call out for all cars. Over.'

'I've done it now.' Kennon chuckled. 'I've got the entire West Mercia force out of bed.'

'Do them good, sir,' Roberts replied. 'Where do you reckon the suspect will head for now?'

'I don't know, Roberts. Where do you reckon?'

'West Bromwich, sir. It's right on the motorway. He won't want to stay on this road any longer than he can help.'

The radio suddenly burst forth with a cacophony of messages crackling over the airwaves. 'It sounds like we've stirred up a hornets' nest,' Kennon said, turning it down. 'Must be every traffic division in the West Midlands.'

'They've got him in their sights now by the sound of it, sir. My bet is he will dump the car and go on foot until he pinches another one. We were lucky to spot him.'

'Damned lucky! That overturned tanker gave us more than we bargained for.'

'There's no sign of him,' Boyd said, as he drove at maximum speed watching the two traffic cars in his mirror.

The Panther was driving like the devil, with his plans gone haywire. As he pushed his speed to the limits the signs for Telford and Cannock loomed up. He passed exit 12 for Cannock, undecided where to come off. His well-ordered strategy was in tatters.

He was involved laying the last of the ransom tapes and making sure everything was ready for the handover. He was now at the critical stage of the handover. He had overrun his time for holding the hostage, and it worried him. Now he had the police on his tail and he had to shake them off at all costs.

The overhead signs loomed up for the West Midlands. This was familiar country to him. Wolverhampton, West Bromwich, Dudley and Walsall. The names conjured up the Black Country, rich in diversity and industrial heritage, all the things he could identify with. Even though he was a Yorkshireman, and a criminal at that, he could still believe he was a working man. Industry was in his blood. Here were his roots in the country he cherished.

In the distance he heard the wail of police sirens as the sign for Walsall came up for the next exit at Maw Green. The traffic was thick with freight lorries as he moved across the lanes. He was conscious of police cars waiting at the exits. He would have to chance it, even if it meant ploughing right through them.

'Here we go...' He began his move among the traffic heading into the slip road and was glad to be leaving the motorway. The distance signs flashed by as the exit loomed up in yards. There was no sign of the police waiting for him. With a bit of luck he could still beat them. He never saw the Rover closing up fast behind him.

He left the slip road and entered the mainstream traffic going into Walsall when he saw two police motorcyclist suddenly move out behind him with sirens wailing. His eyes darted left and right for a turn-off. The traffic was moving briskly on a dual carriage-way and he began to overtake, forcing his way over and weaving in and out, with the two traffic cops in hot pursuit.

He was heading towards the city centre doing 50 mph when he saw traffic lights up ahead on green. The traffic was streaming across as he approached the lights, then with less than twenty yards to go, they suddenly changed to red. Tail lights came on in front and he was forced to slam hard on the brakes. The driver behind did likewise, but too late to avoid a collision, and he was rammed into the car in front.

Tyres squealed on the tarmac as the gaps rapidly closed, and half a dozen cars collided bringing two lanes of traffic to a halt in a tangle of crumpled metal and smashed lights.

Incensed drivers shouted at the man leaving his car, and one even tried to stop him before he went leaping over the roadside railings into the midst of astonished pedestrians.

He ran, clutching the duffel bag to his chest. It contained his shotgun, but he had no desire to use the weapon on a busy street. He dodged in and out of pedestrians, charging them aside as he searched for some sort of sanctuary. He was aware he was among the Asian community in the Muslim area of the city, and it offered the opportunity for an escape. There was a mosque ahead of him across the road, with worshippers going in and, with the wail of police sirens in his ears, his first instinct was to join them.

He ran across the busy street clogged with traffic making direct for the large mosque. Shielded by the worshippers, he disappeared inside. There was no one to stop him as he joined the faithful, falling to his knees and copying their rituals. No one noticed they had an unbeliever among them, and even if they did they welcomed all newcomers to their faith. He was safe among them, and yet he despised them.

No policeman could enter a mosque, and they waited outside as a small crowd gathered to watch. The Rover was stuck in a traffic jam as vehicles were squeezing round the abandoned Austin, while the two traffic cops were trying to deal with it.

Kennon's plan to search Kidsgrove was looking doubtful. It was 11.30 a.m. and they were stuck in Walsall chasing a phantom driver who had outrun them and disappeared.

'We should have left him to the traffic cops,' Kennon grumbled. 'Get us out of here, Boyd, for God's sake.'

'He's abandoned the car, guv. He's caused this bloody pile-up and done a runner,' Boyd replied as he inched through the traffic towards the lights.

'He'll get caught. There's enough police to look for him. We gave them the lead.'

'See the mosque over the road, sir?' Roberts said. 'By the looks of it, that's where he is. Shall we jump out and assist while we're here?'

Kennon looked at the police helmets among the crowd outside the mosque. 'That's an apt way of putting it, Roberts. But if you say so. We're getting out, Boyd. Pick us up as soon as you can.'

The two men jumped out the car and went ahead on foot, making their way to the mosque. They were eager to see the Panther caught and felt compelled to assist in his arrest. They crossed the road to the mosque when a gunshot was fired inside and pandemonium broke. Worshippers came running out, shouting Islamic imprecations, and the waiting police were forced to enter while Kennon and Roberts instinctively followed.

Inside they were met by a gabble of dialects from clerics and worshippers waving their arms about, excoriating the gunman who had defiled their morning worship. The two detectives searched the faces milling around and Kennon addressed one of the bearded clerics in long robes.

'Excuse me, sir. Chief Inspector Kennon, Manchester CID,'

Kennon said, flashing his warrant card. 'Where did the gunman go, sir?'

'This way, Chief Inspector; follow me.'

'Roberts!' Kennon called. 'Bring a couple of constables and follow me.'

'This way, lads!' Roberts beckoned as they followed the cleric through the elaborate gilded mosque decorated with Islamic texts.

They went down a passageway to a back door and stepped outside into a car park at the back of some shops. It was a large site with a hundred cars or more parked up, giving the fugitive ample choice.

'We'll have to make a search,' Kennon said. 'But remember, he's armed and dangerous. We'll split up. If you see him call out. Constables, call up some assistance.'

The constables called for back-up over their radios as they split up to search individually. They moved cautiously among the vehicles, half expecting their quarry to jump out with his shotgun. The police radios crackled with beat bobbies homing in.

The car park was ideal for the Panther. Using his bunch of keys, he seized another car and watched cautiously at the police helmets bobbing above the vehicle roofs. Then Roberts saw him as he started to move and when the car pulled out he made a run at it shouting at him to halt.

The Panther was ready for it and he aimed his semi-automatic pistol out the window straight at the detective and fired two rapid shots. Roberts ran headlong into two bullets and he fell sprawling to the ground. His colleagues heard the shots and came rushing to his aid.

One of the constables gave chase as the car drove straight through the flimsy wooden barrier and out on to the road. The attendant shouted a few choice words as the PC noted the car registration mentally as it was disappearing up the road. He scribbled it down on a pad, 'Beige Austin Allegro', along with the registration number, and passed the details over his radio.

'Call an ambulance!' Kennon shouted, kneeling beside his colleague.

'We lost him, sir,' Roberts groaned. 'The bastard tried to kill me.'

'All right, Roberts, take it easy. Where are you hit?'

'In the chest. But it don't feel too bad.'

'You lie steady. I said he was ruthless. The Walsall constabulary can have him now.'

They waited just eight minutes for an ambulance. The paramedics loaded Roberts inside and Kennon watched him depart for the Royal Hospital. More traffic cars arrived, and all the details of the stolen car were logged before the cars sped away, making for the biggest manhunt yet. Police radios crackled calling up extra men as the hunt resumed at a new pace.

Then Boyd pulled into the busy road and called out to his boss. 'Over here, sir!'

'Roberts has been hit,' Kennon said, climbing in. 'He's on his way to hospital. I think he'll live.'

They sat listening to the crackle of police radios flashing messages of a stolen beige Austin Allegro. 'Suspect is armed and dangerous. Apprehend him at all cost.' The messages were going out over the airwaves to all units.

'Where to now, sir?' Boyd asked. 'The hospital?'

'Any other time I'd say yes. But we've got a young woman to find. Roberts is in good hands. Kidsgrove, Boyd.'

Boyd pulled away and entered the mainstream traffic heading back to the motorway. The time was 1 p.m. They were almost seventy miles off their route thanks to the overturned tanker at Macclesfield. Even if it was a blessing in disguise, Kennon wasn't too pleased. Every hour Julia Woodward was missing was an hour too long.

Chapter Eighteen

'This looks like it, guv,' Boyd said as they turned into Boathorse Lane and entered Bathpool Park at 2.30 p.m. They entered the large park from the east side of the railway and drove slowly up the lane that crossed the rail tunnel marked by two low walls.

'This is a park?' Kennon said. 'I've never seen such a desolate place.'

Without a soul in sight they went across the barren field dissected by the railway cutting until they saw they weren't the only ones there. The presence of a large drain-cleaning tanker operating at the spillway gave cause for concern.

'This doesn't look too good,' Boyd said, pulling up alongside the tanker.

They climbed out and showed their warrant cards to one of the two-man crew operating the levers. 'Manchester CID. What's going on?' Kennon shouted above the noise of the compressor.

'We're maintenance, extracting the silt from the drainage tunnel. We do it twice a year,' the man replied.

'Where does the silt come from?'

The man beckoned them away from the vehicle. 'It runs out the slag heaps. This used to be a coal mine years back. All these hillocks you see are grassed over slag heaps with saplings planted on them.'

'How long does the job take?'

'About three hours. We're almost finished.' The man called to his mate in the cab, 'All right, Harry! Turn it off! We suck it out by hose, Inspector. We must take out a ton of thick sludge every time.'

They walked back as the flexible hose was being withdrawn out of the manhole by hydraulic pump into its metal casing. 'This is the spillway shaft, Inspector, known as the Glory Hole, from all the rubbish chucked down it. Now and again we clear it out. It's usually old wood and scrap metal.'

'Can I take a look down?'

'Of course you can. It's clear now. Here, borrow the torch. You won't see much without it.'

Kennon walked to the concrete pillbox with its railing removed and climbed up three steps to where the manhole cover was open. He peered down into a black hole probing with the torch. At the very bottom he saw a twisted bicycle wheel among the pieces of scrap wood and metal that had been pushed through the narrow side opening. At the very bottom Kennon could hear water running through the tunnel from the reservoir overflow. A dank fetid smell wafted up as he probed with the torch in the vain hope of discovering something.

It was inconceivable that a young woman could be kept down here. He turned to his colleague and handed Boyd the torch. 'Take a look,' he said, shaking his head.

'I'm told there's three shafts here,' he said to the maintenance men. 'Where are they?'

'Three? I never knew that. Did you, Harry?'

'No, I didn't. There's only ever been two as far I know. The other one is across the railway up that bank. That's a deep one, that is.'

'Can we take a look down?' Kennon asked.

'Of course, but I can't think what you'll see down it. What is it you're looking for, Inspector?'

'A woman! That surprises you, eh? You must know about the kidnapping in Manchester last week.'

'Stone me! And you think she might be down here?'

'It's possible. Is there a ladder down this other shaft?'

'There is. But you're not thinking of going down, are you?'

'Why not?'

'Because it ain't healthy, Inspector. There's a build-up of gas down there.'

'I thought you said you clear out the rubbish now and again.'

'We have to test it first with a meter. Sometimes it's safe and sometimes it's not. It depends on the build-up of methane. I'll fetch the meter and we'll take a look.'

Kennon called Boyd over while the maintenance worker fetched the meter from his cab and the men walked on for about fifty yards across the park to the second shaft on the opposite railway bank. The workmen opened up the heavy manhole cover for the CID men and they peered down into blackness. They were handed a torch each but all they could see was the ladder running down the wall into darkness. Below them the sound of water could be heard running through the tunnel. Boyd shouted a distress call in the hope of an answer, but only his echo resounded back with a hollow ring to it.

Then the meter was lowered, tied to a roll of cable. It went down only twenty feet before the test alarm beeped and a red light flashed. It was hauled back up and the gauge revealed a build-up of noxious gases.

'If there's anyone down there, Inspector, I reckon they're most likely dead by now,' the maintenance worker said. 'This is the deepest shaft and it's more likely for gas to accumulate in. It's rare to get a sounding down the Glory Hole. I don't think we've ever had one.'

'Well, gas or no gas, I'm going down!' Kennon pulled a large handkerchief from his pocket and tied it across his mouth.

'You can't go down there, sir!' the workman said with astonishment. 'It's dangerous. You may not come back up.'

'I'll come back, don't you worry.'

Kennon's voice was muffled as he waved away all the objections. Boyd knew nothing would stop him as he climbed on the ladder.

He looked down with the aid of the torch and began his descent, gripping the ladder tight as he went down. The handkerchief sucked into his mouth as he took shallow breaths and when he reached the first platform halfway down he stepped onto it and felt it move.

Now he knew what the miners experienced as he leaned over the edge of the platform and beamed the torch light down the shaft. The second section of ladder had been prised from the wall and was lying six feet out of reach against the opposite side. This was as far as he could go.

'Shit! The bloody ladder's gone!' He stared down and gave a vain call. 'Julia! Julia Woodward! Are you there?'

The shout was slightly muffled but it carried an echo, and

that's all there was – an echo. He tore off the handkerchief and shouted again. 'Is anyone there?'

He waited in a vain hope for an answer. Above the silence there was only the sound of water flowing in the tunnel twenty feet below.

Kennon was crestfallen as the last ray of hope dwindled. He began his slow climb back up the shaft as anxious faces watched from above.

'He's coming up,' Boyd said. 'It looks pretty well hopeless.'

They helped him off the ladder when he reached the top and he sat down beside the manhole with a visible sweat on his brow.

'I ran out of ladder,' he said with a gulp of fresh air. 'The last section has either fallen off or been removed. I can't see any reason why, though. Kids wouldn't be able to lift this manhole. Are you sure you know of no other shaft?' he said to the workmen.

'Positive. I daresay we could find out back at the depot. But then, what difference would it make now? You've seen for yourself what it's like down there.'

'I couldn't smell any gas. I'd still like to know where the third shaft is. Is it possible it's up that high ridge of ground over there?' Kennon said, pointing towards the thick wooded hill that flanked the eastern side of the park.

'I suppose it might be, but you'll have a tough job finding it, I reckon.'

'OK, lads. Thanks anyway. If you find out back at the depot, ring this number.' Kennon gave his card with the Incident Room number on it. 'Much obliged.'

The manhole cover was closed and they came away, disillusioned and dejected.

'What now, sir?' Boyd asked as they walked back to the car and watched the tanker pull out. 'We seem to have drawn a blank. Shall we take a look up there?'

'We ought to,' Kennon replied, looking at the rain clouds forming. 'But even if we find the other shaft I doubt whether we can go down it.'

'But we can still look for it. There might be a girl down there who is relying on us.'

'You feel the same as I do, Boyd. I've been a policeman all my life and I can't think of a case that has affected me like this one. It's as though I feel personally responsible for her fate.'

'Well, then, let's get up there.'

A black cloud drifted over and the first spots of rain came down. 'Why not? Damn the rain! We will go up there!'

'It could be a tough climb in the wet. Let's see how far we can get in the car.'

They got into the car and pulled out of the park, going back towards the town. Half a mile on they saw a sign that read 'Coal-Pit Hill', and they turned off up a winding road climbing steadily through dense woods. As they neared the top, the sky turned black and the rain fell. They went along the crest of the hill with wipers flapping when suddenly they ran out of road. It stopped abruptly at a set of gates.

They stared bleakly at a steel fence blocking their path with locked gates topped with barbed wire. A 'Keep Out' warning sign hung on the gates and mounted above it was a rusting sign that said 'Nelson Colliery, Kidsgrove'.

'That's put paid to our investigation,' Boyd said, staring at the fence. 'We should have walked up the other side.'

'If we're in the right place,' said Kennon. 'How the devil did the Panther get in? There must be another opening along the fence.'

'I shouldn't think so. Those warning signs on the gate are there for a reason.'

'There must be a way in. The fence can only go so far before it ends. It must end somewhere.'

'Yes, and I've got a good idea where. Probably on the edge of a bloody great cliff!'

'No such thing, Boyd. More likely it goes down the other side of the hill as far as the reservoir.'

'Same thing, guv. We're stuck. Unless you want to swim the reservoir. As for me, I can't swim.'

They sat there watching the rain come down in sheets, neither volunteering to get out. 'Polo mint, guv?' Boyd said, taking a tube out his pocket.

'No thanks. If this bloody rain would stop, I'm willing to go along the fence. We've got about one hour of daylight left.'

'Shall we go back then and climb the hill on the other side?'

'If it was dry. But after this downpour it will be too slippery.'

They gazed up at the clouds beginning to part and a pale sun filtered through as the rain slowed to a drizzle. 'There's our cue, Boyd. It's stopping.'

They climbed out the car, pulling the collars of their raincoats up, gave a swift look at the sky and set off. They went up to the gates locked with padlock and chain and could see where the road, overgrown with weeds, continued through the colliery towards a brick building.

They were looking at the transformer house that had once supplied power. It was the only remains of the pithead. The winding towers were dismantled and the site, turned over to nature, was running wild.

'What a tragic sight,' Kennon said, peering through the gates. 'It's hard to believe that hundreds of men must have come through these gates every day to dig out the coal that we rely on. I wonder how much longer the industry will last?'

'Not long, I reckon,' Boyd said. 'The power stations are turning to gas.'

'The price of progress.'

They turned away and set off along a footpath following the fence along the east slopes of the hill overlooking the Trent Canal. They walked about a quarter of a mile, getting nicked by the bristles and thorns growing all along the fence, until they came to the Trent Viaduct, which literally barred them from going any further.

The curving viaduct crossed the River Trent and they had a clear view of the dales. On the other side of the viaduct was a canal that wound its way towards the river and disappeared behind the hill. If they had followed it they would have seen the canal disappear into a tunnel through the hill, and any Ordnance Survey map would have told them that the tunnel led to the subterranean canal beneath Bathpool Park.

They stood looking across a horseshoe valley spanned by the viaduct, neither quite comprehending what they were looking at in the absence of any landmarks.

'I wouldn't mind betting that canal comes from the old colliery,' Kennon said. 'The drainage water must go somewhere. But we've done enough. Let's get back to the car, Boyd. There's nothing more we can do.'

They turned and walked back to the footpath, retracing their steps, and Kennon endowed his sergeant with a piece of industrial archaeology to lighten the moment.

'Up there is the pithead where the winding towers stood over the deepest shaft. It probably dates back over a century when they had boys hauling carts along the tunnels. Hard to believe a coal mine once stood on this spot, don't you think, Boyd?'

'It is. Why do you reckon it was closed, guv?'

'The coal ran out. That's the only reason a mine closes.'

They reached the gates and stood looking through the over-grown brambles with the light rapidly going. 'We ought to be able to get in there,' Kennon said, still clinging to a piece of hope. 'She's in there. I can feel it.'

'But we don't know for certain, guv? We only assume she is.'

'Where else can she be? We've found this place through police work and now it's our job to take it further. I feel this is the place. When I went down that middle shaft I could sense it. If the ladder hadn't gone I would have gone to the very bottom – gas or no bloody gas! Every fibre of my being tells me this is the place where Julia Woodward is hidden.'

'OK, supposing you're right. We're going to have to get a team of engineers and frogmen to descend the main shaft. We can't go down it.'

'Why the hell not? If the Panther can go down it, why can't we? There must be a bloody ladder down there. Why can't we go down?'

'Well, you won't like this, guv, but I have to say I reckon the girl is dead. She's been down there too long to survive. Can you imagine what it's done to her? The sheer terror of being held underground would be enough to kill her. Do you honestly believe the Panther has been feeding her – because I don't. And what's it going to do to his ransom plans if he knows we've found her? He'll abandon the whole thing and go into hiding. Then we'll never get him, and in a year from now he will do the same thing all over again.'

Kennon fell into a momentary silence as they walked to the car. 'It's a good argument, Boyd, I'll give you that, but I just can't accept the girl is dead.'

'Believe me, guv, I wish she wasn't. And I can't see the Super giving us what we'd need to do a search. It will soon be dark and we'd need floodlights up here, a mobile generator, and all sorts of paraphernalia. The chief won't wear it without concrete evidence.'

'You're right. I just can't admit the girl is dead. I have to believe there's hope. But there will be another ransom demand tonight, and we will be compelled to follow whatever trail has been laid. And the Panther will be watching us from up here.'

'Then we have to get back to HQ and prepare for the call. Because if we're here and the trail leads somewhere else, we're going to have egg all over our faces. We'll have blown all our chances.'

They got in the car and Kennon switched on the short wave radio, fiddling with the frequency until a familiar voice responded.

'Manchester CID Central receiving on 208. Sergeant Walker. Come in, George.'

'Ted! I'm in Kidsgrove with Sergeant Boyd. Have you had any news from West Mercia police on the Panther?'

'Yes, George. He got clean away from Walsall this afternoon in a stolen car. There's been no other report of him since.'

'Have you had any news on DS Roberts, who was gunned down?'

'We have, George. They removed two bullets from his chest and spleen and he's expected to make a full recovery.'

'Pleased to hear it. Is there anything to chase up? Any new developments?'

'Nothing at the moment.'

'We're at Bathpool Park, Kidsgrove, where I'm sure Julia Woodward is being held in a drain. But we cannot reach her. We are coming back in... Over.'

'Hold on, George, the chief wants a word.'

'George! I've got some bad news. Sir Charles Woodward died this afternoon at three o'clock. Both sons were at his side. Come back asap! There are complications.'

Chapter Nineteen

'This is the room, Mr Field. You have your own toilet and shower next door, but I don't allow animals. Will it be suitable?' The landlady was unconcerned as she showed the stranger round the bedsit at 21 Nobes Avenue in the small town of Biddulph, just five miles from Kidsgrove.

'It'll do me, Mrs Bainthorp. I can't say how long I shall need it, but I'll take it for a week to begin with. Five pounds, you say?' The Panther handed over a week's rent to the 55-year-old spinster. 'I shan't be here tonight. I've got a night shift to do at the factory in Fenton.'

'That's fine by me, Mr Field. You'll have your own key. What time do you start work?'

'Ten o'clock. "The graveyard shift", I call it. Still, it's not a bad job. I can't complain. I'll be back by 6.30 a.m. and most probably tumble into bed, dog-tired.'

'I'll leave you to it then. I think we're due some rain by the look of it.'

'It don't look none too good,' he said, looking out the window. 'See you later then.'

The landlady went back downstairs leaving him to make his final preparations for the ransom drop. The car was dumped five miles away in Tunstall and he would be on foot for the entire operation. He had laid the trail just hours after leaving Walsaw and giving the police the slip and had managed to do it without interruptions. He regretted shooting the night foreman in Dudley but he had no choice. The man should not have approached him as he was laying tapes in the phone box.

It was the same with all the shootings. He never killed intentionally. It was just bad luck if people got in his way. The shotgun he carried on his raids was essential to help him take control. He could use just a pistol, he told himself, but it would not have the same effect as the 12-bore.

As he unpacked his bag on the bed he thought about the final night at Kidsgrove. He could not keep the girl much longer. Already he had gone three nights over what he planned, and though she was well hidden it could only be a matter of time before she was discovered. But his plan was simple. The final instructions would be taped on a torch secured to the bars of the spillway. They would read: *Drop bag through the open manhole down shaft. Go home and wait for next call.*

It couldn't be plainer. A section of bars would be removed and the manhole cover would be left open for the bag to be dropped down the spillway. A large holdall would not fit through the letter box opening. There was no ladder in the spillway for Woodward to follow down. Once the ransom was in his hands he would move quickly through the tunnel to the main shaft. He would inform the girl he had the money and she would be free within hours. Then he'd make his escape over the top of the hill in darkness.

If there were police in the area he would give them all the slip. They would be in cars watching the roads and he'd be away across the fields on foot. And if there were dogs, he would cross a canal or stream to lose them. It had never failed him yet.

The time was six o'clock and he turned on his transistor radio and tuned in to the BBC news bulletin while he prepared a meal. He already knew what the news would be as a sombre voice announced:

'A detective from Manchester CID was shot and wounded in Walsall this afternoon by the man widely believed to be the Black Panther. The incident occurred in a car park behind a Walsall mosque after a dramatic chase by three police forces down the M6 motorway. A spokesman for the West Mercia Police said the Panther ditched the stolen car he was driving and escaped by running into a mosque filled with worshipers. Police gave chase through the mosque and Detective Sergeant Roberts from Manchester CID was shot down as the man stole a second car to escape.

'It has been announced that Sir Charles Woodward died at three o'clock this afternoon in Manchester General Hospital. His second wife and two sons were at his bedside. It is now widely believed that the kidnap of Sir Charles's daughter, Julia Woodward, is the work of the Black Panther.'

The last bit of news was disturbing. How would this affect delivery of the ransom now? They could tell him to go to hell. But if they wanted to save their sister they would have to cooperate. Tonight he would have to travel light. There could be no shotgun, no tools and no extra baggage of any kind. He would take one flask of soup for the girl in the duffel bag, which he would transfer the money into for ease of carriage. The only weapon would be the pistol in his pocket, carried as a precaution.

He cooked himself bacon and eggs to be going on with, and marvelled at his skill at outfoxing the police. He couldn't be sure when his next meal would be and when he finally sat down to eat a raft of disturbing thoughts ran through his mind.

His past life flickered through his memory, dragging up things he'd rather forget about. And always, in the background, the spectre of failure haunted him. If everything went well tonight he hoped to move to Northumberland and take his wife and daughter on a short holiday to Scotland. He would give up his post office raids and let the Black Panther fade into memory.

Inside Manchester's CID building, Kennon's description of Bathpool Park sent shivers down the spines of hardened detectives. Most of them had dealt with murderers and rapists at some time, but trying to imagine the underground prison where Julia Woodward was held was something else.

Detective Constable Murray's face wore an expression of horror as the most obvious question being asked was, what evidence was there to support Kidsgrove.

'The café owners,' Kennon replied. 'They gave a description of the man that fits with all the others. He ordered a meal and then jumped up and left before it arrived. The envelopes found in the car at Stafford mark out a route to Kidsgrove, but the most compelling piece in my mind is the actual drainage system beneath Bathpool Park.'

'But it's still not concrete evidence, George,' Bradley insisted. 'You've been down there and had a good look, the same as DCI Morrison, and you've seen nothing positive.'

'But neither of us were able to look at the whole system. We only saw a fraction of it. Of all the locations we have investigated, Bathpool Park stands out as the most likely. It's hidden from view, for a start.'

'How did the Panther find it, then?'

'I don't know. But I have never seen anything like it. It's a mystery to me how anyone would know it's there. It's the sort of place the Panther would choose. We know the pump house on the moors was his first choice. It was isolated and out of use. But it could still be seen from the road. That was a bad choice for him.'

'So, how do you see his plans for the ransom?'

'I reckon he will give instructions for the ransom to be dropped down a shaft. But he won't be down there; that would be too simple. He will be watching from somewhere to see his instructions are carried out. Then, when the coast is clear, he will go down the spillway shaft to retrieve it. But he will exit from the main shaft up on the hill.'

'The non-existent one, you mean?'

'It exists all right. Sergeant Boyd and I came within a whisker of finding it.'

'How will he know when the coast is clear?'

'My bet is he'll have infrared binoculars to scan every hill around for the slightest movement. Once he goes down the shaft, anyone attempting to follow will get a stomach full of lead. All we can do once he's gone is go down and rescue the girl and make sure all roads are blocked.'

'Sounds feasible. But he could choose an entirely different place for the ransom to be delivered. In fact I think that's more likely. We cannot move until we get the ransom phone call,' Bradley asserted.

'No sir, but at least let us be ready for Kidsgrove.' Kennon walked to the map on the board and pointed to the small town thirty miles south of Manchester.

'This hill here, called Mow Cop. It's six miles from the town and high enough to receive clear radio signals. Whoever carries the ransom will have a one-way radio with throat microphone on his person to relay the instructions. He will have another one in his car, so we can track him wherever he is and be there quick. Not even the Panther can beat that.'

'But we've got another problem that's just arisen. Neither of the sons wants to go through with it. Their father's death has been a severe blow. It has set them against the idea of giving the Panther any ransom.'

'Jesus! Have they forgotten their sister already?'

'No, but I think they blame her for their father's death. I know it's unreasonable, but what can we do? Both of them are half convinced their sister is already dead, and I'm inclined to agree.'

'Well, I don't. Her survival instinct will withstand a far greater hardship than normal! We must foster the belief she is still alive!'

'I agree, but we can't force them into it. I have suggested a stand-in, one of us to take their place. In fact I believe it might be better. An armed man with a bullet-proof vest might be the answer.'

'I'll do it, sir,' Boyd said from across the room.

'I'll do it, sir! I'm doing a firearms course,' Detective Sergeant Macnally chimed in.

'What an eager bunch we've got here!' Bradley commented. 'Someone already trained in firearms would be better. We don't want anyone getting their head blown off.'

'We don't want a shooting match down there, either,' Kennon said. 'Let's get this thing into perspective. We've got a young woman to save. I think Ian Woodward can be persuaded. We will provide all the back-up he needs. A radio van on high ground at Mow Cop out of the Panther's range. On top of that we shall need around twenty men in positions all round the park to move in at a moment's notice.'

'Fine, if it's all done in the right place, but if it's not...'

'We don't do this single-handed, sir. We've got to share this with West Mercia and Staffordshire and probably the Derbyshire force. They will be the outer ring and they will have their own traps set up. We're up against the most formidable criminal it's ever been our misfortune to encounter. He's been loose for five years. It's time we brought him in.'

Kennon looked at his watch: seven o'clock. 'I will personally go to Bridlington Hall and encourage Ian Woodward to cooperate. I also suggest we have an incident room set up at Kidsgrove.'

'I'll say this for you, George, you certainly know how to organise,' Bradley said, walking over to look out of the window at the rain streaming down. 'We need to inform their divisional headquarters now before it's too late. Give them time to organise. We don't want to be accused by the media of being unprepared.'

At 9 p.m. the Panther left the house in Nobes Avenue for his final journey to Kidsgrove. Although there was no real need for all his Panther baggage, it came second nature to him to wear his combat jacket beneath his raincoat. He donned his cap and, with the duffel bag slung over his shoulder, he walked to the railway station five minutes away and stepped into a phone box outside.

He dialled the Bridlington number directly and waited patiently. The phone was picked up by the butler and then passed to Ian Woodward, still distressed over the loss of his father. 'Ian Woodward,' he answered.

The reply was short, in a West Indian accent. 'Go to phone box outside Denton Green Line Bus station and wait for call at midnight. Have money in bag as requested. No police. No tricks or death will come.'

'You bastard! I've just lost my father because of you!' Ian replied angrily.

'I am sorry. That was nothing to do with me. You must look to sister now.'

'I want confirmation my sister is still alive!'

'You shall have it.' There was a click on the line and Julia's voice came on. 'Ian, this is Julia. I am all right, just a bit cold and hungry. Do as he says, Ian. Go to the Denton phone box outside the bus station and wait for the call.'

The message had got through. The Panther stepped out of the box and hurled the cassette player onto some waste ground, and then he walked into the station to buy a ticket for Crewe.

He waited ten minutes for the train and boarded it along with a few passengers going out for an evening's entertainment. He had the misfortune to share a carriage with a Pakistani, who smiled graciously at him and attempted to make conversation.

'Hello, sir. You look wet,' the man said.

'What do you mean, I look wet?' the Panther retorted angrily.

'No offence, sir. I meant wet from rain.'

'You want to be careful how you speak the Queen's English.'

'I speak it very good. It is my second language.'

'Has to be, don't it! How else are you going to claim your welfare assistance?'

'I am working man like you, sir. I have never claimed welfare.'

'You might not, but all the rest of them do. What are you doing here?'

'I am working in car factory in Birmingham. I am proud to be British citizen. It is the mother country. We are an industrious people, that is why we choose to come here to the heart of British industry to live and work. We don't want handouts.'

The Panther didn't reply. He sat staring out the window, ignoring the man for the rest of the short journey until the train pulled into Crewe Central and he alighted on the platform. He left the busy station and walked to the town centre, where he entered an off-licence to purchase a half-bottle of brandy.

The man behind the counter had no notion of the identity of the customer he was serving, but he thought it odd the man was wearing two wristwatches. They were synchronised in order to give the exact time, and as a precaution against a stopped watch. This was just a part of the Panther's fastidious military discipline about security. Almost everything was duplicated against loss, from sticking plasters to hidden razor blades, lighters for lamps, and two wire-thin flexible saws secreted in his coat collar.

He left the off-licence, made his way through the town and found a café where he could while away an hour or more. His intention was to arrive back at Kidsgrove at midnight for the last phone call to Ian Woodward with more instructions.

He purchased a cup of tea and a bun and sat at a small table in the window where he could watch the world go by.

Two tartily dressed women were first to catch his eye. They swayed across the road on high heels, laughing and giggling, and entered a pub. They were shortly followed by two young West Indians, who seemed to be doing a kind of rumba as they danced along the street making erratic movements to a transistor radio. They bypassed the pub and went round the corner into an Indian restaurant, that other symbol of foreign enterprise the Panther detested.

There wasn't that much to do in Crewe. It was a railway town with plenty of clubs and pubs and a few cinemas, but it had everything Wilson desired. He had no need for nightclubs or casinos or expensive restaurants.

He was an outdoor man with a zest for dramatics, playing at soldiers using maps to track the enemy. He'd cut their communications and destroyed their base with home-made hand grenades. He made inquiries during his national service about joining the SAS, but he wasn't taken seriously.

He readily acknowledged he liked to jump out of bed in the middle of the night and grab a weapon. The army gave him a licence to kill and a desire to do something big. He bolstered his own confidence setting himself high goals to the extent of raising the criteria every time he had passed the previous goal.

At eleven o'clock the pubs emptied and he made his way back through the town, avoiding the drunks as far as possible. He approached one boisterous chucking-out, where a brawl was going on between half a dozen drunks, and found the pavement blocked. There were people watching and his only option was to cross the road just as a police patrol van arrived on the scene. Half a dozen coppers jumped out and began rounding up the trouble-makers and bundling them into the van.

As he stood watching the police at work, a big burly sergeant came along the pavement and grabbed him by the arm with a ferocious bark. 'You! Where are you going?'

'To t'station, Sergeant,' he answered in a Lancashire accent. 'Giz a lift!'

'You'll get my bloody boot up you if you don't move!' the sergeant said, pushing him off. 'Come along, you lot. Move along!'

He walked away, amazed at how the police failed to spot him despite all the photofits, and he entered the station at 11.30 to buy a ticket for Kidsgrove. The train meant a five-minute wait and he went aboard the slow shuttle, stopping at every station up the line. He got out at the small halt of Harding Wood, one stop short of Kidsgrove, and stepped into a phone box just before midnight.

Then he dialled the number he had written down for the public phone box at Denton.

The phone was picked up by a desperate Ian Woodward, who had been waiting twenty minutes hoping this was the genuine kidnapper and not another hoax.

It was the same West Indian voice on the line. 'Look behind the back panel, left side, for message on Dymo tape,' the voice said. 'I will hold the line.' He listened to Ian fumbling about until he came back on the phone to say he'd found the strip. 'Follow the instructions. Do not, I repeat, do not bring the police.'

Ian stared at the message. *Take M6 motorway to Newcastle-under-Lyme. Leave M6 at Clayton exit 15. Go to A34 for Kidsgrove. Phone box outside post office. Instructions under shelf.*

It was clear enough. It seemed that the roundabout journey, which doubled back, was a precaution to spot if the police were following him, which the Panther suspected. Ian lifted the receiver and phoned George Kennon at Manchester to relay the message before stepping into his car for the journey south.

The Panther stepped out the box, turned his collar up against the rain, and set off for the two-mile walk to Bathpool Park. The time was midnight exactly. The timing was going to plan, and he estimated how long it would take Ian Woodward to cover the distances following his instructions.

Kennon rang Stafford CID divisional headquarters to confirm his intentions, and asked them to hold back unless they were called for. But they were already ignoring Bradley's call to hold back and form an outer defence, with the obstinate rebuttal that Manchester had no right to demand it. It was this pig-headed rivalry between forces that hampered the capture of the Black Panther more than anything.

The Panther reached Bathpool Park in fifteen minutes, entering from Boathorse Lane. The park stood empty and almost silent in the darkness, with only the patter of light rain as he made his way to the spillway shaft to lay his last set of instructions.

He eased a section of the top bars away from the pillbox and pulled it along a couple of feet to expose the opening. From his pocket he took a torch that had a strip of Dymo tape attached, and wedged the torch between the bars. He switched it on so that the light could be seen from a fair distance.

Ian Woodward would be told where to look for it, and it should be there for no more than an hour, with new batteries in it to ensure it didn't dim. This was the place for the ransom to be dropped down the shaft. Satisfied it could not be missed, the Panther walked briskly away. He crossed the railway tunnel and looked back for the light before going on across a wide expanse of open ground towards Coal-Pit Hill.

The rain had stopped, which made the arduous climb a bit easier up the slope. When he reached the top of the ridge he walked along the track where the road once was to the old brick transformer house. He reached the main shaft and stepped up onto the raised plinth for a good view of the park through his infrared binoculars.

He had a panoramic view in dark red. The dark shapes of the hillocks loomed large, some more than a mile off, with young trees growing tall on them. It was hard to believe these were once slag heaps on a working colliery. He could see clear across the park to the town itself in a surreal image of red light. All was quiet under a cloak of darkness, and he was confident that this was the night he would pull it off. He heaved the manhole cover up and climbed onto the ladder.

He switched on his torch and swept it down the shaft, casting an array of deathly shadows. Then he began his descent, pulling the manhole cover closed to seal the tomb.

There was no movement below him as he reached the first platform twenty-three feet down. He swung to the next ladder opposite and continued his descent, flashing the beam of his torch to let her know he was coming. Normally he would hear her move. But not this time. His boots sounded heavy on the ladder as he descended, and for the very first time, he called her by name. 'Miss Woodward!'

There was no reply as he stepped onto the next platform at the end of the dry culvert, now forty-six feet down, and gazed over the edge. She was ten feet below, lying still on her two-foot-wide platform wrapped in her sleeping bag.

She was sleeping, and he felt it almost an intrusion as he stepped down heavily onto the platform and felt it move under his weight. He lit the oil lamp and pulled his hood down before shaking her and rousing her from a sound sleep.

'I've brought you some food,' he said, leaning back on the ladder to give her some space. She blinked into the flashlight to adjust her vision. 'Not long to go now. He's on his way.'

'Who is?' she mumbled. Her face had a sickly pallor from lack of daylight and fresh air. She felt drawn and tired and, though not emaciated, she was weak from hunger, and the extreme temperature had caused an aching cramp in her legs.

'Your brother – Ian. He's the one bringing the ransom. He should be here soon. I just hope he follows the instructions. No police and no tricks. If he obeys, you'll soon be free. If not…' he hesitated, '…things will not bode well for you.'

'Will you kill me?' she asked, staring blankly into his hooded face.

'It is not a matter for discussion. Here, have some soup,' he said, pouring her a cup from the flask.

She took a sip and grimaced, handing it back. 'Oxtail! I don't like it.'

'Come on! You must have nourishment. That's all there is.'

'I'd sooner starve.' She was deliberately being uncooperative. 'I'll ask again. What will you do if you don't get the money?'

'I told you, it's not open to discussion! If I were going to kill you why would I have this hood on? There would be no need. Now drink the soup. You will be glad of it.'

Julia took the soup and sipped it, slowly feeling the warming effects as it went down to her stomach, but still she felt lifeless from her seven days of captivity. She pulled herself to an upright sitting position in her sleeping bag, but even with the padded survival blanket and her coat on she could feel the cold concrete on her back.

There may have been no noxious gas down here, but the rank atmosphere from the sludge in the tunnel and a fear of rats preyed on her mind. The constant running of water flowing down the tunnel was all there was to break the monotonous silence as the overflow of rain flowed into the subterranean canal. She slept most of the long hours to rid herself of the boredom, or lie there with her eyes shut thinking of pleasant things – and sometimes not so pleasant. Though he had left her a torch and a book, she had no desire to read.

She watched him raise his hood to take a swig of brandy and he offered her the bottle. She shook her head, pointing to the bottle in her sleeping bag. There was an awkward period of silence between them as neither could think of anything to say.

He was preoccupied, thinking of the ransom and his escape, knowing that it had to come tonight. This was the big job he'd yearned to do to give him the money to boost his business, buy a new van, and give his wife and daughter a holiday. He didn't think of it as crime. It was a way of life.

Julia had her own private thoughts about her father and brothers. She was not that close to Peter; he had too many lofty ideas, whereas Ian was more the rebellious student type that she admired. She got on well enough with Veronica, although there were times when she thought she was only after the family silver. The one thing she had never found was happiness with a perfect man, and she ached for some true love.

The Panther checked his watch every few minutes and then, fiddling with the binoculars hung round his neck, he decided he had better go up to the spillway to check for activity. He mumbled something about the foul weather outside before climbing the ladder into the dry culvert and disappeared along the tunnel. It would be some time before he came back.

Ian Woodward's Mini Cooper travelled south on the M6 motorway in driving rain, tailed by one Manchester Q car keeping a discreet distance. He had agreed to carry the ransom, despite his brother's warnings. Peter was still nursing his wound from the shopping centre debacle, and was unforgiving in his remonstrations.

'You are heading for another disaster,' he told his brother. 'You will get nothing in return for all that money! You might as well throw it down a drain.'

'That's just what I intend to do with it,' Ian replied as he went out the door.

His first stop had been at Manchester Central CID, where he was fitted with two radios, one for him and one for the car. Two cars from the Staffordshire force were waiting along the route in radio contact at all-night service stations ready to join the convoy.

Kennon, who was back at Kidsgrove, had no knowledge about two cars and had warned his colleagues to watch for just one Stafford car that would follow.

The sign for Newcastle-under-Lyme loomed up and Ian Woodward left the motorway at Clayton and picked up the A34, which took him back to Kidsgrove. The first part of the journey had gone smoothly, but the rest of it would not be so easy.

The two Stafford cars were now on his tail behind the Manchester car, while more were moving in from the Derbyshire force. Ian was heading for a prearranged contact with Kennon for the final stage of the journey. As they passed Chesterton, two Derbyshire Q cars pulled out on the tail of the convoy, and a trail of red lights could be seen for miles.

Just before Kidsgrove, Ian pulled into the Audley service station, where Kennon waited with Sergeant Boyd to check he had not met with any mishap on the way. Although Kennon expected a Staffordshire car, not even he suspected five cars would follow him in and pull up on the car park.

'Bloody hell, what's this?' Kennon said. 'They've broken their word not to follow him!' Kennon got out and walked over to Ian's Mini Cooper.

'I haven't got a clue where I am, Chief Inspector,' he said sliding back the window.

'You're eight miles from Kidsgrove, Ian. Turn off at the next exit and head for Harding Wood. It's about four miles. When you get there follow the sign for Kidsgrove town centre. Where are the next set of instructions?'

'The phone box outside the post office.'

'I thought so. From now on you will be in radio contact with our listening post on Mow Cop. Repeat all instructions and remember, any sign of trouble, and we'll be with you in two minutes. I wish it could it be quicker, but we dare not come in too close. Best of luck, Ian.'

'Thanks, Chief Inspector,' Ian replied, and he drove out.

Bob Morrison noted the exchange and, unsure what it meant, got out of his car to investigate. He walked over to Kennon's Rover parked near the entrance as Kennon wound down his window and called out, 'Bloody hell, Bob! You've brought the whole bloody force with you!'

'Don't worry, George. They'll move off in a few minutes to block the exit roads. I thought it was better to come in closer than lie too far out. So it is Bathpool Park after all. I had a feeling it was.'

'It had to be, but it will be touch and go. I just hope the bloody Panther hasn't seen us. Don't you realise he will be watching?'

'Not at this distance he won't. Give us some credit for tactics. It's not obvious. My lads will be outside the town anyway.'

'Bob Renshaw of Derby has promised his men will stay east side of the Trent Canal. He's putting up a cordon from Tunstall to Macclesfield with a dozen cars on the most likely roads, although even that won't be enough, I fear.'

'I think we've got him tonight, George. This man's reign is coming to an end.'

'I hope so. Let's hope we're in time to save the girl. He could still kill her. An animal is more dangerous when it's trapped. What's your destination from here?'

'I thought the town centre would be best, where the lad's heading.'

'Keep well back from the park. Ian Woodward will be in touch with our radio van on Mow Cop and you should be able to pick up the frequency, so listen in.'

The cars moved off at five-minute intervals heading for Kidsgrove, hoping the Panther was not in a position to see them. For the moment they maintained radio silence. They were taking no chances.

Kennon approached Kidsgrove driving past the deserted park before branching off at Coal-Pit Hill going up to the colliery's main gate and there he parked to get a panoramic view. The time was 12.50 a.m.

Meanwhile Ian Woodward was having trouble finding the town centre where he was supposed to find his next instructions in the phone box outside the post office. He had missed the Harding Wood turn-off in the dark and was going towards Tunstall when he realised his mistake. He drove on looking for somewhere to turn on the narrow road, but it was no good; the hedgerows were sweeping both sides of his car and he kept going to the next turn-off.

He drove for five miles in the wrong direction with wipers flapping back and forth until he arrived at Tunstall, where two police cars were waiting in the village square. He drove slowly into the old village, searching for a road sign, when suddenly a car pulled across his path blocking his progress. Then another car arrived and six officers jumped out and surrounded him. Two of them were armed marksmen and as they pointed their Webley pistols at him, the car door was wrenched open and he was forced out at gunpoint.

'I'm Ian Woodward!' he protested, as he was forced to lie flat on the wet road and a hefty man knelt on his back to snap on a pair of handcuffs. 'You guys are making a mistake!' he told them. 'I'm searching for Kidsgrove. I got lost.'

'What do you reckon, Sarge?' one of the two constables said as they hauled him to his feet.

A torch was directed in his face as the sergeant carefully weighed up his captive. Ian Woodward's light beard and tousle of wet hair looked darker than normal and gave him a similar appearance to the police photofit.

'Where have you just come from?' the sergeant inquired, keeping the torch on him.

'Bridlington Hall at Brighouse,' Ian blustered giving the wrong answer. 'I came up the motorway. I'm on my way to Kidsgrove. I'm carrying the ransom. It's in the boot. Take a look.'

'It's locked, Sarge,' a constable said, before removing the ignition key and unlocking the boot. He lifted out the holdall and brought it across to the sergeant and opened it.

'Strewth!' the sergeant wheezed, as several torches picked out the bundles of banknotes. 'How do we know you're not the Panther with his ill-gotten gains?'

'Take a look in my inside jacket pocket and look at my driving licence.'

The licence was examined and Ian Woodward's name confirmed his story. He said, 'Can you direct me to Kidsgrove from here? I'm already late. I must deliver this ransom.'

'I'll have to check with the chief inspector. You hold on.' The sergeant went to his radio, and after what seemed an immeasurable amount of time-wasting, he was finally cleared to let Ian carry on.

'We'll escort you, Mr Woodward,' the sergeant said. 'We can't afford to have you getting lost.'

Ian didn't argue, and as the bag was put back in the boot he climbed into his Mini Cooper and pulled out of Tunstall with two police cars escorting him to Kidsgrove.

Kennon was now showing a grave concern at the absence of the Mini. 'I don't like it, Boyd. He should have been here by now.'

'I reckon he's got lost, guv,' Boyd replied. 'Maybe we should have stuck with him on the last leg.'

'Inform the radio van while I keep watch.'

Six miles away on Mow Cop, the radio van was picking up Ian Woodward as he made his first contact via the car radio that was fixed to his dashboard. He explained he had got lost and was on his way, escorted by two police cars. The message was relayed to the cars in the area and Boyd could hear the alarm bells as he reported to Kennon.

'I was right. He got lost. Worse still, he's now got two police cars escorting him into the town.'

'*Blasted fools!*' Kennon exploded. 'If the Panther's watching we could be heading for disaster.'

Kennon's fears were now reflected in the Panther as he watched from the top of the centre shaft. He had leaned the ladder against the wall of the shaft and bridged the gap to the top ladder with a length of rope. It was the best place to watch from. He cursed as he feared a crisis looming. The time was now 2.30 a.m. and the ransom was an hour late. He would give it a bit longer; he had no choice but to wait.

He was already agitated because a car had come in earlier and parked up. Through his binoculars he spied on a courting couple having sex in the car, and though it might have been good voyeurism it infuriated him. This randy pair could jeopardise the ransom delivery… Fortunately it was over in half an hour and the car pulled out.

But he was getting more desperate by the minute. Woodward should be here by now, he told himself over and over. If he brings the police with him he will have to suffer the consequences. Inwardly, the Panther seethed.

He had not planned to kill his hostage but he could not help thinking of the possibility that he might have to. His plans for escape seemed even more risky as the time ticked by. He was flooded with fears of the police casting a net over the entire Midlands. But he had beaten them before, and he could do it again.

At 2.45 a.m. the three cars entered Kidsgrove town centre and Ian Woodward was guided to the telephone box outside the post office by the police sergeant. He entered the box and searched under the parcel shelf for the Dymo tape. He removed it from its taped position and read the message. *Go straight on for Boathorse Lane. Go to end of lane and enter Bathpool Park by low wall. Look for torch light. Instructions on torch.*

The instructions seemed straightforward and Ian walked to the waiting police car to tell them where he was going, adding, 'Don't follow me! I have to do this alone. I'm now relaying this message to the radio van.'

Every word was picked up on Mow Cop and relayed over the network to the ring of police waiting around the town and strung out over miles of roads leading out of Kidsgrove.

Ian proceeded driving towards Boathorse Lane and then he saw the entrance. He drove in as the rain fell steadily and missed the low wall which would have guided him over the railway. Instead he turned left, keeping to the south side of the park where it was not possible to see the torch light. The Panther watched in frustration as he disappeared, but he came back again, going slowly over the same ground searching for a light.

He stopped the car and got out, looking all round with rain streaking his face. Then he took the ransom bag out the boot and in desperation he yelled, 'I'm here! Where are you? I'm here! I can't see a light!' He shouted several times in frustration, and all the time he was talking into his throat microphone to the radio van, telling them he couldn't find his final message.

The radio van picked up static and lost him for a while as he walked round in the rain getting ever more exasperated, unaware that he was being watched. Kennon watched the small figure wandering around in the dark and then lost sight of him as he went over the bank and down to the railway. He walked along the bank and thought he saw a light across the track. The torch was still glowing wedged in the spillway bars, and then he realised he was on the wrong side of the park.

He turned to go back up the bank and slipped on the wet grass. He went down heavily on his stomach and slid back down the bank, dropping the holdall. He grabbed at tufts of wet grass that slipped out of his hands as he went further back, getting dangerously close to the edge. He managed to halt himself just yards from the last drop onto the track where a live rail carried 6,000 volts. The holdall had miraculously stopped just below him, and he edged his way down to grab it as it balanced on the edge. Then slowly he crawled his way back up the bank, soaked to the skin.

On Mow Cop there was panic as radio contact was lost for several minutes, and the police began their advance on the park. Kennon too felt something had gone wrong, and he and Boyd got back into the car. They turned around and sped back down the hill as the radio crackled with emergency signals. They had promised Ian Woodward they would be with him in two minutes if they felt he was in danger. They were now acting on their word, racing to the park.

Down in the tunnel, the Panther was wading back through the water, cursing and swearing out loud as he saw his ransom disappearing down a hole. He had lost the criteria for safe delivery and he had no choice but to abandon the whole thing. This was his first mistake. He felt the whole episode was a failure, and that was the one thing he couldn't abide. Failure was an unacceptable virus that had to be beaten. He'd had too many failures in the past; he could not tolerate any more. He was obsessive and paranoid about failure.

He went through the dry culvert, swearing loudly, and swung onto the ladder. 'That brother of yours is stupid!' he shouted at his captive. 'The instructions were plain enough!'

He had removed his hood and she was looking straight into his face – a face that was unforgettable in its entirety.

'Look for the light, I said! Look for the bloody light! I wonder whether he's even bothered about you! If he's not, why should I worry? You're an outcast!'

He jumped down heavily on the platform and there was a sharp crack of metal as the support stanchion, riddled with rust, snapped in half, and the platform suddenly gave way. It took only an instant for Julia to slip over the edge, as the Panther lunged forward with his arm outstretched in a futile bid to save her.

He was too late. The five-foot drop snapped her neck, triggering a heart attack, and Julia was hanged by the wire loop cutting into her neck. She died instantly – a tragic, bitter end to her life. He pulled himself back on the ladder and stared down at her lifeless body, seeing the results of his heinous crime with a stark sense of horror.

Unable to comprehend what he had done, he panicked and made his escape up the main shaft. He came out at the top into darkness, and immediately he could see the police cars swarming all over the park. He climbed off the ladder, closed the manhole cover down and made off in the night down the far side of the hill.

The final scene had been played out with disastrous consequences. The instructions taped to the torch on the spillway had fallen to the ground. The message lay unseen as police torches probed along the railway where Ian Woodward fell. It was the final ignominy in a police operation that had gone badly wrong and cost the life of a beautiful and courageous woman. The Panther knew now he would be hunted mercilessly. His crime was unforgivable. From now on he was a fugitive on the run. He had precipitated the largest police manhunt on record.

Chapter Twenty

The following day, Kennon was forced to admit the inevitable. The Panther had beaten the police trap and Julia Woodward was dead. He was loath to admit that with all the resources at his disposal he could not catch the one man he most desperately wanted brought to justice.

He sat in his office writing up reports to account for the investigation by his team after a lengthy debriefing with them, and then he had to let them go. They were now dispersed for other more urgent inquiries, chiefly concerning the IRA. The hunt for the bombers had suddenly taken precedence, and if that wasn't the final slap in the face, the arrival of Scotland Yard certainly was.

Detective Chief Superintendent Douglas Patterson, Head of Scotland Yard's National Crime Bureau, was called in by the West Mercia force. He brought with him members of the Yard's criminal investigation bureau to assist in covert electronic surveillance, voice recognition, ballistics, and fingerprints, and to sift through hundreds of witness statements over the Panther's five-year reign.

Patterson chose Bridgnorth in Shropshire as centre of operations, since most sightings of the Panther came from the Black Country and all the recorded telephone messages were, according to the voice experts, from a man with a Birmingham accent. His first task was to impose a complete news blackout so as not to hamper police inquiries as he undertook the mammoth task of tracing every man who had worked on the Bathpool Park project.

Within days of setting up his centre of operations, Patterson was given a boost when the abandoned Ford Transit van was found in the lane at Codsall, where it had been dumped after the shopping centre fiasco.

The vehicle underwent a thorough search but yielded only a minute amount of information. An old notebook found under the dash revealed the Panther's former occupation as a jobbing carpenter. It held the names and addresses of dozens of past customers. The most prominent was Buxton Manor, for an attic conversion. It was assumed rightly that this is where the chess set originated, stolen by the Panther as he worked on the house.

Kennon had to bow to Patterson's senior command in ruling the murder inquiry. He would still have a hand on the tiller, but he felt the case slipping from his grasp. As the days dragged by without any real progress his spirits sagged and he was in need of a lift, and there was only one person who could do it. He phoned Suzanne at her office at the *Evening Standard* and was told the chief crime reporter was away for the day working in London.

He phoned her again the next day, and just hearing the sound of her voice gave him an instant lift. She told him she had been to London to look up the National Census archives and had found some information that might interest him.

'What sort of information?' Kennon inquired.

'I think I may have the name of the Black Panther. He is Derek Wilson and he lives in Bradford.'

'Derek Wilson? That name rings a bell…'

'It should do. He was the number one suspect for the murder of a prostitute, Harriet Saunders, in 1965.'

'The Harriet Saunders case,' Kennon recalled. 'The girl fished out the Trent. I remember it now. She was badly scarred by acid. But Wilson was never charged, for lack of evidence. Wait a minute, there was a different name on his driving license, if I remember.'

'Exactly. But why? Meet me for lunch at the usual place.'

'The theatre café at one o'clock. I'll be there.'

Kennon felt his spirits soaring as he finished his routine paper-work and left the building at 12.35 p.m. for his lunch date in Victoria Square. The Palace Theatre was a twenty-minute walk along Piccadilly Street, and the balcony café was a popular meeting place. The theatre had just been renovated and its café provided a simple lunch in pleasant surroundings.

Suzanne was waiting outside looking elegant in a three-quarter-length beige coat and high-heeled boots. Her fair hair was tucked under a felt hat and she was smiling as Kennon approached. He greeted her with a kiss on the cheek and apologised for keeping her waiting two minutes. Then they entered the theatre and climbed the wide curved staircase with thick carpet and brass handrail up to the café behind the dress circle.

They ordered tea and tuna sandwiches and sat at a table with the sunlight streaming in through the large windows. The atmosphere was pleasant, if not to say a trifle thespian, with one wall covered in photos of music hall stars from earlier times.

'Now, Suzanne,' Kennon asked. 'How on earth do you link Derek Wilson to the Panther?'

'It was the girl recently fished out the Trent that set me thinking about the Harriet Saunders case. I went down to our archive section and looked up the back numbers for 1965 and found the article that mentioned the name of Derek Wilson. Back then the girls worked on the streets, usually in pairs, for safety reasons. According to Saunders' friend, June Covington, Harriet was approached by a man in a white van. He argued over the price, saying she was a damned sight more expensive than the Bradford girls, and he drove off. Half an hour later he came back and agreed Saunders' price, and she got in the van with him. He drove off with her and that was the last time she was seen alive.'

'Yes, I remember that,' Kennon said, as the waiter appeared with their order.

He set down a pot of tea with milk and sugar and a plate of tuna sandwiches. Kennon picked up the bill and noticed it was almost double the price of most cafés, but he reckoned it was worth it.

'Now, where was I?' Suzanne said, pouring the tea.

'June Covington was the last person to see her, you said.'

'Oh, yes. Anyway, June Covington gave the police most of the licence plate number and it was eventually traced to Bradford, belonging to a man by the name of Derek Wilson. She also told the police the man spoke with a West Indian accent. Witnesses from the post office raids have attributed the same accent to the Black Panther. Too much of a coincidence, don't you think?'

'Not really, given the amount of West Indians there are in Bradford.'

Suzanne responded with daggers and Kennon quickly corrected himself.

'Well, it could be. But it's also been stated the Panther has a Birmingham accent. Wilson was a Yorkshireman.'

'I know. It was also said that Wilson was a jobbing carpenter, the same occupation that has just been revealed that was the Panther's. That's another coincidence.'

'True, but it's still not conclusive. There are hundreds of jobbing carpenters around.'

'I can see you're going to take a lot of convincing, Chief Inspector!' Suzanne retorted, blowing hot. 'The coroner's report on Saunders said her face had come into contact with some strong industrial ammonia. It's been reported the Panther uses ammonia on dogs. He used it on several occasions in post office robberies.'

'He did indeed. You're thorough, Suzanne. I'll give you that. But what was the purpose of searching the National Census?'

'Wilson's driving license with the name of Wyllie set me thinking. Why change his name? I wanted to find out his address. I figured you wouldn't have it on file.'

'Not after all this time we wouldn't. Anyway, he was cleared. That's why there's no police record on him.'

'Precisely. No record; no address. I looked up the 1961 census for Bradford and sure enough found the name Derek Wilson at 13 Radcliff Avenue. Wilson had a wife and daughter listed on the form. Then I checked it against the 1971 census to see if he was still there and found the same details adding ten years to their ages. But why did he change his name?'

'Maybe he didn't like Wyllie. It can be pronounced differently.'

'I know what you mean. But it's more likely he was changing his identity for a career in crime. But he slipped up with his driving license. So you don't think it's worth checking out?'

'It's not conclusive, but it takes us nearer to the Panther's identity. I hadn't thought of the census or checking his handwriting on official forms. We have several samples of his handwriting turned up of odd envelopes. You may have given us a vital lead, Suzanne.'

'I hope so. I badly need a story and this one's gone cold. So will you act on the information? You can't ignore it. You have to follow it up.'

'I will do. But the first thing is to put the house under surveillance.'

'Why? That's a waste of time, isn't it?'

'No it's not. If the Panther lives at that address, don't you think he would cover his tracks by staying clear of it? We've had reports of him using rented lock-ups to store equipment and vehicles. If we want to catch this bloke, we're going to have to be as cunning as he is. Bradford has been suggested more than once as his base.'

'He has to go back some time. How's the investigation going now Scotland Yard has been called in?'

'Painfully slow. We're getting scraps of information from Bathpool Park and from a van he dumped at Codsall, but my team has been drastically cut. The IRA are suddenly more important.'

'I thought they might be. Have you got anything on the bombers' identification?'

'Nope. Not a thing.'

'I don't believe it. You're covering something up, aren't you?'

'I am not. You're pumping me, young lady. I can sniff out the reporter in you.'

'Of course I am, that's my job. You give me information on the IRA and I'll help you catch the Panther. How's that?'

'Let me take you out for dinner tonight and I'll think about it.'

'That sounds a good idea. I thought you'd never ask!'

They left the café in good spirits and stepped into the busy Piccadilly Road where Suzanne's car was parked. This part of Manchester around Smithfield Market was heavily built-up and Kennon could see why the IRA chose the city to plant their bombs. They were not far from the stock exchange financial centre, where a bomb had ripped open the pub named after it. If it had been placed on the trading floor itself it could have brought even more chaos.

But that wasn't Kennon's problem. He had the Panther to worry about, and he was concerned where his next strike would be. He wouldn't be silent for long, that was for sure. And constantly nagging him was the thought of Julia Woodward's body still lying undiscovered.

As the weeks went by, the sinister secrets of Bathpool Park came to light. Objects found in the undergrowth included crumpled cassette tapes, a smashed tape recorder, a brandy bottle, a stop-watch and a plastic raincoat worn by the Panther.

Nothing of such magnitude had ever been left behind from the post office robberies. Could this simply be carelessness? It was as if the man wanted to be caught, as if it was his final act, and he was coming in from the cold; although privately it was felt more likely to be attributable to a spate of frustrated anger.

Repeated calls to the National Coal Board's head office for plans of the conversion of the Nelson Colliery by Scotland Yard finally paid off. They were delivered by courier service from the Midlands Regional Board in Birmingham, along with the names of several contractors who had carried out the work. The plans showed in graphic detail the conversion of the colliery, with its three vertical shafts connected by the tunnel to take the Trent's floodwaters into the subterranean Brindley Canal running through it.

Only now was the significance of police failures to carry out a wide-ranging search of the park and its surrounding area apparent. Patterson blamed the West Mercia force for the failure, while they in turn accused Scotland Yard of rank incompetence. It was an argument that would rumble on long after the investigation was over.

Police officers expressed amazement at finding the main pit-head shaft on top of the hill inside a fenced enclosure half-buried in brambles. The undergrowth was cleared away, the railings were removed, and the cover was raised for the first time in six weeks, emitting a foul stench.

The first thing DCS Patterson did was to send for a police diver; then he informed Kennon and other senior detectives that the third shaft had been discovered. Kennon rushed to Kidsgrove, making it there in less than an hour.

He arrived on the hill to find the old colliery gates were open and a small army of men inside. Several vehicles were parked on the road by the transformer house. He parked his car and made his way along the road to where the Yard men in raincoats were standing round the pit-head.

It was easy to see now from this vantage point, which over-looked the railway and the park, why the Panther had chosen this spot to bring his victim. It was screened from the rest of the park by trees, and nothing of what remained of the colliery could be seen from the road that bordered the park. Apart from the old transformer house and the railing around the main shaft, there was no evidence of a coal mine ever having been here.

As Kennon walked up to the pithead he noted the police specialist diving unit vehicle parked up. It was mounted with a small derrick crane used for lifting objects from rivers and lakes, the objects usually being bodies of drowned victims.

He was surprised to learn that the frogman was already down the main shaft. Patterson had gone over the top in summoning a diver for two feet of water, but Kennon kept his opinions to himself. He spoke with Patterson and other senior detectives, all waiting patiently for the outcome and then he stood watching, feeling the self-recriminations sweeping him: why did he not search?

Down below, the diver's torch picked out some objects left behind sitting on a ledge. There were two lanterns, a pair of leather gloves and a flask, and then came the most fateful discovery of all, unfolding like a Shakespeare tragedy: Julia Woodward was found hanging from the wire noose. Her shoeless bare feet were dangling in the water just six inches from the bottom.

The diver was used to such sights but it was still shocking just the same. He attached his own tackle to her limp body and managed to raise her into the dry culvert before cutting the wire that was wrapped around the stanchion. Then he went back up to call for the mechanical lifting gear. The rescue vehicle was backed up to the open manhole and a harness for lifting human bodies, attached by a wire cable, was lowered down the shaft.

Kennon stood silently, watching grim-faced as her body was slowly raised up the death shaft. The self-recriminations were turning to anger for failing to search as he watched the body brought up and then laid on the ground. To see her condition was pitiful. Her darkened face, turned blue, was serene even in death and bore no signs of injury.

Clearly she had not been beaten, as some officers suggested. Her suede coat was stained with dirt, and though undone at the belt there were no signs of any sexual interference.

The police pathologist gave the all-clear before she was lifted gently into a coffin and six men carried her down a muddy slope to the police mortuary van to be taken away for a post-mortem.

The death shaft was covered with a tent and a mobile incident unit was on hand to sift the evidence that was brought up. It included most of the survival gear and a pair of slippers the Panther had given her. But the most poignant of all the objects was the diary in which she had written down her thoughts as she lay hostage waiting for rescue.

To unmask the Panther was Kennon's personal goal. If he never solved another case he had to solve this one. He had the house in Radcliff Avenue put under surveillance by three of his former team, including Boyd, who was pulled off another murder inquiry.

They kept vigil for over a week from parked cars, and the telephone was tapped. But it revealed nothing. The only people seen coming and going were Wilson's wife and eighteen-year-old daughter.

At the same time, every self-employed jobbing carpenter and small builder was paid a visit by the Bradford police. Workshops were visited, trade adverts were followed up at addresses, and gradually the net closed around Radcliff Avenue.

But it was Detective Sergeant Stacey and DC Murray who had the honour of the final accolade. They were in Radcliff Avenue just a few doors along from Number 13 when a neighbour approached them in an excited manner.

'Excuse me, officers. I hear you're looking for the bloke they call the Black Panther.'

'That's right,' Stacey replied. 'Who are you, sir?'

'I'm Ken Bradbury. I live at Number 15. The bloke you're looking for lives next door to me at Number 13, name of Wilson, Derek Wilson.'

'Derek Wilson,' Murray said, writing the name down. 'What else can you tell us about Derek Wilson, Mr Bradbury?'

'He's an oddball. In all the years I've lived next door to him I can't have spoken more than a couple of words with him. He's got a high opinion of himself, as if he's superior to everybody else. He's a self-employed jobbing builder, so he reckons. He's forever banging around in his house fixing things, and he comes and goes at all hours of the day and night.'

'A jobbing builder?' Stacey felt a surge of adrenalin. 'Is he in the house now, sir?'

'He could be. I saw a bloke go in at about seven o'clock this morning but it could have been the lodger. They've had several come and go over the years, but whether they still have I'm not sure.'

'Why has it taken you so long to report this man?' Stacey inquired, his suspicions aroused now that there was an easy £25,000 reward money.

'I never thought it was serious enough until now, what with all the media attention, and then I saw all the police in the area.'

'What makes you so sure he's the Black Panther?' Stacey asked, still suspicious.

'Look, I'm trying to help you! I don't know!' Bradbury replied in a rattled tone. 'I thought you'd appreciate my help. I was obviously wrong!'

'Not at all, sir,' Murray replied, reassuring the man. 'The Black Panther is wanted right across the land. There's a huge reward for his capture. We want to make sure it goes to the rightful claimant. Let us hope you are right.'

'So long as you appreciate my efforts. I could have said nowt. Then where would you be? Up the creek without a paddle!'

'We'll investigate this Mr Wilson, sir. So he's a married man, I take it?'

'I thought I made that clear! I said they had lodgers! Blimey, no wonder you can't catch the bloke!'

'Thank you, sir!' Stacey countered. 'We shall investigate your information, but you have to understand we can't go after every oddball reported by the neighbours.'

'They don't come much odder than this bloke. He's got a teenage daughter who he rules with a rod of iron. And his wife's cowed by his temper. Don't forget my name! Ken Bradbury, 15 Radcliff Avenue. I'm the one who's given you the lead.'

They moved along to Number 13 and stood outside taking in the house, which had a home-made 'For Sale' sign in the forecourt. The house was a two-storey Edwardian dwelling with a bleak frontage of Yorkshire stone and a glass porch. They went through the front gate up to the door and gave a loud knock.

There was no reply and no sign of movement from inside. Stacey rapped the knocker again, and through the stained glass window saw someone approach the door. It was opened by a dark-haired woman in her mid-thirties, a picture of domesticity.

'Yes?' she said with a weary expression on her face.

'Mrs Wilson? I'm Detective Sergeant Stacey from Manchester CID. Is your husband in?' Stacey said, holding his police warrant card up. 'We'd like a word with him.'

'No, he's not, and hasn't been for two years! We're separated.'

'May we come in? You might be able to answer our inquiries.'

'No. I'm busy – can't you come back later?'

'I'm afraid not. This won't take long. I can enforce it, Mrs Wilson.'

'Come in, then. What's it all about?' She led them into the neatly furnished front room with a gas fire glowing in the hearth. 'Take a seat.'

'Do you know where your estranged husband is living, Mrs Wilson?' Murray inquired, feeling some sympathy for the woman.

'No, I don't! And I don't get any maintenance from him. Not a penny! But then he was always tight with money. I shouldn't wonder if the taxman's after him. What's this all about?'

'We're investigating a kidnap. You may have read about it. The Julia Woodward girl, abducted in Manchester,' Stacey explained. 'The man responsible is a self-employed jobbing carpenter. Our inquiries have led us here. That was your husband's job, we believe.'

'He did a bit of it. He was self-employed.'

'One of the neighbours says he saw a man enter the house at seven o'clock this morning, Mrs Wilson.'

'I can guess who that was! The nosey parker next door. That was most probably my lodger. Yes, I believe he did come in about that time. He goes out for a paper most mornings. But he's gone out again. I don't see much of him.'

'Do you mind if we take a look at his room? I can get a warrant if you refuse, Mrs Wilson.'

'I shall have to check first if he's in.' She went to the door. 'Wait here, please.'

They waited, looking carefully round the room. On the mantelpiece was a framed wedding photograph of the newly-weds. Derek Wilson was in army uniform during his national service days and appeared to be about twenty. Iris was all in white, smiling with a bouquet of flowers. The photo corroborated the marriage but appeared to deny any separation by the fact that it was still on show. It also verified Kennon's assumption the Panther was a man with military training and survival experience.

DC Murray felt the surge of adrenalin coursing through her veins that always came when a suspect was in their sights. They waited ten minutes, with growing suspicion, and Stacey stepped into the hall to look up the staircase just as Iris was coming down. Her cheeks were flushed and her calm composure was ruffled. 'He's just coming down. He's not feeling too well.'

'What's his name and occupation, Mrs Wilson?'

'Mr Davis. He's Welsh. He's with the Inland Revenue.'

'Inland Revenue! What's he doing here? Seems a bit odd, doesn't it?' Stacey said, now even more suspicious.

'I don't know. I don't ask. It's nothing to do with me what he does for a living,' she said, ushering Stacey back in the room. 'Why don't you come back later when he's feeling better?'

'No need for that, Iris.' A smartly dressed man stepped into the room wearing a suit with a collar and tie. His face was grey behind tinted spectacles, with dark greying hair, and he held an unlit pipe in his hand. 'Now what's all this about, Sergeant? I'm Bryon Davis of Her Majesty's Inland Revenue, Gwent Division,' he said, speaking with a pronounced Welsh accent.

'So I'm told. What are you doing here in Bradford, Mr Davis?'

'I'm a tax fraud investigator, Sergeant. I'm after a bloke who owes us thousands of pounds. Barry Appleyard's his name. We think he's gone to ground here.'

'Have you got any proof of identity, Mr Davis?' Stacey asked.

'Of course I have. Here's my card.' Davis handed Stacey his ID with his name on an official card bearing the address of the Welsh tax office in Newport, Gwent.

Stacey looked at it with an inquisitive eye as he handed it to Murray. 'Can we keep this card?'

'By all means, Sergeant! I've got dozens of them. Now what exactly are you looking for? Mrs Wilson tells me you're after this Black Panther criminal that's on the loose. I thought he was in the Black Country, down in Birmingham.'

'What led you to believe that?'

'That's where he comes from, isn't it? At least, according to all the papers it is.'

'He's here in Bradford. What time did you go out this morning?'

'Just after seven. I went to get a paper. I always do. Is there anything wrong?'

'There might be. How long have you been lodging here?'

'Only a few weeks. Once I get this tax fraudster I shall be off again. I travel all over the place.'

'Do you mind if I take a look in your room, Mr Davis?'

'Not at all. What are you looking for?'

'Evidence of criminal activity, Mr Davis.'

'Why the devil am I under suspicion, then? I'm no criminal.'

'No, but you might be in a criminal's room.'

'Unless the previous lodger was a criminal, I'd say that's highly improbable, wouldn't you, Mrs Wilson?'

'It's always been let out, Sergeant. I would never rent to a criminal.'

'I'd still like to check, if you don't mind.'

'I'll take you up there, Sergeant. You too, Constable. Better safe than sorry, I always say.'

'You stay here, Murray. I can manage. Lead the way, Mr Davis.'

Stacey was hedging his bets and hoping he would find something as he followed Davis up the stairs to the landing, but he was taking a risk he should not have done. The house had four bedrooms and a bathroom with a separate toilet. There was an added open-tread staircase to the attic room, which was kept firmly locked. Davis took a key from his pocket and unlocked his room. They stepped inside a neatly furnished room with a single bed, a wardrobe and a chest of drawers. On the top was a shaving kit with brush, an electric razor, a jar of Brylcreem, a comb, some money and a Mars bar.

Everything seemed normal, but Stacey could see no sign of a suitcase. He looked under the bed and on top the wardrobe. 'No suitcase, Mr Davis? Unusual for a lodger not to have a suitcase. Do you mind if I look in the wardrobe?'

'Help yourself.'

Stacey looked inside to see an array of men's clothing hanging up, which included a pair of dark blue needlecord trousers, a brown corduroy jacket, shirts and jumpers and a pair of muddy shoes in the bottom. There was nothing to connect this man to the Black Panther, but still Stacey wasn't satisfied. Something told him that Davis was false. He noticed a scar on Davis's right hand behind the thumb, consistent with the ejector mechanism of a semi-automatic pistol. But it was hardly enough to warrant an arrest.

'I'll look in the chest of drawers, if you don't mind.'

'Not at all, Sergeant. What exactly are you looking for?'

'The proceeds of the post office robberies, a cash bag, or anything that indicates the Panther might have been here recently as a lodger.'

Stacey took a hurried look in the drawers and then stepped out to the landing. He was interested in the attic room.

'Satisfied, Sergeant?'

'Not quite. Can you show me the attic room?'

'No, I can't. I don't have a key for it.'

'Why's it kept locked? Unusual, isn't it?'

'I've no idea. You'll have to ask Mrs Wilson that.'

'I will do. But I'll take a look in the other rooms first.'

Davis shrugged as Stacey looked in the front bedroom. It was neatly furnished with a double bed, wardrobe and dressing table with nothing out of place. Then he looked in the daughter's bedroom, which was also neat and orderly, with not a thing out of place. It was certainly not typical of a teenager's usually untidy room. It reinforced Wilson's known obsession with discipline and order of neatness, which he pressured his own daughter with.

'Nice and tidy,' Stacey remarked, closing the door. 'What's in here?' he said making for the spare room next door and turning the key in the lock.

He opened the door to a dark room with the curtains drawn and when he switched on the light he stared incredulously at what he saw. On a bunk bed there was a jumble of clothes, battle fatigues, hats and gloves, notebooks and Ordnance Survey maps. An array of keep-fit equipment, including a Bullworker, weights and chest expanders, littered the floor. On a table was a hi-fi stereo with speakers, a duffel bag, rolls of tape, a torch and two false number plates.

'Blimey! What have we here?' Stacey exclaimed, standing in the doorway of the cluttered room.

'Take a good look, Sergeant.'

Stacey was suddenly hit hard on the head with the butt of a pistol and he collapsed into the room. His arms were pulled behind him and his wrists were bound with strong insulation tape. Wilson then bound his ankles with the tape before dragging the unconscious detective into the former lodging room. Then he came out, locked the door and went downstairs clutching the semi-automatic pistol in his hand.

He paused at the half-open lounge door to listen to the two women talking before stepping inside with the pistol raised directly at Murray. 'On the floor – face down and hands behind back!' he ordered. 'Tie her hands, Iris,' he said, throwing at her the roll of tape.

'Derek, no!'

'Do it, woman!'

She obeyed without question, taping Murray's wrists tight behind her back. 'What are you going to do, Derek?' she asked in a weak voice.

'You'll see,' he said, taping over the policewoman's mouth with a strip of Elastoplast. 'Right – help me get her upstairs.'

They hauled Murray to her feet and forced her upstairs. She was put in the same room as Stacey, and Wilson locked them both in before passing the key to his wife.

'I've got to get away from here, and you're going to help me. I can only take so much, but it will be enough for now.' He opened a cupboard and brought out a battered suitcase. 'This will do. I'm going up to the attic. I want you to fill the flasks with soup and make me a few sandwiches, and anything else you've got.'

'Derek!' Iris was guilt-ridden, her face crumpled with anxiety. 'What's going to happen when you're gone? I shall have to free the two detectives.'

'Of course you will, but only after I'm well away. Don't worry, Iris, they can't touch you. I coerced you into this. You were the loyal wife. That's your defence. Now see to my soup.'

Wilson went up to the attic room where his deadly secrets lay hidden. Besides all the Panther paraphernalia, he had a secret store of weapons and ammunition which included an assault rifle and several hand-guns. He took only the essentials he needed for a long absence. He was going on the run and might not return for a year or two... or maybe never. But it didn't matter either way. He knew his wife would keep faithful, wherever he was.

He kept his false identity as Bryon Davis knowing he would need it on the road. He had used theatrical make-up on his face and hair and the rest was easy. He could imitate most accents, and often did so on his post office raids. That made it harder for the police to pin him down, with confusing witness statements. He was a master of subterfuge and techniques that came second nature to him. But his one priority now was to get away and do some more robberies. Even now, he wasn't prepared to give up what he was good at – not yet at least.

After packing everything he needed he went down to the kitchen where Iris had the flasks and sandwiches for him packed in his duffel bag. He gave her a peck on the cheek. 'Take care, Iris. Give Karen my love. I'll try and be in touch later.'

Then he went out of the back door, down the neat garden and left by the back gate. He was on his way to the lock-up garage he rented two streets away, where his blue Ford Transit van, recently purchased second-hand, was kept off the road.

Iris watched him leave and returned to the kitchen, She would have to give him at least an hour before she could free the two detectives. She made a cup of tea and sat down, working out her story about how her husband dominated her life and Karen's. She obeyed him without question as a loyal wife, even though she was half aware of his criminal activities. The shootings were all accidents, he told her. There was never any intention to kill. She was trapped by his deceit, whatever she did. But he was on the run and she knew that it was going to be the hardest task of all for her to give him up. His protection was gone now. She had been his shield.

Chapter Twenty-one

Kennon arrived in Bridgnorth the same morning for a meeting with Patterson to pool the information coming in slowly concerning the Black Panther. He was not all that impressed by the team from Scotland Yard, for all their special equipment. Their lines of inquiry were pre-determined by voice recognitions indicating that the Panther was from Birmingham.

It was also the view held by the West Mercia force, who were determined to see the Panther caught on their patch. Kennon was anxious to expose the serious flaw in the constabularies' modus operandi relating to sharing information. This was subject to serious errors of management, which allowed the Panther a free run.

Accusations about why Bathpool Park wasn't searched the day after the Panther took off led to an acrimonious encounter between the two men concerning the cause of the long delay in finding the body. Even as they were speaking, another piece of evidence was brought in. It was the Dymo tape machine, which had spelt out the complex ransom trails. It was found among the pile of debris at the bottom of the spillway.

'It was not the job of Scotland Yard to search Bathpool Park,' Patterson argued. 'We were not brought in for that. We offered our expertise in the latest scientific methods of criminal investigation to help you catch this man.'

'I agree,' Kennon replied, 'but it was a serious error, and one that we should all be ashamed of. How could we let six weeks pass before finding the body? We failed dismally in our methods of operation because we had no central planning. All the high-tech equipment in the world means nothing without good organisation. And that will only come with information channelled into a central unit.'

'And how are you supposed to arrange central planning around one man, Chief Inspector? Especially one who moved about so much and was never in the same place twice.'

'Precisely! That's my point. If the information had been channelled through a national incident room, we could have better studied the Panther's movements and methods. In that way we might well have predicted his next move.'

'We already have it, Chief Inspector. It's called Scotland Yard and it deals with all national crimes,' Patterson argued. 'The problem was that the Panther was never regarded as a national case. Perhaps he should have been, but who decides what is national?'

'That's exactly what I mean. We didn't take the Panther seriously enough. What it requires, Superintendent, is a moral code that is measured for its impact on society and how we react to it. In other words how it offends the national conscience.'

'You mean in the way we measure burglary against armed robbery, or manslaughter against murder. We already do that. It's enshrined in the law.'

'But that's judicial law against specific crimes. I'm talking about moral law and how it reflects on us as a society in the way we treat it. For instance, we treat the murder of a policeman far more seriously than the murder of a member of the public. Why's that? Because one is more shocking than the other, and the lesser killing doesn't have the same impact on our morals, and therefore should be treated differently. The murder of a policeman is a national crime, while the other killing is regarded a regional one. Yet both are murder. Both crimes should be morally equal and warrant the same treatment.'

'I take your point, Chief Inspector. But the murder of a policeman strikes against authority and is therefore a greater offence. You can't have it any other way.'

'But we should do! A serial armed robber who murders four sub-postmasters should breach the moral code by a stack, and thus commit a *national* crime!'

With those words ringing in his ears, Kennon returned to Manchester, determined to push for better police communications and better coordination between the regional crime squads. But did Patterson have a point. Who decides what is a national crime?

Kennon arrived back at his headquarters in a morose mood to find Suzanne waiting for him in the car park. He waved at her before he parked and he suddenly found himself in more buoyant spirits as he walked back and greeted her in the car.

'Hello Suzanne. Are you waiting for me?' he said, leaning in the window to give her a kiss on the cheek.

'Who else would I wait for? You look a bit glum. What's wrong?'

'Nothing that can't be fixed. It's just taking a long time to fix it.'

'What about the address I gave you? Don't tell me you haven't checked it out…'

'We're doing it today. But don't hold your breath. Eight days of surveillance revealed nothing. Derek Wyllie must have moved.'

'He's not *Wyllie*! He's Derek *Wilson*. Couldn't you even check?'

'I said we are checking. You have to understand, Suzanne, that we are getting sightings from all over the country and we have to follow them. We had the house in Radcliff Avenue under surveillance and it revealed nothing.'

'Well, I suggest you go inside the house. You won't see anything outside. Anyway, that's not all I'm here for. My newspaper is prepared to double the reward money to help catch the Panther.'

'It's not necessary. I'd rather it didn't.'

'Why on earth not?'

'We're closing in on him in Bradford. I don't want bogus calls to flood in. And I certainly don't want his morale boosted by a huge reward, because it would be, and then he could turn really dangerous.'

'He already *is* dangerous! How much more do you want?'

'How often do you hear of a reward catching someone? It has a negative effect.'

'Well, I'm flummoxed, George, I really am! I thought you'd welcome the offer. It was me who suggested it. What do I tell my editor now?'

'Tell him the truth, what I said: that it would boost his ego and lead him to do something more destructive, maybe another kidnap to make up for the failed one. Believe me, this man wants an audience, and doubling his reward will guarantee it. But thanks for the offer anyway.'

'Thanks a bundle, George. I really can't make you out sometimes.'

Suzanne drove away and Kennon went back to his office. He'd no sooner got inside when the telephone rang. He picked it up to hear a familiar voice.

'Sir, it's Sergeant Stacey. I'm inside the Panther's house in Bradford with Constable Murray. We have just learned his name as Derek Wilson. He lives at 13 Radcliff Avenue. Murray and me were locked in a room and have just been released by his wife after he did a runner.'

'How the hell did that happen!' Kennon could feel his blood pressure rising. 'You didn't follow a laid-down procedure, did you?'

'He fooled us into thinking he was the lodger and then pulled a gun.'

Stacey was overwhelmed by a wave of embarrassment. His blunder would have severe repercussions. He'd disobeyed police rules by going into a suspect's house without back-up. That could be excused for a minor criminal, but not for someone like the Black Panther, who was wanted by half the police forces in England for five murders.

'Have you got back-up now?' Kennon asked.

'Yes, sir. I've got the Bradford CID here going over the house.'

'I'll be there in two shakes.'

One hour later Kennon coasted in with two regional crime squads hastily brought in from the Greater Manchester and West Yorkshire constabularies. Forty police officers and CID men descended on Radcliff Avenue, accompanied by a contingent of Bradford police, and swarmed all over the house. Cordons were set up around the house as they searched it from top to bottom and kept the newsmen at arm's length.

The locked attic room revealed the most astonishing collection of military hardware Kennon had ever set eyes on. Aside from all the Panther's unique workwear, the search revealed a cache of weapons which included a high-powered crossbow, ammunition pouches for shotgun cartridges, and hundreds of rounds of .22 and 9 mm bullets for a Walther PPK, a Browning and a Hi Standard semi-automatic.

The house yielded up secrets like an Aladdin's cave. Notebooks, maps, compasses and survival rations were found in drawers and cupboards. A stiff-cover book contained newspaper cuttings of the Panther's crimes dating from when he started in 1968, along with notes about the difficulties encountered. The names of the victims who were shot were recorded with 'accidental discharge' written in brackets. Pinned on the wall was a large-scale map of the Midlands and the Pennines. Written across the top were the words 'Modus Operandi: method of operation'.

Kennon studied it with interest. A hundred or more village sub-post offices spread across six counties were ringed with a red pen. Wilson's methodical planning had a line drawn through them to indicate the ones that had been raided. The rest were still waiting for the hooded serial robber to resume where he left off.

As the exhibits were taken out to be loaded into two security vans, Kennon remonstrated with Stacey for not carrying out a proper procedure of arrest.

'Your gung-ho go-it-alone actions may well have lost us the Panther, Stacey. Not only did you risk your own life but you risked Constable Murray's as well!'

'I know sir. I didn't think.'

'Didn't think! I never thought I'd hear that from a detective! The man may go into hiding almost anywhere in the country and we might never find him! Didn't you realise that! Or did you think he wasn't capable of it?'

'It was a spontaneous action, sir. I didn't know the man could be such a class actor. There is nothing in the files to suggest he takes on a different persona apart from that of a serial robber with a Black Country accent, and even that's not true. He fooled me completely.'

'But you knew he adopted different accents, and as for being a tax fraud inspector...' Kennon shook his head. 'Didn't you ask for proof?'

'I did. And he gave it to me. Here's his card.'

Stacey handed the card to Kennon, who viewed it suspiciously, noting it as a fake.

'Well, he can't have got far in a couple of hours. There's a massive hunt out for him. Roads, railway stations and ferry ports, just in case he decides to leave the country.'

'Well, at least I got a good description of him as Bryon Davis, and I shouldn't think he will change it. He's too well known as the Panther from all the police photofits.'

'With a damned hood on, he is! He's hardly likely to be wearing it in a railway carriage. Has his wife said anything to give him away?'

'Nothing I could tell, but Constable Murray might have something – she's still questioning her.'

'The wife intrigues me. I'll see how she's getting on. Give the searchers a hand.'

Kennon went through to the lounge, where Murray was sitting with Iris Wilson, who was beginning to show signs of distress. 'I'd like a word with Mrs Wilson, Constable, if you could leave us a while.'

'Yes sir.'

'Mrs Wilson, I'm Chief Inspector Kennon of Manchester CID. I'd like some information on your husband's background. Where did you meet him?' Kennon asked, seating himself opposite in an armchair.

'In the local dance hall at Bradford Textile Hall. I was eighteen, and we got married two years later at Morley. He was still in uniform doing his national service. Twenty years married next month it will be, Chief Inspector.'

'Congratulations. Has it been a good marriage?'

'Oh, yes. We've had our ups and downs over money, like most couples do over the years, but all in all I can't complain. He was self-employed and he worked hard, but he could never earn enough to satisfy him. I never complained. I told him whatever he earned I was happy.'

'Did you have any idea of his criminal activities, Mrs Wilson?'

'No, I didn't. I never looked in the attic. It was his work room and he liked a bit of privacy. He used to be away for days working all over the country. He could be in Birmingham one day and Leeds the next.'

'You must have had some idea of his criminal activities, Mrs Wilson. A man can't hide that from his own wife.'

'I didn't, sir. I had no idea.'

'Then why did you tell Sergeant Stacey he had run off and left you, and you hadn't seen him for two years?'

'I thought he was wanted for income tax evasion. He told me to be wary of the Inland Revenue checking up on him. I have to protect my own husband – surely you can understand that, Chief Inspector. A wife has a duty to her husband.'

'Have you any idea where he could have gone? I don't have to spell out how serious this is.'

'I've no idea, Chief Inspector. No more idea than you have.'

'You do realise that withholding information can land you in a criminal court, Mrs Wilson?'

'I'm sure it can. But I honestly don't know.'

'Did you know anything about the kidnapping of Julia Woodward from her shop in Manchester? Or how we have only just found her body six weeks later in a drainage shaft? She was imprisoned underground in darkness. She must have been terrified. Can you imagine her terror? Never in all my years with the police force have I ever encountered a crime as bad as this.'

'No, I didn't,' Iris replied, her voice growing weaker. Her distress was telling on her and beginning to give her away, as Kennon stared hard and relentlessly at her. While her face was lined with worry, his was set in stone, grim and forbidding.

'I'll ask you again, Mrs Wilson, and I want the truth. Are you honestly telling me you knew nothing at all of the Julia Woodward kidnapping?'

'I am, Chief Inspector. I had no idea Derek was responsible.'

'I never said he was.'

'But you did… You said it was the worst crime you had ever seen.'

'I did say that. But I never said your husband did it. Yet you knew it all along, didn't you? You knew your husband was a serial robber. You knew he was the Black Panther, and you knew he was capable of murder, didn't you, Mrs Wilson? *Didn't you!*'

'I didn't, I tell you! I didn't!' Iris's head fell into her hands and she sobbed uncontrollably. The strain had broken her down.

DC Murray stood in the doorway watching and noting how her boss had taken his time by asking about her personal background before going for the jugular with point-blank questions. Kennon beckoned her into the room and nodded as she laid a comforting hand on the woman's shoulder. Kennon waited as Iris cried out all her pent-up emotions. He knew the strain she was under.

'I'll ask you again, Iris,' he said in a gentler voice. 'Do you have any idea where your husband has gone?'

She looked up with tears streaming down her face. 'Catterick, Chief Inspector. You'll find him in Catterick.'

'Where in Catterick, Iris?'

'The army base, where he did his national service. It's where he goes when he wants to reconcile his life with nature. It's the one place he remembers with pride. The only place where he can be at peace with himself.'

'Can you be more precise? Where will he stay in the town – with an old army friend?'

'No, Chief Inspector, not with a friend. He will roam the moors and sleep rough. He may even use a vehicle to sleep in. He's done it before, when we had a row. He was gone three weeks, but he comes back a different person. He comes back the man I married.'

'Can you tell me what type of vehicle he's using and what colour it is. Is it a van or a car?'

'It's a dark blue van – a Ford Transit, I think. I've only seen it once or twice. I don't know where he got it from, only that he bought it legally.'

'Here in Bradford, from a dealer?'

'No. He never trusted dealers. He would have bought it from the ads in the local paper about a month ago. I'm sorry I cannot be more precise.' She looked up with her eyes ringed red. 'What's going to happen to me now, Chief Inspector?'

'Nothing for the moment, Mrs Wilson. But you must realise that when we catch your husband, as we surely will, you will be called upon as a witness at his trial. I don't believe you are guilty of anything, but that's not for me to decide. I'm going to ask you now to make a full written statement to Constable Murray.'

Kennon nodded to Murray, who took the distraught woman over to the table where she could make her statement, while the police were still emptying the upstairs rooms for evidence. Kennon watched as a large cash box was brought down containing hundreds of postal orders found in a drawer, along with a post office stamp. Without the stamp they could not be cashed. The Panther thought of everything.

In the front room, Iris's statement would fill a dozen sheets of paper over four hours, as the woman poured out every detail of her life story from the day she married Wilson in 1955 while he was still doing his national service. And a bizarre story it was.

Wilson made it all the way to Catterick Camp in North Yorkshire up the A1 in his dark blue Ford Transit. He arrived at the large army camp looking for work just two hours after fleeing Bradford. He was chasing up the newspaper ad he'd seen for carpenters.

The work was already in progress by Willet Construction, the firm that was contracted for a new mess hall and canteen on the camp, and he hoped he wasn't too late.

Using a false name, he furnished details of his skill as a jobbing carpenter to the site foreman, who explained what was required and showed him the plans.

'The whole roof needs renewing on the existing structure, cross-jigged with the new extensions. Other requirements are new windows and doors, skirting boards and solid floors. You'll be working with about twenty skilled chippies under me, all responsible for their own job sheets, which will be regularly inspected. When can you start?'

'Any time you like. But I don't want wages paid through the tax system. I work on the lump from one job to the next. I find that makes it easier all round.'

'It can be arranged. When were you last paid weekly wages on the cards?'

'My last waged employment was on the Swan Shopping Centre, Bridgnorth, working for Johnson Construction.'

'That must be all of ten years ago. I don't suppose you've got a reference – not that it matters. What made you leave?'

'I was paid off when the job finished. Since then I've been jobbing all over the place on loft conversions and house extensions mostly.'

'Johnson's good enough for me. Start Monday, 8 a.m.'

Wilson's carpentry skills paid off when it suited him. He had indeed worked on the Swan Shopping Centre, which was how he came to know the layout so well.

'Oh, just one more thing before you go,' the foreman said. 'Can I have your fingerprints in this book.'

'Fingerprints! What the hell for?'

'It's the new regulations. All men working on the site have to give a sample of fingerprints for examination by the police. It's all to do with this Black Panther who's on the run. Just touch that ink pad lightly and then the book.'

'If you say so.' Wilson had no reason to refuse, since he had no police record. 'What happens to this book?' he asked afterwards, wiping his hands on a towel.

'The police collect it the end of the week and leave us a fresh pad,' the foreman replied, adding the name of Barry Field on the page. The book held the fingerprints of over a hundred men.

Wilson came out the Portakabin with a job under his belt on his former army camp. It was easier than he imagined to work on the lump, avoiding tax and national insurance. He wasn't entirely happy about leaving his fingerprints but he knew it would take a long time for the police to check the thousands being investigated.

But he could bank on three months' work with good pay to see him through the summer months. His strategy was unchanged: paid work through the summer until September, before resuming his post office robberies across the entire north of England and Midlands.

He was hoping to avoid a return to his criminal life but the failed kidnap had left him no option. If he was to make it big in life with his own business he needed capital. He couldn't even return to his house in Bradford. He could only phone to see if Iris had sold the house, although he doubted she would now; she was never keen on moving from Bradford.

But he was determined to move to a different town, although he wasn't sure where. He climbed back in his van and drove the three miles into Richmond, heading for the Coach and Horses pub. Although not normally a drinking man, it was the one place he had fond memories of during his national service days, and he'd kept loosely in touch with the single landlady ever since.

It was lunch time when he arrived at the eighteenth-century oak-beamed tavern in the square and parked his van in the pub car park. In the back were two padlocked boxes containing his carpentry tools and Panther gear, his clothes and weapons, consisting of two handguns with 200 rounds of live ammunition and the 12-bore shotgun. He was still the Panther, whatever else he did.

When he entered the pub he found it busy and noisy. Apart from the usual regulars there was a crowd of boisterous workers from the camp enjoying their lunch-time drink. There was even a few regular soldiers in uniform who were breaking the rules of no uniforms to be worn off duty, enforced since the IRA pub bombings.

Wilson felt a cold sweat, as though he'd been dumped in a bath of icy water, and had to literally fight his inner self from walking out. A crowd of people was the last thing he wanted.

He searched for the landlady, who was the main reason for his coming in, and saw her serving as he walked up to the bar. Lesley Thompson was forty-two but still had the allure of a girl half her age. She had taken the pub over from her parents ten years previously when they retired, and was now the licensed landlady with a small bar staff.

Wilson knew her from his national service days, when she served behind the bar with her parents, who then still ran the pub. On the odd occasions he came in, almost always by himself, he found her pleasant to chat with and he secretly fancied her. He would have liked nothing better than to take her out on a date, but he had never summoned the courage to ask her.

Even after he married and was still serving, he came in for a pint of shandy and a chat. When he settled in Bradford he lost touch completely, and it wasn't until ten years later he saw her again. He was working in the area when he decided to look her up to see if she was still there. He got a better reception than he'd hoped. She was pleased to see him and he was astounded she still remembered him. From then on he kept in touch with odd visits when he was in the area, and now he hoped for it to pay off.

As he forced a way through the throng a young barmaid stepped in. 'Yes sir. What can I get you?' she said.

'A pint of mild, please,' Wilson replied. He was normally a non-drinker, but there were occasions when he had to make an exception, and this was one of them. He paid for the pint and looked round for a seat away from the bar before going to a corner table where a man wearing a brown leather bomber jacket and jeans sat reading the *Irish Times*.

'I see you're from the Emerald Isle,' Wilson said using a soft Irish accent. 'I'm from Dublin myself. Name's Mick O'Grady. Mind if I sit here?'

'Help yourself. I'm Sean Hannigan,' said the fair-haired man. 'So what are you doing here, O'Grady. Looking for work?'

'I was, but I just found it up at the army camp. I start next Monday.'

'Was it easy to get?'

'Dead easy if you've got the skills they want. I'm working on the new mess hall as a carpenter. Strictly on the lump, between you and me. Why should I pay taxes to the bloody British government?'

'The easiest way is not to work for them. But we all need a job. My mate's up there now after one – and here he is, talk of the devil!'

The door opened and Martin McDonald entered, going straight to the bar. He bought a pint of Guinness and then looked round for Hannigan before coming over. 'No good, Sean!' he said with a scowl. 'The bloody jobs have all gone. Not even a labouring job could I get.'

'Never mind, something will turn up,' Hannigan said, sounding not in the least disappointed. 'This is Mike O'Grady. He's from Dublin, working up at the camp.'

'Well, don't that beat all! I'm Martin McDonald. Is your job legitimate, on the cards?'

'No sir, it is not! I told them I'm working on the lump like the rest of them. Cash only. That's what I've always done.'

'Same here. I'm a bricky, but they've got all the brickies they need. But me and Sean here have another interest in the camp, isn't that so, Sean?'

'We do. But it doesn't do to talk about it to every Tom, Dick and Harry. That's unless of course you have a special interest for Ireland, Mr O'Grady, and would like to see the Brits out.'

'Out of Belfast, you mean! Oh sure, but I don't reckon even the IRA will shift them.'

'They will. And it won't be too long, either. Me and Martin here will see to that. We're looking for recruits, O'Grady, to fight for the Cause.'

'Well, don't look at me, I'm a peaceful man. I don't go in for all that IRA stuff.'

'You should think about it. We're willing to pay for good men…'

Wilson could see what Hannigan was driving at and for a brief moment he could see another opportunity opening up. There could be a profit in it. But dare he commit himself? The kidnap failure had left him bereft of ideas and he was grabbing at straws.

'I'll give it some thought,' he said at length. 'Where can I get in touch?'

'Oh no, we come to you when we're absolutely sure. We'll be here next Friday, same time.'

The two Irishman left, leaving Wilson to weigh up the implications of getting involved with a terrorist job for a quick profit. But the most glaring omission from what they'd said was that once you were in, you'd never get out. The pub gradually cleared as the workers went back to their jobs. The soldiers were the last group to leave, and as the pub emptied out from the lunch-time session, Wilson approached the bar.

'I've called time, sir,' Lesley said without really seeing him. She was busy clearing the empty glasses from the counter to put in the dishwasher.

'Hello Lesley. Yes, I heard you.'

She stopped and looked up. 'Derek! What are you doing here?' she said, beaming a smile at him. 'I was only thinking of you the other day.'

'Nothing bad, I hope,' Wilson replied, shaking hands with her across the bar.

'No, of course not. It's just that we're getting a crowd of guys in here from the building site up at the army camp. I thought I might see you, as it's your line of work.'

'I've just joined them. I start Monday as a sub-contractor.'

'Good for you. It must have been an omen, then. Where are you staying?'

'I shall have to find somewhere. I don't suppose you've got a spare room I could rent for a few weeks? I don't fancy sleeping in a Portakabin every night with a load of sweaty men.'

'I do, as a matter of fact, if you don't mind sharing with a rumbustious Alsatian. I had to get a dog in because of this Black Panther bloke. They still haven't caught him.'

'I don't reckon they ever will. But he's not anywhere near this area, is he?'

'No, but it doesn't mean he never will be. The post office is putting up shutters over the road. If he can rob a post office, he can rob a pub. Have you come across him on your travels?'

'Me! How the devil could I come across him?'

'Don't you ever get called in by the post office to fix the damage he does breaking in?'

'No, I don't. Anyway, I don't think he does any damage, or at least nothing major. He must be pretty good at it by now.'

'He's had enough experience at it! Five years, one of the papers said the other day. And wasn't that kidnap horrible. That poor girl! What she must have suffered.'

'I blame the police for that. They were too slow. They worry to much about how they look to the media. They're all bloody show with no substance. How much is the room? I can give you two weeks' rent in advance.'

'Oh, don't worry about that now. Ten quid a week will do me.'

'Nonsense! Twenty quid at least. You've got to make a profit. Nobody does anything for nothing these days.'

'That's true enough. But it's still a tenner. How's that wife of yours – Iris? You're still married, I presume?'

'Yeah, but not for much longer, the rows we're having lately. I think Iris would be glad to see the back of me. I can't blame her. The hours I work must drive her barmy. I'm hardly ever home. What about you? Are you still single?'

'I am. I threw out the last bloke I had living with me, or living *off* me, I should say. The lazy sod never did any work, he just sat about all day picking winners on the horses. Or so he thought. They were mostly losers, like him.'

'You did the right thing. I come across plenty of work-shy blokes in my business. Idlers and dole cheats. Immigrants are the worst of all. You can't move in Bradford without bumping into a Paki or a West Indian bleeding the country dry. I wish I had half the benefits they get.'

'They're not all bad, Derek. There must be a few among them who want a job to make a decent living. Excuse me a minute, I must let the dog out; I can hear her whining at the back door.'

Derek sat drinking in the nostalgia when the lads of B Company would pile in the door to get drunk. But it was the nostalgia for a rifle on the firing range or on manoeuvres over the moors that came more readily to him. They were the days that shaped him into the man he was and made him better equipped to face the world.

He felt pleased that his charm with the women still worked. He did the right thing, keeping in touch with Lesley. He had somewhere to stay and lie low for a while. But he was apprehensive about the job on the camp. If the police came searching for him and checking on the workers, eliminating them one by one, it was only a matter of time before they caught him. He must avoid detection at all costs.

His thoughts went back to Kidsgrove and the failed ransom delivery. He was plagued by the death of Julia Woodward and, though he felt no blame for her slipping off the platform, he knew others would see it different. They would claim it was premeditated murder, that he had no choice but to kill her.

If he was ever called to trial that would be the one crime the media would focus on, and the one he would be ultimately judged on over all the others. It was now official that the kidnapper and the Black Panther were the same person. He'd committed the ultimate crime that gave him the publicity he craved, and still he had not achieved enough to make him quit his double life.

Lesley returned after letting the dog out, and then saw the

barmaids out of the front door locking it behind them. They were now the only two in the pub. 'Would you like to see the room now, Derek?' she asked. It was an open invitation.

He followed her up the creaking stairs of the 200-year-old pub, along the narrow passage and into the spare front bedroom, with its oak beams and hard wooden floor preserved over the years with umpteen layers of varnish. The double bedstead was fairly modern and made up with a table lamp each side. There was a shagpile rug on the floor in front of a chest of drawers and the velvet curtains covered a lead-light window with sparse daylight coming in.

'I'll open the window and let out that musty smell,' Lesley said, twitching her nose. 'That's the only trouble with these old properties. They look nice but it's what you don't see that is the problem. You'd be surprised what eats away at the old oak beams.'

'I've seen it. I've replaced hundreds of dry rot timbers in houses half this age.'

'Of course you have; I was forgetting you're a carpenter. Is it a good living, Derek?'

'Not bad. I do all right. But I'm still looking for the big job. The one that will set me up for life.'

'You'll find it soon. You've got the drive in you to succeed. It only takes a bit of courage to go it alone. I had to face it when I took this pub over from Mum and Dad. I thought at first it would be impossible. I thought, how on earth am I going to manage it single-handed? But I did it. I told the brewers where to get off when they offered to buy me out. It was a good enough offer but I thought, No, I'll bloody do it alone – and I did!'

'It's because you're good at it, Lesley. There's not many women could manage a pub single-handed.'

'They wouldn't want to, either, if they saw the work involved. Still, now you're here I might get a real man's help. You could even serve behind the bar on a Saturday night.'

'I don't know about that, Lesley. I wouldn't be any good at bar work. I don't mind humping a few barrels in the cellar.'

'I can show you the ropes. Once you've served a few customers you soon get into the swing of it. It's a good social life as well. It will bring you out of that shyness of yours. I've noticed it, you know.'

Wilson suddenly felt a wave of sexual desire and he drew her close as they stood by the window. 'Shall we draw the curtains, Lesley?' he said, pulling one half across.

'What a good idea! I thought you'd never ask,' she replied, and she pulled the other half across, plunging the room into darkness.

They kissed passionately for several minutes before undressing down to their underwear, and then fell on the bed together in a clinch. 'I think you've persuaded me, Lesley. I didn't realise pub work had advantages like this!'

'Oh, you'd be surprised, Derek. Anything can happen after closing time. I think you'll find I'm a good teacher.'

'It's all par for the course then, is it?'

They made love for the next hour, resting briefly between bouts of passion, panting hotly as if they had run a marathon and collapsed at the finish. It was around 4 p.m. when they heard a screech of cars pulling up outside.

Wilson leaped off the bed and, pulling his trousers on, he went to the window to peer out. As he looked down on three police cars drawn up in the square, a dozen men of the North Yorkshire regional crime squad came tumbling out. He knew by instinct they were searching for him; it was obvious. He wondered if they had gone to the camp. Then he realised they must have received a call from the Bradford CID. Iris's protective shield was crumbling.

'What is it, Derek?' Lesley said, sitting on the bed with a sheet draped round her.

'It's the police. I think they must be looking for someone.'

'Let me see,' she said climbing off the bed. 'Who can they possibly want?'

'Stay there!' he shouted. 'Get dressed quickly!'

Wilson was dressing quickly, pulling everything out of his duffel bag. 'I'm going to have to leave you, Lesley. Sorry about that,' he said, zipping up his combat jacket.

'Leave? What for? Oh no! It's you they're after!' Lesley looked horrified as Wilson put on his black hood. 'You're the Black Panther!'

'I am indeed. I'm not so shy now Lesley!' He sprang at her, grabbing her tightly by the arms. 'We could have made a good pair, you and me. But I was too reserved, too timid to ask you out! Too bloody timid! See this?' He pulled the semi-automatic pistol from his jacket pocket. 'This is what rules my life now, Lesley! I live by the gun!'

Lesley could hardly find words to express herself as she finished dressing while Wilson fished out a roll of Elastoplast from the bag. Then he grabbed her by the arm and held her tight. 'You're going to get me out of here. Downstairs now, Lesley, nice and easy. Don't do anything foolish.' He guided her down the stairs, gripping her arm while holding the pistol at her head, and then came the rap on the door.

'Police! Open up!'

As soon as they were down, Wilson forced her hands behind her back and bound her wrists together. Then the door was rapped hard again.

'Police! Open up!'

'It's too late, Derek. Give yourself up,' Lesley implored. 'I'll stick by you.'

'Shut up! Just do as I say.' Beads of sweat burst out on his forehead as he gripped her tightly by the arm and they made their way to the kitchen. Outside, the police waited while a marksman crouched behind a bench-table in the pub garden aiming a rifle with a telescopic sight.

She felt the gun on the back of her neck as they reached the kitchen door. 'Open the door slowly, Lesley.'

She opened the door halfway until it stopped against his boot. He stared hard over her shoulder and saw the glint of a rifle in the garden. 'Stay back!' he yelled. 'Or she gets a bullet in the head!'

The two figures emerged from the doorway and the police held back as Wilson kept his human shield in front of him. 'Put down the gun, Wilson!' a detective sergeant shouted. 'You can't escape! You are surrounded!'

'Stay back! Make one move and I'll shoot her!' Wilson barked.

The police were stymied. They were forced to hold their fire as Wilson kept Lesley in his grip. They went through the garden archway and walked slowly across the car park, where the van stood unlocked. Wilson had anticipated a quick getaway. He already had the ignition key in his hand.

'I'm sorry this had to happen, Lesley. I'll let you go as soon as we're clear.'

'You had bloody better! I thought there was something odd about you the first time we met. I should have trusted my own instincts!'

A dozen police looked on helpless as the couple reached the van and Wilson opened the door, still holding Lesley in front of him. Dusk was falling and the police marksmen were severely hampered for a clean shot. Wilson forced Lesley into the driving seat while he crammed in behind her and cut the tape binding her hands with his sheath knife. 'Now start up and drive out of here, turning left!'

As she started the engine, Wilson called a final warning, 'Any attempt to follow us and I will shoot her!'

As Lesley drove out the car park, three police marksmen opened fire on the vehicle as a warning. One bullet sliced through the tread of a tyre without puncturing it, and two bullets went harmlessly into the side of the van as token hits.

Wilson's response was to shoot the tyres on the three police cars as they went by, with Lesley deliberately meshing the gears in an attempt to stall. He jammed the hot gun barrel into the back of her neck for an immediate prompt, and she sped off down the road. The police were soon running for their cars, with front tyres deflating fast. As they set about changing wheels they radioed to headquarters to send some back-up.

The van headed out the town and joined the A1, heading north across the moors for Darlington. It wasn't a place Wilson particularly wanted to go but he didn't have much choice. He was on unfamiliar ground, and there was no other main road to take, not even a country lane he could recognise.

'Drop me off, Derek! I don't want to go to bloody Darling-ton!' Lesley moaned.

'Keep driving! You're not getting off anywhere!' Wilson snapped as he peered into the side mirrors, checking for police cars. There were none to be seen but he knew they would soon catch up. They passed a road sign indicating the A1(M) with Darlington just ten miles away.

'I haven't been to Darlington since my army service,' Wilson said with a melancholy tone. 'It's not a bad place. We only went there for the hop dances and the women.'

'What are your intentions when we get there?'

'I don't know yet. I'll have to look at the place.'

'Well, let me bloody know, won't you!' said Lesley scornfully as she entered the slip road.

They joined the motorway with no sign of any police cars following and filtered into the traffic going across the dales. Dark clouds were scudding over the hills and Wilson rightly reckoned on about an hour of daylight left. He was already planning ahead for another job, only this one would be much bigger, involving bigger risks. He imagined there might be a reception waiting for him in Darlington, and he didn't fancy going round the town looking for somewhere to stay.

'Turn off at the next intersection,' Wilson said as a road sign loomed up.

A mile further on, and Lesley turned off the motorway on to the slip road. As they approached the roundabout under a motorway bridge they saw the police car sitting on it. They were seen as they passed below and Wilson's worst fears were dawning as he gazed up at the two traffic cops on the bridge. He knew they'd been spotted. They approached the town at Blackwell, and Wilson remembered the railway station he once used as a squaddie.

'Pull over Lesley,' he said as they approached the railway gates. 'This is where we part company.'

Lesley pulled into the small station car park. 'Thank God for that!' she said with relief. 'How do I get home from here?'

'On the train. Here's the fare.' Wilson handed her a fiver. 'That will cover it amply. It's been nice meeting you, Lesley. Sorry about the rapid departure. But you'll have something to talk about with the customers.'

'Where are you going now?'

'I can't tell you that. I'll be seeing you!' he revved the engine and drove out the car park, doing a U-turn across the busy road and heading back the way he came.

She watched him enter the traffic flow until he disappeared. Then the police traffic car from the bridge approached pulling into the car park. It stopped right by her and a burly six-foot officer scrambled out. 'Have you just got out of a blue Ford Transit van, miss?' the officer inquired.

'I have, Officer. And if you want to catch him, you'd better hurry.'

'Where's he gone?'

'I don't know. He didn't say.'

'Right, miss, you'd better come with me!' he said, forcibly putting her into the car. 'Put out a call, Harry. The Panther's disappeared. We've lost the bugger!'

Chapter Twenty-two

Wilson drove west across the North Yorkshire Moors taking a circular route to avoid going back through Richmond. He was heading for a place that was little known, yet held a wartime secret that attracted him like a magnet. The dusk was fading with a curtain of darkness descending as he approached the ruins of an old abbey. Egglestone Abbey was the landmark that guided him as he drove on past the ruins heading towards the village of Greta Bridge.

He went straight through the village and crossed the River Tees, heading for the great limestone ridge that bordered the Stang Forest. He was now travelling over the high moors, racing on before the light vanished until he reached the high limestone ridge of Great Haw on the River Greta. The thunder of a waterfall was music to his ears and soon he could see the dark shape of Great Haw, which so fascinated him.

Even though water was pouring over it, it could not disguise the bizarre shape of the rock thrusting out of the craggy cliff like a panther's head, shaped by the elements over time. This was the Panther's spiritual home, where man and the elements were in harmony. Here he stopped in the cleft of a dale to gaze up at the waterfall cascading into the River Greta from a high scar. A fine spray of mist swirled over the rocks and hung in the air like a witch's brew.

The swirling waters tumbled over the rocks, chasing the salmon, and went flowing down a sloping aqueduct to meet the Tees at Greta Bridge. From whatever angle he looked at the Great Haw, he saw the smooth-shaped head of the black panther thrust forward, with water cascading from its open jaw.

He never ceased to be amazed by its perennial beauty. But time was pressing and he had to leave. Darkness was closing in and he climbed back in the van to drive another two miles across High Scargill Moor through the forest.

It was some time since he was last here, and the metal markers he tied to trees years earlier were still there guiding him along the track until he reached a Nissen hut set in a clearing of forest. A large sign on the fenced enclosure read 'MOD PROPERTY – KEEP OUT'. The fence was all but collapsed as he pushed open the gate and drove on through to the mysterious hut surrounded by trees.

This was the place he used as his headquarters during the war games with his family. He had found it by accident as he drove around looking for a place to build a makeshift cabin years earlier. It was a perfect location, well hidden away from any habitat, and was one of the many secret locations set aside by Churchill and the wartime leaders in the event of a German invasion.

Wilson had long replaced the old rusty padlock with his own, and now as he opened the hut door and stepped inside he felt secure. Here was his new base until the heat died down, and it was only ten miles from the army camp – a reasonable distance to travel each day to his job, and ideal for his night excursions into isolated villages.

He switched on the dim electric light that was connected to the mains power supply and looked around. The hut was bare but for a table and four chairs and a threadbare carpet on the bare boards. Just two small windows each side of the hut admitted some light, and there was a cold-water tap over the sink next to a small cupboard where a Primus stove stood. A final touch was an old bookcase with a few dusty books and a *Daily Mirror* dated August 1940, when invasion looked highly probable.

But the real home comforts were below ground in the secret bunker. Before taking a look, he unloaded everything from his van that he needed to bring inside, and only when the door was locked did he venture below. He unlocked the steel partition door of the Nissen hut that hid the concrete pillbox under its roof with a two-inch-thick iron door.

Wilson pulled back the bolts and opened the door to reveal the bunker steps, and down he went using a torch to light the way. When he reached the bottom he switched on the lights to reveal a time capsule. Spread before him was a wartime bunker some thirty feet below ground. The 65-foot-long bunker had a ventilation shaft and was furnished with easy chairs and double bunks for around twenty of Churchill's closest advisers. In addition it had an escape tunnel, entered behind a bookcase, which ran for fifty yards and came up in a pillbox deep in the forest.

On the wall was a large map of Hitler's Atlantic Wall, pin-pointing all the heavy gun emplacements and Panzer divisions in occupied France. There was a dust-laden telephone switchboard with direct lines to all the military bases across the north of England, for keeping in touch with the commanders in the event of invasion. Ironically all this was never used, and it stood as a testimony to the real possibility of invasion in 1940.

Wilson felt privileged to be standing in a piece of history. Here was his HQ, where he could plan his operations until he himself was forced to surrender. His fantasy knew no bounds.

The next few days saw Wilson travelling back and forth to Catterick, carrying out his job on the army camp and getting to know his fellow workers, but never too intimately. He was nicknamed 'The Bodger' simply because of the state of his blunt tools, and the foreman warned him unless he replaced them with new ones he would be flung off the site.

He finished work at lunch time on Friday and travelled into Richmond to buy his new tools from a reputable builders' merchant. He then decided to visit the Coach and Horses. He felt Lesley would understand his predicament and overlook the previous incident. But just to make sure, he telephoned her at opening time. It was a mistake. She swore a stream of abuse down the phone and cut him off dead.

Whether he was naive or just plain stubborn, he went ahead with the visit to smooth her over. When he entered the busy pub it was virtually the same as his last visit, with a crowded bar. All the same faces as before were there, and when he saw Lesley he was suddenly swept by a wave of embarrassment. He slipped surreptitiously in behind a corner table and was suddenly taken by surprise at seeing the two Irishmen. He had put them at the back of his mind and had literally forgotten all about them.

'Hello O'Grady,' Hannigan said. 'We knew you'd show up. You've come round to our way of thinking, then? I knew you would. What are you drinking?'

'I'm not stopping!' he blustered, and started to get up to leave. McDonald pulled him down with a sharp grip on his elbow.

'That's better! Now, you were asked what you're drinking!' McDonald hissed.

'The same as you.'

'Three pints of Guinness all round, Martin,' Hannigan said slipping a fiver across the table to McDonald.

'What exactly do you want from me?' Wilson asked, keeping his Irish accent up. 'I told you I don't go in for this stuff. I'm settled in the job now.'

'I know. That's just what we want from a loyal comrade-in-arms.'

'You've got the wrong bloke,' Wilson reverted to his natural Yorkshire accent over the pub noise. 'I'm not even Irish.'

'I know. I can tell a phoney accent when I hear it, and you're not O'Grady either. But it makes no difference. You're working for us or we tip off the police about who you really are. We saw your dramatic departure from here last week, and after what we read in the papers… well it didn't take a genius to work it out. Welcome to the rebel clan, Mr Panther.'

'Shush! Keep your bloody voice down!' Wilson looked all about him at the other drinkers. They were too engrossed in their own conversations to hear anyone else's private discussions. 'All right, what do you want?'

'That's better. I knew you'd help our cause. He's decided to lend a hand, Martin,' Hannigan said as his mate came back with the drinks.

'Well, that's mighty good of you! I'll drink to that.' They raised their glasses and drank the Irish brew to cement the occasion, and Wilson realised he was trapped. To cross these two men could be fatal. But he had only himself to blame. He had allowed himself to become deluded by their talk of fighting for Ireland for his own ends, and there was no backing out now.

He kept his back turned to the bar to avoid Lesley seeing him and leaned across to the two Irishmen. 'What is it you want, then?'

'We want you to plant a package on the army base where it can't be seen by anyone,' Hannigan replied. 'We want it placed in the new mess that's being built, for maximum impact.'

'OK. Then what?'

'Then you plant a second package and get the hell out before it goes up! The whole bloody works. Boom!'

'I don't see any profit in that,' Wilson replied. 'Have you thought this out properly?'

'It's the way we do it. We're not interested in profit.'

'You should be. It's the way I work. Let's go outside. We can't talk in here.'

The three men finished their drinks in a rush before leaving, and Wilson saw Lesley staring at him across the bar. If looks could kill he'd be dead by now. He mouthed a silent 'I'm sorry' to her and gave a shrug.

She sneered back at him and the three men left the pub leaving Lesley growling under her breath. Outside they went across the car park and sat in Wilson's van.

'Right! Let's hear what you're proposing,' Hannigan said. 'It had better be good.'

'As I said – you blow up the mess and maybe a few blokes with it, and what have you achieved?'

'What have we achieved?' McDonald replied. 'We've struck a blow for Ireland! That's what we've achieved!'

'But why not get more out of it? As I understand, the IRA always gives a warning before it detonates a bomb, right?'

'Right. But not that good a warning. It creates more of a spectacle, helps get the message across.'

'So why not give a warning with a ransom attached? We plant the bomb under the new mess hall, and with it we issue a 24-hour warning. We want £100,000 to give the exact location of the bomb or we detonate it by remote control within the next couple of hours. I'm sure you boys can arrange to have a device sent over.'

'We'd never get one. The IRA doesn't accept a failed operation.'

'It's not a failure. £50,000 in IRA coffers buys a lot of weapons. We split the proceeds fifty-fifty.'

'It won't do,' McDonald said, shaking his head. 'The British government negotiating with terrorists? Never.'

'They will if it saves lives. You get the bomb ready and I'll do the rest. There's one snag. The new mess won't be ready for another three weeks, maybe four. We shall have to wait till then.'

'We can't wait that long,' Hannigan replied. 'We have to be back in Ireland for the next round of talks by next week.'

'It won't work, then. Because all you'll achieve is blowing up an empty building.'

'So we put the bomb somewhere else. The officers' mess. That's even better, I reckon.'

'It won't be so easy to put it there, that's the problem. I can try... What type of bomb is it?'

'A case bomb. Sixty pounds of gelignite with an electronic timer fixed to it inside a briefcase. Easy enough to hide under a seat.'

Wilson thought about the implications. This could be the big job he'd always hoped for, the one to set him up for life with a new start. 'I'll need a week to suss out the location and how to get it there. Security is tight in the camp.'

'Two days! I'll give you two days, otherwise we turn you over to the cops and do it ourselves,' Hannigan told him. 'We'll find another courier. I'm sure there'll be no shortage of volunteers among the Irish workers.'

'They won't have the expertise that I have. They'll make a blunder and you'll all be caught. It only takes one mistake. They talk about it in the pub. Tongues wag with the drink. Whereas with me, I'm normally a teetotal. No slip of the tongue with me, and no risk involved.'

'We don't shy away from risks. We take a bloody risk with every job,' McDonald retorted. 'Bugger the ransom! We strike a blow for Ireland!'

'Go ahead and do it without the ransom, then. But you'll count me out. I'll take my chances with the law.'

'Why, you scumbag! We could finish you off ourselves,' McDonald threatened pulling a revolver from inside his jacket pocket. He pointed it at Wilson and made a clicking noise with his tongue in a mock execution. 'One shot through the back of the head and you're yesterday's news.'

'All right, Martin,' Hannigan said. 'Let's keep our heads. We need the funds. So how do you get them to deliver the ransom then? I read as how you failed on the kidnap, and you killed the girl.'

'That's a lie!' Wilson snapped. 'I tried to save her. She slipped off the platform. It was a mistake I don't intend to repeat. I have another place hidden below ground for the ransom drop. We observe from a distance and when the drop is made and all parties have withdrawn we collect. £100,000 split fifty-fifty. Think what that'll do to your reputation!'

Hannigan thought about it. 'What about the bomb? We still have to explode it. It's our job. We cannot walk away without exploding the bomb.'

'I know, but you have to convince the negotiators that it won't go off, otherwise you won't collect.'

'We don't negotiate. We issue an ultimatum! They deliver the money and have a few hours to find the bomb, after we give a rough location miles out. Then the bomb goes off. We give twelve hours' warning. That gives them ample time to get the money.'

Wilson nodded. 'Agreed! When do I get to see this bomb?'

'It's not yet complete. Give us two days to finish it and we will deliver it to your place. Where is it, by the way?'

'Ten miles from here, in a secret location. I can't say more than that at this stage. I'll collect the bomb from you when it's ready. I suggest the Catterick Bridge pub car park at nine o'clock next Monday evening. That's two days from now. Then we will discuss the final plan for detonation and where to collect.'

'Nine o'clock in the evening? That's no good!' Hannigan replied. 'That's the time I want the bloody bomb to go off! Nine o'clock in the morning! But remember, if you cross us, it will be curtains for you. We'll hunt you down. There'll be no hiding place anywhere.'

On Monday morning in Manchester's CID headquarters, Kennon studied the photographs of Wilson found at his house and compared them with the five different photofits on the incident board. Only one of the photofits bore a slight resemblance, with the same shaped face and eyes. But the photographs did reveal Wilson's penchant for playing army war games with his wife and daughter on the moors.

The photos were fairly recent, showing his daughter at the age of fifteen dressed up in combat fatigues, leaning against the family's Austin Champ jeep. His wife was sitting behind the wheel, smiling for the camera – even though she couldn't drive and had no licence. Another photo which baffled Kennon showed Iris's body slumped half out of the vehicle with smoke rising from the burned-out Champ as though it had been hit by shellfire. Another showed Wilson and his wife raising a telegraph pole as part of the communications post for their headquarters. They were stage-managed photos which served to highlight Wilson's obsession with all things military.

'It gives an insight into what makes the man tick,' Kennon said, passing the photos to Dr Erwin. 'But how he persuaded his wife and daughter to join in, I can't fathom.'

'Because he orders them to and they're compelled to obey. It's military law. The paramilitary uniform gives him the power he craves,' Erwin said. 'It's just one step away from his criminal activities with a shotgun that puts him squarely in control. That's the man's vice. He has to be dominant, completely in control.'

Kennon gazed round the office at the few staff working on the Panther file. Murray was still there in the outer office working diligently on records. DS Roberts, now recovered from his wounds, was back at a desk job. The priority had shifted to the IRA, and Kennon feared the Panther inquiry was running out of steam.

Even the press had lost interest, although they did report on the Richmond pub incident. There hadn't even been a single post office raid, and it seemed the Panther really had gone to ground.

The telephone rang and Kennon picked it up. It was Sergeant Walker downstairs, reporting from the radio room that Sergeant Boyd was on his way back from Bradford with a new piece of evidence.

'Not another bloody torn envelope with a scrawl on it, I hope.'

'Better than that, George. It's Wilson's notebook of codes appertaining to the post office raids found in a cubbyhole in his house.'

Kennon put the phone down. 'Sergeant Boyd's on his way with Wilson's code book. But I can't see that of being any use.'

'I can't wait to see this,' Dr Erwin replied. 'It should unravel a lot about the man.'

'Can there be much more we don't already know?'

'Definitely. These photos tell us something of the man's military obsession, but that only scratches the surface. If my understanding of military codes is right they give a message by spelling out modes of operating. For instance, take the mnemonic for Panther. P is for post office. A is for armed. N is for no accomplice. T is for timing. H is for early hours. E is for entry, and R is for… that one escapes me for the moment.'

'How about repugnant? So what sort of codes do you expect to see, Doctor?'

'Similar types of mnemonics that have a link with military history and tie in with his own personal traits, I imagine. That's the usual pattern.'

'I see. I take that to mean the ravings of a military fanatic, Dr Erwin. This man won't have anything new or intelligent to say. The average criminal is no better informed than the rest of us. But they like to think they are.'

'That's true, George. I agree wholeheartedly, but men like Wilson are not the average criminal. They have the ability to see what others don't. They have a sharper instinct for survival, taking all the risks into account so that you and I will never suspect them. Their weakness is their vanity. It urges them on to bigger things. They don't know when to stop, so sooner or later they get caught by the law.'

'True. Wilson probably thrives on the media attention he gets. It glamorises him. But I don't believe he possesses any magic ability to see more than I do. Nor does he take all the risks into account. He failed in his kidnapping venture and now he's on the run.'

'But you haven't caught him, and you won't until you understand him and his motives – and you don't have any real strategy to do it with, have you, George?'

'No, but I'm coming round to one. I see his weakness in all things military, those photos prove that. He can't resist playing at battles. I think we are going to have to meet on his terms.'

'What for? Playing at soldiers?'

'Sir! There's a visitor for you,' Murray said, coming back in the room with her file. 'It's Wilson's daughter, Karen. She's in the interview room.'

'Wilson's daughter!' Kennon felt a surge of new blood. 'Did she say what she wants?'

'Only that she wants to talk to the man in charge of the investigations.'

'If there's anything interesting, Doctor, I'll give you a buzz,' Kennon said, slipping the photographs back into the file. 'You'd better come with me, Murray. She will talk more freely with a woman in the room.'

They made their way downstairs to the lobby and along the corridor to the interview room reserved for visitors. Karen Wilson sat on the upholstered seat clutching a package in nervous apprehension.

'Miss Wilson. I'm Chief Inspector Kennon from CID,' Kennon said shaking hands with the girl. 'This is Detective Constable Murray. She will take notes as a formality. Now, what can I do for you?'

'I've come to give you this, Chief Inspector,' she said, handing over the package. 'My father collected them during his National Service. He kept them hidden.'

Kennon took the loosely wrapped package over to a table and unwrapped a shoebox. He lifted the lid and stared in disbelief at a collection of Second World War weapons and badges. There were swastikas from German POWs, several British Paratrooper cap badges, an army revolver and a Nazi ceremonial dagger in a leather sheath. But what caught his eye was a grooved dull-metal hand grenade with the pin still in it. 'Bloody hell! Did you carry this on public transport, young lady?'

'I did, sir. But I don't believe the grenade is real. It's most probably a dummy. My father used to make them. He was fascinated by explosives.'

'By God, I hope you're right.' Kennon lifted the hand grenade out the box, keeping firm hold of it. 'See this, Constable Murray. If I were to accidentally drop this we could all be blown up.'

'It doesn't look a fake to me, sir. But then I've never seen a hand grenade. Don't drop it, for God's sake!'

Kennon wrapped it in brown paper and put it back in the box. 'Is there any more of this stuff back home, Karen?'

'I don't think so. I've had a good look in the attic. I had to hide this from Mum; she would not have approved me bringing it. She doesn't know I'm here. She thinks I'm at a friend's house.'

'Just as well. I don't think my superintendent will be too pleased when I tell him, either. I shall have to call the bomb squad. Is there anything else you wish to say? Feel free to talk – there's nothing to fear.'

'I'd just like to say that whatever my father has done – and I don't condone it for one minute – he is not a bad man. But he has delusions and fantasies. He can be obsessive, especially with me, and he has sometimes treated me harshly, but I believe he did it through misguided principles. He wanted to protect me.'

'I understand, Karen. Most fathers want to protect their daughters from the harsh realities of life. But nevertheless, he's still a dangerous man to the public, and we have to capture him and bring him to trial.'

'Did you know Wilson is not his real name, Chief Inspector?'

'Yes. I do know he changed it from Wyllie.'

'Wyllie… I know it sounds ridiculous. He did it for my sake. He didn't want me ridiculed at school like he was. That's how much he thought of me and why he was so possessive. When I left school he didn't want me to find a proper job. He wanted me to work for him. He even used to pick my friends for me.'

'That doesn't surprise me, Karen. He sounds just the type to be over-protective. He does it for his sake as much as yours.'

There was a long silence while Karen sat staring at the floor. 'Is there anything more you'd like to tell us?'

'There's so much, I don't know where to begin.' Karen's face was etched with pain. 'I feel blighted by his crimes, as if my whole life has been screwed up. Can you imagine what that's like? My own father has committed murder.' Tears welled in her eyes.

'All right, take your time. Would you like Constable Murray to get you a cup of tea?'

'No thank you, I'll be OK. When I read in the papers that my father was the Black Panther, and responsible for the kidnapping, I wept. But the tears were not for him, Mr Kennon. They were tears for my mother. I cried for her.'

'I understand, Karen. You've been through a tough ordeal. Your father was last seen in Darlington. Can you throw any light on why he should go there? Does he have any friends in that area?'

'No, I don't know why he's gone there. He used to take me and Mum to Catterick several times to look at his old army base but it was usually on our way to the Yorkshire Dales for a boring week of army games. Dad found an old army hut we used as headquarters. He said he was going to do it up as a summer retreat for us. I didn't enjoy my holidays with him. It was all so silly when I look back.'

'Where is this hut, Karen? Do you know the name of the place?'

'It's not far from Greta Bridge at Great Haw on Scargill Moor in the middle of nowhere. It wasn't much to look at. A bit of a dump, really.'

'So it's quite possible he might have gone back there,' Kennon said. 'Is it near any major road or village?'

'The main road goes through Greta Bridge. You turn off there for Scargill in a remote area on the edge of Stang Forest surrounded by limestone clefts and potholing caves. Caves are another of his fascinations. He can stay down them for days. You'll have a hard job catching him if he's on the moors. He can go for days on small packs of survival rations.'

'Can he indeed? I shall have to take a look at this place. I'm going to have to leave you, Karen. Constable Murray will look after you. Thanks for coming in.'

Kennon left the room and went along to the radio control room just as Sergeant Walker was on his way out to the canteen.

'Ted, I've got some urgent business. I want four men, two of them armed.'

'It's a bit tight, George. They're tied up with the IRA business, and there's been another bomb warning at Warrington.'

'Merseyside can deal with that. All right, get me two detective sergeants from Number 4 squad. Leave the marksmen out; Stacey and Kelly will do, and tell them I need them urgently. Ah, there's Boyd coming in.'

Kennon caught up with Boyd on the stairs. 'Boyd! What have you got?'

'You won't believe the stuff we're turning up at the house, guv. Survey maps, letters, detailed descriptions of breaking and entering – and to top it all, this year's diary of the Panther's post office raids!' Boyd said, handing it over.

Kennon flipped through the first two months of dates, which listed several rural sub-post offices, complete with the addresses, plus a baffling code of letters alongside in brackets.

'These are jobs that have either occurred or been abandoned, by the look of it,' Kennon said. 'The code of letters is baffling but I daresay Doctor Erwin might make something of it. I've asked for Sergeants Stacey and Kelly to report in. How good are you at potholing, Boyd? Ever done any?'

'Are you serious? No, I haven't,' Boyd replied as they entered the department. 'Why? Are you thinking of taking it up, sir?'

'Superficially. Wilson's daughter, Karen, has been in, and she's blown Wilson's cover. It's just possible he's in an old army hut on the Yorkshire Moors at Scargill. I want to see this place. The four of us will descend on it in stout walking boots to look the part of serious potholers. It's the only way I can think of getting close to the man. We must bring the Panther in, Boyd, before he strikes again.'

'If he's down a pothole you can count me out. I've got a thing about confined spaces.'

They walked to the Kidnap Incident Room and Kennon passed the code book to Dr Erwin. 'There you are, Doc. See what you can make of that.'

'I will, George,' Erwin replied, getting up to leave. 'Did the daughter have anything useful to say?'

'She brought a box of weapons, including a hand grenade, still with the pin in it, and a few medals. Oh, and Wilson changed his name from Wyllie some time ago.'

'Did he indeed! That shows the trait of a very disturbed mind.'

'That should get the old juices flowing for you,' Kennon said, turning to the map.

'Here it is, Boyd. "Great Haw" – it's marked as a cave, by the looks of it, just outside Greta Bridge. This area is Scargill Moor, deeply wooded, where Wilson has his headquarters, according to his daughter. We shall probably have to hunt around for it.'

'What is it we're looking for?'

'An old army hut, probably a Nissen hut left over from the

war. It would make an ideal hideout for a military fanatic like Wilson.'

'Why do we have to dress up as potholers? Why can't we just storm the place and arrest him?'

'For one, we don't know whether he's there or not; and two, he's armed to the bloody teeth! I don't want to get shot, and I don't suppose you do either. He's a killer, Boyd. As potholers, we pose no threat. As police we do, and I don't want him taking off again. If we need armed back-up, we'll send for it.'

'How? By carrier pigeon?' Boyd said, thinking his boss had lost his marbles.

At eleven o'clock, Stacey and Kelly arrived and were briefed on Kennon's plan to capture the Panther. They were left in no doubt as to the risk they faced that was driven home by their boss.

'Make no mistake. This man is dangerous,' Kennon warned. 'He's a military fanatic fighting his own war, and unless we corner him we're never going to catch him. We are breaking from police convention and I take full responsibility for it. Police convention has failed, now let's try the Panther's way, with a false identity.'

Before they left the building, Kennon briefed Sergeant Walker about his mission and circled the area on a map. He anticipated they might be gone a day or two, and so questions would be asked. He was staking his career on catching the Panther, but it was worth it. He felt the pressure taking its toll on him after three months of his most difficult case yet.

There was no time for delay, so Kennon drove out and headed for a large outdoor sportswear shop on Liverpool Road to buy the kit they needed. They received personal attention from two of the staff, who gave them advice on the correct clothing required for potholing, and there was not a hint they were detectives.

They purchased trousers made of tough flannel, waterproof coats, walking boots, thick wool socks and bobble hats. On top of that there were climbing picks and tackle to hang on their belts, with a coil of yellow waxed rope for each man. There were no half measures. They had to look genuine. It was all paid for on expenses, and Kennon realised he would have some explaining to do to Bradley.

They came out the sports shop carrying their suits and shoes in carrier bags which they put in the boot. They looked the part, dressed as potholers with all the attendant apparatus of ropes and tackle, but they didn't quite have the same enthusiasm. They climbed into Kennon's own Rover, trying to forget they were detectives and set off on the long journey to the North Yorkshire Moors.

It was 2.30 p.m. when they arrived at the tiny village of Greta Bridge and pulled into the pub car park of the Traveller's Inn. They went inside the pub and inquired about a room for the night. Kennon anticipated they would need it, and he maintained their cover as potholers exploring new caves.

'I can put you up, gents. But I thought you potholers roughed it in tents,' the landlord said, pulling them pints.

'We do normally, landlord, but we thought we'd have a change this time round,' Kennon replied. 'We're looking for the Great Haw cave; do you know of it?'

'Great Haw! That's the deep one. There's been a few accidents up there, I can tell you. It's in the Great Limestone Ridge of Scargill Moor. I've heard it's sixty foot deep and half a mile long. It's about four miles from here, gents. It's marked by a waterfall with a panther-shaped head thrusting out of the limestone – one of the wonders of Scargill Moor, which spawned a folklore legend of a prowling panther.'

'That should be easy to find, then. Do you know of any refuge huts up there, in case the weather turns?'

'No, I don't. There's an army Nissen hut nearby, but whether it's for potholers' use, I doubt very much.'

'Have you any idea who owns it?'

'It's MOD property. During the war there was talk of building a secret underground bunker up there for Churchill in case the Germans landed. Now, whether they did or not I don't know. But I suppose that was the whole purpose to keep it secret.'

'That's interesting. Have you seen or heard of anyone using it recently?'

'No, I haven't. But there was a bloke who used it for war games with his wife and daughter a few years back, so I heard.

Amazing what some people do in their spare time! But it can't be very secure if it's open for anyone to use.'

'I suppose not. How far is it from the Great Haw cave, in case we have to use it as a base?'

'Not far. About a mile into the Stang Forest. It's in a fenced enclosure.'

'Can we use your car park for a while? I think we'll set off on foot from here.'

'Of course. But watch out for some of those caves out there. They can be damned dangerous.'

'We will. Thanks, landlord.'

They stepped outside into the chilly air, picked up their ropes and tackle, and set off for a four-mile walk, conscious they had only about three hours of daylight left. They crossed the ancient stone Greta Bridge where two rivers, the Greta and the Tees, met with a dull roar of water thrashing below them in a foaming whirlpool before slipping, quietly and unhurried, along a natural sloping aqueduct.

They walked in single file up the narrow road to Scargill that branched off the A66, taking in the scenery crossing brooks and streams. The Greta River was swollen by heavy rains and they were forced to cross some dangerous bogs, sinking up to their ankles. The landscape was varied, with a range of hills and caves on the limestone scars, and they were grateful for their stout walking boots and waterproof jackets, which gave good insulation against the cold.

Scargill village was little more than a few crofters' cottages on the edge of Scargill High Moor, which was a track of thick forest. Soon they were walking towards the ridge that was Great Haw, and when they reached the waterfall they stood gazing up at the thrusting rock in the shape of a panther's head. The jaws were open, with water pouring out and flowing on each side of the glistening head with a dull roar as it tumbled fifty feet over the rocks into the River Greta.

'This must be the Panther's spiritual home,' Kennon said, checking the map as they stood gazing at the unique feature. 'We're on the right course, lads. Let's get moving.'

They walked on through the village and entered the Stang Forest, where tall pines cut out the last of the dying light. They carried on for half a mile up the twisting road until they reached a clearing with a gated entrance to what appeared to be a private road. A large board on one side read 'MOD PROPERTY – KEEP OUT'.

'This must be it, lads,' Kennon said, surveying the dense wood. 'You wouldn't find this place in the dark.'

'How the hell would anyone find it?' Stacey replied. 'Wilson must have a nose like a bloodhound.'

'He probably heard of it doing his national service,' Kelly observed. 'He could have even trained in this area.'

'Right, let's take a look at it,' Kennon said, slipping the rope off the gatepost. 'We'll ignore the sign. There's been a vehicle up here. See the tyre tracks? We'll follow them.'

They followed the tracks for a short distance and stopped just before a clearing. They could see the hut as plain as day through the trees. As they moved around it, they saw a blue Ford Transit van parked just behind under the trees.

'That's his van all right,' Kennon said. 'Kelly, you play the injured party. Put your arms round me and Boyd. Stacey, rub some dirt on his face and cut the sleeve of his jacket.'

'It'll ruin a good coat, sir,' Stacey said putting a penknife through the material and ripping it open.

They moved on to the mysterious hut and saw it was fenced off by a wire-mesh fence. It was an enclosure inside an enclosure. On what was once a gate, but now looked like part of the sagging fence secured by a chain, another sign read 'MOD PROPERTY – KEEP OUT'.

'That's a nice welcome! Here we go then,' Kennon said, pushing open the rickety fence gate. Suddenly the hut door banged open and an unshaven tramp of a man shouted, 'Can't you read! What do you want?'

It was Wilson, and he was brandishing a 12-bore sawn-off double-barrelled shotgun. He looked a physical wreck. His face was drawn and sallow, he had bags under his eyes from lack of sleep, and his hair was a tangled mess.

The four men froze in their tracks, staring into the glaring eyes of the man who had evaded capture for four long years. And though they didn't know it, he in turn had a gun pointing at him – from two IRA men hidden inside, out of sight.

'We're potholers!' Kennon shouted back. 'We've got an injured man here who needs medical help. I insist we come inside.'

'This is MOD property!' Wilson angrily retorted. 'I'm the official keeper of it. So you can find somewhere else to take him! Now get out!'

'Be reasonable, man! We've just walked ten miles with him, we can't go on. We have to lay him here. Have you got a phone we can use?'

'No. There's nothing here! The nearest phone is at Greta Bridge, a few miles up the road. Now shove off! I won't tell you again!' Wilson pointed his gun at Kennon.

'All right, if you won't help we'll go! But I'll be back, and I'll bring the police with me! You're no more the official keeper of this old shack than I'm Jack the Ripper.' They turned round, still holding Kelly between them.

'Wait! Bring him in. I don't want no trouble.'

Kennon turned back, hardly believing what he heard.

'Thank you! What's brought this sudden change? What are you hiding? Escaped prisoner on the run, are you?'

'Never mind all that! I'm letting you in. Just two of you!' he said, indicating Kennon and the injured Kelly. 'You other two can go back to the village and get an ambulance… if you're lucky.'

Boyd hesitated. 'We can't leave you here, guv,' he said under his breath.

'It's all right,' Kennon whispered. 'We can manage. Get some back-up.'

'What are you jabbering about! Are you coming or not?' Wilson shouted.

'I'm coming,' Kennon called back. 'Get an ambulance, lads,' he shouted after them.

Boyd and Stacey hurried away as Kennon turned back with Kelly and dragged him towards the hut door. Kelly moaned about his back with every step. He had no visible injuries and the back was all he could play on.

Wilson watched every move, standing back as they came through the door. 'Lay him on the bunk,' he said pointing to a corner where there was a bunk which he had dragged up the steps from below. He knew where he had to sleep at night, and it wasn't the bunker.

Kennon laid Kelly on the bunk and he groaned like a seasoned actor.

'It's his back. He slipped on a rock inside the cave,' Kennon explained, hoping to God Wilson didn't ask him which cave. 'All right, mate. Take it easy. The ambulance is on its way.'

He straightened up, and when he looked round he got the shock of his life.

Sitting in the far corner at a table in the dim light he saw two men watching with loaded revolvers pointing straight at him. They were Hannigan and McDonald, and they had just secured themselves the first IRA arms dump on the British mainland.

Chapter Twenty-three

'What the devil is this?' Kennon said. 'I was right. You're escaped prisoners.'

'Sit down and shut up!' Hannigan said. 'We're the IRA. You've got us to thank for letting you in. But we're big-hearted like that. Isn't that right, Martin?'

'It is, Sean. We're a couple of big-hearted fellows.'

'All right, let's cut the crap. What do you two big-hearted fellows want from me?'

'Just a wee favour, nothing too big. You see, our friend Derek here is not exactly straight with the law himself. That's why he carries a shotgun. But we stick by him because he is doing us a favour tonight, isn't that right, Derek?'

'If you say so. But it's bloody risky. Why can't I do it tomorrow, like we agreed?'

'Because time is of the essence, and we don't have a lot of time… What's your name, feller?' Sean pointed the question at Kennon.

'Russel. George Russel.'

'I'm Sean Hannigan, my mate here is Martin McDonald. You'll be hearing a lot more of us. Now, George, the problem we have at the moment is this: Derek here has agreed to plant a package containing a bomb in the middle of Catterick Camp. He knows the layout as he works there on a building contract for the new mess hall, which is where we originally wanted the bomb to go. But there's been a change of plans, and the new target is the officers' mess. But we're thinking one bomb will not make such a big impression as two bombs. The second target is the armoury. We were content to leave it at that, but Derek wants big bucks for it. He's of the opinion that the British government will pay out a hundred grand to stop the bombs from going off, isn't that right, Derek?'

'I said it's possible if we show a commitment to say precisely where the bombs can be found once the money is cleared.'

'But you see, George, as I have already explained to Derek, that is not the way the IRA works, and my commanders would roast me alive if I failed the campaign for the sake of a few lousy grand. They don't want money, they want blood – soldiers' blood. I have to strike a blow for liberty. So that's the dilemma we face. Now, I'm not against making a profit by any means, but my self-logic tells me the British government won't pay a terrorist, nor would they even negotiate, so we have no choice but to go ahead with the bombing as originally planned.'

'And you want me to assist! No way! I don't do the IRA's dirty work.'

'Yes, I thought you'd say that. So what can I do? I have to go ahead without the ransom, which was never realistic from the start. But I can't trust Derek to plant the bombs if he's not getting anything out of it. So how can I trust him to do the job? I could blow his head off, but that won't solve my problem. I need an inside man to carry it out.'

'Why don't you plant the bomb yourself? That's what you usually do, isn't it?'

'Because I don't know the camp layout. Catterick is the largest army base there is, and heavily guarded. If I get caught the job's a failure, and the IRA doesn't tolerate failures. They'd dispatch me and I'd never see the light of day again. Things were looking bad until you showed up. You've given us another hand to play. You'll plant the bomb, George, and to show our appreciation, I'll let your injured colleague over there off from an early grave. Otherwise I shall have no choice but to blow his head off, and yours with it. You get my meaning?'

'Only too well. But you'll blow our heads off anyway, even if the bombs do go off. You can't afford to let us go free.'

'You're wrong there, George. When this job is done we will disappear. We have no roots in this country. It makes no difference whether you run to the police or Special Branch with my name. In fact it would be an honour to be placed on the list with a bounty on my head. That gives me a greater standing in the IRA. I'm a hero overnight! You have my word you go free if you do the job. Otherwise I shall have to dispatch you. So what do you say? Will you do it?'

'It doesn't look as if I've got much choice. But how are we supposed to get inside?'

'That's the easy bit. You'll be going in wearing the uniform of the British Army. We even provide a car. Derek will be Captain Somerset, and you will be his driver. You will carry a forged pass each in case you're stopped, but our experience tells us that's highly unlikely. The guards tend to get a bit lazy at this time and they just wave through any man in uniform without bothering to check the pass. Derek will direct you to the officers' mess and the armoury, and you will wait outside while he goes in and plants the bomb. Then when he's done that you will drive him back out of the camp to base. But it won't be here; oh no. It will be the Traveller's Inn at Greta Bridge to drink a pint of Guinness and watch the BBC Ten O'clock News on the bar TV.'

'You're willing to step inside a pub after a bomb outrage, and order a pint with an Irish accent? You're mad!'

'Aye, lad. You have nothing to fear from the Scots,' Hannigan replied in an authentic Scots accent. 'It's a fine pub ye have here, landlord.'

'Very droll… That won't convince him!'

'I think it will. And you can't blow the whistle either, or he gets it in the head. If it's the right news we want to hear on the TV we all disperse and you won't see us again.'

'What's to stop me driving straight to the nearest police station once we leave here?'

'Because we shall be coming with you to make sure you don't. You will drop us twenty yards from the camp entrance and we shall be watching to make sure you drive inside. The perfect job. You'll be striking a blow for Ireland.'

'What time are we supposed to strike this "blow for Ireland"?'

'Eight o'clock. That's three hours from now – plenty of time. I suggest you get into uniform ready to go while we prepare the bomb. It's a thirty-minute drive to Catterick. Of course, your injured colleague will have to stay behind tied up so he can't escape.'

'You've overlooked the ambulance that's on its way.'

'By, God, Sean, he's right! What are we going to do about the bloody ambulance?'

'We'll have to wait and see. I reckon we can bluff it out. We tell the crew they both left. The injured man felt able to walk after a little rest. What can they do? They'll have to take our word.'

Dusk was falling as Sergeants Boyd and Stacey, both nursing sore feet after their long hike, limped into the pub car park at Greta Bridge. The Traveller's Inn was closed until six o'clock, with almost an hour to go, and neither man had the car keys to sit inside the car out of the biting cold.

'We'll have to knock the landlord up, Jack,' Stacey said, resting on the stone wall.

'It will blow our cover if we do. Still, I don't suppose the boss will worry about that now. Isn't there a blasted telephone box in this village?' Boyd replied, looking round for a phone.

'We're in the outback, mate. I'll be surprised if the inn's even got one.'

'Right, let's knock him up and see.' Boyd gave a loud knock on the front door and after a few minutes they heard the bolts slide back.

'Hello, boys! Where's the other two?' the landlord said opening up. 'Don't say there's been an accident.'

'You could say that, landlord. We need a phone urgently. We apologise for the deceit, but we're not real cavers. We're detective sergeants from Manchester CID, and the boss is in trouble up at that MOD place.'

'I didn't think you were real cavers, somehow. This way, boys.' The landlord led the way through the public bar, ignoring the payphone on the wall, and through to his comfortable lounge. 'There you are, boys. Help yourself,' he said, pointing to the phone on a small table. 'I'll get the kettle going for some tea.'

Boyd dialled the desk number and got straight through to Sergeant Walker. 'Ted! It's Jack Boyd. You know where we are. We need back-up divisional firearms officers, asap. The location is the village of Greta Bridge on the A66, ten miles from Catterick Camp. The boss is in trouble. I'm at the Traveller's Inn with Sergeant Stacey.'

Walker responded with a prompt radio call for Number 6 Regional Crime Squad to return from the city centre where, ironically, they were on IRA watch. Then he called Divisional Firearms based across the city at the police training centre before reporting to Superintendent Bradley. As the mechanisms of law enforcement swung into action there was a crucial element missing. No one was leading the operation, and so it passed to Bradley, who was pleased to put his paperwork to one side and lead from the front.

Six cars left Manchester with twenty-four men, including four firearms officers for the eighty-mile drive north. Headlights stabbed the darkness as the cars sped across to Leeds and on to the Great North Road, the A1. They were heading into a prolonged operation of catching the Panther which they hadn't envisaged.

'Where the hell did this uniform come from?' Kennon asked, feeling the rough khaki itching and making his skin crawl. He was looking for a diversion to distract McDonald, who was sat in a corner of the hut holding a pistol on them. He could still hardly believe he was this close to the Panther. All the statistics concerning the man's height and weight were correct. His darker skin tone and permanent five o'clock shadow were other features identified on the photofits. But the most prominent feature were his eyes, which glared like a cat.

'It's my old uniform,' Wilson replied. 'I slipped the quartermaster a couple of quid to wangle it out when I was demobbed after national service.'

'Couldn't bear to let it go, eh,' Kennon commented. 'And where did that one come from you're wearing?'

'We got it from an army and navy store for five quid. Not bad value, when you consider how much a new one costs,' Hannigan said. 'That's what I can't understand about you British. You let your country's uniform end up in a second-hand store! No wonder the country is in such a state.'

'It's in better shape than Ireland,' Wilson responded. 'We don't resort to terrorism on our Celtic neighbours.'

'That's because your country's not occupied. Have you noticed right through history how the British never leave a colony unless they're forced out?'

'You're making too much of an issue out of it. When I was in

Belfast the two sides got along perfectly well, Catholic and Protestant. There was no bitterness, no hatred, just a good friendly atmosphere.'

'Sure they did. But didn't you notice the Protestants got a better class of service wherever you went – from jobs to decent housing – while we Catholics were shunned. Sectarianism has bubbled under the surface for years and it's up to us, the IRA, to put it right.'

'You won't put it right your way,' Kennon said, unable to stay out of the talk. 'And I doubt whether politics will do it. But try integrating your culture and you'll see the difference. People only go to war when they fail to understand each other.'

'Oh, we understand all right! We have a free state that ends at the border, and that can't be allowed to continue.'

Hannigan opened the briefcase on the table to reveal sixty-pounds of gelignite sealed in two packets, each wired to a small 24-hour digital detonator. 'This is what will make the difference. Timed to go off at exactly 9 p.m. when the mess is full of British officers drinking their gin and tonics. Well, this will make an even bigger mess, and save them the trouble of building a new one. Now remember, Derek, you have to take one of these packets out for the armoury and leave the one for the mess in the briefcase. I'm setting them both now.'

Hannigan pushed the timer buttons on each bomb and shut the case. 'You've got two hours. Now let's get going.'

'Hold on, Sean. What about him?' McDonald said, pointing to Kelly laid on the bunk.

'You're right. Now where did I put that bit of rope? There it is, on the bloody floor.' Hannigan picked up the rope, and as he bent over Kelly to tie him up, the sergeant suddenly grabbed him by his coat and pulled him down. In one fluid movement he was off the bunk and swung the startled Irishman round onto McDonald with a force that sent them crashing against the wall.

As the two men collided, Kennon leaped at McDonald, grabbing his gun hand and forcing it up. A shot was fired through the roof at the sudden jolt on his arm as Kennon pushed the man backwards off the chair and tore the pistol from his hand. Hannigan regained his balance and took a wild swing at Kennon as Kelly charged him to the ground. Both crashed to the floor and Kelly, the bigger man, had Hannigan pinned under him.

McDonald was pinned under both men, staring down the barrel of his own gun.

'I've got him covered, Kelly!' Kennon said, thrusting the pistol out in both hands.

Kelly got to his feet, still holding Hannigan in an armlock that kept him down while McDonald lay sprawled on the floor with blood trickling from his lip. Kennon held the pistol on them and then realised there was a man missing.

'Wilson! He's gone!' Kennon shouted, keeping the pistol trained on the IRA men.

'I'll get him, boss!' Kelly flew out the door and rushed outside into the darkness, unable to see a damned thing. 'Bloody hell! Where'd he go?'

He searched round the back of the hut, assuming it was the most likely path Wilson would take, and peered into the dark woods. He thought he saw a movement in the trees and he shouted at a dark shape moving away. 'Wilson! Give up now!'

The next thing he heard was the snap of a shotgun being closed after loading, followed by a blast of a shot that tore through the trees as Kelly threw himself flat on the ground. Then he heard the van start up. He scrambled to his feet in a last-ditch effort to stop him, but he was just too late. The van was moving away with its engine racing. It flattened the fence and bounced wildly out the compound and down the track heading for the road.

Kelly went back inside the hut. 'He's gone, boss. He took a shot at me and then got away in the van.'

'Yes, I heard it. You OK?' Kennon asked, keeping the gun trained.

'Yeah, I'm OK. We almost had him too,' Kelly said, staring at the empty table. 'Jesus Christ! He's taken the bomb with him as well.'

'You're bloody coppers!' Hannigan said. 'I might have guessed. And you were after the other feller. Bloody hell!'

'We were. Ironic, isn't it. You picked the wrong man, Hannigan.'

They hustled the men outside with their hands tied behind their backs and padlocked the door of the hut. Then they walked to the IRA car, which was parked further back under the trees.

Kennon had already extricated Hannigan's car keys from his pocket and the two IRA men were forced into the back, tied together for extra security. The two detectives climbed into the front with Kelly at the wheel and Kennon in the passenger seat still keeping the pistol trained on the captives.

Kelly started the car and switched the headlights on full beam, illuminating the forest. The car left the woods at the end of the forest track and pulled out on to the road heading for the village of Greta Bridge.

Chief Superintendent Bradley listened in disbelief as Boyd spilled out the story in the pub car park. Four of his detectives masquerading as potholers had travelled eighty miles to capture Wilson and bring him in and two were now trapped by the man.

He heaved his shoulders like a prizefighter in a boxing ring and sighed. Even the men from Kennon's own regional crime squad were of the opinion their boss had made a grave error and would not get off lightly.

'Didn't you realise you were breaking with police convention?' Bradley seethed in the cold night air. 'By discarding with warrant cards and IDs, you were acting without proper authority. Supposing Wilson had gunned you all down? There would have been no grounds for charging him with malicious wounding. He could simply claim he thought you were out to rob him.'

'That's a risk we were all prepared to take, sir,' Boyd replied.

'Oh, yes! You got that off pat, Sergeant!' Bradley's breath seemed to freeze in the night air. 'I wonder at the workings of the Chief Inspector lately, I honestly do. Rules and regulations are there to be observed, not discarded on a whim! So now we've got to rescue him and Sergeant Kelly from some Nissen hut in the middle of nowhere!'

Bradley glared at all the men gathered around him. Privately, every man was backing their boss, hoping he'd come out trumps. He usually did, even when he discarded proper procedures.

'I've taken men off IRA watch to come here. If the Chief Constable hears of this, there will be one hell of a political storm over it. And he ran up a bill…'

Bradley's words were lost against the sound of a car horn and a blaze of headlights speeding towards them. Kennon had expected the back-up would have arrived by now, and when he saw the men crowding the area he waved an arm out of the window as the car turned into the car park with flashing lights and came to a stop. All eyes peered to see through the mud-splattered windscreen as the two men climbed out.

'How the devil did you get out, sir?' Boyd asked holding the door open.

'Wasn't easy, but the game's not over yet!' Kennon said as his eyes fell on Bradley. 'I see the chief is here. Good evening, sir.'

'Never mind good evening! What the devil's going on?'

'We came here on a tip-off to capture the Black Panther, sir. But things didn't go quite as planned and we've caught the wrong man. Two of them, in fact.'

'What are you talking about, Chief Inspector? And why are you wearing an army uniform! Is this another one of your stunts?'

'Stunt? Certainly not!' Kennon was going to savour the next piece. 'We lost Wilson, sir. He's on the run again. But to compensate for it, we've brought in two IRA terrorists. They're in the back of the car.'

'Two IRA terrorists!' Bradley blustered.

'That's right. They were all set to blow up Catterick Army Camp.'

The rear doors were opened, and the two IRA men were discovered tied together. They were hauled out and held for inspection, and a body search conducted for weapons. 'They're clean. Who are they?' a detective said as he searched Hannigan's pockets for a gun.

'Sean Hannigan and Martin McDonald,' Kennon said. 'And if it hadn't been for the quick thinking of Sergeant Kelly here, we might still be under a death sentence. Now, if we act fast we might still catch Wilson. He's escaped in his Ford van and he's carrying the IRA bomb. It's my guess he's heading back home to Bradford. What he intends to do now is anybody's guess.'

Chapter Twenty-four

Wilson drove like the wind. He was heading south with an erratic plan forming in his head. The past events had stirred his mind into a seething cauldron of rage over his past failures. He nursed a burning sense of social injustice that had grown into a malign and twisted hatred – and someone had to pay for it, and pay heavily. There had to be an account for a life of hard work, so that he could justify the end and say it was worth it.

The plan forming in his mind revolved around the bomb he was carrying in the briefcase. He had removed the detonator and it could easily be put back while he made a demand for a large sum of money. He wasn't greedy: £100,000 was all he wanted. It was a realistic amount, besides being all he could carry.

The place would have to be a public place somewhere busy where a lot of lives could be threatened. Manchester seemed the most obvious place, because of its size and large population, where he could outsmart the police. He would give a warning like the IRA, but make it longer; twenty-four hours, as opposed to the IRA's maximum two hours.

He drove on, thinking out the details of where and how to place the bomb unseen, but collecting the ransom caused him more concern. Who would pay, and how, required a carefully laid plan that might take several days to work out. In the meantime he needed somewhere to stay.

He was consciously heading towards Bradford on the A1 with no direct route to Manchester. He would have to take the Leeds ring road to pick up the road across the Pennines and as he approached the overhead sign for Bradford he felt the lure of home. Dare he risk it? The police search of his house must be finished, but how would Iris receive him? He would chance it and find out.

At the Wetherby junction for Leeds and Bradford, a new danger threatened. A police roadblock was waiting for him, and as the traffic began to slow he realised he had no option but to dump the van. As the tail lights came on in front he immediately pulled over on to the hard shoulder with less than 200 yards to the police checkpoint.

He grabbed everything he needed, including his shotgun, from behind the passenger seat, and stuffed it into his large duffel bag. All his survival equipment – his rations and blankets – and his tools would have to be left behind. Then he climbed out the cab, taking the briefcase bomb with him, and fled across open country.

It was 2 a.m. when he arrived at Radcliff Avenue, tired and hungry and let himself in with his own key. The house was in darkness and he guessed Iris and Karen were asleep in their own rooms. Karen always wanted her own space. He went through to the kitchen, closing the door behind him, before switching on the light, and drank a glass of water from the tap before searching for something to eat.

A cheese sandwich seemed the only available choice as he searched the fridge and took out some cheddar and margarine. He took a couple of slices of bread from the bread box and made the sandwich with some pickle. Then, taking a half-bottle of brandy from his pocket, he took a swig and sat content in his own kitchen, pondering his plans for his last job.

He was focused on Manchester Central Station for a bomb plot to have any impact. It would have a terrorist foundation with the added impetus of a ransom attached to it. He would lay the trail as he'd done for the kidnapping on Dymo tape at varied locations for the police to chase on a strict timetable before the bomb went off.

He had visions of Manchester's top detective, George Kennon, carrying the ransom whilst trying to pin him down at the same time. It would be the classic case of 'Police versus the Black Panther' before he quit the role for good. He would go down in the annals of crime history.

As he sat there contemplating with his back to the door and feeling the brandy take effect he was unaware of a young woman creeping stealthily down the stairs with a gun in her hand. It was Karen, and she had woken at her father entering the house.

She approached the kitchen seeing the light under the door, which was slightly ajar, and she slipped in behind the figure slumped on the table drifting into sleep. She stared at him a full minute trying to decide what to do, and then she shook him. He stirred and looked up through hooded eyes to see his daughter holding a gun on him.

'Karen. Where's your mum?'

'What are you doing here, Dad! Why did you come back?' Karen asked in a less than welcoming voice.

'This is my home. I live here.'

'Not any more it's not. We don't want you here!'

'Put that gun down. Where did you get it from?'

'From your secret room. The one you kept locked and forbade anyone to enter. Now I know why – you're a murderer! I hate you!'

'No, you don't. But you must let me explain the circumstances in which I acted.'

'I don't want to hear it!'

'You have to! Put the kettle on and we'll talk!' he ordered her.

'No! You don't order me about any more. I'm eighteen and I live my own life. Why did you have to come back? I thought we were rid of you for good.'

'You don't mean that. I'm your father. I did everything for you. I gave you a good home and brought you up to show respect for your elders.'

'Oh, don't give me all that shit! You did it for yourself!'

Wilson was shocked. Karen had radically changed, and he didn't like it.

'You be careful how you speak to me, young lady. I'm still your father and you'll do as your told. Now sit down and listen! And put that bloody gun down before you have an accident.'

'An accident! That's a laugh. It was you who taught me how to use one on those bloody manoeuvres you dragged me and Mum on.'

'I did that to help you cope with life. There are people in this world who would take advantage of you. You're a better person for it. I didn't want my daughter hanging round with the wrong kind, taking drugs. It's an unfair world out there!'

'Spare me the grief! It's all about having the right attitude. And

I don't see you as a role model. You let go of life when you took up robbing innocent people and shooting them. But the worst crime for me was the kidnapping of Julia Woodward. What possessed you to do such a thing? You revolt me!'

'I did not kill her! It was an accident. I swear to you on my life I did not kill Julia Woodward. She slipped off the platform. I tried to save her. As for the other killings, I used a gun when I was forced into a corner. I had no choice.'

'You did have a choice! You could have chosen to give yourself up, but you didn't! You carried on with it, you got a kick out of it. How do you think Mum feels, knowing she was married to the Black Panther? She's sick with worry! We want you out of our lives. Go, Dad! Go now!'

Karen pointed the gun at her father, her hand trembling.

'Don't be silly, Karen. You won't use that. Do you think I don't know my own daughter? Come on, give it to me.'

'Yes! You don't know your own daughter. You never have done. You're oblivious to others while you dream in your own little world, acting out fantasies that have nothing to do with real life! When did you ever take Mum on a proper holiday, after all she did for you? Every year was the bloody same – on the moors playing at soldiers, while you gave the orders. But no more, Dad. Those days are gone.'

The door opened and Iris stepped into the kitchen. 'Put the gun down, Karen,' Iris said with a calm voice. 'Hello Derek. I didn't expect to see you so soon.'

'Hello Iris. They can't keep me away from my home. Now tell that daughter of ours to behave herself.'

'Don't listen to him, Mum! He's evil!' Karen urged, her hand shaking. 'He'll worm his way back and we'll never get rid of him! You don't want him, do you?'

'Come on, Karen. Let's sit down and talk about it. We don't want a scene.'

Iris filled the electric kettle and switched it on. 'Let's have a cup of tea and talk it over.'

'Oh, for Christ's sake, Mum!' Karen banged the pistol down on the worktop. 'I'm going to bed! You two sort it out!' Then she rushed out of the room.

They listened as she stomped up the stairs to her room and heard her door slam. They looked at each other with a resigned shrug of the shoulders as if to suggest she was an impossible teenager going through a phase, but both knew different. Their little girl had grown up remarkably fast.

'She'll get over it,' Iris said. 'I'll make the tea. Where have you been, Derek?'

'Catterick. I went back to the headquarters to have a look at it. You remember the fun we had up there, Iris. You liked it, didn't you?'

'It was different. But it was a bit over my head, all that army stuff. What's it like there now? All overgrown, I expect.'

'It's just the same as ever. The hidden bunker is still there. No one's been there, so it's still our little secret. But I had a bit of trouble. I ran into the IRA, who wanted it for an arms dump. I got tangled with two of them. They wanted me to plant a bomb in the barracks. Well, I couldn't do that, but I had to go along with them, or they threatened to shoot me.'

'Goodness me! I hope you told them where to go.'

'No Iris. You don't tell the IRA where to go. But I managed to escape when the police closed in. That's where I've just come from. At first I thought it was a stroke of bad luck, the police tailing the IRA to our HQ; then I realised it must have been Karen who told them. That was the bitter part for me. But I came away with a bonus. I pinched their bloody bomb.' He chuckled. 'Here it is in this briefcase.'

'No! Don't open it!' Iris shrieked, knocking a cup into the sink and smashing it.

'Don't worry, it's harmless. I've defused it.' Wilson opened the case. 'Sixty pounds of lethal gelignite. It don't look much, but it's enough to blow up an entire building. This is what they used on the three pubs in Manchester.'

'But what are you going to do with it?' Iris asked meekly.

'Use it on my next and last job. Yes, Iris, this is my last job. If I get this one right we don't have to work any more. We'll have made it.'

'Where are you going to put it?'

'I don't know. But I reckon Manchester's Central Station

would be as good as anywhere. Plant it in the left luggage lockers. I could then issue an IRA warning and hold British Rail to ransom: £100,000 or the bomb goes off.'

'You can't do that! It's wicked.'

'Don't tell me what I can and can't do! You're as bad as Karen. I hope you haven't been turning her against me.'

'Of course I haven't. But she's growing up. Give it up now, Derek! Haven't you done enough damage?'

'No! I'm not finished yet! This has got to be the big one. If I can pull this off we can retire. I must do it. I don't want to be remembered as a failed kidnapper. I didn't kill that girl, but who will believe me?'

'Nobody, Derek, because you caused it to happen. That's the difference.'

'One day I'll tell the world how it really happened. Why I was forced into crime, how life conspires against you... I'll let them know that the powers that be in this country are morally corrupt. Twenty years from now it won't be safe to walk the streets for fear of black muggers and rapists.'

'I'll stand by you, Derek, but I won't get involved with a bomb plot.'

'I need an alibi to collect the ransom. No one's going to get hurt. I'm not going to blow anyone up.'

'How are you going to get the ransom if you pose as the IRA?'

'I don't know yet! Don't ask so many questions, woman!'

'There's no need to get angry. When are you going to do it?'

'Soon. I need to lay low for a while until the heat dies off over the pub bombings. They'll have every copper on the street asking questions.'

'You'll have to hide the bomb somewhere safe. I don't want Karen to know about it.'

'She won't know a thing. How much cash have you got? I need some money.'

'About £100. There's no more postal orders. The police took them all.'

'That will do. I need to have at least seventy quid. Can you spare it?'

'I suppose I'll have to. Where are you sleeping tonight, Derek?'

'I can't stay here. I shall have to use the lock-up in Leeds Road.'

'You can't do that! You'll freeze to death in there. Let me phone my sister.'

'At this time? Don't be daft! I'll use the lock-up. Get my body warmer and scarf.'

Iris trotted off to get the body warmer and the money while Wilson checked the contents of his duffel bag. He was checking to make sure he had all the essential items in case he had to do another post office raid. Money was getting tight, and if he had to resume his work he would do so. Everything was there, from his brace and bit to his black hood and the sawn-off shotgun.

Iris returned with the body warmer and scarf squashed into a rucksack and the seventy pounds. She helped him on with his rucksack over his raincoat and gave him the money. He took a swig of brandy and was ready to leave. Then he noticed the pistol that Karen had brought down lying on the kitchen worktop.

He picked it up and ejected the magazine clip. It held just one bullet. 'Dear Karen,' he said putting the gun in his duffel bag. 'She wouldn't have fired it.'

He turned and went to the front door pulling his cap on as he went.

'Take care, Derek,' Iris said. She was still desperately trying to keep their marriage together. 'When will I hear from you?'

'I'll be in touch.'

He gave her a peck on the cheek and turned away, going out of the gate with a final wave. Then he was gone into the night.

The streets of Bradford were quiet as he briskly walked the two miles to the Leeds Road. A full moon was shining over the rooftops on this calm March evening, and the wet streets were drying after the rain. He was loaded up with rucksack on his back, the duffel bag over his shoulder, and the bomb briefcase in his hand, walking at a steady pace.

As he reached the halfway mark, a Panda car turned out of a side street just ahead of him of him and passed on the opposite side of the road. The constable had noticed him, and decided that a man loaded up with bags walking around at 3 a.m. needed checking out, and he turned in the road. He came back slowly, catching up with the walker. Then, leaning across to wind down the window, he stopped him.

'Excuse me, sir!' the constable called over. 'Mind telling me where you are going at this time of the morning?'

Wilson hesitated. 'Wortley. I'm going to Wortley.'

'That's a fair old distance. Mind telling me what you've got in the bags? Only at this hour I have to check people walking the streets.'

Wilson stopped and looked the young constable square in the eyes. 'Personal possessions. I've had a row with the missus and I've left home.'

'A marital tiff! That's sad. But I still have to be sure.' The constable got out of the car. 'Mind showing me what's in the duffel bag, sir?'

Wilson dumped the bag on the ground and in one swift movement he pulled the shotgun out, gripping it in both hands and pointed it straight at the policeman.

'Hands up!' he ordered. 'Make one wrong move and you're a dead man.'

'Now h-hold on, sir,' the constable stammered. 'Let's be sensible.'

'Handcuffs! Put them on!'

The constable took the handcuffs off his belt and snapped one on his wrist as Wilson looked around for an anchor point. The only thing in range was a door handle on a nearby betting shop, and he ordered the policeman over to it.

'Snap the other end on here and give me the key!' Wilson ordered.

The constable did as he was told and Wilson dropped the key down a drain before sliding the shotgun back inside the duffel bag. He had won a small triumph, and it boosted his ego to go still further, so he checked the car to see if the key was in the ignition. It was, and he threw his bags inside and climbed in behind the wheel. He started the engine and without a glance at the stranded policeman shackled to the door he drove away, jumping a red traffic light, and headed for the city centre.

Wilson drove up Canal Road, went through the deserted city centre, jumping two more sets of lights, and turned on to the Manchester Road. He was in two minds whether to head for

Huddersfield and look up an old army pal, but he wasn't sure of the address. He knew he had to find somewhere to stay, and friends were few and far between. In fact there was only one person in his life he could rely on, and that was his wife.

He felt the pull of Manchester as he approached the ring road and headed for the A58 to Halifax. He had twenty-five miles to go on a clear road and he drove on, ignoring the crackle of police messages on the short-wave radio as he crossed the Pennines.

As calls came through for the constable to report in to his station he knew he would have to dump the car pretty soon and walk. Miles of dark road went flashing by until Rochdale offered the first stretch of lights with an orange glow over the endless empty carriageway.

Just below Rochdale he turned off for Oldham and drove through the old town just to have a look at it before driving on for Manchester. He had some fond memories of Oldham from just after the war, where he played on bombsites as a kid. He was subconsciously searching for his aunt's house, where his mother took him to visit when they lived in Rochdale for a while just after the war.

But so many years had passed he couldn't remember where it was, and he drove on towards the big city. He drove through Moston and carried on until he was around three miles from the city centre, then he turned off the Oldham Road and headed for Ancoats Hospital. He knew roughly where he was east of the city, and he drove into the hospital car park and pulled up close to the west wing. It was not yet 4 a.m. and still dark, and he felt himself fighting against sleep.

As much as he wanted a short nap, he couldn't stay in the car and he climbed out with all his baggage and walked away out of the hospital grounds. He walked for three miles, keeping off the main roads as far as possible, until he came to Piccadilly Station which was a terminal for southbound trains.

He entered the station, walked across the concourse and found a seat in one of the far corners and slumped down to wait for the buffet to open. He catnapped for an hour until six o'clock when the station came alive with the buffet opening, and he shook himself awake for a cup of tea.

The hot cup of tea warmed his bones after the cold night, and as early morning passengers came into the buffet he realised he must look a bit of a tramp after his hectic journey all the way from Catterick. He rubbed his chin, felt a growth of stubble and then decided he had better move on.

But where to go was the question. Outside the station he entered a phone box to look at the small card adverts that were on display. He glanced at the ones offering a special massage for gentlemen at Cynthia's, and other delights on offer, as he scanned the small cards. Apart from students' bedsits in a hostel there was nothing in the way of a private room.

He stepped outside the box and walked on down the Piccadilly Road heading for the Market. The dawn was rising and he stopped at a newsagent's to look at the ads. There was one that caught his eye: a room to rent for ten pounds a week at 44 Stretford Road, Salford. He entered the shop to ask for directions and came out with a newspaper. He glanced at the front page to read of another IRA bomb explosion in a Birmingham pub, and then set off as the dawn rose slowly over the city.

It was a long walk of nearly four miles, and when he reached the run-down district he was half inclined to turn back, but he had come this far and decided it might be ideal after all. Stretford Road was terraced on both sides with small two-up and two-down houses with tiled forecourts. He found Number 44 and knocked.

A young woman of around thirty, wearing jeans and a roll-neck jumper, opened the door with a cigarette in her hand.

'I've come about the room for rent,' Wilson said. 'It was in the newsagent's window.'

'A bit early, innit? Where'dya come from?'

'Catterick Army Camp. I've been hitchhiking all night. I've just been demobbed.'

'Come in, then.' She closed the door and led Wilson down a short passage to the stairs. 'This way.' She led him up the stairs and they stepped into the small bedsit with a portable electric stove, a wardrobe, a chest of drawers and a single bed on a lino-covered floor. 'This is it. We share the bathroom and toilet along the landing. It's not much, but it's only ten quid a week.'

'Is there anyone else to share it with in the family?'

'Nope. Just me. I split with my old man two years ago when I found out he was seeing another woman. I've been taking in lodgers to help pay the bills. What's your name?'

'Field. Barry Field.'

'I'm Maureen. Are you married, Barry?'

'No. I was living in army married quarters, but me and my missus split up just recent. Now I'm out the army I have to look for work and somewhere to stay. I might not be here long, depending on what I find.'

'That's not much good to me then, is it? You might be gone in a couple of weeks. I need someone more permanent.'

'I know, I'm sorry. But I need a place badly. I'll give you fifteen quid a week if you'll let me stay.'

'Fifteen quid! Bloody 'ell! I'll even do your cooking for that.'

'There's no need for that; I know how to cook, and I see there's a small stove here.'

'Well, perhaps the odd meal, just now and again. I wouldn't mind a bit of company. It gets boring being stuck in on your own. I work odd hours, cleaning, and sometimes I do a bit of bar work in the evenings. Keeps me busy.'

'That's life,' Wilson said, taking out a roll of notes from his pocket and peeling off three fivers. 'Here you are. Fifteen quid in advance.'

'Ta very much. You are a gent,' she said, eyeing the wad of notes. 'Here's your room key. I expect you want a rest now. You carry on. I'm going out for a bit; I'll see you later.'

The door was shut and Wilson shoved all his kit in the wardrobe before flopping on the bed. He lay there, gazing up at the ceiling. He reckoned this place would be ideal. Only one person in the house suited him. As he lay on the bed his eyelids grew heavy and he fell asleep within minutes.

He slept soundly for five hours and woke at 2 p.m. to see pale sunlight filtering in through the net curtains. It was the first bit of sunshine in weeks. He raised himself off the bed and went to the door opening it a little. He could hear voices downstairs which sounded like two women chatting and figured it must be a neighbour dropped in.

Then he looked at himself in the mirror and decided his first job was to wash and shave. He rummaged in his rucksack for his electric razor, plus soap and towel, and then padded along to the bathroom.

Ten minutes later, looking a lot more respectable in a clean shirt and trousers, he was back in his room with the electric kettle switched on while he rummaged for a small jar of instant coffee. He made himself a cup of black coffee, using packs of sugar pinched from roadside cafés, and then sat on the bed with his road map to work out his plan.

The most difficult of any demand crime, whether it be kidnapping or blackmail, was how to collect the ransom. He had already tried once with a live hostage and failed. How would he manage with a similar situation? The more he thought about different ways to collect the ransom, the more impossible it seemed.

Any drop point could be easily covered by police, as it was at Bathpool Park. Even so, Bathpool Park seemed the best option. He had spent weeks looking for it and it could have worked if the instructions had been followed properly.

He decided he would use it again, only this time he would have a different escape route through the subterranean canal. He had no idea where it emerged. The only way to find out was by going back there at night with a powerful torch and going right through it. He was pretty sure the water in it was only waist deep, but the real problem was where exactly did it emerge – if at all – and how long was the tunnel?

He looked at his watch; it was 2.40. Now was as good a time as any, and it was only a short train journey to Kidsgrove. Then he realised there might be a problem. Would the area be sealed off to the police? It was two months since the kidnapping; surely they must have finished by now. Anyway, they were hardly likely to be there at night. He would have to risk it. He checked his rucksack for a good torch, a hand mallet and a hand towel that Iris had thoughtfully packed. That was all he needed. Then he left the room, locking it behind him and went downstairs.

He could still hear the women talking in the kitchen and he knocked and poked his head round the door. 'I'm just going out, Maureen. I might be late back.'

'Hello Barry. This is my next-door neighbour, Carol. You'll need a key for the front door, then.'

'Yes, please.'

'Pleased to meet you, Barry. Maureen tells me you're ex-army,' Carol said in a flirtatious manner. 'Are you from Manchester?'

'No. I'm from Leeds, but I thought I'd have a look at Manchester before I decide what to do about a job. They don't teach you much in the army. You know how it is.'

'There you are, Derek,' Maureen said handing over a front door key. 'What time do you expect to be back? Only I normally bolt the door at midnight.'

'I could be very late, 2 a.m. most probably.'

'I'm normally in bed by midnight. I could wait up, though.'

'You go to bed and lock up. I'll stay with a friend back in Leeds.'

'Don't be daft! You're paying enough for your lodgings. I'll wait up, it won't kill me.'

'Well, if you don't mind. If it's not any trouble... See you later, then.'

Wilson left the room and the two women listened for the front door to close.

'He's gone! Well, what do you reckon! Is it him?' Maureen asked.

'Bloody 'ell, Maureen,' Carol said, looking as if she'd seen a ghost, 'that's him all right! That's the face in all the papers, and in the post office. You've only gone and let your room to a bloody murderer!'

'But he seems such a nice bloke. I don't know whether it's him or not. I still can't really believe it.'

'Of course it's him! All that about being ex-army is bullshit! How many soldiers have you seen with hair that long? They all sport a short back and sides. It's definitely him.'

'What are we gonna do? I'm sleeping under the same roof with a bloody murderer.'

'Think of the reward though. Twenty-five grand split down the middle. We'll be quids in.'

'How we gonna get it, though? If we report him to the police and it's not him we're gonna look a right couple of chumps.'

'We need to pump him a bit. Get him to talk. How about dressing up tonight in a bit of sexy gear. Black stockings and short skirt… plus a few drinks… that ought to do it.'

'What – both of us? Look a bit suspicious, won't it?'

'Why? I live next door. I stayed up with you to keep you company.'

'What's your old man gonna say?'

'He won't mind. You know Steve, soft as putty. Besides, when he sees the reward, he'll be over the moon.'

At three o'clock, in the city centre, Wilson left Hargreaves' sports shop on Oldham Street carrying a large plastic carrier bag. He had just purchased an inflatable mattress and a foot pump to inflate it with, but he had no intention of bathing. He had no idea of the depth of the water in the canal. If it was too deep to wade through then he would float through it on the rubber raft.

With his cap pulled down across his brow, he walked along the busy street with no one giving him a second glance. The man wanted by half the police forces in the country could go shopping in city centres and no one recognised him.

He reached Piccadilly Station and bought a return ticket to Kidsgrove and checked on the last train back, which was 11.30 p.m.: much earlier than he thought. That meant he would have to go down the tunnel at about nine o'clock at the latest in order to catch the last train, or wait for the morning one. Either way, it wasn't a problem and he boarded the train that was standing in the station waiting to leave in five minutes.

He found an empty compartment and sat thinking over his plan as the train pulled out, clattering over the points and heading for Birmingham. The plan would run very similarly to the kidnapping. First a phone call to the station manager warning of a bomb, followed by explicit instructions to go to a phone box, where the ransom trail would begin on a strip of Dymo tape.

The phone call would be the acid test. Would the manager take it seriously or dismiss it as a prank? Given the spate of recent IRA bombings, he couldn't dismiss it. He dared not. The bomb would be delivered on the same day and placed into a left luggage box on the station concourse.

His one other concern was a vehicle to carry the large amount of money. £100,000 was the sum he would demand. It would require at least six suitcases, but he would demand that the cash be put into canvas holdalls. It would probably go into three or four large bags.

The weight would be considerably more than he could carry, so he would have to devise a way to drag them through the tunnel, over 150 yards to the canal tunnel entrance. From there they would go onto the lilo and then floated down the canal.

Once that bit was done he would have to transfer the money to a vehicle parked somewhere along the open canal bank and make his escape. It sounded too easy. What could possibly go wrong?

When the train pulled into Kidsgrove at 3.45 p.m. Wilson alighted and left the station to stroll round the small town centre. He was anxious to see if there was any police activity in and around the police station, as well as being curious to see how the police worked. As he expected, he saw posters of himself pinned up all over the town in shop windows, and it made him appreciate how much of a campaign had been generated since the kidnapping. The publicity he'd always craved was the only consolation in his long catalogue of crimes; he certainly wasn't proud of himself for it.

There didn't appear to be much police activity around the police station or anywhere else, but he was perturbed to see huge stretches of water in the High Street from recent flooding. It didn't surprise him, given the amount of rain that had fallen lately. The drains weren't coping, and he was concerned about the drainage system under the park. Had it coped?

He headed into a small bakery-cum-café, which had a pleasant atmosphere inside. The smell of fresh baked bread and a wide choice of pastries and cream sponge cakes on offer were tempting, but he still ordered his customary cup of tea and a currant bun and took them to a small table.

There were a few customers in the café. They didn't pay him the slightest attention, and he sat looking at the framed photos on the wall of old Kidsgrove at the turn of the century. Dusk was approaching and he had a few hours to kill before going to Bathpool Park, where he expected police activity might be more visible.

As he sat there thinking out his plan he realised he needed something more than just a plain set of instructions on Dymo tape and a name popped into his head: Harry Farr, the ex-miner, who lived in Bridge Street. It was Harry Farr who'd told him about Bathpool Park when he bumped into him five or six years back working as a postman. He was still bitter over the mine closing, even though he was over sixty and had failing eyesight. He lived at the other end of town and he was worth a visit.

He finished his tea and was about to leave when the door opened and a policeman came striding in. This was all he needed. The constable's cape was dripping water all over the place, and only then did Wilson realise it was pouring with rain outside.

'I advise all you people in here to go home quick,' the constable told everyone. 'The river has burst its banks and the High Street is flooding.'

Wilson kept his face turned away from the policeman as he picked up his rucksack and plastic bag and made for the door. Outside, the rain was falling steadily, and he walked briskly away down the High Street where the water was bubbling up the drains and collecting in great pools over the road and pavement.

It was a two-mile walk to Bridge Street, and Wilson stepped into a phone box on the chance that Harry might have acquired a telephone by now. He looked in the phone book, ran his finger down the page and found the address: H Farr, 44 Bridge Street. He thought he'd phone first to make sure he was in and he dialled the number.

The phone rang several times before it was answered by a gravelly voice. 'Farr! State your business.'

'Hello, Harry. It's Derek Wilson. I'm in town and I thought I'd look you up. I see you're still in Bridge Street.'

'Derek Wilson! What are you doing in Kidsgrove? Bodging up someone's house?'

'Something like that. Interested in earning a bit of cash – a tidy sum?'

'Depends. I had to quit the post office. Sight got so bad I couldn't read the damned addresses. Ended up putting everything through the wrong doors.'

'Not your fault, mate. It happens to the best of us. I'll pop round and see you.'

Wilson stepped out the box and walked up the High Street, counting his blessings. Harry Farr unemployed… couldn't be better! He wouldn't see his face clearly and wouldn't even connect him to the kidnapping. But would he go for the plan to earn a tidy sum? Of course he would, after he'd heard the fake story Wilson was putting together.

It was just after nine o'clock when Wilson arrived in Bathpool Park from Boathorse Lane. Harry Farr had accepted his offer without any doubts, and now it was time to put the next bit of the plan to the test.

It was a desolate place, and Wilson sensed some of the park's sinister secrets rustling in the trees as he walked along the lane with his head bent against the rain. The park was deserted with no sign of police activity when he entered by the low wall. There were no cordoned off areas, and even the tent was removed from the hill over the death shaft. He followed the track towards the railway embankment until he saw the dark hump of the centre shaft, and then he was suddenly overwhelmed by trepidation. For two months this place had become a scene of intense activity, and it all came flooding back, filling his mind with things he'd sooner forget. He had still not laid the ghosts to rest.

He knelt over the manhole cover to insert his turnkey, and then with one heave he pulled the cover up to its full height and stared down into a black hole. He pulled his torch out his pocket and climbed onto the ladder, beaming the light down before dropping the plastic bag twenty feet down to the platform. Then he began his descent down the shaft, closing the lid behind him.

As he shone the torch down he was amazed to see the second ladder he had wrenched from the wall had been put back. That was the one thing he was unsure of. He assumed the police must have had it put back, but he wasn't complaining. He dropped his plastic bag with the lilo down to the next platform before his final descent to the bottom. He shone his torch down into the rushing water below and he realised the drain was taking a huge amount of flood water down the spillway.

He pulled the lilo out of its bag and laid it out on the platform before attaching the foot pump. Then he began pumping the pedal vigorously up and down, forcing air into the limp shape while watching it gradually inflate. It took ten minutes of hard pumping to fully inflate the five-foot-long mattress and press home the valve.

Then he climbed down the last few feet into the surging water until his feet were firmly on the bottom. He was standing on six inches of glutinous muddy silt clinging to his boots in freezing water up to his waist.

He pushed the lilo underneath him and, holding it against the flow, he eased himself onto it and then pushed himself away to go drifting down the tunnel in darkness. The beam of his torch lit the way ahead. Forty yards on he approached the main shaft with just the torch beam guiding him and the light picked out something hanging at the foot of the main shaft. He pushed his feet against the wall to slow up, and then he saw beneath the collapsed platform a sleeping bag caught round a stanchion, hanging limp. It was a painful reminder of the fate suffered by Julia Woodward entombed in this ghastly place.

The next thing he knew, the tunnel suddenly dropped and he hurtled downwards into the blackness of the Brindley Canal. He was immediately swept into the canal tunnel in a whirlpool of rushing water, going rapidly out of control.

He bumped against the sides of the tunnel scraping his bare knuckles on the concrete and almost capsizing as he gripped the lilo, swept along in a torrent of water. The torch threw a circle of light on the roof just two feet above his head as he flashed the beam in all directions, bumping into the tunnel sides, skinning the backs of his hands and spinning round out of control.

As he went on, he felt the tunnel closing in on him. It was getting smaller. His head hit the roof and he dropped his torch in the water. Now he was in darkness being carried along in a fast-flowing tide clinging onto the lilo like a shipwrecked mariner, buffeted and pushed against the tunnel sides in the swirling waters.

Never for one minute did he imagine the water could be so fierce underground, and he began to wish he'd heeded the constable's warning of the burst river banks. Bathpool Park was taking an unprecedented overflow through the surface drains, which was precisely what it was meant to do. He was in a subterranean canal a hundred feet underground and it might well be his last journey...

The thought of ending up trapped in a deep pothole seized his imagination. He had no idea of the depth of water beneath him and as the tunnel roof came lower he was confronted with the thought of drowning. He was drifting faster now and he sensed the canal must be nearing its end as it flowed towards the Trent.

Without the torch he was in total darkness, swept along in dirty water, and he felt like a rat down a sewer. There had to be an end somewhere. Then it appeared – a small pinprick of light far off as he approached the end of the tunnel.

As he clung to the lilo he saw a barrier up ahead. An iron grill almost like a portcullis covered the end of the tunnel to prevent anything going up it. His worst fears were coming true as he was swept towards the end of the tunnel and suddenly brought to an abrupt halt as he bumped up against the ironwork.

Here the water was deep and the fierce current was pulling him down as he slipped off the lilo, clinging hold of the bars. A close inspection of the grill revealed it to be a trellis of flat iron bars with six-inch square openings large enough to poke an arm through. It was firmly bolted in place to the brickwork, with five-inch bolts set into wall brackets. He reached for the mallet in his rucksack, as his feet found a ledge on the tunnel side on which to stand. He was now standing in four feet of freezing water on a sound footing, which enabled him to work on the grill.

He lifted the mallet and struck hard against the grill, sending a sharp clanging noise echoing up the tunnel. Then he brought another blow to bear against the edge of the grill, followed by another, until he was smashing at it, constantly trying to prise it off the wall. Suddenly he felt it give and he carried on banging over and over, and he could feel the wall brackets beginning to loosen out of the concrete.

He must have struck it for fifteen minutes continuously before stopping for a breather. He was sweating in the freezing water but the grill was coming loose. He carried on raining blow after blow onto it until it suddenly gave way and the whole thing came out of the wall and crashed into the water. The entrance was clear.

He waded through into the open country, looking up at the railway viaduct that stretched across Brindley Ford, and could just make out the route of the canal stretching away across open land until it reached the River Trent. The rain was still falling. He grabbed hold of the lilo and began to wade across the canal, with soft mud clinging to his boots almost dragging him back. He reached the bank among some rushes and hauled himself out onto the land.

He was sweating as he stood looking at the fast-flowing tide and he couldn't believe his luck. He had a fear of drowning that haunted him from boyhood, and for a moment back there he'd had visions of a watery grave in the depths of the tunnel.

But he had done it. He had found his escape route. He reckoned he must have travelled two miles or more from the park, and he now had to make his way back. Soaked to the skin and shivering with the cold, he deflated the lilo and folded it up into a compact size to fit it back into the plastic bag.

Away in the distance some lights were glowing across the low-lying fields. He reckoned it must be Kidsgrove, and he set off in that direction in darkness to catch the train back to Manchester.

Chapter Twenty-five

'You did what?' Suzanne said in astonishment. 'You masqueraded as a potholer to arrest Wilson? I don't believe it!'

'Don't you dare print a word of it,' Kennon said across the dining-room table.

They were in Suzanne's flat on the very same evening after Kennon had accepted her invitation at the police press conference where it was announced that the Black Panther was in Manchester carrying an IRA bomb.

'If you knew where he was, why couldn't you make a police arrest? It couldn't be that difficult, surely.'

'It would have been. For one, I wasn't absolutely sure he was in the cabin; second he would have seen us coming; and thirdly he's armed. I couldn't risk the lives of my detectives and I couldn't call for an armed unit without being sure.'

'You're telling me he saw you coming,' Suzanne said as she refilled the wine glasses. 'But still, it wasn't a total loss, with two IRA men captured. But how the devil did the Panther get involved with the IRA?'

'God knows. But it just goes to show how far their tentacles reach. They would have blown up Catterick Army Camp if we hadn't been on the scene. It was a chance in a million.'

'And it got you off the hook with your boss as well. I didn't know the police used those methods.'

'We don't normally, so don't advertise it. You'd be surprised what we do to catch criminals. We visit pubs to eavesdrop and have conversations with known villains; it's all part of the job. It carries a risk, but then police work always has done.'

'But what happens now with the Panther? He's more dangerous than ever, isn't he, with an IRA bomb?'

'I didn't think it was possible for him to be more dangerous. But yes, you're right. He will strike again. But where and at whom is the question. I think he will use the bomb to extort a ransom. He's got no reason to use it any other way.'

'What on earth drives this man? He must be the most dangerous criminal you've ever come up against.'

'Not the most dangerous, but he's certainly the most formidable in his planning and execution, all done with military precision. He's not quite another Brady, but he's got more nerve than him. He works to a set pattern of tactics, changing them when it suits him to lay a false trail.'

'A bit like the police then, dressing up as potholers.'

'Oh dear, I asked for that! No, we only do that for the IRA. Specialist tactics.'

'Is that so? Well, you'll have to do it again now. How about posing as a film director on the lookout for new talent? You never know, Wilson might come along for an audition.'

'No, it would never work. But if you were to put an ad in a telephone box offering a luxury massage I reckon you could haul him in.'

'Oh, this is getting serious! How did you know I could do a massage?'

'I didn't, but I'm willing to find out.'

'Ah… I asked for that,' Suzanne said, as she opened a bottle of port. 'I might take you up on it. I usually start with both knees in the back, it's very effective for stiff joints.'

The following day, Kennon was back at his job, cajoling his team to work at the new threat posed by the Black Panther.

'He's going to strike again. You can bet on it. And this time it won't be one life threatened but dozens. He will demand a ransom to make up for the failed kidnapping.'

'But at least he'll give a warning,' Boyd replied, 'so we can avert a disaster, unlike anything we get from the real IRA.'

'Providing he gets his ransom, and even then it's not guaranteed. He didn't tell us where Julia Woodward was after his plan failed, so why should he this time?'

'So how's he going to do it, guv?' Kelly asked. 'IRA-style, do you reckon?'

'Yes, Kelly, IRA-style, but with strings attached. However, until he makes the call we're stuck. All we can do is search for him. But we need to search in the right places. Where's he most likely to be in a city this size? Come on – think!'

'In lodgings, guv,' DS Myers replied, 'unless he's sleeping rough.'

'That's right, Myers: lodgings. But where in lodgings?'

'It could be anywhere in Salford or Moss Side.'

'Working-class areas, right. But not too far from the city centre, if he's relying on public transport.'

'What do think his likely target will be, guv?' Stacey inquired. 'Do you think it will be a pub?'

'Definitely not a pub, Stacey. Somewhere much larger than a pub. Although it's possible if he wants to hold a brewery to ransom... No, it won't be a pub. More likely a railway station, but which one? Right, we'll have to start searching for his lodgings. It's better than sitting on our bums.'

'I'll take Salford area, if it's all right with you, guv.'

'Why's that, Myers?'

'I know the area very well, guv. I used to live there.'

'Very well. You and Stacey take Salford.' Kennon circled the area on the map in a blue felt-tip pen. 'Johnson and Kelly can do Moston. Roberts and Stevens can do Rusholme, and myself and Boyd will do the Gorton area. Oh, and Murray and Baxter can do Cheetham Hill. Is that everyone?' Kennon drew the circles on the map. 'Target only known bedsits and similar rented rooms. It won't be easy, but local shops will be a big help. Work with beat constables wherever you can, and make a note of all premises visited.'

'What happens if we find him, guv? Do we arrest him, or keep him under surveillance?'

'If he's in his lodgings, arrest him, Kelly! Have I got to teach you to suck eggs?'

'But what about the bomb? He could have planted it,' Kelly countered.

'If he has, he has. We can't let him go free. Weigh it up and assess on balance what is likely to get the best results. It will depend on the circumstances and the place he's in. If you're unsure, call for back-up. But remember, he's armed.'

The news of the Panther carrying a briefcase bomb had been broadcast on TV the previous night as an essential part of informing the public, since the IRA bombings virtually demanded it.

Down in the front car park a knot of reporters were waiting for more information. It was now almost a daily ritual for the media to turn up in force whenever a new piece of evidence or a rumour relating to the Black Panther surfaced. And the rumour this time was that the man was in Manchester.

As Kennon came out the front door with Boyd he faced a barrage of questions that sounded like a babble of baboons fighting over a dead carcass. But one question came through loud and clear, from a woman, and Kennon was immediately drawn to Suzanne.

'What was that again?' he said, holding his hands up to the others to calm them.

'I said, can you confirm the Black Panther is holding a new hostage, Chief Inspector?'

'No, I can't. Where did you get that from?'

'I'm afraid I can't reveal my source.' She smiled teasingly.

'You little devil! Take over, Boyd,' Kennon said, steering Suzanne to one side.

'I had a call just half an hour ago at my office telling me the Black Panther is in Kidsgrove,' Suzanne told him in a hushed voice. 'He's returned to Bathpool Park.'

'Bloody hell! Who was that?'

'A man's voice; he didn't give his name. I had only just arrived at work when the phone rang. I nearly dismissed it as a hoax, but it sounded authentic. His message carried a sinister tone. He said, "People think the Black Panther is finished, but he's not. He has returned to Bathpool Park with a new hostage. Tell Chief Inspector George Kennon of Manchester CID he has no chance against the Panther." He rang off before I could ask a question. Do you think it was a spoof?'

'No, I don't. Thanks for telling me, Suzanne.'

'Do you think it was him, the Panther himself?'

'It sounds very likely. But why tell us where he is? He's taunting us in order to provoke a reaction and heighten the tension.'

'But who's the hostage he's holding?'

'The hostage? The general public at large, that's his hostage! And this time, he's got a bomb to do it with. There's your story, Suzanne. Print it. I'll catch up with you later.'

'What about his name? Can I print that too?'

'Yes, Suzanne, you can. And his face! Put it on the front page!'

Kennon returned to the desk to use the phone. He called Kidsgrove police station first rather than Patterson at Bridgnorth. He wanted first-hand information. He spoke with the desk sergeant and was told it was highly unlikely because of severe flooding in the town from the night's downpour.

'It's impossible, sir,' the desk sergeant explained. 'The town's half flooded. It's a regular occurrence in Kidsgrove this time of the year.'

'But you will check it out, Sergeant, and let me know,' Kennon practically ordered the sergeant.

'Of course, Chief Inspector, though I can't imagine anyone going down there unless they're a frogman. But we'll get it checked.'

Kennon then phoned Patterson at Bridgnorth to let him know of the fresh developments, which now landed Manchester at the hub of inquiries.

'I've checked at Kidsgrove, Superintendent, and they tell me the park is most likely to be taking the brunt of last night's downpour. But we can't dismiss the message out of hand. I'm inclined to believe the hostage he referred to is the public, and that was his way of putting it.'

'You could well be right, Chief Inspector,' Patterson replied. 'But I fail to see how he could use Bathpool Park if it's flooded, and in any case it's too well known now, and we can easily put a cordon round it. He'd be mad to use it for a ransom drop. And why would he tell the local paper?'

'Because he craves publicity. He could be laying a false trail, but I think it's more likely he's giving definite clues to boost his reputation. He's out to prove he can beat us, even when he's given us the clues to follow.'

'I've never known it in all my experience, Chief Inspector,' Patterson replied. 'I'm sending you a police bomb disposal unit from the Yard. They will be highly visible visiting all public areas with a new sonar detection device. They'll also be posting notices informing the public of the need to be vigilant. I'll keep you informed.'

Kennon put the phone down. 'Well, he won't take any lessons from us, Boyd. But then I've come to expect that of the Yard. He's sending a bomb disposal team. I can't see that helping much after the bomb's gone off.'

'Pity he didn't send it when we had the real IRA threats. It might have saved a few lives. But when can we expect the next bomb warning? That's the pressing question. And how much time will he give us?'

A police car stood outside 44 Stretford Road in Salford while two uniformed officers knocked at the front door. It was just after ten o'clock and they were responding to an incoherent phone call from the woman householder, Mrs Maureen Jackson.

The door was opened and an inebriated Maureen beckoned them inside. 'Hello, boys. That was quick. Come in.'

'Are you Mrs Jackson?' the officer inquired.

'That's me. Come in lads. He's upstairs in his room.'

'Who is?'

'The bloke you're chasing. He's my lodger.'

The two officers stepped inside and Maureen ushered them into the front room.

'So, who exactly is the lodger?' Sergeant Bob Broom inquired.

'He arrived yesterday morning and took the room upstairs. I'm single, and a bit of extra helps to pay the bills. I wasn't sure who he was. It was my neighbour who noticed he was a bit queer – well, not queer, more suspicious, I suppose.'

'What's his name, Mrs Jackson?' Broom inquired.

'He said his name was Barry Field. But I bet that's a lie.'

'So what makes you suspicious of him? Has he committed a crime?'

'What?' Maureen said, lighting a cigarette. 'He's that bloke, the Black Panther who everyone's chasing!'

'The Black Panther. How do you know he is?'

'Cos I've seen him in the paper, that's how! Blimey, you're slow.'

'Did he leave the house at any time after he arrived?'

'He went out last night and got back just before midnight. I stayed up waiting for him. I had to find out who he was. We 'ad a few drinks, and then he tells me he's the Black Panther wanted by the police. Well, I was flabbergasted.'

'He told you he was the Black Panther over a few drinks. Are you sure you weren't just a bit drunk, Mrs Jackson?'

'Me drunk? Never! I can hold my drink. It's true, I tell you! He told me he was the Black Panther and he was on the run. He's up there now.'

Maureen swayed as she stood up. 'Well, go on then. Go up there and get him!'

'All in good time, madam,' the officer replied poking his head down the passage. 'Did he tell you where he came from, Mrs Jackson?'

'Yes. And I didn't 'ave to ask, either. He's just been demobbed from the army and split up with his wife.'

'Just been demobbed. How old is he? Any idea?'

'About forty, I reckon. He tried it on with me, of course. All men do at some time. But he was rough. I told him straight, I wasn't 'avin' none of it. Then he got all moody and went to bed.'

'All right. We'll go up. You're sure he's in the room now?'

'Of course I am. I ain't heard him go out or nuffink. He's probably still in bed. You follow me. I'll show you the way.'

Maureen led the two police officers up the narrow stairs and onto the landing. 'That's his room. Shall I call him?'

'No! Leave him to us! Ready, Ron?' The two officers drew their truncheons and listened at the door. There was no sound from within and the sergeant turned the handle slowly.

'Careful, Bob. I reckon we ought to call for back-up,' Ron whispered to his mate.

Broom shook his head as he turned the door knob slowly. The door opened an inch and then both men burst through like an avalanche.

'Police! Drop the gun!' they both yelled.

They stood in the empty room with truncheons raised, looking all about them while Maureen's pet cat, curled up on the bed, stared back at them. They looked under the bed, in the wardrobe and every other small space they could think of.

'He's gone! He's not here, Mrs Jackson.'

'Well, he was here. Honest – I swear to you he was here this morning.'

'Well, he's not here now, and as far as I can see there's no trace of anyone ever being here. He's done a moonlight on you, missus.'

'What's that note there, Bob?' Ron said, pointing to a piece of paper pinned to the inside of the wardrobe door that had just swung open.

The sergeant pulled it off the door and read the message out to an embarrassed Maureen.

'*Sorry I had to leave, Maureen. Thanks for the shag. The Black Panther.*'

Wilson strode across Central Station with his duffel bag over his shoulder and the briefcase in his hand heading for the public toilets. Just along the west wall was a large recess containing the left luggage lockers he would use for the bomb. The station clock said twelve noon and the timing was just right for his plan.

He entered the gents' toilets, went down some steps and made for one of the vacant cubicles. He locked the door, seated himself on the pan and opened the briefcase on his lap. Inside were two thirty-pound packs of gelignite, capable of a massive destructive force, twice the power of the pub bombs. He reconnected the detonators with a 24-hour clock and set the detonation for eighteen hours. If his plan failed the bombs would explode at 6 a.m. He shut the briefcase up and spun the combination to lock it.

The next job was to plant it where it could do maximum damage. He stepped out the cubicle and left the toilets for the station concourse. The station was busy, with a lot of people coming and going to the trains along four platforms. The buffet was busy and so were the shops. It was like that every day.

Wilson knew that a bomb warning would cause chaos, following in the wake of the IRA bombings. That alone would guarantee the ransom he was demanding. All it required was the nerve to do it. He made his way to the left luggage lockers where he had a choice from about 200 along two walls. He selected No. 68 and dropped a fifty pence piece into the slot to open it. He placed the briefcase inside and locked it.

Then he had a brainwave. He went to another locker, put his money in and removed the key. Then he went to another one and repeated it. He finally opened six lockers and removed the keys, noting, to his advantage, that over half the lockers were in use.

Then, with six keys in his pocket, he walked away, confident that no one recognised him. It was unlikely, dressed as he was in raincoat and cap. He disliked having to wear this humble appearance in public and much preferred the tough macho image of the Panther.

He revelled in the name 'Black Panther' and, though it was coined by the media, he did much to promote it with armed robbery by stealth in the middle of the night. The paramilitary clothes he wore were carefully selected after studying pictures of terrorists, and in particular the IRA. If the next job was successful he could put the Panther to sleep, and that was not the most comforting of thoughts. He would rather keep the game going. He had come to realise he was obsessed with it and it had taken him over.

As he walked through the busy station he was struck by another thought. How could he make doubly sure the ransom was paid? And if it wasn't, would he still allow the bomb to go off? He pushed the latter question to the back of his mind and concentrated on the ransom payment.

He calculated that the £100,000 demand would go first to the station manager and from there up to the higher echelons of British Rail, the Board. But would they take it seriously? They would have to if they wanted to stop the bomb. In theory they would have eighteen hours to pay up, but realistically he would have only about fourteen hours until 2 a.m. to collect the ransom and get away.

He left the station and walked to the bank of telephone boxes outside on the station entrance. In his pocket he had the message written out on a piece of paper and the station telephone number. He entered the only available phone box and pulled the message from his pocket, and then he dialled the number.

After three rings the phone was picked up by an inquiry clerk. She was asked for the station manager on a matter of great importance and Wilson was put through. The manager answered the phone and heard the sinister voice speaking with a West Indian accent.

'This is a bomb warning. Get a pen and paper,' Wilson said, acting the part to the full and brushing aside the manager's objections. 'I am dead serious. You listen up, man, before I get mad. There is a bomb in your station. I want £100,000 in used notes or the bomb goes off. The money is to be put into canvas holdalls and delivered by midnight. You got that? There will be no negotiating, man, I am calling the tune here. Take the money to Derby Central Station and wait for the next call at 11.30 p.m. at the phone box outside, number 664309. You got that, man? I will repeat once more.'

The manager repeated the phone number of the box whilst still protesting. 'It can't be done,' he said, 'I need more time. The Board will object.'

'You have till midnight to save your station or the bomb goes off.'

Wilson cut him off, satisfied the message had sunk in. He left the phone box and walked up Princes Street to purchase his equipment for the next stage of his operation.

In a sports shop he bought another beach lilo and a coil of climbing rope. The rope was needed to pull the estimated four holdalls of cash through the tunnel. He also bought a thinner coil of rope to lash the holdalls to the mattress, and he purchased two heavy torches which were most essential.

He had calculated the bags of money would weigh about ten stone and take up the entire raft. He would take the second lilo and ease them both through the canal. He now had everything he needed, including his weapons, which were in his duffel bag. Now he set off for Piccadilly Station to catch the next train to Derby.

The station manager's first response was to phone directly to his head office in Derby, stating the ransom demand with a warning of a bomb at the Central Station. Then he dialled 999 and called the police. The call was then relayed to Manchester CID, where Bradley took control in the absence of a senior detective in the building.

Over the radio, he ordered Kennon to go straight to Central Railway Station, and instructed the team to carry on with their search for the Panther's lodgings. No sooner had he done that than he got a call from the Uniform Division stating the Panther's lodgings had been discovered in Salford.

Kennon arrived on the station with Boyd at just after 1 p.m. and they went straight to the manager's office for an interview. Richard Sedgemore, the station manager, relayed the Panther's message word for word.

'I was stunned, Chief Inspector,' Sedgemore said, lighting a cigarette with a trembling hand. 'I've never had a bomb warning, especially one from the IRA.'

'That message came from the Black Panther,' Kennon replied. 'We know the man is in Manchester and we know he has a bomb in a briefcase.'

'He never said who he was. He certainly wasn't Irish, but he did sound a bit foreign. West Indian, I would have said.'

'That's his trademark. It was the Black Panther, no doubt about it. What did the Railway Board say about it? Are they sending an official?'

'They are indeed. He's coming from Derby. He should be here soon. I got the distinct impression they would not bow to the bomber's demand. I shall have to close the station, Chief Inspector. They won't like it, but I've no choice.'

'But not yet. He's given you twelve hours to deliver the ransom. Now, I suspect there will be a few more hours added to that for him to get away. So we have time. Now where's the most likely place he could plant a bomb on this station?'

'If it's in a briefcase, left luggage, I should think. But we have over 200 lockers on the platform and probably over half that number are in use, so they won't have a key.'

'But you have a master key, I presume?'

'There is no master key! The lockers are treated as private property. It's always been that way. The keyholder is the only person who can open it.'

'That's a daft idea! We may have to force them open. Is there another place the bomb could be hidden where we don't need a key?'

'The station buffet, beneath one of the seats, is possible. Or in one of the shops. A search would soon find it.'

'That seems a bit too obvious. There must be another place,

not so obvious. This man has a sharp brain; he will know a search would most likely find it.'

Sedgemore's secretary gave a knock at the door and admitted the man from the British Rail Board. Henry Thomas introduced himself and took advantage of the manager's seat behind the desk as Sedgemore vacated it.

'Disturbing news, gentlemen, I'm afraid to say,' Thomas said with a stony face. 'I and my directors of the British Rail Board have had a meeting and the Board have decided it will not acquiesce to a ransom demand.'

'Would the Board sooner see innocent lives lost, Mr Thomas?' Kennon replied. 'Because that's what could happen if we don't find the bomb.'

'There will be no innocent lives lost, Chief Inspector,' Thomas replied in a functionary manner. 'The station will have to be closed down, if necessary. The Board won't budge. We do not negotiate with terrorists.'

'How long will it be closed for? A few hours, a whole day, a week? The bomb may have a radio-controlled detonator that can be switched on and off at will. The man operating it is one of the most intelligent criminals I've ever come across. He will tie you up in knots, Mr Thomas. You could be closing down every other day until his demands are met. Believe me, I know.'

'I'm sure the bomb will be found long before that happens. And that's another thing, Chief Inspector,' Thomas replied brusquely. 'Why did I not see dozens of police here when I arrived? I saw one solitary policeman strolling up and down outside near the entrance, making no attempt to stop and search.'

'It's probably because they're too busy looking for the IRA bombers who have wrecked three pubs in the city. There will be more police when it's required. But I must say I am not happy over the stubborn decision taken by the Rail Board. You have a chance to avert danger, and you refuse. You have a choice, the pubs didn't.'

'You may have a point, Chief Inspector. But this man – the Black Panther, whoever he is – must be stopped. He's had four years' free rein. Don't you think he should be caught by now?'

'He should have been, but the fact is he hasn't. He plans

meticulously, right down to his escape. That's how he's acquired his formidable reputation. You play your part and deliver the ransom, and I'll catch him for you. Now I must go and speak with Scotland Yard colleagues at Bridgnorth. In the meantime, gentlemen, I suggest you get those luggage lockers open. You've got ten hours.'

Outside the station, Boyd and Kennon discussed the next move as they walked to the car parked inside the forecourt entrance.

'Where to, guv? Kidsgrove?' Boyd said as they got in the car.

'Kidsgrove, Boyd? I thought I said Scotland Yard. That's Bridgnorth.'

'I know, guv, but you don't want them telling us what to do, do you?'

'You must be a mind-reader, Boyd. Kidsgrove it is, and step on it!'

It was raining hard when they arrived in Bathpool Park. They drove slowly round the deserted ground, which was half flooded with large pools of water. A chill wind rippled the pools giving an air of desolation and there was an emptiness over the park that would never quite diminish even with time.

There were no police cordons or danger signs to keep people off the manholes, and not even a public notice to say what had happened here on that fateful week in January.

They stopped by the centre shaft manhole just below the embankment and got out the car. Kennon had a manhole key and a standard police torch, but wished he had one that was more powerful. Both men stepped up onto the concrete plinth and heaved open the heavy cast-iron manhole cover to look down into the black hole.

Kennon pulled the torch from his raincoat pocket and directed the light beam down the shaft. The light reflected off the water running through the tunnel forty feet below.

'I can't tell the depth from here, Boyd. I'll have to go down and take a proper look. That's if I can get on the second ladder.'

'I forgot about the ladder. Let me go, guv. I'm younger than you.'

Kennon gave Boyd a withering look, worthy of James Bond. 'You're not implying I'm past it I hope, are you, Boyd? Because I can assure you I'm not. I can reach the damned ladder.'

'Of course, guv. I was only offering out of duty. How are you going to measure the depth?'

'I'll have to stick my bloody foot in, won't I? Here, hold this torch.' Kennon climbed down on the ladder. 'OK, give it here.'

Then he began his descent as Boyd watched him, occasionally peering round the park in case someone was coming, not that he was likely to see a soul out in this weather. Kennon reached the first platform and felt it firm under his feet. He beamed his torch down looking for the second ladder and was surprised to see it firmly back in place on the opposite wall. He carried on down into an even blacker hole, beaming his torch as he went. He reached the bottom rung, which was just below the tunnel roof and about four feet above the water. If he wanted to test the depth he would literally have to drop down into the tunnel.

But he could tell just by the sound that it was deeper than the last time he was there. He could also tell, by the distance it reached up the curved sides of the tunnel, that it was three or four foot deep. The system was designed to take not just the reservoir overflow but the River Trent as well.

He stood on the ladder peering down with the torch and could see pieces of driftwood floating by; more rubbish from the spillway, he imagined. He stepped down onto a ledge and crouched on the ladder to get his head down below the roof in order to look up the tunnel.

He directed the torch into the blackness and for the first time he got some idea of the living conditions that Julia Woodward had endured for six nights. Then something caught his eye dangling from the main shaft. It was her sleeping bag hanging down, caught on the edge of the platform.

He stood looking at it, trying to imagine what it must have been like for her in this underworld dungeon, terrified and alone in the darkness. He switched off the torch to get a better idea and was immediately engulfed in a tomblike blackness. It felt like oppression pressing in on all sides.

He switched the torch back on and swore he would not rest until he caught the man responsible. Then he began the climb back up.

Boyd was couched over the manhole with his raincoat over his head keeping a watchful eye as his boss came slowly up. Kennon wore a grim face as he climbed out of the shaft and stepped back onto firm ground.

'It's taking a damned lot of water down there,' he said, closing down the lid with a clang. 'But it's certainly not flooded beyond use.'

They scrambled back in the car and dried their faces with a box of Kleenex tissues.

'What's it like down there, guv?' Boyd asked.

'Bloody awful is the only way to describe it. The water looks about waist-deep in the tunnel, which would probably hinder Wilson if he's using it for the drop.'

'So, do you reckon he will use it and return here?'

'I do, Boyd. I certainly wouldn't rule it out. He knows this place. This is what he chose for the last ransom. I reckon he will use it again.'

'But surely he must know that his escape will be made impossible now we know of it.'

'We don't know it! We don't know where the tunnel goes. That water must go somewhere. It can't just disappear into the hill. Wait a minute… there's a canal. I remember reading about it. There was a controversy over filling it in from the environmentalists' lobby. Head for Bridgnorth, Boyd. I need to see those plans that Patterson managed to acquire from the Coal Board. Why didn't I get hold of them?'

It was forty miles to Bridgnorth and dusk was falling as they pulled into the central police station at four o'clock. Superintendent Patterson made them welcome and ordered up some tea while they sat and discussed the drama unfolding with the bomb. The Nelson Colliery plans were rolled out on a table for Kennon to look at, and he saw what he suspected drawn clearly on the conversion plans: the Brindley Canal.

'There it is, Boyd! The Brindley Canal. I knew I was right,' Kennon said, stabbing his finger at the spot. 'It even "Brindley Canal Tunnel". It goes under the hill. Pity it doesn't say where it comes out.'

'What's special about that, Chief Inspector?' Patterson asked.

'It vindicates my belief that the Panther will use it again for the next ransom drop.'

'What ransom drop? There won't be one! I've spoken with Thomas from the BR Board and he tells me they will not countenance a ransom demand from a terrorist. He says it's against BR policy.'

'Well, he's a fool then. If his station gets blown up he will wish he'd taken my advice.'

'You advised him to pay up?'

'I did indeed. It's the only way we're going to catch the Panther. I can't see any other way, though I'd be happy to hear one.'

'You know we can't give in to the demands of criminals, Chief Inspector. Whatever possessed you to give that advice?'

'Common sense, Superintendent. I want this man caught. This is the only way we're ever going to catch him.'

'Nonsense! Once we've located the bomb, the game's up. He's finished!'

'Once we've located the bomb! It will have gone off long before then. Are you willing to risk it?'

'Thomas assured me the station can be cleared of people and closed down while a search is made for a whole day, if it's absolutely necessary.'

'When will he close it? Ten o'clock tonight, or ten o'clock tomorrow morning, when we're picking up pieces of bodies? We don't know what sort of detonator is on the bomb or what time it is set for. It could be a remote control device, switched on and off at random when it suits the bomber.'

'That's a risk we'll have take. I have no control over British Rail. It's up to them what they do.'

'You do have the authority where public safety is concerned. This is a police matter.'

'Yes, I could do. But BR would have to shut down half the network for it to work. But let's return to the Black Panther. I'm sworn to catching this man. We owe it to Julia Woodward and her family. Let's assume the ransom is put up and it follows the Panther's instructions. Where do you think it will lead to?'

'Bathpool Park. That's where it will lead to, Superintendent.

I'm convinced of it. He's even told us it will be. He phoned the *Manchester Standard* and boasted he would return there.'

'Yes, I heard about it. It's on the front page. But that's obviously the ravings of a crank. Besides, the amount he's asking for will be impossible for one man to carry. It would fill four or five holdalls. That alone rules out Bathpool Park. He would never climb the ladders.'

'He doesn't have to, Superintendent. My guess is he will take it out via the Brindley Canal. He could use a boat or a raft of some kind, and float it out. All we have to do is find where the canal comes out and wait for him.'

'That's absurd, Chief Inspector. I've never heard of anything so bizarre. How is he going to get a boat from a river up a subterranean canal? It's impossible. Besides, the ransom will not be paid, so he won't be going anywhere.'

'So what do we do? Sit and do nothing – and face a blunder like last time?' Kennon looked at his watch. 'We've got six hours to find the bomb. I'm returning to Manchester. If you need me you know where to find me.'

'Hold on, George,' Patterson said changing his form of address. 'What do you propose to do?'

'I'm going to headquarters to get backing from my chief for a surveillance team at Kidsgrove. We will stake out the park and wait for the Panther to show. How I'm going to manage it without a ransom, I don't know. I shall have to convince BR to pay up and promise them strictly confidentially that no word will leak to the press.'

'OK, you win. Leave BR to me, and I shall convince them to play ball with the Panther's demands, in the interest of public safety. If they still refuse to pay the ransom I shall have to go to the Commissioner at the Yard to force their hand. You get your team and I'll give you the backing.'

Chapter Twenty-six

It was eight o'clock when they arrived back in Manchester at the Central Station. A dozen or more uniformed police were on duty, watching and waiting for developments to materialise, though what they expected was never fully explained.

Kennon and Boyd went straight to the manager's office and burst in after knocking on the door without waiting for a reply.

Sedgemore was alone and appeared to be biting his nails down to the roots with a half bottle of whisky in front of him. He looked nervous and was surprised to see the two detectives had come back.

'Ah, gentlemen. Take a seat. Would you like a drink?'

'No thanks,' Kennon replied. 'Where's Thomas?'

'He's gone back to head office to try and convince the Board to pay the ransom. We had a call from a Scotland Yard man who told us we should pay the ransom demand in the interest of public safety or we could face a criminal liability charge.'

'He's right. I take it then you haven't searched the luggage lockers?' Kennon replied knowing full well they hadn't.

'No, we haven't. Mr Thomas forbade it on the grounds that it—'

'Was private property!' Kennon finished the sentence for him. 'The man's an imbecile. If he won't conduct a search, I shall bloody well do it.'

'You won't get them open without doing a lot of damage, Chief Inspector. And besides that, how are we going to make secure all the contents that get pulled out and strewn over the floor? We will lay ourselves open for prosecution.'

'Never mind about that! We have to find that briefcase. Do you realise what an IRA bomb can do? It will kill and maim. Have you had a police bomb squad arrive yet?'

'No. I haven't been told anything of a bomb squad. Where is it coming from?'

'That's another thing he's failed us on, Boyd. Can you wonder at the man? I thought he was supposed to be the elite.'

'Maybe they're at the wrong station, sir. It'll be ironic if they're searching at Victoria or Piccadilly.'

'Ironic? I can think of a better word. *Incompetent!*'

'I can phone the other stations and find out,' Sedgemore suggested.

'Later. Can I borrow your phone a minute?'

'By all means. Help yourself.'

Kennon dialled Bradley's number at CID headquarters and hoped to God he was still there. Fortunately he was, working late, compiling a quarterly report.

'CID Central. Superintendent Bradley,' he answered.

'Chief, this is DCI Kennon. I'm at Central Station conducting inquiries. I am one hundred per cent certain the Panther is behind the bomb and he will use Bathpool Park for the ransom drop. I need a dozen men to stake it out tonight. I want every man to carry a large spotlight, not a skimpy torch; it must be a spotlight and a radio as well. And I want at least four marksmen from the firearms division. Is that possible?'

'Of course it is. Have you seen tonight's *Standard*? Wilson's on the front page with three columns of his history. How is it the press can get all this information on the man and we can't?'

'They have an excellent chief crime reporter who knows her job. She's very useful to my inquiries. I want the team to muster at the Central Station where I will meet them. This is operation "Catching the Black Panther". I have every reason to believe we can catch him tonight and put an end to this saga once and for all.'

Kennon replaced the receiver. 'Can you phone your head office, Mr Sedgemore, and see what's happening about the ransom?'

'I can, but I doubt whether they will tell me. Mr Thomas was most insistent I wait for his call. He says the Board will have to get the Transport Minister's approval, and even then it may still be subject to a Commons select committee.'

'I might have known! We shall have to search for the bomb ourselves.' Kennon looked at his watch. 'Eight o'clock. Time is running out.'

'Sir, shall I make a start on the lockers?' Boyd said. 'I'll get one of the staff from the luggage department to assist. We'll break them open.'

'No, Boyd. I've just thought – if it has a trembler device you could set it off. We're going to need the bomb unit's sonar equipment. I'll give Patterson a ring.'

Kennon dialled the Bridgnorth number, feeling the sweat running down his face. 'Superintendent! DCI Kennon here. What happened to the bomb squad you said was coming?'

'They were diverted to Birmingham after the pub bombing there,' Patterson replied. 'Do you need them?'

'Of course I do. I wouldn't be asking otherwise. It's possible we might have eight hours. But I'm only guessing. So it's pretty urgent.'

'OK, I'll see what I can do. What's the news on the ransom?'

'Stalemate. I'd appreciate it if you can persuade them to hurry up. My team is heading for Kidsgrove tonight for an all-out effort. I'll keep you informed. If you do manage to get the bomb squad to come here, tell them to beware of a trembler. Bye for now.'

Kennon put the phone down. 'I'll have that drink now, Mr Sedgemore, if you don't mind?'

'Sir, what about the ransom?' Boyd asked. 'We still have to follow Wilson's instructions.'

'You're right, Boyd. I'd forgotten that. Mr Sedgemore, I want you to phone your head office and make it clear that we must have the ransom right now.'

'I don't think they will agree, but I can try.'

Sedgemore dialled the number and waited. A secretary answered and told him to hold while she fetched someone. Thomas came back on the line in an angry mood.

'Thank you for calling in the middle of a meeting, Sedgemore! I told you to wait for my call! No decision has been reached by the Board, and may not be for several hours. The Chairman looks unlikely to approve and the Board will have to accept his decision. Goodbye!'

'It's no go, Chief Inspector,' Sedgemore said, replacing the phone with a hangdog expression. 'Mr Thomas tells me the Chairman looks unlikely to approve.'

'Bloody typical! No wonder the railways are in such a state. Your Board is stuck in the Stone Age.'

'I shall have to close the station, Chief Inspector,' Sedgemore said dolefully. 'They won't be pleased but I have no choice.'

'You do what you have to do. Where are the instructions you wrote down? Boyd, you'll have to follow this,' Kennon said, handing him the note. 'You take the Panther's instructions and relay them to me over the car radio. It's the only way.'

Boyd read the instructions. ' "Go to Newcastle-under-Lyme and wait for call at box outside Central Railway Station. Number 664309 at 11.30 p.m." Looks straightforward enough, sir. Where will you be at that time?'

'I'll be on the hill in Bathpool Park in a patrol car. You should be well in range from Newcastle. Wherever he directs you to go, radio me and let me know the details.'

'What if he sends me in the opposite direction?'

'Follow it, Boyd. If we have to move to another place then we will. But I'm confident he'll bring you back to Bathpool Park.'

'But I'll have no ransom to deliver…'

'We shall have to chance without it. He will use the same method as before. Drop the ransom in bags down the spillway. When he doesn't get it he will be one angry man. He will have to come out, and he will come out shooting with a shotgun. That's why I need the marksmen. We may have to kill him.'

'But what if he uses the subterranean canal? We still don't know the exact place it comes out at.'

'I'm pretty sure it comes out near the railway viaduct, Mr Sedgemore. Have you got an Ordnance Survey map?'

'I have, sir.' Sedgemore opened a drawer in his desk and produced several maps. 'Take your pick, Chief Inspector. There's the Manchester Ship Canal among that lot. We use them for maintenance.'

Kennon eagerly opened the one for North Staffordshire Potteries with Kidsgrove and Stoke-on-Trent clearly marked on it.

'By God, there it is, Boyd! I was right,' Kennon said, running his finger down the River Trent. 'Brindley Ford and the Trent Viaduct, clearly marked by Coal-Pit Hill on the dotted line. We were within an ace of it. I'll have that place covered as well. Half a dozen men at each possible exit with an armed back-up should do it. Let's go and meet the team. They should be on their way. Clear this station of all passengers at midnight, Mr Sedgemore. But let the bomb squad on if they turn up.'

Bradley got the team assembled in double quick time. He gave the job to Sergeant Walker, believing the Uniform Branch was better able to deal with it.

'But they'll be in marked cars, sir!' Walker exclaimed.

'All the better, Ted. It will light a beacon for the Manchester Police,' Bradley replied. 'Besides, from what DCI Kennon tells me, Wilson will be underground.'

Radio calls were put out calling in six regional cars selected by Walker from the suburbs. When they arrived, twelve men volunteered to lend the CID a hand, and there was a definite hint of triumph on their faces over their CID colleagues.

They all carried powerful spotlights and the two-way radios which were part of their equipment anyway. They were given a quick briefing by Bradley that the operation for catching the Panther was in deadly earnest to counter a bomb plot. Then the firearms division arrived in their own vehicle with Parker-Hale T4 sniper rifles with infrared telescopic sights.

Trained to shoot to kill, they were told it was more prudent to maim the target in this case, in order for Wilson to disclose where the bomb was.

At 8.30 p.m. they left for the city's Central Station in five cars to meet with Kennon, who was already outside talking with an unofficial member of his team. Suzanne had been made aware of police activities and she had found out where Kennon was located from Sergeant Walker before heading to the railway station.

She pulled up in her white Mini looking sensational in a fashionable suede coat with black trousers. Her fair hair shimmered in the light.

'You look very attractive tonight,' Kennon said, pleased at seeing her. 'What are you doing here?'

'I've come to see you,' she replied, smiling at the compliment. 'And why are you wearing casuals? You look like a hiker in that gear.'

'It's the latest fashion in potholer's gear. I may need it where I'm going, tonight.'

'Oh, yes, where's that? Down a pothole?'

'Down a drain. I'm going to Bathpool Park as soon as the team arrives.'

'You're going after the Panther?' Suzanne could hardly contain her excitement and her journalist's enthusiasm. 'Can I come? You promised me a story!'

'I know, but this is strictly police work. I can't take you along. I've just had a BR official tell me that it's not their policy to deal with terrorists. I've now got to get the Panther without the ransom. I'll have to use bluff.'

'Well, they would, wouldn't they! Can't you fake a ransom? A bag full of newspaper with some real cash on top might do it.'

'It wouldn't work, Suzanne. The Panther's not stupid. He will check to see if every note is there, and if it's not, he won't reveal where the bomb is, and sixty pounds of gelignite will blow this station apart.'

'How are you going to bluff him without it?'

'Once we're at the drop-off point we shall have to force him up with a show of arms. It's about the only thing we have left. We have to catch this man and force him to tell us where the bomb is. What else can we do?'

'Then I have a solution.'

'Oh yes, what's that?'

'I phone my managing director for the newspaper to put up the money.'

'Be realistic, Suzanne. He will no more put up a hundred grand than I will fly to the moon.'

'He will. I know he will. I've had countless meetings with him and he always said if ever the paper could avert danger by using its financial muscle he would do it. He was, of course, referring to the Aberfan tragedy in '66.'

'Noble words, Suzanne, that's all that was. The Prime Minister said exactly the same thing on the Six O'clock News if I remember rightly. It always takes a disaster to move these people after the event.'

'Well, let me at least try. I have his home number in my diary.

I will remind him of Aberfan. What have we got to lose?'

'OK, go ahead. But I think I know what the answer will be.'

'You come to the phone with me and tell him how the money is to be delivered.'

'Oh, no! Don't drag me in. I'm not allowed to ask for cash, it's against police rules. No, I'm sorry, Suzanne. It won't work.'

'So how are you going to catch Wilson without it?'

'We shall have to either go down the main shaft and get him or spray tear gas down to get him up.'

'Tear gas down a huge drainage system? By the time it reaches him it will have dispersed. That won't work either.'

'Then we'll go down and physically get him up.'

'What if he removes the ladders, or padlocks the manhole covers? How will you go down then?'

'Christ – I don't know, Suzanne! We shall just have to wait for him to come up. He can't stay down there indefinitely.'

'Is there another way that you haven't covered?'

'There's a subterranean canal under the hill. That's the route he will take if he gets the ransom. But it's been dismissed by my superiors as absurd. I'm sure that's the escape route.'

'Then let's prove them wrong, George.' Suzanne looked at her watch. 'How much time have you got?'

'About four hours to deliver the ransom and find out the bomb's exact location. Failing that, I've no idea, but I imagine about another four hours before the bomb explodes. That's an optimistic view.'

'OK. You go ahead and I'll meet you in Kidsgrove at about eleven o'clock. Where's the best place to meet?'

'Hang on! What are you doing?'

'I'm going to get the money.' Suzanne got back into her Mini. 'I'll be at Kidsgrove police station at eleven o'clock. I like the gear. See you!'

'Wait!'

There was no time for a protest. Suzanne drove off at speed, leaving Kennon to gaze after her. 'By God, I reckon she will and all!' he said to himself.

A few moments later five marked police cars arrived and pulled into the station forecourt.

'This looks like our team arrived, sir,' Boyd said, climbing out of the car in his weatherproof potholer's gear. 'And not a CID man among them.'

'Just as well, the way we're dressed. The CID won't make much difference now,' Kennon replied.

They gathered on the station forecourt to hear Kennon outline the operation at Bathpool Park in terms that made them feel vital to a successful operation.

The plan that Kennon outlined was simple. They were all to be in position at eleven o'clock and wait for Wilson to emerge either from one of the mine shafts or at Brindley Ford. As soon as he was in full view and standing on firm ground, he would be blinded by the spotlights all around him and he would be ordered to surrender. If he attempted to fire a weapon, the marksmen would shoot to maim, or kill if necessary.

'But I hope that doesn't happen,' Kennon said. 'As a last resort I will even go down and get him. I want this man to answer in a court of law for his crimes. Any questions?'

'Yes, sir. How long do we wait for him to show himself?' an officer asked.

'About two hours, I imagine. It is possible he might not appear at all. He's a master at deception, but I'm staking everything he will show.'

'Is there a ransom involved, sir?'

'Not at this stage, but that might change.'

'If there is, would it be possible to put a homing bug in with it?' one of the officers said. 'That way you'd know the Panther's every movement.'

'If we had a homing bug, but we haven't. Besides, he'd find it and chuck it out. OK. Follow me to Kidsgrove police station – and keep close! I don't want anyone getting lost.'

The cars pulled out and entered the flow of traffic heading south out of Manchester. The weather had cleared, but rain still threatened according to the forecast. As they left the city behind, Kennon was thinking of Suzanne. She was the best thing to happen to him. She was vibrant and alive with ideas. She was intelligent as well. How did she know tear gas was easily dispersed? And what if she was right about Wilson padlocking the manholes? But Kennon's overriding thought was if it wasn't for the Panther they might not have ever come together.

It was 8.45 p.m., and as the cars headed into Staffordshire, the Panther was putting together the finishing touches to his complicated ransom trail.

Chapter Twenty-seven

'£100,000 at this time of night! You must be joking, Suzanne!' Peter Graves, Managing Director of the *Manchester Standard*, said down the telephone.

'It's not impossible though, is it, Peter?' Suzanne replied. 'Most banks will open their vaults at a moment's notice if they have to. You told me that yourself when Julia Woodward was kidnapped.'

'I know, but I was referring to her wealthy father. A title carries a bit more clout than a humble newspaper proprietor.'

'Well, if we don't get it tonight, you can kiss goodbye to the Central Station. You know the damage an IRA bomb can do. And it's not as if you'll lose the money. Once the Panther is caught, which he will be, you will have it returned.'

'That's not the point. Throwing money at a lost cause is not a good idea. It won't guarantee his capture, will it?'

'No, but it will shame British Rail. That's worth a story, isn't it? And you have just admitted that the money could be got for a lost cause. But this is not a lost cause. The man in charge of the operation, DCI George Kennon, is determined to catch the Black Panther tonight, but he needs the ransom to do it.'

'What time does he need it by?'

'Thank you, Peter! Midnight is the deadline, Kidsgrove police station is the place.'

'I can't guarantee it. But I'll see what I can do.'

'Do you want me to come over with the holdalls? I need four. I think the press room might have some.'

'No. Meet me at the front entrance in one hour. But not a word to anyone, you understand. This is strictly off limits. One hour. That's ten o'clock.'

'I'll be there. Thank you again, Peter.'

Suzanne was over the moon. She replaced the receiver, poured herself a gin and tonic and switched on the television for the BBC Nine O'clock News.

The headline news was mostly about the Watergate scandal, involving a call by the US Senate to impeach President Nixon. Several items later the newsreader announced a muddled report that the Black Panther was involved in a bomb plot with the IRA. Then it went on to declare that the British Rail Board was refusing the ransom demand to defuse a plot to blow up Manchester's Central Station. There was not a word on the Panther's return to Kidsgrove. But then there wouldn't be.

'God, I hope I'm right,' Suzanne said, turning the TV off. She slipped her coat on and left her flat in the borough of Audenshaw for the newspaper office in central Manchester. It was about a twenty-minute drive at this time, with light traffic to contend with. It could be twice that time in the rush hour.

She reached the newspaper building of the *Manchester Evening Standard* at 9.50 p.m. and parked in the management bay to wait for the managing director to arrive. Peter Graves was head of the Board of the Manchester and Sunderland Newspaper group, which began as a family-run business seventy-odd years previously. By all accounts he was a wealthy man in his own right.

The paper had gone from strength to strength under Graves' management and he had personally promoted Suzanne to head the crime department, recognising her hard work over a decade of reporting for the paper, including her biggest scoop on the Woodward Fraud inquiry.

Ten o'clock passed and Graves had not shown. There were a few lights on in the building as staff worked late, usually sub-editors and the sports department. The presses were running and Suzanne could feel the ground tremble as she got out of her car and paced up and down the front car park.

10.30 arrived and still no sign of Graves. She lit a cigarette and began to worry. He must be having trouble getting the money. What if he couldn't get it? He would let her know either way. She decided to enter the building to use a phone as the time drew near eleven o'clock, when suddenly she heard a toot of a car horn and Graves' luxury Mercedes came through the gate.

'Sorry I'm late, old girl,' Graves said as he powered the window down. 'I had to get this from a private source. I said the bank wouldn't open up for me – and they bloody well wouldn't!'

'I thought that was the case. I was getting worried,' Suzanne replied as Graves climbed out.

He opened the boot of his Mercedes. 'How about that?' he said. Suzanne gazed at the four bulky holdalls stuffed with cash, every bundled wrapped in polythene. 'All bagged up and ready to go.'

'Crikey! Is that what £100,000 looks like?'

'It is indeed. All in large notes as well, mainly tens and twenties. It would take all night to count it, so I don't know how the Panther's going to manage it. I can only presume he will take our word for it.'

'But how on earth is he going to carry it?' Suzanne replied incredulously. 'You know where he is, don't you? Bathpool Park, the same place as he hid Julia Woodward.'

'I thought that was the place when you mentioned Kidsgrove. Incredible! Right, jump in, time's getting on.'

'What? Are you coming with me?'

'Of course I am! I can't let you take this on your own. Besides, I wouldn't miss this for the world. This'll be the scoop of the year. Jump in, we'll be there in no time.'

Suzanne climbed into the luxurious Mercedes with her boss and the car sped away out of the gate heading for the motorway. They had twenty-eight miles to go, and Suzanne was praying they would make it in time. But she had never been to Kidsgrove, and had no idea where the park was.

'Do you know Kidsgrove, Peter? I've never been there,' she said as they sped along.

'I've been through it several times but I don't really know it. It's a small commuter town.'

'Do you know where Bathpool Park is?'

'No, I don't. Is that the place we're going?'

'Yes. I told Chief Inspector George Kennon I'd meet him at the police station at eleven o'clock. But we've missed that deadline, so I imagine he will be at the park.'

'How many police will be at the park?'

'I've no idea. I think we had better go to the police station and get help. It would be a disaster if we went to the park and alerted Wilson to a police trap.'

'I'd like to know how Kennon believes the Panther will be in the same place as the kidnapped girl was. We could use him on the paper. He must be telepathic?'

At precisely 11.30, Boyd reached the phone box outside the Central Station in Newcastle-under-Lyme. He was using Kennon's Rover with a police driver. The phone was already ringing when he stepped in the box and lifted the receiver. The voice he heard was the Panther's, relaying the next message in a West Indian accent.

'You are to go to phone box outside the Nelson Arms in Kidsgrove, in the high street. The message you need is taped under the parcel shelf. That is all.'

Boyd went back to the car and called up Kennon on the radio. He waited listening to a blur of static, then a reply came through.

'DCI Kennon. I've got you loud and clear, Boyd.'

'Sir, the next stop is the phone box outside the Nelson Arms, Kidsgrove. You were right.'

'Don't celebrate just yet. Call me when you get there. Over.'

The Rover pulled out of the station forecourt and headed out of the city centre, following the signs for Kidsgrove ten miles away. So far the rain had stayed off, but dark clouds were rolling in from the west, threatening another downpour.

Twenty minutes later, Boyd entered Kidsgrove and went slowly down the high street, searching for the Nelson Arms. It was easy enough to find and they pulled up at the phone box outside. This was the easy part. Soon it would become complicated, and he began his search under the parcel shelf. His fingers touched something and he peeled off a strip of Dymo tape bearing the next message. When he read it he was stunned.

Go to 12 Bridge Street and knock. The man who answers is blind. Give him £1,000 and say this is from Reg. He will direct you on.

Boyd rushed to the car and relayed the message to Kennon over the radio. He spoke over a blur of static. 'It's Boyd, guv. I'm to go to Bridge Street and I need a thousand pounds to hand over to a blind man. What the hell do I do?'

'Bloody hell! He's testing us. He's making sure we have the ransom. Go to the police station. I'll meet you there in ten minutes.'

The driver set off for Kidsgrove police station, and they arrived to see a large Mercedes parked outside with two policeman guarding it. Boyd flashed his warrant card and went inside, to find Suzanne and her boss talking to a uniformed chief inspector.

'Hello, Miss Thornton,' Boyd said. 'What are you doing here?'

'Sergeant Boyd, do you know where Chief Inspector Kennon is? Is he in the Park?'

'He was. He's on his way here now.'

'Oh, good. We've got him, Peter. This is Peter Graves, the Managing Director of the *Manchester Standard*. We've got the ransom with us.'

'You've got the ransom? What – how?' said Boyd, flustered. 'What are you doing with it?'

'The *Standard* is paying the bill, Sergeant,' Graves answered. 'We assumed British Rail wouldn't pay, so we're putting them to shame. Am I right?'

'Yes, you are. Well, stone me! We thought we could do without it but we can't. I'm following the Panther's crazy ransom trail and have just been told to pay £1,000 to a blind man before I can proceed to the next message.'

'A blind man? An accomplice, I imagine. Is that usual in a ransom case?'

'No, it's not. The boss reckons the Panther is testing us to see if we have the ransom. That's why he's on his way. We're in radio contact.'

'Could this blind man actually be the Panther, do you think?'

'I never thought of that! He's not known to use an accomplice, so it's quite possible. Unless he's hoodwinked the blind man into doing it.'

'I'll get you the cash, Sergeant. You're going to need it.'

Graves stepped outside to his car and opened up the boot just as Kennon arrived in a marked squad car. Graves introduced himself and explained what he was doing there with the ransom, and the two men entered the station.

'Suzanne, you are brilliant!' Kennon said. 'The Panther is playing cagey. He wants proof of the ransom. But I can't guarantee the result.'

'Yes you can. You can outwit him.'

'Here's the £1,000, Sergeant,' Graves said, handing it over. 'I was just saying, Chief Inspector, could this blind man be the Panther?'

'I shouldn't think so. He would never risk getting that close. We will have to assume it's not and follow his instructions. He's holding a bomb over our heads. If I don't get him tonight he will win every time. This won't be the last of him.'

'Then I suggest we transfer the money for your sergeant to deliver. I've come here for that reason, and we shall see it through. You have a better chance with it than without it.'

'Thank you, sir. But I have no guarantees to offer. You could lose it.'

'I fully expect to. I just want this man caught. If the money helps do it that's enough reward for me. The Woodward family come out the poorer in all this.'

They went outside and transferred the four holdalls of cash to Boyd's Rover and Kennon felt the weight of each bag.

'He certainly won't get this out very easy. He will be using the canal… Boyd! I've just decided. I'm coming with you! You can't do this alone. If the blind man's the Panther, he's tricked us. You'll finish up shot and he'll seize the car and the ransom.'

'I can handle him, guv. He won't get one over on me.'

'We can't risk it. I'll stay in the car while you hand the money over.'

'What can you do if he's armed? Nothing!'

'Damn! I should have brought one of the armed squad with me.'

'I'll come with you, Chief Inspector,' said Graves. 'Two of us should be able to take him. I've got a golf club in the boot. One good swing will do it. A hole in one!'

'Nice thought, Mr Graves, but I can't let you do it. Police rules.'

'Hang the damned rules! It's my money. I insist on full citizen's rights.'

Kennon was stumped. 'What can I do? No… I shall have to go back and fetch one of the armed squad.'

'You haven't got time for that. I take full responsibility for my own actions. Now let's get on with it,' Graves urged.

'I shall be hung, drawn and quartered if this goes wrong.'

'Get in the front, Chief Inspector, we're wasting time.'

'Suzanne, I'll see you when I get back.'

'Take care, George.'

She gave him a kiss on the cheek and watched him get in the front and crouch in the floor well, shutting the door on him. Graves got in the back and gave her a mock demonstration, tapping himself on the head with his club as Boyd pulled away.

They arrived at 44 Bridge Street, and pulled up at a small terraced cottage shrouded in darkness with one light in the window.

'There's a light on,' Boyd said. 'Why would a blind man want the light on?'

'He has to read Braille, doesn't he?' Kennon replied. 'Get a good look at him, Boyd. But don't go inside the house.'

Boyd got out and walked up the path to knock at the door. He waited and knocked again. It was a full two minutes before the door opened and a tall, grey-bearded man with a white stick stood before him wearing dark glasses.

'Yes. Who is it?' the man said staring straight ahead.

'Reg sends you a gift,' Boyd said handing over the wad of notes. 'Have you a message for me?'

'Hold on a minute.' The man took the money, shut the door, and returned to the front room. Four minutes seemed like ten before he came back and handed over an envelope. 'I believe this is what you want. Reg left it for you. He said you'd come for it. Have a safe journey.'

The man shut the door and Boyd walked back to the car. 'That was the blind man all right. He was too tall for the Panther,' he said, getting in and opening the envelope. He removed a Dymo tape and switched on the interior light to read it out.

Go to Bathpool Park and enter by Boathorse Lane. Look for light straight ahead. Go to light and find next instructions on torch.

'Bathpool Park it is, gents. This is getting all too familiar.'

They turned the car round before heading back to the main road that would take them back through the centre of town and on to Bathpool Park.

'I'd like to know who that blind man was,' Kennon said, pulling himself back onto the seat.

'A relation. A long lost cousin, perhaps,' Boyd said. 'He might even be an ex-miner.'

'An ex-miner,' Kennon murmured. 'That might explain how Wilson found the place.'

As they went through the town centre, just recovered from the recent local flooding, the heavens opened and the expected downpour came. A flash of lightning lit the sky and Boyd drove on through the downpour, wipers flapping back and forth.

'God, this is all we need!'

A roll of thunder sounded an ominous prelude as they approached Boathorse Lane and drove slowly down it, passing one parked police car in the shadows. Two more were parked up at the gates on the hill.

Boyd turned into the park and drove slowly towards a light shining from the top bars of the spillway on the far side. This was the light that Ian Woodward missed on his visit. Now there was a more powerful torch and it was tied more firmly to the bars.

They crossed the railway cutting, passing the shadowy figures of police crouched behind the low wall holding their spotlights as they waited for the Panther to emerge from the centre shaft on the embankment. Up on the hill, twenty yards from the main shaft, two marksmen waited patiently, viewing the park through their infrared night sights. They were well within range of the centre shaft, if that was where Wilson chose to exit by. The other two marksmen were on the other side of the hill waiting at Brindley Ford.

Now they approached the ugly pillbox that marked the spillway. Boyd parked within ten yards and waited a few minutes for the rain to ease off, then he got out and walked towards the torch. He had to cut the tightly bound cord with a penknife and then he unwound the Dymo tape to read it in the torchlight.

The message was blunt. *Drop the holdalls of cash down through the open manhole and go home. I'm watching you.*

Boyd looked up and saw the manhole cover standing open on the top of the pillbox. He went back to the car. 'I'm to drop the bags down the spillway, guv. Do I carry it out?'

'Of course. I'll give you a hand. Stay here, Mr Graves. No need for you to get wet.'

'Stay here? If you're getting wet, so am I,' Graves replied bluntly. 'This is my money, remember.'

'No talking, then. Only one or two men should really be here.'

The three men went to the boot and each lifted a bag out and carried them over to the pillbox in silence. Boyd climbed up on top and the bags were handed up to him. He shone the torch down the dark hole and could see water pouring in through the reservoir overflow pipe. Then he lifted the first bag over the manhole and dropped it.

Standing at the bottom, getting wet, was the Panther. The first bag dropped with a thump at his feet and he lifted it and swung it to one side. Then the second bag came down and also landed with a thump. He swung that to one side and waited for the third bag. Nothing came and he stood looking up the twenty-foot shaft in darkness.

The torch switched on, blinding him, and then the next bag came down, landing on his back as he ducked to avoid it. It was a savage blow and he swore loudly. The sound echoed up to the men on top and Boyd smiled triumphantly, knowing he had hit him.

Then the fourth bag dropped. It landed with another thump and the Panther quickly threaded a length of rope through the leather handles. He pulled the two ends over his shoulder, wrapping the rope around one wrist as he held a torch firmly in one hand. Then he began to drag the heavy load down the tunnel, pulling over a hundred pounds of dead weight a distance of 150 yards.

Wilson was physically fit, which was just as well since the load required a man of some physical strength to pull it all through the thick sludge of accumulated silt. The water was up to his thighs and he was wearing his all-weather paramilitary fatigues, which kept him dry. It was only his boots that were letting in water.

He felt like a packhorse pulling the heavy load and he could appreciate the sheer hard work of the coal miners who had once worked down here. The torch beam disappeared into the blackness, and then he was stopped as the bags snagged on debris buried in the silt. It required a superhuman effort to pull them free, and he grimaced at the thought of a bag ripping open.

After one hundred yards he paused for a breather. He looked over his shoulder back up the tunnel as if half expecting someone to be following him. He knew they were up there, but he knew that it was highly unlikely they would come down. They would be watching and waiting for him to come up, but they would wait a long time. His exit was the Brindley Canal.

He carried on dragging his load down the tunnel, passing under the dry culvert and on to the foot of the main shaft where the two inflated lilos were tied to the ladder. He was now at the critical stage where the bags had to be loaded onto their raft at a point where the tunnel sloped down to the canal.

He reached up and pulled one of the lilos down with a coil of rope attached to it and held it firmly as he felt the water pulling it. Then with one hand he lifted the first holdall out of the water and onto the raft, placing it dead centre, while keeping a firm hold on it. The bag was now a minimal weight, as it floated with buoyancy. He groped for the next bag resting on the bottom and lifted that onto the raft, keeping as near centre as he could to avoid it tipping over.

Then, passing the rope across the top, he began lashing the holdalls to the lilo wrapping it round tight and then securing it with a couple of reef knots. Then he lifted the third bag onto the raft and tied it to the others. He was working just by the light of the torch and he was conscious of the sleeping bag hanging down from the rusting steel platform, which was resting on its broken stanchion hanging precariously by two loose bolts.

More than once the sleeping bag hindered him as he turned into it and it swept across his face like a giant cobweb. In frustration he would give it a pull only to find it snagged on something. He swore as he lifted the last bag onto the lilo and began to lash it down with the rope. All four bags were perfectly balanced on the makeshift raft, and it floated with ease.

Holding the precious cargo against the flow of water pouring into the canal, he reached up for the second lilo, which he would have to somehow board and lie flat on. As he reached up for it, he grabbed the sleeping bag by mistake and, in a fit of frustration, he pulled it hard to tear it down. It was a fatal move – one that would seal his fate.

The fierce tug on the sleeping bag was enough to break the precarious hold of the platform resting on its broken stanchion. The bolts pulled out of their housing and the five-foot platform came crashing down on him. It struck the top of his head, gashing a deep wound before slicing into his shoulder and pushing him under the water.

Suddenly his grip on the lilo was gone and the precious cargo went down into the foaming waters of the Brindley Canal. He made a vain grab, cursing loudly as he came up from his soaking and watched it disappear down the tunnel.

Pain throbbed through him as he pulled himself up by the ladder, cursing loudly. Then he saw the second lilo floating away. In sheer panic he made a grab for it with an outstretched hand, only to lose his footing and fall backwards into the water.

He went under in pitch blackness and then emerged unsteadily, grabbing at the sides of the tunnel for support. The platform was wedged against one side of the shaft and he swore blindly, kicking it furiously out the way. Then, reaching for the ladder, he felt the depth of pain in his neck and shoulder as he began to pull himself up.

His head throbbed from the severe gash, oozing a sticky blood down his face, and his shoulder felt as though it was broken.

It took sheer effort to pull himself up the ladder and he man-aged to crawl into the dry culvert where his duffel bag was stored. He lay there clutching his bag, battered and bruised but not yet defeated.

Up on the surface the police waited around the two manholes, watching for one to open. Boyd had taken the car back to Boathorse Lane and the three men walked back and waited behind the wall over the railway tunnel. The rain had stopped and a stillness settled over the park. They were less than twenty yards from the centre shaft looking down on it. At the first sign of Wilson emerging he would be instantly blinded by light.

They waited fifteen minutes before the news reached them via the radios from the men on the far side of the hill. A raft had drifted out of the canal tunnel carrying a bulky object. It was stopped at Brindley Ford by four constables and dragged out onto the bank. The ransom was saved. Meanwhile, at the tunnel entrance two marksmen waited with their rifles for the Panther to emerge. He didn't, and it was assumed he was choosing another exit.

'He'll be coming up the centre shaft, I'm sure of it,' Kennon said. 'But what the hell's gone wrong?'

'He's waiting us out, guv,' Boyd replied. 'That bag I dropped on him must have injured him.'

'How the devil can there be a canal down there?' Graves inquired, fascinated at the prospect of a story. 'How did you know about it, Chief Inspector?'

'It was in your paper ten years ago when the mine was converted into this park. It's an artificial canal constructed for the drainage system. It connects with the original canal at Brindley Ford.'

'I can't believe a man would take a woman down there and hold her captive. How deep is the tunnel, did you say?'

'It varies. At the spillway it's about twenty feet. The centre shaft is double that. But it's the main shaft that's about sixty foot deep and emerges up on the hill where we brought out Julia Woodward.'

'Incredible.'

The waiting went on with restlessness beginning to creep in and Boyd suggested going down. 'We can take him, guv. There's enough of us.'

'If he's injured he will come up. He will have to emerge soon,' Kennon said. 'He relies on darkness.'

'It's five hours till daylight,' Boyd observed dryly.

'I know, Boyd. We'll just have to wait.'

'Yes, guv. But will the bomb wait?'

It was 3 a.m. when a car pulled into the park and stopped just inside the entrance. The driver flashed his lights and the three occupants got out and walked towards them. It was Patterson and two of his team coming to check on the progress. They had spent the last hour at Kidsgrove police station liaising with the bomb squad in Manchester, and had now come to watch the net close.

They crouched behind the wall and chatted quietly and Kennon felt the whole weight of Wilson's capture fall on his shoulders. It was as though the Scotland Yard men had conceded to his infinite wisdom in predicting where the Panther would be and how best to trap him.

'What's happening, Chief Inspector?' Patterson asked. 'Is he down there?'

'He's holed up below. The ransom's back in our hands. It floated out the Brindley Canal on a beach lilo on the far side of the hill, but without Wilson.'

'So you were right. I never thought it was possible. But why hasn't Wilson followed it? Could he be injured, do you think?'

'I reckon that's exactly what's happened. He's fouled up somewhere in his plan. It's not exactly a safe place down there. Any news on the bomb search?'

'The bomb squad are still looking. They've been right through the luggage lockers and there's no trace of it yet. They're now searching the whole station. If they get a bleep it will show up on the X-ray monitor. Are you sure this man has actually left a bomb and isn't just bluffing?'

'No, I'm not. But can we afford to take that chance?'

'No, we can't. But let's pray we get a result, or we're going to look damned silly.'

'Right!' Kennon jumped up as another shower of rain fell. 'I'm going down after him. He's had enough time to show himself. Boyd! Fetch two volunteers and an extra spotlight and follow me. I'll radio up for a marksman to come down.'

'Yes, sir!'

Kennon turned to Patterson, who seemed to have lost the power of communication. 'You want a result, Superintendent. I'll give you one. I'm going down for him even if I have to drag the blighter out.'

He called up for a marksman over the radio before removing his raincoat to reveal his zip-up nylon jacket and rough cord trousers with walking boots. Patterson watched incredulously as Kennon strode off towards the centre shaft with the rain beating down, before scampering up the low railway embankment. He dropped down low at the top where he could keep his eye on the centre shaft and waited for his colleagues to catch up while searching his pocket for the T-shaped manhole key.

Boyd brought Sergeant Watson and a PC with him, and the marksman arrived carrying his rifle with a night sight. Boyd handed his boss a spare spotlight. Then they climbed up on the round concrete plinth and raised up the heavy manhole cover. They moved it right back and directed their powerful light beams down the shaft.

'Wilson!' Kennon shouted down. 'The game's over! We're coming down!'

There was no reply, not that Kennon expected one, and only the sound of water was heard gushing through the tunnel. Kennon stepped onto the ladder and started down, with the others following; the constable stayed at the top as a lookout. When all four men reached the bottom they stood in two feet of freezing water listening for sounds of movement. The spotlights blazed bright over the walls and low ceiling in the tunnel as Kennon allowed the two volunteers to adjust to the grim surroundings.

'Not very pleasant, is it, fellers? Now you know the kind of man we're up against.'

Kennon pointed the way and they set off down the tunnel with the marksman out in front wearing a bullet-proof vest.

They reached the steps of the dry culvert and the light beams picked out the rusty metal platform half submerged some fifteen metres ahead. Beyond that there was nothing except empty blackness and they felt a sense of entombment down here, sixty feet underground.

'He's waiting for us somewhere,' Kennon said, pointing up the steps. He directed his light beam up to the dry culvert and called out, 'Wilson! I have an armed man with me! Are you coming quietly? It's over!'

There was no movement of any kind, apart from a brown rat that scampered along a ledge and plopped into the water. Boyd shuddered when suddenly the silence was shattered by the blast of the shotgun. The four men instantly ducked below the steps as a curious zinging of lead pellets resounded off the walls in all directions and a plume of smoke drifted over them carrying a smell of cordite. They crouched on the steps waiting for the next shot, breathing in the acrid scent that hung heavily in the air. Then Kennon raised his head a fraction.

'Give up, Wilson!' he shouted. 'You can't go anywhere! You may as well surrender.'

'Never! For six years I've had you beat!' Wilson shouted back, his voice echoing down the tunnel. 'I've raided post offices across six counties and confounded all your efforts at capture! You won't take me alive!'

'Then we shall have to kill you! The choice is yours!'

'Listen to me, Kennon. I know it's you. I want you to know I did not murder Julia Woodward! She died because of your mistakes! You killed her – not me!'

'Then tell me where the bomb is!'

'There is no bomb! I fooled you into believing it. You see how I always have control.'

'Do you? You've just lost the ransom. It went through the tunnel and has been recovered. Weren't you supposed to follow it?'

There was no reply and Kennon ordered the spotlights out as they went slowly up the steps keeping close to the wall with the marksman to Kennon's right.

They kept their heads down listening to Wilson's laboured breathing, which was amplified in the tunnel. Gingerly they crept up and then stood peering over the top of the steps into the darkness. There was no movement and nothing to see before Kennon switched on his light and directed it down the culvert.

Caught in the full glare of the lamp, Wilson was on his knees facing them, the shotgun was at his side, while in his left hand he held his pistol to his head. He was just seconds from blowing his brains out.

'Put the gun down, Wilson!' Kennon shouted. 'You tell me what went wrong with the kidnapping and I'll listen. I want to hear it.'

'It's too late for that! You came the closest to catching me Mr Kennon. You were the most persistent, and you nearly had me a couple of times, but it's over now.'

'It's not over! I want to hear your side of the story. You want to tell it, don't you?'

Through his telescopic sight the marksman could see Wilson's finger closing round the trigger of the gun pressing against the side of his temple, and he was forced to make a split-second decision. He squeezed the trigger and fired. The bullet struck Wilson in his left thigh and he let out a low groan, suppressing the pain as far as possible. He stayed on his knees through spasms of sweeping paralysis, fighting the pain, and then the pistol dropped from his hand with a clatter and he fell forward on his face.

Kennon's team rushed up the steps beaming their spotlights on their quarry as they went through the culvert to take their charge in hand. Wilson groaned with pain as they leaned down and turned him on his back, and discovered him wearing his hood. It was his last defiant act to keep his face hidden. Then they lifted him by his feet and arms and carried him away back down the culvert.

The men up top had heard the shots ring out and quickly moved in around the centre shaft and peered down into the black hole. Two powerful spotlights beamed down from the hill above, two more came from the opposite embankment and all around the centre shaft was illuminated in bright lights.

Down below they carried Wilson along the tunnel to the centre shaft and lowered his legs into the water holding him up straight, as Sergeant Watson hoisted him onto his shoulder with a fireman's lift. Kennon lent a hand as he placed one foot on the ladder.

'I can manage, sir,' Watson said. 'It's a pleasure to bring this bastard up.'

Then he started up the ladder with Kennon following, lighting the way with the spotlight. Carrying an eleven-stone man up a vertical ladder was no mean feat. Watson brought him up as hands reached down to take over the burden of lifting Wilson. They lifted him through the opening and then down off the plinth. They laid him out on the wet grass and Kennon knelt down to remove his black Lycra hood, revealing Wilson's bruised face and bloody nose where he had fallen forward. He could hardly believe he had the Black Panther caged at last.

'Call an ambulance, somebody,' Kennon said, feeling the wounded man's pulse as the team crowded round. 'Superintendent, you can call the bomb squad off. He never planted the bomb.'

'He didn't! What the hell did he do with it, then?'

'He didn't say. Take a good look, everyone,' Kennon said, looking up at them. 'This is Derek Wilson, alias the Black Panther. You won't see another man like this again.'

Boyd was going through Wilson's coat pockets, pulling out packs of high protein tablets and other items before going through his trouser pockets. He removed fourteen pounds in notes and loose change, along with the keys to six lockers.

'Look at this guv!' Boyd said. 'The keys to the lockers. He was lying!'

'I don't think so,' Kennon said taking a close look at them. 'They're locker keys all right. But I reckon he changed his mind afterwards.'

'Why would he do that?'

'I don't know… just a hunch. But you'd better take them up to the bomb squad in case they've missed the bomb. I'll phone ahead and tell them you're on your way.'

'You're not coming, then?'

'No. I'll see Wilson loaded into an ambulance with a police escort, then I'm meeting the *Standard*'s chief crime reporter. I promised her a story, and by God, she will get one now!'

'We done it, boss! We wouldn't have done without you.'

'And I wouldn't have done it without all you here and the help of two special women.'

'Two women?'

'Yes, Boyd, two women. Suzanne Thornton and Julia Woodward. They gave me that extra burst of energy when I needed it. Without their urgings to keep going we might never had caught him. I reckon I'll take a holiday now. They say Venice is nice at this time of the year.'

Author's Note

Donald Neilson, born Donald Nappey on 1 August 1936, nicknamed the Black Panther, changed his name by deed poll because he did not want his daughter to suffer the same humiliation that he did at school.

He turned to crime to bolster his earnings as a jobbing carpenter as early as 1968. Sub-post offices were his target, since they were lightly defended and easy to rob, and he had over 23,000 to choose from. It is not clear how he acquired his nickname 'Black Panther', but it was a name he aspired to. Five people died at Neilson's hands; three were sub-postmasters and one a night foreman of a freight depot in Dudley. The fifth person was eighteen-year-old Lesley Whittle, heiress to a small fortune left to her by her deceased father. The two water company men are not included in the toll and are entirely the author's creation.

Lesley's father, George Whittle, ran a long-distance coach company with his son, Ronald, who took over after his father's death. Neilson read the story of the family's wealth in a newspaper and kidnapped Lesley in the middle of the night from her home in Highley, Shropshire. She was wearing only her nightdress when he took her away.

He took her to Bathpool Park in Kidsgrove and hid her in the drainage system, leaving her on the narrow platform in the main shaft with a sleeping bag and survival blankets. His intended target was Ronald Whittle, who was married and lived in the next village. Lesley's stepmother was out for the evening when Neilson broke in and found Lesley alone in the house.

He took her without a struggle and punched out the ransom message on Dymo tape, with instructions that were not followed up properly. The first demand by public phone at the Swan Shopping Centre in Kidderminster went unanswered through police failures and misinterpretations. Two more attempts by Neilson to seize the cash failed, and the ransom was never paid.

Neilson allowed a period of three days to exchange his victim before she died and he abandoned the site. It was six weeks before Lesley's body was found hanging in the death shaft with a wire noose round her neck. It was claimed that Neilson murdered her by pushing her off the ledge – a claim that he strongly denied at his trial. He claimed she fell off by accident, and it was never proved one way or the other.

Neilson remained free for almost a year after the kidnap and returned to post office raids. He was captured by two constables on night duty in a Panda car who saw him acting suspiciously following one of his night excursions. When they questioned him he pulled a gun on them and forced them to drive him to Biddulph in Nottinghamshire. The two constables overpowered him when they reached his destination, where he put up a tremendous fight in order to escape. The following day his bruised and battered face with swollen lips appeared in all the national newspapers. The kidnapping and subsequent murder of Lesley Whittle shocked the nation as a barbaric crime on a defenceless girl.

Neilson was sent for trial at Oxford Crown Court in June 1976. Such was the aura created in the public image for the Black Panther that the queue to see him stretched round the block. He was found guilty on all counts and sentenced to thirty years in prison.

Neilson finally got the publicity he craved through a special exhibition by Scotland Yard in their infamous Black Museum.

Printed in the United Kingdom
by Lightning Source UK Ltd.
135624UK00001B/7-27/A